THE KILLING HOUR

EAGLE BROTHERHOOD SERIES

KAT LE VEQUE

OLIVERHEBERBOOKS

This title was previously published as Darkling, I Listen

Cover design by Kim Killion

Published by Oliver-Heber Books

0 9 8 7 6 5 4 3 2 1

AUTHOR'S NOTE

They call themselves the Eagle Brotherhood.

We've all got 'that' group of friends. People we've bonded with that just 'get' you and you get them. Whether you bond over common interests, or a job, of even just mutual friends, we've all found that connection at one time or another.

Same with the Eagle Brotherhood.

It started with five Americans. They were young, brilliant, idealistic, and met during a semester abroad. When I first wrote this series, many years ago, it was originally called the American Heroes series. It was supposed to be about guys who knew each other as young men, but who went on to live their own lives and have their own adventures. Ordinary guys in extraordinary circumstances was how I described it. There were only five in the beginning, but somewhere along the line, we added two Brits as 'honorary' members. There are actually more books slated to be written, but I just haven't gotten around to it yet. One of the Eagle Brotherhood — Nash Aury — even has a sequel mostly written to his book, so this is really a series that has a lot of growth potential. And why not? It centers around men who are honorable, chivalric, and end up facing some really stressful and, in a few cases, dangerous situations. Some explainable, some not. That's the fun of it.

But it all had to start somewhere.

Each Eagle Brotherhood book starts out with the same *"How it began"* preface so you, as the reader, knows where these guys connect because they don't appear in each other's stories. It's a rather interesting connection, but one that opens up the hero of each tale — and eventually the heroine — to one heck of a story. These guys are connected to me as much as to each other.

They really are a true brotherhood.

I hope you enjoy the stories in this series because they were a labor of love to write. You don't have to read them in any particular order:

The Burning Hour
The Sunset Hour
The Secret Hour
The Unholy Hour
The Devil's Hour
The Killing Hour
The Ancient Hour

Happy reading,

AQUILA FRATRUM

Seven men.
Each with a story to tell.
Welcome to the world of the Eagle Brotherhood.

Years ago, five Americans on a semester abroad met at the home of their sponsor in Yorkshire, England. They were taking the same course at the University of York, including the son of their host. But it wasn't the course in International Law that bonded them. It was an incident from that time, something that happened on a dark and stormy night in an alley behind a bar in York called *The Calcaria.*

It is something that changed their perspectives forever.

These days, the men who once called themselves the *Aquila Fratrum* or the Eagle Brotherhood — a name based on the Americans who were military-based at that time — have gone forth in their lives. They are men in normal, everyday professions who succeed in extraordinary things. Their paths aren't smooth, and they aren't perfect, but they understand more than most that life is never about the smooth or the perfect. It is about the imperfect and the difficult. It's even about the unexplainable.

And, above all else, light overcomes the darkness.

Aquila Fratrum.

Ordinary men who have lived extraordinary circumstances.

And the women who love them.

HOW IT BEGAN
MORE THEN TWENTY YEARS AGO, THE CALCARIA, YORK

MICK MCCONNELL, PROPRIETOR

"Beck." A big man with a crown of auburn hair spoke with a drunken slur to his words. "Beck. *Seavington!*"

The blond Californian on the other side of the table, who had been half-lidded as he watched a group of women across the darkened room of the pub, jerked at the sound of his name as if he'd just been slapped.

"What?" he said, looking at the man with the auburn hair. "Christ, Phipps. Can't you just leave me alone for a minute?"

Archer Phipps struggled not to laugh. "Why?"

"Because you're breaking my powers of concentration, you ass."

That broke the table out in snorts of laughter. The man seated next to Beck, big and blond and with a mega-watt smile, put a hand on Beck's shoulder.

"What in the hell are you concentrating on?" he said, leaning over to see what Beck might be seeing. When he spied it, he gestured. "Over there?"

Beck full-on pointed to the women across the pub. "There."

"Those?"

"*Those.*"

"Well... what are you trying to do by staring at them? Just go talk to them."

Beck scowled at the man. "Because I'm trying to lure them with the power of suggestion, Trevor," he said. Then, he looked around the table and pointed. "It works. Colt over there has a laser stare. He doesn't even have to say anything — women know what he's thinking just by the expression on his face. Isn't that right, Sheridan?"

Colt Sheridan, clean-cut and square-jawed, waved an annoyed hand at the man he'd spent nearly every day with for the past six months. "Some of us don't have to be obvious," he said. "Look at Nash. All he has to do is give them one of those sexy, down-home expressions and they're falling all over themselves. I don't have anything on him."

Across the table, Nash Aury, the quiet and diplomatic sort with a Louisiana drawl, laughed softly. "It's all in the face," he said, gesturing to the big dimples in each cheek. "I don't have anything y'all don't have, but we don't have anything that Serreaux has, so maybe we should just give it up and let him take the lead."

The group looked over at Ethan Serreaux, a man with a French parents even though he was born in America. Dark-eyed and dark-haired, he looked like he'd just come off the pages of a men's magazine. When he saw that the entire table of semi-drunks was looking at him, he smiled lasciviously.

"*Belle fille,*" he said in his best Maurice Chevalier impression. "*Asseyez-vous sur mes genoux et dites-moi à quel point vous me voulez.*"

Everyone burst out laughing except for Beck, who slowly banged his forehead on the table. "You sound like Pepe Le Pew," he said. "Shut *up!*"

More laughter, most especially from Archer and the last man of their group, a giant of a figure who wasn't part of their academic group. Fox Henredon was in the process of obtaining his Ph.D. in Archaeology with an emphasis in Egyptology from Oxford. In fact, he'd come back a few months ago from a dig near Aswan and when he visited his best friend from grade school, Archer, he'd come across the Americans temporarily housed in Archer's pad. He'd gotten on so well with them that they'd made him an honorary member of their group. But not just the group — of their secret society, as well.

Aquila Fratrum.

The Eagle Brotherhood.

The whole secret group was really meant as a joke, but the basis of it — the honor, the patriotism — they took seriously. Three out of the five Americans had come from Annapolis and all five of them were majoring in International Law, hence the purpose of the semester abroad course. Archer was taking the same course, and he'd been the host house, and given that they were all within a few years of each other age-wise, they'd all bonded over common likes, common dislikes, and a passion for adventure.

It was a guy gang like no other.

But tonight, they were drinking to the group that would soon be separating. The course at the University of York was finished and the Americans would soon be heading back to their native lands, but promises of reciprocal visits had abound all evening. Nash, in particular, had invited everyone to New Orleans for the holidays because his family, having made their money in sugar, had a massive house that could accommodate everyone. Beck, Cord, and Colt had already committed to it, but Ethan had family obligations he needed to get out of. Archer was trying to figure out how to break the news to his parents, who were possessive of his time, while Fox was on the verge of committing. He'd never been to New Orleans and a street named after liquor intrigued him. As the Brotherhood planned their next gathering, Beck stood up from the table.

"I need to find the loo," he said, looking around. "Where is it? Back behind the bar?"

The problem was that he was drunker than the rest of them and probably not in great shape to find anything, so Cord stood up next to him.

"Back in the corner," he said. "Come on, little brother."

He had Beck by the neck, pulling him back behind the bar where there was a dark corridor that led to bathrooms and the kitchen. The term 'little brother' was essentially referring to Beck's age because he happened to be the youngest out of their group. But he was also the toughest. Beck Seavington could out-fight anybody, Fox included, and Fox had participated in underground fight clubs during his earlier college days. He'd won money at it, too.

But Beck's fists were quite lethal.

The Navy wanted him that way.

Cord went with Beck so he wouldn't get into any trouble. Cord was an enormous man, having played football, and the rumor was that he was being scouted by the NFL. He wasn't a fighter by nature, but no one was going to test of man of that size. He'd just push the scrapper, Beck, in front of him, anyway, and let the career Navy man do the damage.

Every group had a scrapper.

It smelled like stale booze and bleach back here and the door to the men's room was locked. Beck rattled it but it remained fixed. With a heavy sigh, he looked at Cord.

"I can't wait," he muttered.

Cord tipped his head in the direction of the door to the alley out back, which was next to the kitchen door.

"Outside?" he said.

Beck nodded, which nearly threw him off balance, and charged through the back door. Cord followed him and they ended up in the dirty, damp alley behind the bar. It smelled worse out here, like garbage and animals. There were crates against the wall, broken down cardboard boxes, and little else. There were two ends to the alley, but they were standing closer to the end that dumped out onto the street where *The Calcaria* was located. Beck was looking for a discreet place to relieve himself when the back door smacked back on its hinges again, spilling forth the rest of their group.

"I think we're done with this place," Archer said, rubbing his eyes because the alcohol was messing with his vision. "There's another pub down the way called Valhalla. Let's go there."

Beck had found a spot behind some crates. "Are the women more proactive there?" he asked. "I mean, will they actually come up and talk to you? I don't think my mind control is working."

Archer grinned. "Do you seriously want a woman that approaches you?" he said. "The wooing of a woman is an art, Beck. You don't want some nervy woman up in your grill, do you?"

The others snorted in agreement. Ethan and Nash were by the back door, leaning back against the wall, as Colt went to stand next to Beck. Fox went to stand with Cord, maybe as a lookout since they really shouldn't be pissing in an alley, when three men suddenly appeared from what was a small walkway between buildings. It was dark, so no one really noticed, until one of the men walked up behind Colt and put a knife to the man's back.

Then, everything changed.

The drunken, happy mood was gone.

"Easy, big man," the man said. He was short, with a dirty

jacket, but the knife he'd produced was quite large. "If you want to keep your kidney, you'll relax, mate."

Everyone froze — Ethan, Nash, Archer, Fox, Cord, Beck, and most of all, Colt. But his features never changed expression, even as he felt the prick of cold steel against his right kidney.

"If you're looking for money, you're too late," he said steadily. "We're coming out of the bar, not going into it. We've spent our money."

The man in the dirty jacket grunted as his friends also produced big knives. "Somehow, I doubt it," he said. "We were watching you inside. I think you're from money, so you've got more where that came from, Yank. I think all of you have more."

With that, his friends began to move. One of them was heading for Ethan while the other one was heading for Archer. The group, as a whole, instinctively started to back away from the men approaching, but Fox refused to budge. At seven inches over six feet, he had that luxury of being stubborn.

"You blokes really think you're going to rob guys who are twice your size?" he said incredulously. "You're either incredibly stupid or way too overconfident."

"I'll go with stupid," Cord muttered.

Fox quickly agreed with him. "Stupid, for sure," he said. "There are seven of us and three of you. You may be able to take out a couple of us, but there are five of us left who will break your fucking necks. Are you ready for that?"

That brought some pause to the man's companions, but the man in the dirty jacket poked Colt enough to draw blood.

"Give me your fucking money!" he hissed. "Another word and I'll cut a hole in this man big enough to stick my hand through!"

Colt didn't even flinch when the man jabbed him. He kept his right hand up while his left once reached into his pocket for his wallet. But as he was doing that, and the other two men with knives were advancing on Ethan and Archer, no one happened to be watching Cord.

And that would be their fatal mistake.

"*Quaere ferro scopum tuum,*" Cord suddenly mumbled. "*Oboedite mihi!*"

Inexplicably, the man holding the knife to Colt's back jerked. He jolted. His hand flew up and the big blade he'd been forcing on Colt flew up and into his own throat, straight back through so that the tip came out of the back of his neck. It went through him like a bullet. As he staggered back and fell to the ground, his friends were momentarily startled and that gave Cord the opportunity to turn against them.

"*In molles venter it ferrum,*" he growled, lifting a big fist as if to punch the men straight in the face. "*Utrumque vestrum!*"

The men screamed as the hands holding the knives came up and plunged the blades into their bellies as if they had a mind of their own. They went down as Ethan, Nash, Archer, Fox, Beck and Colt made haste to back up, away from what was evidently going on. No one knew what was happening and it was best to get clear considering knives were slashing all over the place.

At least, everyone but Cord backed up. He pointed a finger at the men who had just stabbed themselves in the belly.

"*Ferro ad carnem, ferrum ad os,*" he said in a low tone. "*Collum secari debet.*"

The men with knives in their bellies suddenly withdrew those knives and stabbed themselves in the neck, three or four times, until they could stab no more. They simply lay there and bled as Cord turned to his stunned group of friends.

"We need to get out of here," he said quietly. "Before the cops come. *Quickly.*"

No one moved. They stood there, eyes wide at what they'd just seen. Colt, who was the closest to Cord, grabbed him by the arm.

"What in the hell just happened?" he asked in awe. "What did you do?"

Cord looked back at the men bleeding out on the alley floor. "I protected us," he said simply. "We really need to go."

"Protected us *how*?" Fox was at Cord's side, his handsome face seriously. "What did we just see, Cord? Hypnosis of some kind?"

Cord scratched his head. "No," he said reluctantly, looking at the curious group. "Can we just get out of here, please?"

"Not until you explain," Fox said.

He was serious. No one was moving, not really. Exasperated, Cord sighed heavily. "Fine," he said. "I did it to save Colt's life. That guy was going to kill him."

Colt, who had blood running down the right side of his torso, stepped forward. "He probably was," he said. "Nobody is disputing that. But *what* did you do?"

Cord looked at his friend. "It's not something I really talk about," he said hesitantly. "I haven't... I haven't done that stuff since I was younger, but you all know I'm descended from Abigail Williams. When we all talked about our families and stuff, I told you guys that I was descended from one of the chief accusers of the Salem Witch Trails."

"You did," Colt said as his gaze moved to the men on the ground. "But what does that have to do with it? And done *what* stuff?"

Cord was clearly reluctant. "My dad likes to call us Casters," he said. "Abigail Williams was an accomplished witch and that trait is passed down in my family, like red hair or freckles. Only it's some kind of power we can summon. What you saw was a spell. I turned their knives against them."

"You're a witch?" Colt repeated in shock. "Seriously, Cord? Like — magic?"

Cord didn't answer. He just started walking, very quickly,

and the others instinctively followed. They came to a walkway that led out onto the street and, nearly running, they headed up towards the main road.

"Yeah, like magic," Cord finally said as they came to the main avenue. "You saw it. I can't explain it more than that, but I wouldn't have done it if I thought we could have gotten out of that without Sheridan missing a kidney. Just... do yourself a favor. Forget you ever saw it."

"Wait," Ethan said as they began to walk, very quickly, towards the area with the car park. "We can't just leave. No matter what happened, or how it happened, we have to call the police."

"And tell them what?" Cord said. "That we got attacked and that I used a spell to turn the weapons against the guys who attacked us? They would think we were nuts."

As Ethan shook his head in disagreement, Archer grabbed him by the arm and pulled him along. "They would want to know who stabbed those guys," he said. "They'd take our finger-prints and find out that none of our fingerprints were on the weapons. How in the hell are we going to explain that?"

Ethan wasn't sure, but he didn't like running from a crime scene. "Guys, we can't leave," he said, trying to drag his feet. "We were witnesses to what happened. We have to..."

Cord suddenly came to a halt and grabbed Ethan by the shirt. "What do you think is going to happen?" he hissed. "Ethan, I don't want to run any more than you do, but I'm the one who killed those guys. That's the bottom line. And I'm not doing time for it and I'm not going to show the York Police how I turned those weapons against them, so forget it. We're not calling anyone. We're getting out of here and you are giving me your word that you'll never repeat what you saw. I need you to swear that to me."

Ethan could see how upset Cord was and he put up his

hands in a gesture of surrender. "I swear that I'll never repeat it," he said. "Don't worry about that. But if anyone else saw us..."

"Who is going to see us?" Cord said, letting go of his shirt. "No one saw us. We're going to fly home tomorrow, anyway, and we'll be out of here. Done."

Ethan nodded, but he wasn't happy about it. Even if he wasn't happy, at least he understood. The entire group began walking again, very quickly, with the car park in sight. Beyond that, freedom.

Freedom from something they hoped wouldn't come back to haunt them.

Cord most of all.

"You... you really *did* that?" Beck finally said. He was still astonished by what he'd witnessed. "How in the hell did you learn how to cast spells?"

Cord school his head. "I told you," he said. "It's in my blood. But I don't like talking about it, so let's just drop it... okay?"

"But we saw it."

They had reached the car park by now and Cord came to an abrupt halt, facing the group. He was normally a congenial guy, but the event had him spooked.

"I know you guys saw it," he said. "But you need to swear that you will never repeat it. You will never tell anyone. Because if you do, I'm going to be in a shitload of trouble. How in the hell am I going to explain to anyone that I used witchcraft to kill some criminals?"

"But it was in self-defense," Ethan stressed. "No one is going to convict you, or any of us for that matter."

Cord's frustration bled through. "But we would have to explain *how* it happened," he said. "Don't you get it? One question would lead to another, questions you don't want to answer. Trust me."

Nash, who had been silent for the most part, put a hand on

Cord's shoulder. "Cord, where I'm from, voodoo and witchcraft are part of the culture," he said quietly. "I've seen things I can't explain, so I believe what you're saying. I know what I saw. You have a gift, but it's a gift people don't understand. We've all witnessed something tonight that was... well, pretty damn amazing."

Cord registered some relief as he realized he had the support of Nash. The guy wasn't going to hound him. After a moment, he looked at the rest of the group. "You know, we've joked about calling ourselves the Eagle Brotherhood, but I think we really *are* a brotherhood now," he said. "We've experienced something that could have cost us our lives. It was small, but it happened. You saw something you shouldn't have seen because I did something I shouldn't have done. But to protect you guys... I'd do it again. I hope you know that."

"I feel like I owe my life to you," Colt said, reaching out to shake Cord's hand. "You were brave to do what you did, Cord, knowing... well, knowing that it wasn't something for all to see. But you did it and I'm grateful. I'll take an oath of silence on the Eagle Brotherhood if that's what it'll take. To protect you because you saved my life, I'll do anything. And if you ever need me, no matter where I am, I'll come. That's a promise."

More hands began shooting out, covering Colt and Cord's hands. It was a vow, a promise, not to discuss the event that bonded them more than a school or allied nations could. It was a bond that went deeper now because they harbored a secret. More than that, they had crossed into the realm of a brotherhood that would protect or kill for one another.

The true test of a brotherhood.

It was an oath that would take to their graves.

Wherever life would take them.

ONE
NORTH YORKSHIRE, ENGLAND, PRESENT DAY, THE MONTH OF AUGUST

IT WAS a dark and stormy night.

Seriously, it was a very dark and very stormy night. Scarlett Ward stood at the window of the old rectory she had so recently purchased, trying to stuff rags in the corner of an old window that was leaking profusely. The walls of the old home had to be a foot thick, heavy grade stone and mortar that had held the rectory together since the late eighteenth century, but years of neglect had taken its toll.

It wasn't the house's fault. It was hers. Scarlett had bought the house based on pictures and several telephone conversations, desperate to get out of Southern California by doing something completely over the top. She bought an old rectory on the North Yorkshire moors. Still, she thought maybe the real estate agent should have been more open about the condition of the house, but maybe she saw dollar signs from America more than she thought about her own sense of integrity. Whatever the reason, Scarlett had walked into a mess.

The house was in moderately bad shape and everything leaked. Scarlett had only arrived that morning, but she quickly discovered that water of some kind came spurting, squirting or dripping out of everything that had anything to do with water. As Scarlett held rags up to the dripping window caulk, her youngest daughter came racing in from the kitchen.

"Here, Mom!" Alexandra Ward was nine years old, with long dark hair like her mother. She had brought wads of paper towels and thrust them at her mother. "Use these!"

Scarlett knew that Alexandra meant well. She tried to be tactful in the face of her frustration. "Honey, those paper towels won't do any good," she said. "I need cloth rags."

Alexandra was undeterred as she mopped up the water running down the old and cracked wall. "I couldn't find any," she said. "I think they're in boxes."

Scarlett struggled with her patience. "Do you think you could start opening boxes in the kitchen to see where they might be?" she asked through clenched teeth. "I could really use them."

Alexandra dropped the paper towels and ran off again, tracking water across the old plank floors. Upstairs, Scarlett could hear her older daughter, Morgan, as she squealed about water coming in through the ceiling and the woman simply had to shake her head. The entire place was coming apart and there wasn't a damn thing she could do about it.

Out in the kitchen, or what pretended to pass for a kitchen, Alexandra suddenly let out a loud scream. Startled, because Alexandra wasn't usually the screaming kind, Scarlett dropped the wet rags she had been holding up against the torrent and bolted into the big central hall that connected to the kitchen. Racing into the kitchen, there was a back door leading into a small utility area where the back door was wide open and rain was hammering in.

Alexandra was standing in the open doorway, yelling, but Scarlett couldn't hear what she was saying above the wind and rain. She raced to the open door and slammed it shut, turning to her soaking daughter but being interrupted by the sound of breaking glass coming from the kitchen. Scarlett and Alexandra ran into the kitchen to see that something had crashed through the big window over the sink. Water and wind whistled in through the broken glass.

"Get me the tape!" Scarlett yelled. "Hurry up!"

Alexandra went on the run as Scarlett grabbed one of the recently unpacked kitchen knives and ran into the utility room where there were a few unpacked and flattened boxes. She grabbed one of the boxes and hacked away at it, eventually pulling free one of the cardboard sides and running back into the kitchen. Climbing up on the old Formica counter, she pushed the cardboard against the broken window.

"Alex!" she cried. "Hurry!"

A few seconds later, Alexandra came running into the kitchen, followed by her older sister. Morgan Ward was fourteen years of age, elegant and long-limbed, with glistening brown hair. Her pretty face was wide with shock.

"What happened?" she demanded.

Scarlett turned her head when a big gust of wind blew rain into her face. "Something broke the window," she yelled above the noise. "Go cut another piece of cardboard from the box on the back porch. Hurry!"

Alexandra handed her mother the only tape she could find, duct tape from one of their open and unpacked boxes. Scarlett had her daughter rip off big strips of it, handing them to her mother as the woman held the cardboard over the open window. Everything was wet, including the cardboard, but Scarlett managed to tape it up over the window in a moderately effective fashion.

By the time the first cardboard was semi-secured, Morgan returned with another big piece of cardboard and Scarlett taped the second piece over the first, reinforcing the breach. As Scarlett and Morgan duct-taped cardboard over the window, Alexandra began to inspect the broken glass and wood on the old kitchen floor.

"Mom," she reached down and gingerly picked up a big, wet rock. She held it up to the weak light of the old kitchen fixture. "Look at this – someone threw a rock!"

Still on her knees on the Formica counter, Scarlett peered at her daughter. "What do you mean someone threw a rock?" she nearly demanded. "And what were you doing with the back door wide open like that?"

Alexandra was still holding the rock. "I saw someone in the kitchen window," she insisted. "Someone was looking in but they ran off when they saw me."

Startled, not to mention feeling vastly uneasy, Scarlett climbed off the counter. "Are you sure?" she asked. "How could you tell? There are no lights outside."

Alexandra inspected the wet rock. "I could see them from the light here in the kitchen," she told her mother. "It was like a face and then it was gone. And then they threw this rock."

Scarlett looked at the rock in her daughter's hand, now feeling some confusion in the mix. "Why would they throw a rock in our window?" she asked, more to herself than to the girls. "That doesn't make any sense. No one knows us. We just moved here."

Morgan climbed off the counter and went to her mother. "I don't like that someone threw a rock in our window," she was near tears, as the teenager was often. Raging young hormones made her emotional. "I'm scared."

Scarlett put her arm around her daughter, who was almost taller than she was. "It's okay," she assured her quickly before Morgan's emotions got out of hand. "It has to be a mistake. There's no reason why someone would want to throw a rock in our window. The wind must have blown it in."

"A rock?" Alexandra wasn't catching on to the attempt to calm her sister. "This is a heavy rock. The wind can't blow it in."

Scarlett gave her younger daughter a threatening expression. "If the wind is strong enough, it can blow around a lot of things," she said deliberately so Alexandra, her logical child, would take the hint. "For now, we need to check to see where all of the leaks are and plug them up for the night. We'll call a repair guy tomorrow."

Alexandra was starting to realize how upset her older sister was so she bit her tongue, taking the rock with her as she went back into the central hallway that linked up with the lower living spaces. The hall was dark and creepy; smelling of dust and the passage of time, and Alexandra clutched her rock as if ready to throw it at the first ghost that jumped out at her. Scarlett and Morgan were right behind her, Scarlett still comforting her older daughter, when the sound of breaking glass again pierced the sounds of the storm.

Alexandra was the first one into the room that the real estate agent had called the garden room, a massive chamber adjacent to the kitchen. There were big windows and a big French door, which now had a broken pane in it. Scarlett pushed past her younger daughter, inspecting yet another rock on the floor as wind and rain whistled in through the breach. She stood there a moment, staring at the rock. She didn't even try to pick it up or cover up the broken glass. After a moment, she turned to her girls.

"Get in the car."

TWO

"LOOK," Scarlett was trying not to lose her temper. "We just moved here today. I don't know a soul in this town, so how could I have any idea who might be throwing rocks into my window? That's *your* job; to find out who did it and punish them."

Scarlett and the girls were sitting in a booth at a pub called The Calcaria. It was situated in the nearby and much larger town of Tadcaster, and since Scarlett's new town wasn't so much a town as it was just a village, she didn't know where else to go when the second rock came crashing through the window. She just rushed the girls into the car and started driving south; knowing Tadcaster was a couple of miles away and presumably with police services. She wasn't even sure what number to call for the cops, so she stopped at the first open establishment she came to and asked them to call the police for her. She didn't know what else to do.

The pair of cops, or bobbies, that showed up quickly was young and fairly hot to trot. They took Scarlett very seriously but within the first few minutes of speaking with them, Scarlett got the sense that they were asking a bunch of irrelevant questions. She was trying to urge them to go back to the rectory with her but they seemed to think more questions were in order. Frustrated, she ordered the girls hot cocoa and a sandwich to split between them and continued to try to impart a sense of urgency with the police.

The storm was still raging outside, blasting rain and wind against the fine glass panes of the pub. It was around ten o'clock in the evening and there were several people in the establishment, either at the bar or sitting in clusters around the main tables and booths. It was also a weekend in late August, and there were several teenagers in the pub, which made it rather noisy. Scarlett alternately watched the room and the officers in front of her as they continued with their insipid questions. A half hour into the situation, she'd finally had enough of their apparent unwillingness to take her seriously and asked to speak with a supervisor.

The young officers tried to convince her that a supervisor wasn't necessary, a rookie mistake, which only made her angrier. Her American breeding and fiery personality put the young Brits into groveling mode. Another five minutes went by before they were embarrassed enough to get on the radio and asked for the watch commander, or at least the British equivalent. By that point, Scarlett had lost interest in speaking with them and just sat with her girls as they drank their cocoa and ate their sandwich. It was close to eleven-thirty by the time the supervisor showed up.

At the stroke of half-past the hour, the pub door opened and the lightning flashed, illuminating an enormous figure in the doorway. Everyone in the pub looked up because it was a well-choreographed moment as the wind howled and bolts lit up the sky, giving the figure a striking silhouette.

Scarlett watched, just like everyone else, as a man of tremendous size closed the pub door and shook the water off his coat. The first thing he did was skim the room until his gaze came to rest on the two officers standing a couple of feet away from Scarlett. Then his intense gaze fell on her.

It was a moment that she would remember for the rest of her life.

———

He wasn't just angry; he was bloody well pissed off. He'd been at home trying to settle his six-year-old son down for the night when the call from dispatch came through. *You're needed at The Calcaria in Tadcaster.* Dispatch couldn't tell him why, only that the officers were calling for a supervisor. Being the on-duty watch commander because the shift's usual commander had called out ill, he had no choice. Peeved, frustrated, Deputy Chief Constable Archer Phipps had his mother try to settle the boy down as he pulled on his overcoat and tore out of the court-yard in his police-issue BMW 5 series unmarked police car.

Taking the A64 southwest, it was almost twenty miles to Tadcaster over rain-slicked roads. The very large barrier city of York stood between him and his destination, but the A64 cut around the southern perimeter of the city before continuing onward. He tore through the night, through the bad weather, until he exited the motorway on York Avenue and continued through the town of Tadcaster until the road turned into Commerce Street and then to Bridge Street. He barely saw a soul and, given the bad weather, he wasn't surprised. The night was a mess and here he was out in the middle of it.

Taking a right on Kirkgate Street, The Calcaria came up on his right and he surprisingly found a parking space just across the street. Warm light glowed through the windows of the old pub. As the storm overhead grew worse and lightning was added to the mix, he crossed the street and realized his anger hadn't abated as he entered the warm, stuffy establishment. If anything, it was worse. He began praying this was a damn serious matter with a combative contact because he was ready to tear into them.

Wind and rain followed him inside as he slammed the door behind him. The coat was soaking and he shook it at the door, water droplets spraying on the mat, before lifting his gaze to search out the officers who had called him. The room was fairly crowded for the late hour but he caught sight of two officers off to his left, standing next to a series of booths lined up against the far wall. It wasn't very well lit so he struggled to make them out as his eyes adjusted to the dimness, but he did notice that seated in one of the booths next to the officers was an exquisitely beautiful woman. That, he could clearly see.

The woman was looking at him. He felt a rather odd jolt when their eyes met, something electric and warm, and his anger took an odd pause. Eyes still on the woman, he shook off the last of the water on the arms of his coat and made his way over to where the woman and the two young officers were lingering.

As he drew closer, he could make out the woman's features more clearly although he was genuinely trying not to stare at her. He wasn't the staring kind but, in this case, he would make an exception. The woman had dark hair and alabaster skin, with delicately arched dark eyebrows over big, bottomless hazel eyes. Her face was sweetly-shaped, her perfect bow-shaped lips a faint shade of red. The more he tried not to stare, the more he ended up staring because her beauty was truly astonishing. He'd never seen anything like it in his life.

The two young officers were already fixed on him as he approached and the shorter one, the more chatty of the pair, spoke.

"Good evening, Deputy Chief," he said. "Sorry to pull you out in this weather, but we've got a bit of an issue."

He was pointing to the beautiful woman and Archer's anger took a complete dousing now that he was coming to realize that the woman with the long-lashed eyes was the reason he was called in the first place. It made the inconvenience worth it just to look at her.

"It's the job," Archer replied emotionlessly as he ran a hand over his damp hair, his gaze on his officers. "What's the situation?"

The young officer replied. "This is Ms. Ward," he said, indicating Scarlett. "She just moved here from the States – bought a home in Newton Kyme, you see, and she seems to think someone broke her windows tonight but I've been trying to tell her that this storm...."

Scarlett cut him off. "Storms don't throw five pound rocks through windows," she said firmly, her gaze on the enormous supervisor with the strikingly handsome face. "Look, I know you guys think I'm some American idiot who doesn't know the difference between someone throwing a rock through a window and my own ass, but I'm telling you that someone threw two rocks through my windows tonight and it was *not* my imagination. I've been trying to explain this to your officers but they seem to think I'm full of crap, so rather than continuing to deal with the Keystone Kops, I want to talk to a supervisor."

Archer almost laughed at her animated and angry speech, but he fought it. In fact, he didn't even crack a grin.

"I would be happy to speak with you about it." He extended an enormous hand, which she shook reluctantly. "Deputy Chief Constable Archer Phipps at your service, Ms. Ward. How can I be of assistance?"

Scarlett sighed heavily, struggling to calm down now that the lure of genuine help was within her grasp. "You can tell those two to go back out into their squad car and eat donuts while I talk to you," she said with a cocked eyebrow.

Archer bit his lip to keep from grinning as he glanced at his two officers, now insulted, and jerked his head in the direction of the front door. Peeved, they took their sweet time leaving the pub. They were full of self-importance, now cut down to size by the American woman. Archer watched them until they were about halfway to the door before returning his attention to Scarlett.

"So how can I help you this evening?" he asked.

Now that the two jokers were out of her sight, it did wonders for Scarlett's demeanor and she quickly relaxed. She pointed to the two young officers who were opening the pub door. "Are all of your officers that young and that ridiculous?"

Archer cleared his throat softly, still fighting that urge to grin. "No, mum," he replied. "I'm sorry if they didn't take you seriously. I promise to do better. Now, do you want to start from the beginning?"

His voice was rich, deep and soothing. His manner was calm and reassuring. Scarlett was eased by it and she was starting to realize how harsh her demeanor had been. Her gaze moved over him, briefly, but a brief inspection was all she needed to form an assessment. Archer Phipps was perhaps in his early forties, with close-cropped auburn hair and pale blue eyes. He wore a neatly trimmed mustache and a bit of a fashionable goatee, which she was surprised to see on a usually clean-shaven cop. He was one of those men that made all women take a second look, as if to reaffirm a truly handsome male specimen. And he was absolutely enormous, which was a little intimidating, but she found she rather liked it. His hands were the size of a dinner plate.

"I'm sorry," she finally seemed to let her guard down now that she realized someone was going to help her. "I don't mean to be such a bitch. We just arrived today and we've been traveling for over twenty-four hours and I guess I'm just a little edgy."

Archer smiled, a hugely sexy gesture that sent Scarlett's heart racing. "Don't worry about it," he assured her. "Twenty-four hours of traveling is bound to make anyone edgy. It would probably bloody well make me crazy."

She laughed. "It's just been a long day," she agreed, feeling somewhat at ease with him. Exhaustion swamped her and, with that, she began to ramble. "We took a red-eye flight from Los Angeles to Heathrow, where we then took the Tube into London to London's main train station – I don't even remember what it's called – and then we caught a train to King's Cross and transferred to another train, which took us to York. I had already made arrangements to rent a car, so we got the car and drove to Newton Kyme to see our new house, which wasn't so much a new house as it was a broken down mess of a building that the real estate agent failed to warn me of. It's my fault, really. I should have been more...."

She suddenly realized she was rattling on and she looked at him with some shock and horror. He just grinned. "Go on," he encouraged her. "I'm exhausted simply listening to you."

Scarlett waved him off. "I'm so sorry," she apologized. "I'm completely wasting your time. Look, all I know is that at around nine o'clock tonight, someone threw a rock through our kitchen window. I would have thought the raging hurricane outside blew it through the glass, but another rock came in through a window in another room a few minutes later. One rock is coincidence; two rocks are planned."

Archer nodded as he moved towards the booth she was sitting in and planted himself in the opposite seat. "And you didn't see or hear anything before the rocks broke the glass?"

"I did!" Alexandra, sitting in the next booth, was on her

knees on the seat, looking over the back of the booth. "I saw a face in the window."

Archer looked at the pretty young girl with dark hair and her mother's hazel eyes. "And you are?"

"Alexandra Ward."

He nodded. "Nice to meet you, Alexandra Ward," he said, a faint twinkle in his eye. "What did the face look like?"

Alexandra thought a moment. "Hmmm," she cocked her head. "Like a boy. A man. He just looked in the window and when he saw that I was looking at him, he disappeared."

"Are you sure?"

"Yes."

"Did you see anything else? Like, was he wearing a hat or jacket that you could see?"

Alexandra shook her head. "No," she replied. "But I saved the rock that came in through the kitchen window."

Archer's gaze moved from the girl back to her mother. "Where is your home?"

"Newton Kyme," Scarlett replied, pointing in some direction she assumed was north. "They call it the rectory on Croft Lane. I don't even know if there's a numerical house address."

His attention lingered on her a moment, studying her, and Scarlett could feel the heat. There was something electric in the air between them, something she couldn't put a finger on but could definitely feel. She wondered if he felt it, too, or it was just exhaustion and attraction causing her to imagine it. She thought she had her answer when he abruptly tore his gaze away and stood up from the booth, pulling a portable radio out of his pocket.

It's just my imagination. Scarlett sat back in the booth, feeling somewhat foolish, listening to the Deputy Chief Constable direct units to the rectory on Croft Lane. It was silly, really; she didn't know the first thing about the man other than he was very handsome. Any heat from his gaze was all in her head. As Alexandra climbed out of her booth and came to sit with her mother, Archer gave what description he could over the radio. Alexandra snuggled next to her mother, watching the man in the wet overcoat.

"He's really tall," she whispered to Scarlett.

Scarlett's gaze was lingering on the man, thinking the same thing. "He sure is."

As Archer continued giving information to dispatch, Scarlett left the booth and made her way to the bar where the manager was cleaning dirty glasses. It was the same man who had called the police for her and as she approached, he glanced up from his chore and smiled.

"So everything is okay?" he asked.

Scarlett nodded, glancing back at Archer still on the radio. "It seems to be," she turned back to the manager. "I just wanted to thank you for your help. I'm kind of new around here and I really appreciate it."

The middle-aged bartender with the round face grinned. "You're welcome," he replied. "Hope it all turns out well enough for you."

"Thanks," she replied. "What's your name?"

"Mick," he stuck out a wet hand. "Mick McConnell. I own the place."

Scarlett shook his hand. "Scarlett Ward," she replied. "Thanks, Mick. You've made a loyal customer out of me. I promise I won't go to any other pub but yours."

He grinned. "Good enough." He looked over her shoulder and saw Archer off in the corner of the room, on the radio. He dipped his head in the man's direction. "So they called him, did they? I haven't seen Phipps around here in months."

Scarlett glanced over her shoulder again. "The Deputy Chief Constable?"

Mick snorted as he began to wipe out damp glasses. "He pretends that's what he is."

Scarlett's humor left her and she looked at Mick with some concern. "What?" she demanded. "He's not really a cop?"

Mick continued wiping out glasses. "Oh, he's a bobby, all right," he assured her. "But that's not what he really is. Well, I guess that's not fair; the man has worked hard to get where he's at. He's a good man and the people around here respect him."

"Then why do you keep saying he's not really a cop?"

Mick looked at her. "He's gentry."

"Come again?"

"Nobility," Mick clarified. "That is Henry Archer Bottreaux de Velt Phipps, the seventeenth Earl of Wintringham and Mulgrave. He inherited the title when his father died, oh, about six years ago."

Scarlett's eyes widened. "Seriously? He's an earl?"

Mick continued wiping down the glasses as if discussing a very unimportant subject. "True enough," he confirmed. "He lives in the family estate over on the other side of York. I've never seen it but I hear it's a big place. Phipps' ancestors have owned the land since the days of the Conqueror, so they say. Used to be a big castle out there but now there are just ruins."

Scarlett was astonished. "How would you know all of that?"

Mick looked up at her, a twinkle in his eye. "Most people in these parts know about each other, or at least have heard about each other," he told her. "Especially the nobility; they're a dying breed, they are. I was born and raised here. I remember Phipps when he was just a lad, a big bully of a kid who liked to terrorize his classmates. His father sent him to military school because of it and I heard he did time in the Royal Marines. He came back to us all shaped up and went to work for the North Yorkshire police."

Scarlett was looking at Archer as he wound down his conversation on the radio. She was surprised and intrigued. "Wow," she finally breathed. "It never even occurred to me that I'd meet a real earl. Ever."

Mick pointed at her with his kitchen towel. "I wouldn't mention that I told you. He might not like it."

She shook her head seriously. "I won't, I promise," she said, eyes still on Archer. "But why wouldn't he like it? Is it a big secret?"

Mick shook his head. "No big secret, at least to us locals, but he probably doesn't want me to go blabbing it around."

She returned her focus to Mick. "What else do you know about Deputy Chief Constable Archer Phipps?"

Mick lifted his eyebrows at her. Scarlett just smiled.

———

As Scarlett chatted with Mick, Archer's eyes were riveted to her. Even though he was busy coordinating units, he couldn't take his eyes off the beautiful woman with the silky dark hair. She was a few inches over five feet and fairly top heavy with big lovely breasts, something that had him seriously checking her out even though she was wearing a modest sweater. She wasn't too skinny and he liked that, too. She was a shapely, lovely woman and the more he watched her, the more interested he became.

He didn't know the first thing about her but what he saw, he liked, and he finally admitted to himself that one of the first things he did when he was introduced to her was look at her left ring finger. She wasn't wearing a wedding ring.

"How long have you been a cop?"

The soft question drifted up to Archer, breaking him from his thoughts, and he looked down to see Alexandra staring up at him. He smiled at her.

"A long time," he told her. "Longer than you've been alive."

She cocked her head. "How do you know how old I am?"

He grinned. "Let me see," he pretended to take the question seriously. "I think you're around nine or ten years old."

Alexandra returned his grin. "I'm nine," she said, turning to point at her sister, who had sat silently in the other booth up until this point. "That's my sister, Morgan. She's fourteen."

Archer looked over at the very pretty young woman with the long, straight dark hair and her mother's lovely face. "Hello, Morgan."

Morgan just lifted a hand but didn't say anything. Alexandra continued talking. "I'm going to be starting school next week," she told him. "The schools are kind of different here than they are at home. It was kind of confusing, but I think my mom understands it now. I'm going to be going to Riverside Primary School and Morgan is going to be starting Wetherby High School."

Archer nodded, looking over at the lovely teenager who seemed tired and uncomfortable. "Wetherby is a good school," he told her. "You'll like it there."

Morgan seemed slightly embarrassed that he was talking to her, as if she had hoped to stay out of any conversation. "I guess," she shrugged, looking at her hands. "Maybe."

Archer's gaze lingered on the young woman, thinking she seemed rather morose, before returning his attention to chatty Alexandra.

"Well," he said after a moment. "I hope you both like it here. I'm sure it's much different from America, but I think it's nice."

"My mom thinks so already," Alexandra said. "She kept

saying how beautiful everything is when we took the train up here today. It's really green."

Archer nodded, glancing at his watch and thinking it was time to get a move-on. "It's definitely green," he agreed, thinking of his next question and thinking himself rather caddish for asking but he did it anyway. "So... did your dad move here for a job?"

Alexandra shook her head. "My dad isn't here," she said. "He lives in California."

So she really *wasn't* married; it wasn't simply a matter of neglecting to wear a wedding ring. He felt like a heel for probing a nine-year-old, in the course of a job no less, but he didn't feel bad enough that he wouldn't have done it again given the chance. He wanted to know. In any case, he liked the answer.

"So it's just you, your mom, and your sister?"

"Yes."

"Then your mom must have moved here for a job," he said.

Again, Alexandra shook her head. "She didn't come for a job," she said. "My mom writes songs. She's a singer."

Archer's eyebrows lifted. "Really?" he asked with interest. "What does she sing?"

Alexandra wasn't shy about sharing what she knew, good or bad, having no idea that every question coming from the Deputy Chief was calculated.

"She was famous back in the eighties," she said. "My mom had a lot of albums out, but she didn't use her real name."

Archer was intrigued. "She had another name?"

Alexandra nodded. "Her singer name was Scarlett Starr," she told him. "My grandma has pictures of her singing in malls and at car races. Her hair was all permed and curly, and she wore big bows in it. Her jeans were all ripped and she wore lace gloves. It was funny."

The girl giggled as Archer turned to look at the raven-haired goddess now finishing her conversation with the bartender. *Scarlett Starr*. Now he was captivated as well as interested, a dangerous combination in his opinion. He wasn't ready for another relationship or another woman in his life, not by a long shot. At least, he didn't think he was until Scarlett turned away from the bar and fixed him with her doe-eyed gaze. Then he wasn't quite sure about anything, including his fear of commitment. He watched as she returned to the booth and collected her coat.

"Sorry," she gestured at the bar. "I was just, uh, making sure I paid my bar tab. I'm ready to go if you are."

"Ready, indeed," he replied.

He began to walk back to the pub entrance as Scarlett and her girls followed. He paused by the door as Scarlett put her coat on and bundled up Alexandra, but it was clear by looking at the three that they weren't prepared for England's sometimes harsh and wet climate. Their coats were light and not waterproof. When the girls were all bundled up, he gave Scarlett a polite smile and pushed open the door, letting in the wind and rain as the four of them spilled out into the night.

Archer followed Scarlett the three miles back to Newton Kyme as the sky unleashed above them. She went very slowly in the bad weather, unused to driving in it, so it took them a few long minutes to final enter the village that probably wouldn't have taken more than 10 minutes on a sunny day. She pulled into a long driveway off of Croft Lane and he could see the big, stone Victorian rectory looming dark and empty off to the northwest.

Scarlett was ahead of him in her little rental car, which suddenly came to a halt. Before he realized it, Scarlett was flying out of the car and into the entry vestibule on the side of the house. It took Archer a moment to realize that the entry door to the structure had been wide open, banging about in the wind.

It was obvious by her reaction that it was not how she had left it. He threw his car into park and bolted after her.

The rain was pounding as he entered the cold, dark rectory. Overhead on the second floor, he could hear feet racing across the floorboards so he made a break for the stairs, calling Scarlett's name. He could hear her shouting something and he could make out a curse word now and again. As he neared the top of the stairs, he could hear another voice as well, sounding distressed. Someone was crying out in pain. He reached to his waistband and unsnapped his service weapon.

"Mrs. Ward?" he shouted. "Where are you?"

He could hear her furiously cussing. Suddenly, a figure came bolting out of one of the rooms, running for the stairs with Scarlett in hot pursuit. She had something in her hands and before Archer could stop her, she smacked the figure over the head with it. The figure yelped and ran straight into Archer, standing at the top of the stairs.

"You... you bastard!" she screamed.

Scarlett swung the weapon again but Archer put out a hand and stopped her from crowning whoever it was. Somehow, she'd gotten hold of a piece of wood and was wielding it like a club. Archer pulled it from her grip firmly as he grabbed the sweat-shirted figure by the neck.

"Slow down," he told her, trying to focus on his squirming captive. It took him all of two seconds to recognize the face and he grunted. "Declan Knobbs. I should have known. What in the hell are you doing here?"

The figure in Archer's grip was half-shrouded by the hood from his sweatshirt. The young man fought against the big hand that restrained him. "I'm not doing anything," he shouted. "Let me go or I'll sue you!"

Furious, Scarlett punched the kid in the arm. "You broke

into my house, you jackass," she snarled. "Who in the hell are you and what were you doing in my house?"

Archer pulled the intruder away from Scarlett, who was thoroughly intent on beating him up. Not that Archer blamed her, but it was rather hilarious to watch. The woman was plucky and feisty, and he admired that. But the fact remained that he couldn't let her assault a suspect so when she reached out to smack the kid in the head, he put out an enormous hand and grasped her wrist.

"No more," he told her evenly. "I want you to go back down to the car and sit with your daughters. Please. I'll talk to you in a minute."

Scarlett's cheeks were flushed as she backed off. Archer glanced at her as he began to take his fighting captive down the stairs only to note that her eyes were swimming with tears. He paused, looking at her with some concern. When Scarlett realized his attention was on her, she began to wipe furiously at her eyes.

"He peed on my daughter's suitcase," she was so angry that she was shaking. "Her whole room smells like urine."

Archer came to a halt, forcing his captive to look at him. "Is that true?" he asked in a rumbling voice that sounded deep and dark like the Devil. "Did you urinate on the suitcase?"

The kid spit on the lapel of his overcoat in reply and Archer dragged him down the stairs. By the time he got down to the entry vestibule, wet with incoming rain, at least three police cars were behind his vehicle in the driveway and officers were running in his direction. He handed the suspect off to the first officer to reach him.

"Take him to the Selby station," he told them. "Book him for breaking and entering, and vandalism. I'll be there shortly."

Two officers took the struggling youth to the nearest police car while four other officers approached Archer for instructions. Archer began pointing to the property.

"There may be more than one," he told them. "It'll be hard to find any tracks or evidence in this rain, but see what you can do."

One of the officers glanced up at the wet, gray-stoned structure as rain pelted his face. "Someone actually moved into this place?"

Archer nodded, wiping rainwater from his eyes. "An American woman and her children."

The officer, an older man who had lived in the area all his life, lifted his eyebrows. "Didn't the agent tell her about it?"

Archer lifted his shoulders. "I don't know. What about it?"

The older officer shook his head with regret as his gaze moved over the old place. "It's been vacant for years," he said. "The local kids hang out here and do drugs, or worse. We're always clearing out squatters. That's probably what young Knobbs was doing here."

Archer stared at him for a moment, absorbing the information, before shaking his head with disgust. "I think I heard about a flop house around here, somewhere," he muttered as he turned for the front door. "I didn't realize this was the place."

"It's the place."

Archer's jaw ticked but he remained silent as he went back inside. He stood in the big vestibule entry, looking around at the old rectory that had been standing for at least a couple of hundred years. He knew the area well enough, but not with the detail that the local police did. He had heard about the old rectory in Newton Kyme that was rumored to not only be a flop house, but haunted as well. He just hadn't made the connection. There were a lot of old rectories around.

He peered into the darkened rooms, seeing water damage

from the storm on the walls and floor. Water puddled near the old windows. There were four big rooms downstairs including a kitchen and as he policed the ground floor, he could see the broken windows in a back reception room and also in the kitchen where someone had tried to seal up the breach with cardboard. He didn't touch anything but he made sure the rest of the windows were intact, and the back door locked, before proceeding upstairs.

It was quiet and dark on the second floor, the only sound was that of the storm outside. He hadn't taken two steps into the big central hallway when he began to hear faint weeping. He also heard water running. Following the sounds, he ended up in an old bathroom where Scarlett was running cold water into the bathtub, full-bore, and the bathtub was full of clothes. An empty suitcase was on the old tile floor and she was weeping as she soaked the top of the suitcase with water and some kind of soap. Peering closer, he could see she was using shampoo to clean away the urine. Concerned, he crouched down a few feet away from her.

"Mrs. Ward?" he asked hesitantly. "What are you doing?"

Scarlett was sobbing softly as she scrubbed at the suitcase. "I... I'm trying to clean this," she wept. "I just can't believe... I mean, who in the hell pees on someone's things? This is Morgan's suitcase. She's going to go to pieces when she finds out what's happened. I can't let her... I have to clean this up before she finds out. This is all we brought with us until the rest of our stuff arrives, and that won't be for a couple of days. I can't let her wear clothes that have been peed on."

Archer could see how upset she was. He began to look around at the place, the dilapidated state of it, feeling a good deal of pity for her. She obviously didn't know what she was getting into, as indicated by their conversation earlier in the pub. It seemed like the entire venture hadn't gone as planned and now with the intruder, the woman had reached her limit. He didn't blame her.

"Were you planning on staying here tonight?" he asked.

She nodded, tears and mucus running down her face. "Yes," she sniffled. "I bought the beds a few weeks ago and had them delivered this morning. The real estate agent let them in, so at least we'd have something to sleep on. But I had no idea that this house was in such horrible shape until we got here. I bought the place based on the photos that the real estate agent sent me and she wasn't very honest about it. She just wanted to make the sale. But it's my fault for buying a house I've never even seen and... I'm sorry, I'm sure you don't care about any of this. Don't I have to go down to the station for a statement or something?"

She was looking up at him as she spoke the last few words and his gaze fixed on her face, studying the fine features and porcelain skin. His expression was surprisingly tender.

"Yes, eventually," he said quietly. "It can wait."

"Are you sure?"

"Yes. But may I make a suggestion?"

Scarlett wiped at her dripping nose with the back of her hand. "Sure."

"Why don't you and your girls sleep at a hotel tonight? A hot shower and radiant heat might make a world of difference, at least for the night."

He was very gentle with her and very comforting. Scarlett gazed at the man and her tears began to fade. She could feel the warmth between them, that spark that made her heart jump, but she reminded herself that it was again only her imagination. Archer Phipps was a handsome man, no doubt, but his kindness was only in the line of duty.

"Did that kid say why he threw rocks through my window?" she asked. "Who in the world is he?"

"A local thug," Archer replied. "He's just a troublemaker."

"You know him?"

"I know *of* him."

"But why my house?"

Archer sighed, wondering how much he should tell her. "This house has been vacant for a while," he said carefully. "Local kids used to come and hang out here. Maybe he was just angry that the house finally has an occupant."

She lifted her delicate eyebrows in surprise. "Do you think so?"

"Possibly."

She thought on that. "Well," she muttered, more to herself than to him. "I guess that's as good an explanation as any. Welcome the hell to England."

She said it with quirky sarcasm, which made him smile. "On behalf of the part of England that doesn't break into homes or throw rocks through windows, allow me to say welcome to our country and we're very happy to have you."

She grinned at him. "Thank you," she said, finally feeling some measure of graciousness in her new country. "It's nice to be here."

He was still smiling as he watched her go back to scrubbing the suitcase, but his smile faded as he watched her try to get the urine out of the heavy fabric. "Will you take my advice and go to a hotel for the night?" he asked again.

She shook her head and looked up at him. "I appreciate your concern, but we're going to stay here. This is our home now and I'm not leaving."

He just lifted his eyebrows in defeat. Given what he'd seen about her over the past half hour, he wasn't surprised at her answer. She seemed like a determined woman.

"If that's the way you want it," he said, digging into his coat pocket and pulling forth a business card. He handed it to her. "I guess there's nothing more I can do here tonight, but if you need anything or have any further trouble, please ring me."

Scarlett took his card, looking at the name, the title, the information in general. "Thank you, but I'll be fine."

She was an independent one, he could see. But he realized he was disappointed that she didn't intimate that she would, indeed, call him if needed. He didn't want to walk out of the house and never see her again. Still, he was on duty and didn't want to come across as inappropriate in any way. The woman had already had a bad introduction to the English and he didn't want to compound it.

Realizing there was nothing more to stay, at least nothing more on a professional level, he stood up and turned for the stairs.

"Would you like for me to escort your daughters inside?" he asked. "They're still down in your car."

Scarlett sighed heavily, looking at the clothes, the suitcase. "I suppose there's no way Morgan isn't going to see this," she muttered, standing up. "I'll get them. I'm sure you have more important things to do and we have seriously taken enough of your time tonight. I can't thank you enough for coming out in this weather and helping me out. It means a lot."

He stood his ground as she came to stand next to him. They were in fairly close proximity in the bathroom doorway, enough so that he could see the faint red highlights in her nearly-black hair. She smelled good, too. God, she was an alluring creature.

"You're welcome," he told her. "Honestly, it's the job, but I seem to have better luck at my work than putting my son to bed, so it was no trouble at all. I'm loathed to admit I was glad for the break because he had the better of me. There was a battle and I was losing."

Scarlett grinned. "How old is your son?"

"Six going on seventeen."

She laughed. "I have one of those. Nine going on twenty-nine."

He returned her smile, feeling the warmth spark between them that he had experienced nearly the first time he laid eyes on her. He thought he must have been imagining it because she hadn't given him any indication that she felt the warmth, too.

"I know," he said. "I met her. She's bright and charming."

"Thank you," Scarlett's dark hazel eyes were glimmering at him. "She's my little rock."

"And your older daughter?"

Scarlett shrugged. "To tell you the truth, she's a little more of a challenge than the younger one. She didn't want to move here, so this whole thing with her suitcase... well, it's going to be trouble."

"I'm sorry I couldn't prevent it from happening."

She looked at him seriously. "You've been the most helpful person I've run into since leaving Los Angeles," she said. "I sincerely appreciate everything you've done."

He smiled, being sucked into those beautiful hazel eyes, feeling like he didn't want to go back home at all. He wanted to stay there and talk to her, all night if he could get away with it. But he knew it was impossible so he simply bobbed his head in acknowledgement and headed back to the stairs. Scarlett followed.

"You're very welcome," he replied as they took the stairs. "I'll give you a ring tomorrow about coming down to the station and giving a statement. Do you have a phone?"

Scarlett nodded. "A cell phone I purchased when I got here," she told him. "It's in the car. I'll get you the number."

He pulled a pen and another business card out of his pocket as they made their way out of the rectory. The storm had eased somewhat, although it was still raining. Everything was slippery and wet. Scarlett scurried to the car and opened the door only to be hit in the face by a blast of heat. The motor was running so the girls could turn on the heater, keeping them cozy. She began scrambling around in her purse.

"Mom?" Morgan was in the back seat, looking tired and unhappy. "I don't want to sleep in the house tonight. Can we please go to a hotel?"

Scarlett passed a glance at her daughter and an even longer one at Archer, standing next to her. He did nothing more than wriggle his eyebrows at her, in complete agreement with Morgan, as she found her new phone and pulled it out. She turned it on and the number appeared.

"The number is 07624 442546," she looked over at him writing it down on the back of his business card. "No, 2546. That's right."

Archer finished with the number, put the lid on the pen, and put everything back in his pocket. As he looked up from his coat pocket, he realized there was a hand stuck in his face.

"Thanks again, for everything," Scarlett felt his big, warm hand close around hers and shake it gently. "You've been hugely helpful."

Archer shook her soft hand a little longer than he should have before releasing it. "My pleasure," he replied, very much wanting to say more but refraining. His attraction to the woman was starting to muddle his senses. "If you change your mind about a hotel, there's a Day's Inn right up the main road in Wetherby."

Scarlett smiled at him. "Thanks, but I think we're okay."

There wasn't much more he could say. With a lingering gaze and a faint smile, he forced himself away from her and back to his car where a couple of the officers had gathered to give him a report on their inspection of the property. He was listening to them but he kept glancing over his shoulder at Scarlett and her daughters. It was apparent she was having trouble convincing her children to go back inside and, at one point, he even heard the older girl burst into tears.

But he listened to his officers as they finished their reports, with everyone heading back to the station or to their patrol grids. Archer climbed back in his car, still watching Scarlett's little rental car where she had climbed back inside and shut the door. He sat there a moment, watching, coming to suspect that the lovely Ward women would not be spending the night in the broken down rectory.

It was just a hunch he had.

THREE

SOMEONE WAS POUNDING on the car window.

Startled awake, Scarlett glanced at her watch. *1:54 am*. The rain had stopped and it seemed oddly silent outside now that the tempest had passed. Wiping away the condensation off the window, she was rather surprised to see Archer standing there. She opened the door.

"What's wrong?" she asked, sleepy but alert. "Did something happen?"

He didn't look too pleased. He pulled her door open wider and hit the button to unlock the other car doors. "It's one thing to spend the night in a house with no heat, no electricity, and no hot water," he said as he went around to the other side of the car and opened the passenger door. "But sleeping in a car is unacceptable. I thought you might pull something like this."

Scarlett stood there, open-mouthed with confusion and surprise, as he reached into the passenger seat and scooped up Alexandra, who was half-asleep. Then he used his foot to pop the release on the front seat so it leaned forward, opening up the back seat for Morgan. He peered into the back of the car.

"Come along, young lady," he told her. "Climb on out of there."

"Wait," Scarlett threw out a block as he unloaded her daughters. "What's going on? Where are you taking the girls?"

He reached out and pulled Morgan out of the car when she had difficulty climbing out. With Alexandra in his arms, he began to walk back towards his still-running car, parked in the drive several feet behind Scarlett's vehicle.

"I'm taking all of you to the hotel down the road," he told Scarlett in a tone that dared her to argue with him. When he looked at her and saw the expression on her face, he didn't back down. "I know you're exhausted and I know you don't want to leave your new house, but subjecting your children to sleeping in the car is unacceptable. They're cold, tired, and need a real bed."

Scarlett was watching him, mouth open in outrage, as he took both girls to his BMW and carefully laid Alexandra in the back seat.

"But...," she scooted after him. "We *can't* leave. Everything we have is here and the last time I left, some idiot vandalized it."

Archer was helping Morgan into the car. "I have a panda car stationed at the base of the driveway," he told her calmly. "No one is going to vandalize the house while you're gone, I promise. Does that convince you that going to a hotel for the night is the right thing to do?"

"Panda car?" Alexandra yawned from the back seat. "What's a panda car?"

Archer, leaning on the open passenger door, looked down at her. "A police car," he told her. "You know – black and white, like a panda. In England, we call them panda cars."

Alexandra giggled and yawned again, leaning heavily on her sister. "I like panda cars."

As the girls settled down in the back seat and closed their

eyes, Archer looked at Scarlett. "Well?" he demanded, though it was without force. "Are you just going to stand there or are you coming with us?"

Scarlett was still fairly shocked at the man's actions, but above her outrage, she was coming to understand that he was doing something very nice for them. It was gracious and kind, even if he was being a little forceful about it, making a decision for a woman he just met. So she pushed down her annoyance, her pride even, and took a few steps in his direction.

"Why are you doing this?" she asked, her eyes imploring. "This isn't part of your cop duties."

His forceful demeanor softened as he gazed into her lovely face. "I just don't think it's right for your daughters to spend the night in a cold car when there's a perfectly good hotel a few miles away."

Scarlett sighed. "I know," she said after a moment. "But the girls didn't want to sleep in the house and I was afraid to leave it."

He softened further. "I realize that," he said quietly, "and I'm very sorry about what happened earlier tonight. That's why I stationed a patrol car by the gate. They'll watch out for the house. But you and the girls really should spend the night in better shelter than a car."

She smiled at him. "That's really sweet for you to go to all of this trouble just to make sure the house is safe."

He felt like smiling just because she was. He couldn't look at that exquisite face and not smile like a giddy fool. "I want to make sure you and your children are safe, too," he reminded her.

Her expression, so outraged only moments before, was now warm and appreciative. "That's really kind," she said sincerely. "I... I'm just rather stunned that you would take the trouble to come back for us."

He was starting to feel that electricity again, genuinely

hoping she felt it, too. He was also starting to feel as if he'd been a bit rough on her.

"It seems to me you've had a pretty rough deal since your arrival," he said, a twinkle in his pale blue eyes. "Maybe I feel the need to make up for that."

She laughed again. "Why? You didn't cause any of the problems."

"No, but maybe I can help right them." He paused as he thought carefully on his next words. "I'm sorry if I came across harsh by kidnapping your children out of the vehicle, but the thought of you and your girls sleeping in that cold car all night just didn't sit well with me. Maybe I have old-fashioned ideas of chivalry, but I really couldn't stand by and not help in some way."

By this time, Scarlett was smiling openly at him, the first time since their acquaintance that she actually seemed to warm up.

"I didn't know they made guys like you anymore," she teased, although she was very flattered. "I'd hate for you to go to all this effort for nothing."

"Does that mean you're coming with us?"

"I suppose you'll take my children, anyway, if I don't."

He grinned. "I don't think they'll fight me on it. I think they'd be more likely to fight *you* for permission to go."

She had to agree. "All right," she agreed. "You win. I'll go quietly, officer."

He smiled happily. "Excellent."

He had a very impish grin, one she found charming. She giggled as she turned away from him and went back to her car. Archer watched her go, the soft slope of her torso and the way her dark hair tumbled down her back, before shutting the passenger door so the warm air inside wouldn't escape. As he continued to watch, she pulled her purse out of her car and locked the doors, then held up a finger to him to silently ask him for a minute of patience while she went back in the house.

When Scarlett emerged a short time later, she had a bag full of stuff slung over her shoulder. Archer was still waiting by the passenger door as she approached and he smiled at her, opening the door wide so she could climb inside. Shutting the door behind her, he climbed into the driver's seat, backed out of the drive, and took off into the dark night.

———

Scarlett had no idea how long she'd been asleep or what time it was. It was still very dark in the hotel room thanks to the black-out curtains and a glance at the clock showed it to be very late, indeed. *12:14 pm*. With a sleepy gasp, Scarlett tried to roll herself out of bed.

"Oh, no," she breathed, reaching for the phone and buzzing the front desk. When someone answered, she spoke urgently. "Hi. This is room 238. I'm so sorry, but I just woke up and… what?… really?… are you sure?… well, okay, then. I guess there's nothing more to say. Thank you very much."

She hung up the phone with a peculiar look on her face and then she just sat there on the edge of the bed, pondering what the front desk had just told her. After a moment, she simply fell back on the pillows, wondering if she should simply go back to sleep, when the connecting door between her room and the girls' room opened. Morgan was standing in the doorway, yawning.

"Mom, it's late," she said sleepily. "Do we have to check out?"

Scarlett rolled onto her side, looking at her daughter. "No," she said frankly. "Apparently, Deputy Chief Constable Phipps told the manager that we would need the room for the entire day, so our reservation goes through tomorrow."

Morgan yawned and rubbed her eyes. "Good," she said. "I feel like I could sleep all day."

Scarlett eyed her daughter a moment, feeling pangs of guilt for what she had forced her children to endure. She hadn't really thought about it until last night when Phipps was so adamant about the sleeping conditions. He had been right. She struggled not to feel horrible about it.

"Would you rather stay here while I went back to the house?" she asked Morgan.

Morgan nodded vehemently. "Yes," she said. "Mom, I know that's our house and all, but it's old and dirty and I hate it. I don't like it at all."

Scarlett sighed. "I know," she murmured. "But in all fairness, I had no idea it would be like that. You know that. I would have never knowingly brought you and your sister into a house like that. But now... I don't know what we're going to do. I'm not even sure we can live there the way it is. I have this terrible fear that we're going to spend about a hundred-thousand dollars in renovations to make it habitable."

Morgan yawned again, her hand on the door knob. "I feel bad for you, Mom, but I don't want to go back there right now."

"We can't spend the next six months in a hotel."

Morgan shrugged. "I know," she said, rubbing at her eyes again, but at the same time, she was watching her mother closely. She knew what her mother had been through over the past year and she began to feel bad about being such a pain. "I think the house will be really nice when it's fixed up. I don't mean that I really hate it. I just hate it the way it is now."

"Me, too," Scarlett sighed. "But we'll get it straightened out. I need to call the real estate agent and see if she can hook me up with a contractor."

Morgan wandered into the room, towards her mother's bed. "That would be good," she agreed. "I'm sure the house can be fixed up really nicely. Don't feel bad that you bought it and it turned out to be a heap. You didn't know."

Compassion from Morgan was a rare thing, a sure sign that the usually-selfish teenager was beginning to grow up. Scarlett eyed her older daughter, knowing the girl was going to start stressing out over the house. Morgan was deep-thinking that way. She didn't want Morgan worrying and hastened to reassure her.

"It'll be fine," she said, sitting up in bed and perking up. "Right now, I think I'm going to take a shower and give that agent a call."

Morgan sat down on the bed beside her mother. "Are you okay? I mean, about everything?"

Scarlett put her arm around her child's shoulders and squeezed. "I'm fine."

Morgan snuggled up to her mom. "I know it's been really hard for you with Jerry dying and all. I'm just sorry his kids were so evil, you know, about his will and fighting you about it. I don't mean to be awful to you about moving to England. I know you felt like you had to."

Scarlett's good mood began to fade. "I just thought it would be good for all of us to get a fresh start," she told her what she had told her from the start. "You know, like an adventure. Maybe we won't stay here forever, but maybe we will. Maybe we'll go back to America and tell everyone about the year we spent in England and all of the adventures we had there. I think this will be a really wonderful cultural experience for you and your sister. So don't worry about the house; we'll get it handled. It's all part of the adventure. Okay?"

Morgan nodded and Scarlett kissed her on the forehead and

got up from the bed. She wanted to get off the subject of the past year and the pain it provoked.

"Now," she said, facing her child. "You can go back to bed while I get dressed and go back out to the house. I brought some clothes, so you have something to change into, but...."

"You said that guy peed on my clothes," Morgan said with some suspicion.

Scarlett nodded patiently. "He did," she said, "so I brought you some of my sweats, just until I can get your clothes washed. In fact, that's what I'm going to do first thing – find a laundry mat and clean your clothes."

As Morgan went back to bed, Scarlett showered and shaved, taking the time to relax after such a harrowing previous day. She took her time washing and drying the long dark hair, putting on makeup with red-tinted lipstick, and finally dressing in jeans and a long-sleeved white t-shirt with a deep "V" neck that hugged her slender torso and showed her great breasts without showing too much skin. It was all about the shape and she had a great one that she worked at. Pulling little white tennis shoes on her feet and donning a cute white jacket with rhinestones across the back, she grabbed her purse and stuck her head into the girls' darkened bedroom.

"I'm off," she whispered to Morgan. "I left my new cell number in there by the phone, so call me if you need me."

Morgan was half-asleep. "How do I make a phone call in England?"

"The same way you make it at home."

"I don't have to do anything special?"

"No, baby."

Morgan yawned and pulled the covers up around her neck. "How are you going to get back to the house? That police guy drove us out here."

"I'm going to have the front desk call me a taxi, I guess.

When you guys wake up, call me and I'll bring you back some food, okay?"

"Okay."

"Love you."

"Love you, too."

Scarlett closed the door quietly and quit her hotel room, making sure the "Do Not Disturb" door hanger was on the door of both rooms. Going down to the lobby, she made her way to the front desk where a pale blond girl smiled amiably at her.

"Hello," the girl said cheerily. "How can I help you?"

Scarlett smiled in return. "I was wondering if you could call a taxi for me. I need a ride over to Newton Kyme."

"I'd be happy to give you a lift."

A deep voice came from behind and Scarlett whirled around to find Archer standing behind her. She had to make a conscious effort to prevent her jaw from dropping, not only at his surprising appearance, but also because, in the light of day, the man was exceptionally attractive. She'd only really seen him in the dark and to see him now in the bright sun was something of an experience. Had she not known the man and simply passed him on the street, she would have definitely given him a second glance because he warranted it. He was a looker.

"Well, well, well," she bit off a grin. "Look who showed up... what in the world are you doing here?"

He grinned at her, all straight white teeth with a dimple in his left cheek. "I just happened to be in the neighborhood."

She scowled, although it was done with humor. "Liar," she accused him. "Tell me what you're really doing here."

He laughed. "How do you know I'm lying?"

She shrugged lightly. "I don't," she said, her hazel eyes glimmering. "But I would suspect that you're a busy man and your business doesn't involve hanging around hotel lobbies."

Archer continued to smile at her. In fact, he really couldn't do anything else. If he thought her to be merely beautiful last night, today he was slammed out of his mind. The woman was stunning in every possible way with her luscious dark hair and deep hazel eyes. Coupled with her pale skin and red lips, he wasn't ashamed to admit he was hugely smitten. When he'd gone home last night, she was all he could think of and this morning, he could see why. His attraction to her was almost beyond his control.

"You're right," he finally conceded. "It doesn't. I will admit that I came by to see how you and your girls were after last night."

Scarlett's smile grew. The man made her feel giddy and flirtatious, things she hadn't felt in years. "We're all fine, thanks to you," she said as she sobered. "You were right; making the girls sleep in the car was unacceptable. But I hope you understand I did it because I wanted to protect our things. I was afraid that if I left the house, something else would happen to it."

He sobered as well. "I know," he said somewhat quietly. "That's why I had a car parked in front of it all night. Your house is fine."

She was back to smiling gratefully. "I promised Morgan I'd go back and wash all of her clothes."

"I'd be happy to take you back."

"Really? Then I'd be happy to accept."

His smile returned. "Excellent," he said. Then he looked around. "Should we wait for your girls?"

Scarlett shook her head. "They're still sleeping. I told Morgan I'd wash her clothes and bring them back some food."

He nodded in acknowledgement and, with nothing more to say, they walked from the lobby and out to the car park where his BMW sat illegally parked against the curb near the entry. He opened the door for Scarlett to admit her into the car before sliding into the driver's seat. Turning the car on, he pulled out of the hotel's car park and out onto the main street of Wetherby, heading south.

It was a bright day with brilliant puffy white clouds scooting across the sky. Scarlett kept casting sidelong glances at Archer, looking at him without turning her head, but all she could really see was his left hand and both legs. His hand was resting on the gear knob and she found herself inspecting the size of the man's hand. It was huge. Alone in the car with him had only made her sense of giddiness grow stronger.

"I really appreciate you giving me a ride back to the rectory," she said as they headed through the town's main street. "To tell you the truth, I wasn't quite sure how to get back there. I was really hoping the taxi driver would know."

Archer took a left and headed for the A1 motorway. "You'll figure it out in no time," he said. "Roads and directions aren't complicated like they are back in Los Angeles."

She grinned at him. "I'll admit, they are pretty complicated in L.A.," she said. "I know how to get to the 105 Freeway, the 405, the 110, the 2, the 10, the 57, the 60, the 210, the 91, and everything in between, but the difference is that, unlike here, there are mountains that help you get your sense of direction. There's nothing like that around here."

The on-ramp to the motorway was up ahead. "Whew," he exclaimed. "How can you remember all of those freeways?"

She laughed with some mirth. "I was born there," she replied. "I know Southern California like you know Yorkshire."

He nodded in agreement, taking the on-ramp south. "But you decided to leave it," he ventured. "Any particular reason, other than you were dying to buy a broken-down rectory?"

Scarlett chuckled for a moment before sobering. "Lots of reasons," she said, turning to gaze at the green English countryside passing by. She peered at the land, the sky. "It's so beautiful around here. Who knew that last night a tornado blew through here?"

Archer glanced over at her, sensing that she didn't want to talk about why she came to England. So a lady was entitled to her secrets. He refocused on the road. "The storm last night was nothing but a gentle breeze," he scoffed. "You should see it when it really gets blowing."

Scarlett turned to look at him again. "I don't think I'm looking forward to it," she said, watching him grin. It made her think of last night, of their initial meeting, of pieces of the conversation they'd had. She was very curious to know more about him. "So tell me about your little boy; what's his name?"

"Henry Archer Charles Phipps," he enunciated each name distinctly. "He's with his mother today."

Scarlett regarded him a moment, noting that the man didn't wear a wedding ring. But that didn't mean anything these days.

"How long have you been married?"

He turned to look at her. "I'm not."

"Oh," she replied, thinking he looked a little surprised at the question. Maybe it *had* been too direct. "I'm sorry; I didn't mean to offend you by asking."

He shook his head. "You didn't," he replied, looking back at the road. "But do you really think I'd be driving with a woman I just met, alone in a car, if I was?"

She shook her head. "No," she said. "I didn't mean to question your honor."

His lips twitched with a smile. "You didn't," he said. "We just met, after all. You have no idea what kind of man I am. I could be a sociopath for all you know."

She grinned. "Somehow, I don't think so."

His smile broke through, letting her know that nothing she could say could possibly offend him. "Henry's mother and I divorced almost four years ago. It's a long and boring story."

"I'd like to hear it if you'd like to tell me."

He shrugged, eyes on the road. "Nothing much to tell, really," he replied. "Christiana and I got married when she became pregnant with Henry, although she really wasn't sure she wanted to get married or even have the baby. When he was born, she just up and left us both. Here I was, with a newborn, and had no idea what to do with him. But I figured it out, eventually. I tried to work on the marriage for a couple of years but, in the end, she just didn't want to be married, so we divorced. She's only really taken an interest in her son over the past couple of years and sees him about once a month. She's just not the mothering type."

Scarlett was listening to him seriously. "Oh, my," she said after a moment. "I'm so sorry to hear that. I don't understand how a woman could have a child and then not want to be a part of that child's life."

Archer shrugged, glancing over at her. "She's working on it."

"How is your relationship with her? I mean, is it at least cordial?"

He nodded. "Cordial enough. For Henry's sake, we get along, but there's no love lost. I tolerate her and she tolerates me."

Scarlett nodded in understanding, feeling a good deal of sympathy for the man. It was quite a bit of personal information and she sensed that he was somehow opening a window into his world for her to look into. She was coming to know him a little and trust him in a sense. He had divulged a part of his life that was perhaps not so pleasant; perhaps it was her turn to open up a little. Turning to look out of the window again, she sighed heavily.

"I left Los Angeles because I wanted to get away from some very bad memories," she said after a moment. "I was married once, to the girls' father, but we divorced right after

Alexandra was born. Then I met someone and was in a relationship with him up until last year when he died in a motorcycle accident. He was fairly wealthy and although we weren't married, we did have a domestic partnership. But after he died, his grown children challenged it so I've spent the better part of the past year in court fighting them. When all was said and done, I felt like I just had to get out of Los Angeles, so I took a leap of faith and moved to England. So here I am."

Archer alternately glanced over at her and watched the road. "That's a bum deal," he said. "Greed does terrible things to people."

She nodded. "It certainly does."

"What ended up happening with the grown children?"

Scarlett sighed; feeling depressed simply thinking about what had happened. So many months of her life wasted with bullshit.

"Like I said, Jerry was a very wealthy man," she said. "He knew what his kids were like. So in his will, he left almost everything to me with only small amounts of money left to his three children. I ended up splitting the estate with them just to keep them off my back. Jerry would have killed me for doing it, but I felt it was the right thing to do."

"Was it a big estate?"

"Several million dollars."

He grunted, noting their off-ramp was coming up. "You're generous."

She shook her head as they came off the motorway. "No," she said softly. "Just tired of fighting. I want to get on with my life."

His gaze lingered on her. "So you bought an old rectory in England that turned out to be a dud."

She forced a smile as she turned to him. "It won't be when

I'm finished with it," she said. "I'm going to hire a contractor and renovate the house. I'm actually pretty excited about it."

He took a left turn off the off-ramp and headed east. "Good girl," he applauded. "You're not going to let it get you down. I like that."

Her smile turned real. "The only question is whether or not we can live there while the renovation is going on. If not, we'll have to lease someplace and that could be expensive."

Archer shrugged as they passed through a small town, closing in on Newton Kyme and the ragged rectory. "I wouldn't worry about it until the time comes," he said. "I'll give you the name of a contractor that just did some work on my home. He's reputable and does a good job."

"Thanks," she said, her gaze lingering on him. "You know, you've really gone out of your way for me since last night and I appreciate it so much. You're a pretty nice guy."

He wriggled his eyebrows, eyes ahead on the road. "Don't think I'm so altruistic."

"Why not?"

"I'm not sure I can tell you."

She laughed. "Why not?"

"Because."

She waited for more of a reply but he didn't say anything more. She lifted her eyebrows at him. "Because?" she repeated. "Is that all you're going to say?"

He fought off a grin because she was laughing at him. "For now, that's all I'm going to say."

Chuckling, Scarlett just shook her head and focused on the road ahead. "Okay, so you don't want to talk about it," she said, slouching back against the seat and getting comfortable. "Let's talk about your son. What does he like to do?"

Archer could see their destination in the distance ahead. "He likes to get into mischief," he told her. "He likes Spiderman and Harry Potter. He tells me he's going to be a wizard when he grows up and wants to know how he can get a lightning bolt scar on his forehead like Harry has."

She giggled. "You should just draw one on with an eyebrow pencil."

"I hadn't thought of that."

Scarlett turned to watch a herd of sheep by the fence along the road. "When Morgan was little, she was enamored with *101 Dalmatians*, oddly enough, with Cruella de Vil. She would take my eyebrow pencil and draw those crazy Cruella eyebrows on her forehead and tell me she wanted a dog coat. But then I explained to her that we would have to kill puppies to get her the coat, so she decided she didn't want a dog coat anymore. Funny what kids come up with sometimes."

Archer glanced over at her. "And you?" he asked. "What did you like as a kid? Or even as a teenager? Were you just another normal, All-American girl?"

He'd asked the question with a purpose, mostly because of what Alexandra had told him the night before. He wanted to see if it was true or, more than that, if she would tell him about it. Scarlett sighed heavily, a grin on her lips as she continued to watch the countryside whiz by. She began to fidget.

"You're not going to believe it."

"If you tell me, then I'll believe it."

She shrugged, appearing hesitant. "Well," she said reluctantly. "I was a normal girl, mostly, but when I was about fourteen, I started writing songs. Silly pop songs, you know, that I would record with my keyboard into a tape recorder. It was just for fun, at least to me, but my mom thought I was really good so she gave one of my tapes to this guy at our church who happened to be a record producer. He thought they were good, too, and knew a guy at a local radio station, who took my songs and started playing them on the air. Suddenly, I'm singing in malls all over the state. I began singing at NASCAR races, horse races, and county fairs. I even sang for the first President Bush."

He was looking at her with some astonishment. "You're kidding."

She turned to look at him, grinning with some embarrassment. "No," she assured him. "My stage name was Scarlett Starr because it sounded better than Scarlett Rossheimer. Ward is my first husband's name and I just kept it. Look me up on the internet. I even have a fan site, although I don't have anything to do with it. Some of my old fans run it."

"Would I know any of your songs?"

She cocked her head thoughtfully. "Maybe," she said. "My four top hits were 'Love at the Mall', 'The Heartbreak Store', 'Shoes, Shoes, Shoes' and 'Mom Says No, So I Go'. About five years ago, the Sentai Car Company bought the rights to 'Shoes, Shoes, Shoes' and turned it into their jingle."

She hummed a few bars and he recognized it. Impressed, he shook his head with wonder. "Wow," he said after a moment. "I had no idea you were a celebrity, although I should have guessed."

"Why should you have guessed?"

"Because you're so gorgeous. That kind of beauty isn't wasted incognito."

Her smile turned bashful. "It takes one to know one."

He looked at her, grinning. "I'm gorgeous?"

She just nodded and looked away, playfully, and he was enchanted. He almost missed their turn because he was looking at her. But he made the left hand turn onto Croft Lane and headed to the end of the street, pulling into the uneven driveway. When he glanced over at Scarlett again, she was no longer smiling. Her gaze was riveted to the house.

"Good Lord," she sighed, disappointed. "I'd forgotten how run-down the place looks. It really looks like hell."

He watched her as she climbed out of the car before climbing out himself, following her as she walked up the grassy, muddy drive towards the house. He very much wanted to stay and help her, but he wasn't sure she would be receptive. He'd already made himself pretty obvious by showing up at the hotel and he didn't want to press his luck and end up chasing her off. He just wanted to continue the conversation, to get to know her better. What he knew so far, he liked enormously.

As he debated how to handle it, Scarlett continued to walk to the entry vestibule, inspecting the house, looking up at the roofline and the old windows. He trailed after her as she rounded the side of the house, hearing her suddenly let loose a curse. He picked up the pace and rounded the side of the house to see her staring at the back of the house, pointing at it. It was then he noticed that someone had taken a can of red spray paint and had written on the old stones of the rectory.

Get out, bitch

Archer came to stand next to her, his jaw ticking as he envisioned the messy red letters. "Jesus," he hissed.

Scarlett's gaze lingered on the scrawl before turning to him. "I thought the car you parked out front was supposed to prevent this?"

He felt guilty. "It *was*," he began to head back to his car. "I need to call this in and see who in the hell was sleeping on the job last night. I'm going to have someone's head over this."

"Wait," she ran after him and he stopped, turning around. Scarlett put up her hands and shook her head. "Just forget it. It's not worth it. People don't want me in this house and I get that, but the fact is that I'm going to stay, so just forget about yelling at your officers. It doesn't matter, anyway. I'll just go get some turpentine and scrub it off the walls."

He stood there, puzzled, as she pushed past him and went to

her car, unlocking it. He saw that she was about to climb inside and went after her.

"Hey," he said. "Where are you going?"

Scarlett put the key in the ignition, realizing she was very close to breaking down. "To a hardware store to get turpentine." She suddenly slammed her hands against the steering wheel. "Or maybe I'm going to head back to Heathrow and buy three plane tickets and get the hell out of this damn country."

Her head lobbed forward onto the steering wheel, her forehead against it, and she began to weep softly. Archer sighed heavily and opened up her car door wide, crouching down beside her as she sobbed quietly. He put a big hand on the back of her head comfortingly, thrilled with the first feel of her hair against his skin. It was soft and warm. He almost lost himself in the sensation but forced himself to focus on the fact that she was so upset. He stroked her silky dark hair.

"I'm sorry," he said. "I know this whole experience has been one mess after another. You just sit tight and I'll take care of it."

Scarlett didn't have the will or energy to argue. She thought she was being so strong through the course of everything, but apparently she wasn't as strong as she thought. More than that, his hand on her head sort of undid her. It had been a long time since she'd had male comfort and she realized the moment that he touched her that she had missed it. He was offering to help her and she wasn't going to fight him on it. A large part of her wanted his help. It made her feel like she wasn't so alone, something she had felt keenly for the past year.

So she didn't say anything as he went back to his car and got on the radio, talking to dispatch and finally to the watch commander for the Tadcaster substation. He also got on his cell phone and began calling people, although she didn't know who. She could hear his voice but he was too far away to discern any words. She just sat there with her head on the steering wheel, struggling to compose herself as she listened to his deep, confident voice. It gave her comfort. As she was thinking of the last time she'd found comfort with a man, she heard footsteps approach the car and his big, warm hand was on her head again.

"I've got the wheels in motion," he crouched down in her open car door again as she turned her head, still against the steering wheel, to look at him. "I'll stay here and oversee this, so I want you to go back to the hotel with the girls and stay there. I'll ring you in a little while."

She wiped at her watery eyes. "I can't," she said. "I have to wash Morgan's clothes and…."

He shook his head, interrupting her. "I've got that handled," he said. "You don't have to do anything except go back to the hotel. I'm having food delivered to you and the girls so you'll have something to eat. Just rest and relax, and I'll ring you in a bit."

Scarlett's head came off the steering wheel, looking at him with a mixture of confusion and curiosity. "What do you mean you have the clothes handled?" she wanted to know. "I can't let you do that yourself."

"I'm not going to do it myself."

"Then who's going to do it?"

"My people are calling a cleaning service to come and pick them up," he told her. "They'll be washed and delivered to the hotel this afternoon."

She was genuinely surprised. "But… but the suitcase is soiled, too," she said. "It needs to be…."

He cut her off. "I'll get her a new suitcase. It'll be delivered with the clothes."

Scarlett's jaw dropped when it began to occur to her just how much he was taking on. She put her soft hand on his big, muscular arm.

"Archer, you're a saint for doing all of this, but it really isn't your problem," she insisted. "You don't have to do any of this."

He nodded firmly, putting his big mitt over her hand. "Yes, I do," he countered. "I told you this place would be safe and it obviously wasn't, so I need to make amends. I'll take care of the clothes and suitcase, and I have people coming over here that will clean up the graffiti. I've also got a cleaning crew coming to clean up the inside and repair the broken windows so we can start getting this place livable. You need to let me do this."

She was baffled. "Why?"

He smiled and patted her hand. "Because I want to," he said softly. "Please."

All Scarlett could do was stare at him, torn between wanting to let him do as he said he would and telling him to back off. He was comforting, that was true, but not really knowing the man, it was also too much, too soon. He was taking over. It was starting to scare her a little, so much so that she suddenly climbed out of the car and nearly bowled him over. Archer stumbled back and stood up as she backed away from him.

"I can't," she shook her head, her hazel eyes wide and unsteady. "I can't let you do all of this. Archer, I just met you last night and suddenly, you're taking over this whole situation? You don't even know me and I don't even know you. I just... I just can't let you do all of this. It makes me really uncomfortable."

He could see he had frightened her and hastened to reassure her. "I'm sorry if I'm coming on too strong," he said sincerely. "I don't mean to. I'm just trying to help. You've gotten a bum deal since you got off the plane at Heathrow and I'm just trying to make things a little easier for you. I'm not trying to scare you and I'm not trying to take over. I just want to help."

Scarlett was still guarded. "I believe you," she said quietly.

"But this house is my problem. I can't let you assume the problems of a woman you just met."

"Why not?"

"Because I can't," she declared. "It may be something you later regret. Now, I want you to do me a favor."

"Anything."

"I want you to go."

He looked both hurt and surprised. "Why?"

"Please," she whispered, realizing the tears were returning. "I think you're a sweet, generous and wonderful man, and I've very much enjoyed coming to know you. But you're overwhelming me like an eager puppy and it's just too much for me right now. The last thing I want to do is take advantage of someone I just met and I feel like that's exactly what I would be doing by letting you do all of these things for me. You'll have to let me work them out for myself. If I need help, I'll ask."

He just stared at her, feeling disappointment like he hadn't felt in a very long time. But he realized she was right.

"I'm so sorry," he said after a moment. "I didn't mean to be pushy. As I said, I was just trying to help. The moment I met you last night, I... I was so attracted to you, Scarlett. I don't know how else to say it. This morning, I had been sitting in that hotel lobby for almost two hours waiting for you to come downstairs because I wanted the chance to talk to you again. I realize it sounds freakish, like I'm stalking you, but I assure you I'm not. It just that... well, I've pretty much sworn off all women and then I saw you and knew I had to make an exception."

So he spelled it out, plain and simple. All of the warmth she thought she had imagined between them hadn't been her imagination at all. It had been real. Scarlett was deeply touched, thrilled if she were to admit it, but she was also leery. She wasn't sure she was really ready for something as wonderful as this.

"I don't know...," she hung her head, confused. "I'm so flattered, Archer, but... I'm not sure I'm ready to date anyone, even someone as amazing as you."

His heart fell a little but he didn't give up. "Well," he ventured, "if you *were* ready to date, what would your criteria be?"

She thought a moment. "I wouldn't be looking for something casual," she said. "I won't be a convenience."

"Neither will I."

"If I date someone again, it's with a purpose. I had one domestic partnership and I wouldn't look for another. If I hook up with someone again, it's going to be something well thought out and permanent because I don't take relationships lightly."

"I don't either."

She cocked her head. "So what are you saying?"

"I'm saying that I'd like to get to know you. I don't have to know you weeks or months or years to figure that out. I got a good feeling off you within the first few minutes of meeting you and I trust my gut. It tells me that you're very, very special." He paused, watching the indecision on her face. "I'm not asking for the moon, Scarlett. I'm just asking if you'll let me come around now and again, and treat you the way I think you should be treated. I'd really like to if you'll let me."

It was a sweet and non-pushy way to present his case and she fought off a flattered grin. "I think that would be okay, I guess," she said quietly. "But shouldn't you be focusing on a duchess or princess or something?"

His brow furrowed. "Come again?"

"Aren't you British nobility?"

His features relaxed somewhat, perhaps suspiciously. "Who told you that?"

"It doesn't matter. Is it true?"

He puckered his lips thoughtfully. "Maybe."

"We can't go any further with this unless you tell me the truth."

"If I tell you the truth, will you let me clean up your house and take you out to dinner tonight?"

"I'll let you take me out to dinner."

"What about the house?"

"Let's hear your truth and I'll decide."

He couldn't help but grin, watching her as she struggled not to grin also. There was hope in the air, as if they were both pondering the fact that they were interested in one another and excited, terrified, at the prospect.

"All right, then, if you're going to be difficult about it," he folded his enormous arms over his chest. "I am descended on both sides of the family from British nobility, as my mother's father was Baron Rosedale, and through my father I inherited the title Earl of Wintringham and Mulgrave. I also have a few other sundry titles to go along with that, but the Wintringham earldom merged with the Mulgrave earldom about three hundred years ago, and at the time it was the largest earldom in Yorkshire. Right now, my family still owns the land from Stamford Bridge to Claxton, up to Kirkham and across to Thixendale. We're still a major landholder in the north. I have a younger brother, who is also titled, but in this day and age you can't support your family with a title, which is why I went to work for the North Yorkshire police and my brother became a barrister. Is there anything else you want to know?"

Her eyes were twinkling at him. "How tall are you?"

"Six feet, five and a half inches."

"How much do you weigh?"

"In American terms, about two hundred and sixty pounds. How much do *you* weigh?"

"One hundred and twenty-three pounds."

"Any other questions?"

"Where are you taking me for dinner?"

"Someplace lovely and expensive. Next question?"

"Why aren't you working today?"

"Because I have a rotating schedule and this is my day off. Is that it?"

"For now."

"Good."

He uncrossed his arms and walked over to her, taking her by the hand and leading her back to her rental car. Opening the door, he put her in the driver's seat.

"Now," he said with quiet authority. "You will drive down this driveway and take a right out to the big road. Then you will take another right and go for about five miles until you come to a big motorway. Go north, or right again, and get on the motorway and drive until the signs say Exit Wetherby. Are you with me so far?"

Scarlett nodded. "Yes."

Archer continued. "Get off at the second Wetherby exit and go left on York road, or back over the freeway. When you come to Deighton Road, go right and it will take you straight to the hotel. Do you understand?"

"Aye, captain."

"That's Deputy Chief Constable."

She broke into a grin. "Yes, my lord."

"If you call me that again, I'll spank you."

She giggled uncontrollably, still somewhat apprehensive of the direction her association with him seemed to be taking but realizing she was willing to explore it. If she didn't, she would never forgive herself.

"Okay," she finally gave in. "I'll go back to the hotel and wait for you to call."

He lifted her hand and kissed it, flashing her a bright grin. He closed the car door and stood there while she started up the car and carefully backed it out. Scarlett's last vision of him was as he began to walk towards the house, waving to her as he moved. She waved back, put the car in drive, and went back to the hotel exactly the way he told her to. She wasn't sure how she was going to explain any of this to the girls, so she opted not to, at least until she had to. Truth was, she was still trying to figure it all out.

By early afternoon, things began happening.

———

It all started with a knock on the hotel room door about an hour after Scarlett had returned from the rectory. Morgan opened the door to find two employees from a local restaurant called *Le Bon Appetit* with enough food to feed ten people.

Delighted, and hungry, the girls tore into cinnamon toast, scrambled eggs with ham, roast beef sandwiches, egg mayonnaise sandwiches, chips, and a host of other goodies that had them stuffed and groaning a half hour later. It was a feast that made the young ladies very happy in a day or two that hadn't seen much of that and Scarlett was appreciative. The food was only the appetizer, however; the main course came by early afternoon.

Scarlett had been lying on the bed, surfing the internet learning about the restoration of older homes, when there was a soft knock at the door. Setting her computer aside, she rose to answer the door.

Three people were standing outside in the hallway; two women and one man. The women had what looked like grocery bags in their arms and the man had something big behind him, which upon further inspection, was a very large rolling suitcase. Scarlett lifted her eyebrows at the trio in friendly greeting.

"Can I help you?" she asked politely.

The man spoke; he was slender and silver-haired. "Miss Scarlett?"

"Yes."

"Lord Phipps sent us. We have your laundry."

Scarlett opened the door wide and admitted them into her room. The women were older, rather dowdy, but they moved swiftly and silently into the room and deposited the grocery bags onto the bed. The man came in after them with the big rolling suitcase. As he came into the room, Scarlett got a good look at the suitcase and her eyes bugged.

"That's a Louis Vuitton," she pointed at the suitcase with shock.

The man nodded. "Yes, mum."

Scarlett tore her eyes off the suitcase and looked at the man. "But that's at least twenty-five hundred dollars."

The man looked rather confused as he looked at the suitcase. "I wouldn't know, Mum," he said politely. "We simply picked it up at the store in Leeds. Lord Phipps would know how much it costs."

As Scarlett stood there, astonished, Morgan opened the connecting door between the rooms. "Mom?" she asked. "Is that my clothes?"

Scarlett nodded as Morgan came into the room. Her mother had told her about Archer taking care of the clothes cleaning and arranging to get her a new suitcase, but before Scarlett could hold her off on the suitcase, Morgan got a look at it and shrieked.

"Oh, my gosh!" the girl gasped, falling to her knees beside the suitcase and running her hands all over it. "A Louis Vuitton! Are you kidding me?"

"Hold on," Scarlett admonished. "I'm not sure we can keep...."

"Why not?" Morgan begged. "Mom, Mr. Phipps *gave* this to me so he obviously wanted me to have it. Why can't I keep it?"

Alexandra came into the room, having heard her sister squeal, and gave a serious look to the Louis Vuitton, but it didn't mean much to her, so she looked at the clothes on the bed and then at the people who brought them.

"Hi," she said simply.

The man smiled at her. "Hello, young lady."

Alexandra was curious. "Who are you?"

"I'm Mr. Bayse," he replied, pointing to the women. "That is my wife, Mrs. Bayse, and her sister, Mrs. Pine."

He indicated the women in order, the round brunette and the graying blond. Before Alexandra could ask any more questions, Mr. Bayse turned to Scarlett.

"Lord Phipps has asked me to take you back to the rectory," he said. "When you are ready to leave, we'll be down in the car at the entrance."

Scarlett didn't ask questions. She was truthfully rather anxious to get back to her property and sick of sitting around in a hotel room. She turned to the girls.

"Hurry up," she said. "Get your stuff packed up so we can go."

As Mr. Bayse and the women went downstairs, Scarlett and the girls hurriedly finished packing up what they had brought with them, Morgan with her beautiful new suitcase. She was very proud of it and Scarlett knew she would never be able to give it back to Archer, but she was certainly going to let Archer know what she thought of him giving Morgan such an expensive gift. But she put her annoyance aside as she finished packing and got the girls organized. It took about fifteen minutes for Morgan to change into her own clothing and for all of them to pack up and make it downstairs to the hotel lobby.

Mr. Bayse had a passenger van and, after loading in their

bags and the precious Louis Vuitton suitcase, they climbed in and the van departed for Newton Kyme. Alexandra sat with Scarlett, watching the countryside go by while Morgan sat in the back and messed around on her electronic tablet. She was pretty much glued to the thing. As they headed south, Alexandra noticed the animals in the fields.

"Mom," she pointed out the window. "Look at the horses."

Scarlett had her arm casually around her youngest, toying with the child's hair. "Pretty," she commented.

"Do you think I can have a horse?"

"Maybe," Scarlett replied. "We really need to get the house in order first, though."

Alexandra didn't like that answer too much. "If I can't have a horse right now, do you think we could at least find a stable to rent one? There has to be stables around here."

"Give me a few days to get the house settled, Alexandra. Then we'll look in to it."

Scarlett's tone effectively shut Alexandra down for the moment, but she was still longing after the horses that they passed along the motorway. Morgan was focused on her tablet as the van sped south, retracing the route that Archer had taken that morning on his way to the rectory and Scarlett was beginning to recognize some things and get oriented. She quickly recognized the turn off onto Croft Lane.

As the van pulled into the old driveway, Scarlett immediately noticed at least three contractor's lorries, or trucks, and a bigger lorry that looked like a moving van. There were also a couple of cars on the lawn, one of them being Archer's big BMW. As the passenger van pulled halfway up the driveway and came to a stop, Archer suddenly appeared from the entrance vestibule.

Scarlett watched him approach, her heart fluttering at the sight. He was such a handsome man and although she hadn't known him a full day, still, the more she saw of him, the more enamored she could feel herself becoming.

Mr. Bayse put the van in park and shut down the engine. Alexandra went to open the van door but Archer was there, opening it for her. He smiled at Alexandra and helped her out of the van, followed by Morgan. The older girl gazed at him with warm gratitude.

"I want to thank you for the beautiful suitcase," Morgan gushed. "It's the most beautiful suitcase I've ever seen."

She was smiling at him and Archer realized it was the first time since he'd met the girl that he had seen her smile. She was quite lovely, like her mother.

"You're very welcome," he said. "I'm glad you like it."

"I love it," Morgan insisted, climbing out of the van when he held up his hand and helped her out. "It's just beautiful."

"Good," he said, turning his attention to Scarlett, who was the last one out. His gaze fell on her and his features softened with appreciation. "Hello, Ms. Ward."

His voice was soft, deep, purring. Scarlett felt a chill run through her at the sound. "Hello," she said. Then she fought down the giddiness to focus on something she had been stewing on since the expensive suitcase had showed up. "You're in big trouble, buster."

Archer's smile faded and his eyebrows lifted. "Me?" he asked. "What did I do?"

As the girls went towards the house, Scarlett crooked a finger at Archer, indicating for him to follow her. He did, gladly, as she walked to the rear of the car so they could have more privacy. She came to a halt and faced him.

"Let me preface this by saying your generosity is astounding and you have my deepest thanks for making my daughter so happy," she lowered her voice. "But I ought to punch you right in the nose for buying Morgan a two thousand dollar suitcase. What in the world were you thinking?"

Archer would have thought she was very angry except those deep hazel eyes were twinkling. He bit off a smile. "May I plead my case, Your Honor?"

"You'd better."

His mouth twitched. "I was presented with several different types of suitcases, but everything but the Louis Vuitton seemed very cheap and flimsy. Not wanting to provide your daughter with something that was going to fall apart after a few uses, I wanted to get her something that would last for years to come. I though the quality of it was worth the price."

"How much did you pay for it?"

"It's a gift. Do you always ask how much gifts cost?"

She cocked an eyebrow. "It's a very *expensive* gift and if you don't tell me, I'm going to give it right back to you no matter how much my daughter begs to keep it."

As he'd seen from the beginning of his association with her, she was determined, stubborn and, if one got right down to it, pushy. But he liked those qualities in her. He thought they were very admirable. But he was stubborn, too.

"I'm not going to tell you. Are you still going to give it back?"

Her reply was to turn back for the van and throw open the door. He walked up behind her as she dug around in the back until she got a grip on the handle of the Louis Vuitton. When he saw her wrestling with it and trying to pull it out, he reached over the top of her and grasped both of her wrists, effectively stopping her. He was pressed up against her, her sweet body spooned against his, and he leaned over and put his lips against her right ear.

"Eighteen hundred pounds," he whispered. "Now, can she keep it?"

A violent shudder ran through Scarlett with his hot breath on her ear. Archer felt it and he resisted the urge to wrap his arms around her and kiss her tender neck, so close to his mouth. He wanted to run his tongue and mouth all over every piece of flesh he could come into contact with, in the very worst way. He'd never felt so much desire in his entire life.

"You're telling me that there were no suitcases of decent quality less than eighteen hundred pounds?" she asked breathlessly.

"None that I liked."

Scarlett sighed heavily. The truth was that she couldn't think with him so close against her. His big body and warmth had sucked every thought right out of her head. She let go of the suitcase and tried to stand up, but he was still backed up against her and it was difficult to move.

"All right," she muttered. "She can keep it. But don't try to get away with something like that again."

Archer could feel her trying to stand up but he had no intention of moving. He could feel himself growing aroused as she squirmed against him.

"I swear, I won't," he whispered, his lips still close to her ear. "Unless I have your permission first, of course."

"Just so we understand one another."

"I think we're starting to."

A shout from the house broke Archer from his stance and he stood away from her, looking over to see one of the contractors calling to a colleague. He thought he'd heard his name but had been incorrect. Scarlett, still trying to catch her breath, turned in the direction of the shout also but Archer stopped her. Facing her, he put his big hands on her upper arms, effectively stilling her.

"There's something else we need to discuss before you head over to the house," he was trying to fight down his arousal and focus. "I had a contractor come out earlier today and assess what needs to be done on the rectory. He's made some discoveries, none of which should be particularly surprising given the age of the house, but the biggest problems seem to be the plumbing and electricity. He says it's going to be at least a couple of weeks before those can be ironed out but until then, you can't live in the house. You won't have any plumbing and only limited electricity."

Scarlett wits returned as the impact of his words hit home. "Are you serious?" she asked, then shook her head quickly. "Don't answer that. I know you are. But... I really didn't anticipate not being able to live in the house. I didn't have a Plan B."

"I know," he said patiently. "But I have a proposal if you'll hear it."

She eyed him. "Proposal?" she repeated warily. "Okay... go ahead."

He grinned. "My home is about twenty miles from here," he told her. "It's huge. There's more room than we know what to do with, including an entire wing that isn't being used. You and the girls are welcome to stay there until your house is habitable. I promise, it's a completely chivalrous and platonic offer, and I don't expect anything in return, if you get my meaning. It just seems a shame for you to pay to stay somewhere when I've got perfectly good rooms going to waste. I'd be honored if you'd consider it."

Scarlett's gaze lingered on him and she could tell, simply by the tone of his voice and his body language that he meant what he said. She didn't get the sense that he was trying to get her under his roof to do wicked things to her. As much as the offer appealed to her, she found that she simply couldn't take that leap after only knowing the man a day. She wasn't sure what kind of message that would send to her daughters. So she grasped both of his big hands in her small warm ones and stood on tiptoe, kissing him gently on the cheek.

"That's so sweet of you, thank you," she murmured. "But I'm going to have to decline for now. I'm just not comfortable moving my girls into the home of a man I've known for less than twenty-four hours no matter how much I like him. I very much appreciate the offer, though. It's extremely generous of you."

He had suspected that would be her answer but he was disappointed anyway, even though her refusal had been very kind. He held her hands tightly.

"I thought that might be your answer, but I wanted to make the offer anyway," he said. "Maybe... maybe you'll feel differently next week. Maybe you'll be more comfortable with it as time goes on and we come to know each other better."

"Maybe," she agreed, eyes twinkling.

He smiled in return. "For now, will you let Henry and I at least take our new American friends out to dinner?"

She cocked her head curiously. "I thought you said he was with his mother?"

"She'll bring him home tonight at five."

"Then we'd love to."

Archer was thrilled. He grinned broadly, glancing over at the rectory and noticing that the girls were wandering the front garden, inspecting it. They were trudging through the wet grass, trying not to slip in the mud.

"I suppose you girls will need time to get ready," he said, looking to Scarlett again. "I'll take you back over to the hotel and we can see about arranging an extended stay."

"I think that would be the best option right now."

"Even so, my offer still stands. Just say the word."

"I appreciate that."

It was as much of an answer as she was going to give him so he didn't push. But he did take her hand as they made their way over to house to speak with the contractor. Scarlett relished the feel of his big, warm hand around hers, savoring it, until they neared the rectory and she discreetly pulled her hand away. By then, the contractor was coming over to greet them and Scarlett heard all of the bad news, first hand.

It was bad indeed.

———

Henry Phipps was a handsome lad of six, big for his age with his father's auburn hair. He was dressed in slacks and a sport coat, as was his father, when they came to pick Scarlett and her daughters up at the hotel around seven that evening.

Henry decided very quickly that he was deeply in love with Alexandra. He sat in the back seat of the BMW between Morgan and Alexandra, but his attention was solely on the younger Ward girl. Alexandra wasn't sure how to take the child's attention, eyeing the boy who was staring so openly at her. Scarlett kept glancing back at her daughter, grinning because the girl looked so uncomfortable.

The night was surprisingly calm and pleasant, a far cry from the tempest that had plowed through the night before. Dressed in an elegant black and white dress and black stilettos, Scarlett looked astonishingly beautiful as she sat in the passenger seat. In fact, Archer was having a difficult time keeping his eyes off her as they headed into York.

"I hope you're all hungry," he said to the group. "We have reservations at a very nice restaurant. Their food is excellent."

Alexandra was still eyeing Henry. "What kind of food do they have?"

"Anything you want," Archer replied. "Beef, chicken, fish... you name it."

"I'm a vegetarian," Morgan interjected. "I don't eat meat."

Archer shrugged. "I'm sure they have something for you as well. You won't starve, I promise."

They continued on into the city as early evening descended upon the land. They entered the city limits of York, winding their way across the river and past York Cathedral. Scarlett's eyes were wide on the enormous cathedral.

"My gosh," she breathed. "That thing is enormous. I saw it yesterday when we came in but I really didn't pay much attention to it. It's really beautiful."

Archer glanced up at the towering spires of the Gothic cathedral. "That is York Minster," he told her. "Every child in York is forced to learn about it. A church has been on that site since the Dark Ages, but the structure you see began construction shortly after the Norman invasion. It's one of the biggest churches in Europe."

Scarlett's eyes were still on the minster as they passed by. "I believe it."

They arrived at the restaurant shortly. Called the Lime, it was an upscale experience in imaginative cuisine, some that was a little out of the ordinary for Morgan and Alexandra. Scarlett thoroughly enjoyed the experience in the cozy little restaurant, as the food was delicious and the company divine. She had a wild mushroom risotto that was to die for and a delicious white wine that Archer had selected, and little by little, she was becoming more comfortable with the man she had known only a short day. Halfway through dinner, it was as if she had always known him. She couldn't describe what she felt any other way.

There were a variety of reasons for her sense, the most predominant one being that Archer was a very old fashioned gentleman and had raised his son to be the same way. He opened doors, held out chairs, and rose politely when a lady either left or arrived at the table. He ordered for her, put her napkin in her lap, and did everything but eat the food for her. He was unbelievably attentive, but it wasn't contrived. It was real, the natural actions of a well-mannered man. Sitting in between Alexandra and Morgan again, young Henry behaved exactly the same way.

Henry had held open the door for Alexandra and Morgan almost as an afterthought, but he rushed to pull their chairs out for them, something that confused both of the girls until Archer pulled out the chair for Scarlett and then they started to catch on. Henry was very helpful with the bread basket and in sharing his knowledge of what venison and beetroot were. He even tried to pour sparkling water for Alexandra, but it was fairly heavy for him so his father had to help him.

Still, he was a very polite, kind and intelligent young man. Scarlett knew it was all because of Archer and, with that under-standing, she began to see just what kind of man Archer really was. Only a man of integrity and character would raise his son so thoughtfully and she began to rethink her stance on his offer to allow her and her girls to stay at his home. She was coming to think it might be the opportunity of a lifetime... what had she told her girls? That living in England was a great adventure? Perhaps this is where the adventure started.

By the time dessert came around, they were all getting along quite well with the exception of Morgan, who still seemed quiet and withdrawn. Scarlett was sitting back against her seat, teacup in hand, watching her daughters and Henry interact. Henry was trying to pour Alexandra some tea and Scarlett glanced at Archer, who was watching his son as well. When the boy threatened to spill it from the pot, he put out a big hand and steadied it.

"Henry, you're very helpful," Scarlett said.

Henry looked at her, a pleased smile on his face. He was missing his lower front teeth, making him look adorably juvenile.

"I help my teacher all of the time," he told her. "Miss Peacock is old and sometimes she needs help with things, but she smells funny so sometimes I don't like to get too close to her."

The girls burst out laughing and Scarlett put a hand over her mouth to hide her smile as Archer admonished his son.

"Henry," he said quietly, shaking his head at the boy. "That's not very nice. We don't speak that way of others."

Henry was both defiant and contrite. "But it's true," he insisted weakly. "You told me to always tell the truth, no matter what. Miss Peacock smells like a mush pot sometimes."

Alexandra was far gone with giggles as Morgan looked at Archer. "What's a mush pot?" she wanted to know.

Archer was looking at his son with an eyebrow cocked in disapproval, glancing at Morgan as he answered. "I think he means she smells like mushy flower pot; you know a moldy smell." He leaned forward and looked pointedly at his son, who was giggling because Alexandra was. "Henry, I know I told you that you must always tell the truth, but sometimes you must be careful. Yes, it's the truth that Miss Peacock smells like a mush pot, but is it nice to say so?"

Henry had stopped giggling and was looking at his father with some remorse. "No."

"Would it hurt her feelings?"

"Yes."

"Then you must think before you say things like that. Would you like it if someone told you that you smelled?"

Henry shook his head. "No," he said, then turned to Alexandra. "I have a cat."

The boy had the attention span of a mosquito, which wasn't unusual for a six-year-old. He'd moved on to the next subject as his father sat back in his chair, shook his head reproachfully, and sipped his coffee. But Henry didn't see; he was completely focused on Alexandra.

"What's the cat's name?" she asked.

"Max."

"What kind of cat is he?"

"A big orange one. He likes to chase bugs."

"Oh."

"And I have a pony, too."

That got Alexandra's attention. "You do?" she asked, very interested. "What kind of pony?"

"He's black and his name is Nero," Henry said proudly. "I got him for my birthday."

Scarlett was watching her daughter's reaction to the young boy having a pony. "Nero?" Scarlett looked at Archer with a quirky grin. "Who named him that?"

Archer was sitting very close to her, as close as he possibly could without putting an arm around her. But her right leg and his left leg were butted against one another and it was a supreme effort for him not to put a hand on her knee or touch her in some fashion. As long as he wasn't looking directly at her, he could control it, but the moment their eyes met, his palms began to sweat with want to touch her.

"He came with that name," he replied. "He's a pedigreed Welsh pony and his full name is Nero's Charge of Light. I swear, I didn't name him."

Scarlett was giggling. "That's a good thing," she shook her head. "I'd worry about you if you had. Who in the world would name an animal Nero?"

He snickered in return but was interrupted from replying by Alexandra. She was still fixed on the fact that Henry had a pony.

"Do you keep horses at your house?" she asked Archer.

He nodded, moving to casually put his arm around Scarlett's chair but pulling back when he realized how intimate that would look. "Several," he replied. "Do you like to ride?"

Alexandra's face lit up. "I had a horse back in California but we had to sell him when we moved," she said wistfully. "My mom said that maybe we could get another one after the house was settled, but that could take a really long time now that... well, now that the house is so messed up...."

She trailed off, looking at her mother with tears filling her eyes. It was a sensitive subject with Alexandra. Scarlett set her teacup down and moved to comfort her daughter but Archer interrupted.

"No worries, love." He could see how upset she was. "I have a whole stable full of horses you can pick from. You can ride whenever you want to."

"Really?" Alexandra lit up and the tears vanished. "Can I come tomorrow?"

"Alex," Scarlett admonished. "Honey, you don't invite yourself over to someone's house."

Archer did put a hand on Scarlett's knee, then, simply to quiet her. "You can come whenever your mother will let you," he replied. "I have a couple of gentle mares that you might like."

Alexandra was nearly leaping out of her seat. "I had a jumper at home," she said excitedly. "I did a few competitions with him, just beginning stuff, but I won a couple of times in the five feet and under barriers."

Archer could see how thrilled the girl was. "I have a few jumpers as well," he told her. "They used to be racehorses, but I had them re-trained when their racing days were over. You can come and take a look whenever your mother says it's all right."

Alexandra looked at her mother and Scarlett knew that all was lost. There was no way she could deny or delay the child.

"Can we go tomorrow, Mom?" Alexandra asked eagerly.

Scarlett sighed faintly and sat back in her chair, toying with her teacup. She eyed her daughters, both of them, thinking a lot of things at that moment. Mostly, she was thinking about Archer. At that moment, she could feel her resistance to him fading. He was so incredibly generous with her girls, something they desperately needed from a male figure. Their father was absent in their young lives and they'd lost Jerry just as their mother had. Now, Archer was making his presence known and the girls were succumbing. They all were. Scarlett was losing her control in the situation. Truth was, she wasn't all that upset about it.

"Archer offered to let us come and live at his house while ours is being fixed," she finally said. "He says he has a very big house and an entire wing that's not being used. I told him I'd have to think about it."

Alexandra jumped off her chair. "I want to go!" she squealed. "He has horses there and I could ride them every day!"

"I can ride with you!" Henry started jumping up and down because Alexandra was.

Scarlett looked at Archer, who was gazing back at her with such hope and warmth that it took her breath away.

"You're taking on a lot offering your home to three people you just met," she said.

He smiled broadly. "No decision in my life has ever felt so right. Please come."

Scarlett hesitated for a moment. "Maybe we can come out tomorrow and take a look at the horses," she murmured, "and the house. Maybe we should all see what we're really getting into before we make the final decision."

"Fair enough."

Scarlett regarded him a moment. "I'd really hate to lose you as a friend if this didn't work out."

He shook his head firmly. "That's not going to happen."

"It might. You don't really know us, after all. We could be the Americans your mother warned you about."

He laughed and dared to take her hand, holding it tightly in his big, warm fingers. "My mother loves Americans," he said, sobering. "She'll love you, too."

Scarlett chuckled as he squeezed her hand. She returned her attention to Alexandra and Henry, who were beginning to wander around the restaurant.

"I think we've lost our audience," she said, looking at her oldest daughter, still sitting quiet and subdued at the table. "Except Morgan, of course. What are you doing over there, sweetheart?"

Morgan had been messing around with her new cell phone, looking up when she heard her name. Seeing that her mother and Archer were looking at her, she put the phone back in her purse.

"Nothing," the girl replied. "Mom, I'm kind of tired. Can we go back to the hotel now?"

Archer was standing up before Scarlett could even get a word out. "Of course," he said, waving the server over with the check. "I'm sure you're all exhausted. It's been a busy couple of days."

Scarlett thought their departure was all a little abrupt; she still had a cup of tea in her hand, but she set it down and collected her coat, which Archer helped her put on, and finally her purse. Morgan was already at the door, waiting for them, as Henry followed Alexandra around as the girl inspected some kind of sign near the front door. Archer took Scarlett's elbow politely as they headed for the exit. Before they could get to the door, however, a little old woman seated near the front of the restaurant stopped them.

"I don't mean to interrupt your evening," she said, "but I've been watching you and your lovely family all evening. What wonderful and polite children you have. You must be very proud."

Archer looked rather shocked. Scarlett glanced at him, seeing that he had no idea what to say to the old woman, so she answered.

"Thank you," she said pleasantly. "We are very proud."

The woman sat at the table with an equally old man, her ancient eyes twinkling as she reached up and grasped Scarlett's hand.

"You're American," she murmured. "I could tell. You look like a movie star. How fortunate your husband is."

Now Scarlett was rather speechless, unsure of what to say. Only a moment or two passed before she heard Archer's soft, deep voice next to her.

"I am, indeed, madam," he said quietly. "Deeply fortunate. Thank you for your kind words."

The old woman's gaze moved back and forth between Archer and Scarlett. "You've been together a long time, I can tell," she said, letting go of Scarlett's hand and grasping the old man's hand next to her. "Charles and I have been married for almost sixty years. You two have the same look we had when we were young. There is much love and devotion there, and your children reflect that. It's wonderful to see."

Scarlett was growing increasingly tongue tied. She thought that if she answered the old woman initially, that it would be the end of it, but now they were being pulled deeper into the quagmire of awkwardness. It was Archer who finally put both of his hands on Scarlett's shoulders and gently pushed her along.

"Thank you again," he said as they moved on. "Have a wonderful evening."

Fortunately, the old woman didn't say anything more as Archer herded Scarlett and the children out of the restaurant. As they headed to the car along the lamp-lit street, Archer put his arm around Scarlett's shoulders. He simply couldn't help himself. The kids were walking in various positions up ahead of them as he bent down in Scarlett's ear.

"Sorry about that," he said.

Scarlett looked up at him. "Why?"

He shrugged, watching Henry and Alexandra play on the curb. "Because it was awkward, I suppose," he said. "Old women have great imagination."

Scarlett was watching the sidewalk pass beneath her feet. "Not a problem," she said. "I suppose we do look like a cute couple."

He grinned, the hand on her shoulder now gently caressing her. "I've been trying to tell you that since yesterday."

Scarlett grinned. "I'm starting to see the light."

He came to a halt, facing her, as the smile faded from his face. "I truly, sincerely hope so," he said, seeing that Morgan, several feet ahead of them, had come to a halt also to wait for them to catch up, so he resumed walking. "I have to work tomorrow but I'm thinking that when I'm off, I'll pick you and the girls up, and you can have dinner with us at the house and take a look at the horses. I can also show you the wing I was talking about so you can inspect your potential living quarters. Would that be acceptable?"

Scarlett could hardly turn him down. "Sounds good," she replied. "Your contractor is coming over tomorrow to start on the plumbing, so I'll be busy with that in the morning."

"Are you going to leave the girls at the hotel?"

"Yes," she nodded. "There's no reason for them to come with me to the rectory. I don't think they like it very much, anyway. At least, Morgan doesn't. She says it's too creepy."

"It *is* pretty creepy."

Scarlett snickered, glancing up at him as they drew near to his car, parked along the curb. "Afraid of ghosts much?"

He laughed, stroking her back gently, affectionately, but letting his hand drop as quickly as he touched her. "I could tell you some stories," he alluded. "I've seen a few things in my time that make me believe there are things out there that we don't understand. Years ago, I saw a friend... well, suffice it to say that I've seen things. But those stories will be for another time when we're alone and I can properly comfort you."

She lifted her eyebrows. "Pretty sure of yourself, aren't you?"

His pale blue eyes glittered at her. "Sure enough. Objections?"

"Not so far."

"Good."

They reached the car and Archer unlocked it, opening the door for Scarlett while also helping his son open the heavy door for the girls. Everyone settled, Archer climbed into the driver's seat and turned the car on, pulling away from the curb and heading down the dark, quaint street, returning his dinner guests to their hotel. Truth was, he hated to see the evening end.

In the dark as they drove the motorway back to Wetherby, he dared to put his hand on Scarlett's knee when he was sure the kids couldn't see it. He was surprised and very pleased, when she gripped his fingers tightly.

The evening ended on high note.

———

Phipps Hall was nothing Scarlett had expected.

In truth, she really wasn't sure what she had expected. All of this was so new to her. Therefore, when Archer pulled up a long driveway and onto grounds that looked like a park, she was mildly impressed. The land his family had owned for over five hundred years was beautiful and serene. There were paddocks along the drive and Alexandra grew excited as horses came in to view. The green grass and rolling hills were very picturesque. Scarlett was in the process of inspecting a mare and her tiny foal when the house suddenly appeared over a rise.

The hills seemed to part and a Jacobean jewel of a home appeared. It was a magnificent home of gray stone and glass, looking like it had once been a castle or fortified manor because there were turrets on the corner of the structure. Great stone planters that looked like they had been stolen from the looting of Rome lined the driveway near the house, spitting out sprays of slender yellow flowers and adding to the impressive ambiance. As Scarlett sat there with her mouth hanging open at the sight, she heard breathing in both of her ears.

"Wow," Morgan was by her mother's left ear, sitting forward in the back seat and straining to catch a glimpse. "That house is amazing."

"It looks like a castle," Alexandra concurred in Scarlett's right ear, awestruck.

Archer smiled at the women as they gawked at his ancestral home. "Welcome to Phipps Hall, ladies," he said. "This land has belonged to my family for almost eight hundred years and, for a time, there was a castle not far from here called Steelmoor. It stood from the time of Henry the Second until just after Henry Tudor gained the throne, whereupon my ancestor decided he needed a finer house and not a military garrison, so he began building Phipps Hall."

"It's incredible," Scarlett breathed as they pulled up in the circular driveway. "It looks like something out of a movie set."

Archer grinned as he put the car in park and climbed out. He opened the door for Henry, who ran around to the other side of the car and opened the door for Alexandra and Morgan. Archer opened the door for Scarlett and extended a hand, politely helping her from the car. Dressed in nice black slacks and a sexy black blouse that both titillated and concealed, she looked delicious and he wasn't discreet in his observations of her. But, like a gentleman, he let her hand go so as not to be overly obvious about it, and swept an arm in the direction of the entrance.

It was an entrance vestibule, just like the one at the rectory, only larger and more exquisite. Archer shut the door leading from the drive and then opened the second door, which led into the most enormous living room Scarlett had ever seen. The soft green walls embraced white pillars, white furniture, and magnificent pieces of art spread throughout the room. A fireplace that stood taller than she did was embedded in one of the walls. Scarlett just stood there and gawked.

"Oh, my goodness," she breathed. "This is the most beautiful room I've ever seen."

Archer's gaze moved over the room he'd known since birth. He was used to all of the opulence but he could understand why people were impressed with it.

"When my father passed away several years ago, my mother sank herself into restoring the house room by room with his life insurance," he told her. "The house's last major renovation had been during the nineteen thirties when my grandfather, quite the party animal and wanting to make it a grand party house, completely renovated it from an earlier turn of the century renovation. This house has been renovated many times in the course of the centuries."

Scarlett just shook her head in wonder. "It must have been incredibly expensive," she said. "Your family must have oil wells in Saudi Arabia in order to pay for a house like this. You hear about so many of them being sold because people can't afford to keep them up."

"The North Sea, actually."

Scarlett was still looking at the room but his soft words caught her attention. She turned to look at him. "Pardon?"

He smiled at her. "We have oil wells in the North Sea," he said. "My mother is a de Velt. If you haven't heard the name, you will. The de Velt family has been in northern England since William the Conqueror first came ashore. The family owns a lot of property, still, but back in the nineteen twenties my mother's father did some oil prospecting off the shore between Ashlington and Whitby Bay, and ended up sinking a few wells. The automobile industry was just taking off so, consequently, he had an immediate market for the oil. Over the years, the family has expanded the oil empire and my mother is a shareholder in the company. She's worth a lot."

Scarlett was staring at him in shock. "You said you had to work for a living."

He shrugged. "I do," he replied. "My mother isn't going to just give me money. She expects me to be a contributing member of society and pay my way, but I have my own personal wealth fund that she contributes to, especially now that I bear the ancestral title. Technically, Phipps Hall belongs to me. My mother is just a guest."

Scarlett blinked, overwhelmed by it all. At a loss for words, she simply looked back at the room with a rather started expression.

"Wow," was all she could think to say. "This is all so overwhelming."

He grinned and politely took her elbow. "Let me show you around."

He did. The house had at least four levels, starting in the basement with room after room, like a labyrinth, all of the rooms with names like the Snooker Room or the Party Room, the Wine Room, the Bar Room, the nanny's room and staff quarters, plus a variety of other rooms that she lost count of. The next level was the ground level and room after gorgeous room was connected by doors or halls. There was even a secret staircase embedded in a wall that Alexandra and Henry had great fun with. Everything was exquisitely and expensively furnished, and the rooms smelled of old wood and lemons. It was an interesting and very British combination.

There was a mezzanine level between the first and second floors that contained three bedrooms and three bathrooms, and it was this level that Archer offered to Scarlett and the girls. The bedrooms were enormous and beautifully furnished, including the largest bedroom, which had a massive stone bathtub fixed in a corner by the fireplace. There was still a big bathroom with a shower as well, but the tub was in the bedroom itself. Archer showed off the three bedrooms and within two minutes, the girls were begging to stay. There wasn't much Scarlett could do other than agree. Archer was so pleased that he was beaming from ear to ear.

He finished up the tour on the upper floor which contained four more big bedrooms, including the enormous master's suite which encompassed the entire front side of the house. The bathroom alone was as big as a two-car garage. Archer didn't seem impressed by his bedroom suite but Scarlett clearly was. She'd never seen anything like it.

Henry had taken Alexandra and Morgan into his wonderland-like bedroom to show them his toys and gadgets as Scarlett stood in a round turret-type projection in Archer's room that overlooked the driveway. She just stood there, looking out over the green hills of Yorkshire, seemingly lost to her thoughts. Archer walked up behind her, close enough to brush his body against hers, but made no move to touch her.

"What do you think?" he asked. "Do you think you can stand staying here until the rectory is finished?"

Scarlett sighed, her gaze lingering on the landscape, before turning to Archer. "I think this place is incredibly beautiful," she replied. "I guess I was just standing here, thinking of the past couple of days and wondering how my life came to this point. It seems kind of surreal."

He smiled at her. "For me as well," he said. "I told you this before; I had essentially sworn off women until I saw you. In that instant, it was like everything had changed and now here you are, in my home, where I never expected you to be – not in a million years – and I'm thrilled to death at the prospect."

She looked at him seriously. "Why would you swear off women?"

He sobered. "It's a long story."

She studied him because he didn't seem inclined to elaborate on that remark. She gave him enough of a pause but he didn't speak. Finally, she did. "Can I ask you a question?"

"Certainly."

"You said you wanted to date me."

"I do."

"In your mind, what, exactly, does that mean?"

He cocked his head. "I believe I explained it when I told you that I wanted to treat you like a special lady and see where that takes us."

"And I told you that I wasn't looking for something casual."

"Neither am I."

The conversation was starting to confuse her. Perhaps she was already reading too much in to all of this, confused by her own thoughts and speculations. But she wanted to be absolutely clear about what she was getting herself in to. She finally threw up her hands.

"Archer, you're moving my daughters and me into your home," she began to get animated. "If I were the suspicious type, that would mean far more to me than your simply wanting to date me to 'see where that takes us'. Then you say you're not looking for something casual." She suddenly turned away from him and shook her head. "I'm sorry. I shouldn't be thinking too hard about this, but for my own sense of self protection, I guess I have to. If the girls and I move in here, then people are going to assume that you and I... did you ever think about that? What in the world are people going to think if we move in with you?"

He was back to smiling at her. "They'll think I'm a very lucky man."

He was gently teasing but she didn't take the bait. "And they'll think I'm a tramp." She shook her head, her expression pained. "My girls are going to want to make friends... do things with new people... but if their mother is shacking up with Archer Phipps, I'm afraid that might make it kind of difficult for them. I'm afraid I've let you overwhelm me with your charm and persistence, and I'm afraid I'm going to make a bad decision."

His smile faded. "You and I know that this living arrangement wouldn't be for carnal purposes," he said. "I've told you before, Scarlett; I just want to help you and the girls, and I'd like to get to know a lovely woman very well. I, frankly, don't care what people think. They're going to think what they want, no matter if you're living with me or not. But they wouldn't think anything at all if you and I were engaged."

Scarlett's eyes widened. "What?" she hissed. "Are you crazy?"

He laughed. "No, I'm not," he said. "If you're worried about perception, we can simply tell everyone that we're engaged and leave it at that. It's a little white lie that would make it much easier for your daughters to make friends and assimilate into the community. You, too, for that matter. In fact, it would give you some prestige and people would be more willing to accept you as a member of the community. No one would dare shun the fiancée of the Earl of Wintringham and Mulgrave."

She just stared at him, torn. But she had to admit, it made sense, and she wasn't beyond being secretly titillated by the idea. After a moment, she simply laughed.

"I don't even know what to say," she said. "I guess it sounds logical. I'm probably stupid for saying so, but it does."

He was smiling as he approached her. Before Scarlett could react in any fashion, he pulled her against his broad chest and his mouth slanted hungrily over hers. Momentarily startled, Scarlett's first instinct was to pull away but she found, very quickly, that she couldn't. Archer was a wonderful kisser and his power, his quiet strength, quickly had her succumbing. Her arms began to wind around him, her hands to his face, as his kiss began to grow more forceful. Just as she lost herself completely, he pulled back.

"I was right," he whispered.

Scarlett swallowed, forcing herself to focus on his words because her mind was so muddled. "What... what do you mean?"

"You are as delicious as you look."

She just stared up at him, wrapped up in his big arms and struggling to collect her thoughts. "So are you."

He grinned seductively and moved in for another kiss, but they both heard voices out in the corridor and he let her go to see what the commotion was. Scarlett was still standing by the window, struggling to catch her breath, as Archer stepped out into the corridor and began speaking with someone. Just about the time Scarlett reached the bedroom door to see what was going on, Archer approached with an older woman on his arm.

"Mother," he was smiling at Scarlett. "This is Ms. Scarlett Ward, and those young ladies are her daughters. Scarlett and her family arrived from America a couple of days ago. She bought an old rectory over in Newton Kyme. Scarlett, this is my mother, the Lady Arabella de Velt Phipps."

Scarlett smiled at the very attractive blond woman and extended her hand. "It's so nice to meet you," she said. "Your home is so lovely."

Arabella was refined and slender. Her pale blue eyes studied Scarlett intently as she shook the outstretched hand. "Thank you," she said. "It's very nice to meet you also. You purchased a home locally, did you?"

Scarlett nodded. "An old rectory," she replied, glancing at Archer. "It needs some... work."

Archer snorted. "That's putting it mildly," he was looking at his mother. "The place is falling apart, although the let agent didn't bother to tell her that during the sales process. She arrived to a mess."

His mother's brow furrowed as she looked between her son and the beautiful American woman. "That's awful," she declared. "I'm so sorry to hear that. What are you going to do?"

Scarlett tried to be positive. "Well," she cocked her head thoughtfully. "Your son has referred me to a contractor who seems to think he can have it all repaired in the next few weeks. It really is a lovely place; it just needs a little help."

Arabella smiled because Scarlett was being rather upbeat about it. "I'm glad to hear you're not packing up and going home," she said. "It's a lovely community around here. I do hope you'll like it."

Scarlett smiled broadly. "I already do," she said, glancing at Archer. "Your son had been wonderful in helping me acclimate. I don't know what I would have done without him."

Arabella turned her proud smile to her son. "He's very helpful that way," she said, watching Henry and Alexandra make a dash past them for the secret staircase. The children were giggling, having fun. "Oh, my. Henry has found a friend."

Archer watched the kids clamor at the secret door. "Henry, carefully, please," he admonished his son before he answered his mother. "Indeed, he and Alexandra seem to be getting along famously."

Arabella smiled at the children. "She's a lovely girl," she returned her attention to Scarlett. "Can you stay for tea or must you rush off?"

"She's staying for dinner," Archer answered for her. "In fact, Scarlett and her girls are going to be our guests for a short while, at least until the rectory is in habitable condition. I've offered them use of the mezzanine."

Arabella's smile froze on her face as she turned to look at her son. "Use... of the mezzanine?"

Archer nodded. "Three big bedrooms and no one to use them," he said. "There's no reason why Scarlett and her girls can't. Besides, the youngest girl is a horse enthusiast and Henry is thrilled with the prospect of having someone to ride with."

By this time, Arabella's smile was quickly fading. She stared at her son. "But...," she was struggling to be tactful in Scarlett's presence. "Uh... may I have a word with you in private, Archer? Please excuse us for a moment, Scarlett."

Arabella was already pulling him with her, heading for a corridor that disappeared off into darkness. Archer winked at Scarlett as he followed his mother.

"Of course, Mother Dear," he had her by the elbow. "Whatever you wish."

Scarlett stood there in the entryway to the master suite as Archer and his mother faded down the corridor. She didn't think much of their swift exit until she heard voices. The second they were out of sight, Arabella's raised voice could be heard.

"Are you mad?" the woman hissed loudly. "You don't even know this woman yet you would bring her into our home?"

Archer's voice was much calmer. "Please don't upset yourself," he said. "She's a very decent woman and I've spent a lot of time with her over the past few days. I think you'll like her a great deal and appreciate the companionship."

"Pah!" Arabella spat. "Having her visit our home is one thing, but living here is quite another. We know nothing about her, Archer. She cannot stay here."

"I've already offered."

"Then un-offer."

"Mother, I can't."

"You can and you will. Tell her to go to a hotel. I'm not running a boarding house for stray women and children."

"Now you're being cruel."

"I'm being sensible. I thought you were sensible, too, after your experience with Christiana, but I see I was wrong. Another beautiful face to turn your head, Archer. You're acting like a fool."

That was all Scarlett could stand to hear. Quickly, quietly, she went downstairs and out the big front entryway door. Once on the gravel drive outside, she pulled out her cell phone and called information for the nearest cab company. They connected her with a company in York who dispatched a taxi out to Phipps Hall.

Archer went looking for Scarlett about fifteen minutes later. He walked the entire upper floor, the mezzanine, and was starting in on the ground floor when he caught sight of his son in one of the front windows, looking forlornly out into the drive.

"Henry?" Archer entered the room. "What are you looking at? Have you seen Miss Scarlett?"

Henry nodded and pointed out of the window. "She's out there."

Archer's brow furrowed with curiosity as he made his way over to the window to see what Henry was seeing. He could see all three women standing outside in the darkness in the driveway. The furrow in his brow deepened.

"What's she doing out there?" he asked.

Henry lifted his shoulders, looking glum. "I don't know," he sighed. "But she took Alexandra with her."

Archer didn't say anything more to his son as he made his way outside. Just as he opened the entry door, he could see headlights down the drive. They drew closer as he came outside to where Scarlett and the girls were standing, but still, he paid little attention. He was solely focused on Scarlett.

She saw him from the corner of her eye, moving towards him before he could say anything. Scarlett didn't want their conversation overheard by Morgan or Alexandra. She didn't want a scene, in any fashion, but knowing Archer as she had come to, she suspected he wasn't beyond creating one if she went against his wishes.

"Hi," she said simply.

Archer looked genuinely perplexed. "Hi," he replied, reaching out to grasp her hand. "What are you doing out here?"

Just as he said it, he noticed the taxi as it drew near. His sense of confusion grew as Scarlett spoke.

"We're going back to the hotel," she said softly, forcing a brave but hollow smile. "Archer, you're so sweet to offer to let us stay here, but it's apparent that it's caused some friction with your mother. I wouldn't dream of upsetting her, so I think it's best if you just let us return to the hotel for now. We'll figure this all out later."

He was in offensive mode. "No," he said flatly. "We'll figure it out now. Were you simply going to leave and not discuss this with me?"

She nodded, putting her hands on his chest to calm him because he seemed to be growing agitated. "I was just trying to give you and your mother some space," she insisted. "I think it's best if you just let us go back for now."

He was quickly growing outraged. "No," he insisted. "You're staying for dinner."

Scarlett stood her ground. "I don't think that's a good idea," she said. "You and your mother need to get things straightened out and I think you'll understand when I say I'm really not comfortable staying for dinner. My girls and I don't need to be in the middle of family tension with people we really don't even know."

His blooming fury took a hit and he just looked at her as if she had grievously hurt him. "You don't feel like you know me?"

She could see that was the only thing he was focused on; the fact that there was a tense situation with his mother didn't seem to faze him. It was all about Archer and his feelings, his wants.

"I've known you for three days," she pointed out. "I keep trying to tell you that. How much can we really know about one another in that short amount of time?"

She took all of the wind out of his sails. He just looked at her before finally shaking his head. "You're right," he whispered. "I guess... I guess I was just fooling myself. It's just that I want to be with you so badly, to know you. I guess I've sort of forced all of this on you, haven't I?"

She nodded, a smile playing on her lips. "Your mother is showing some common sense. It was kind of the same thing I've been trying to tell you, only you're so overwhelmingly persuasive that it was hard to turn you down. Maybe... maybe we just need to cool things for a couple of days."

He shook his head. "I don't want to cool it," he whispered. "I don't want to go a couple of days without seeing you. Please."

The taxi had pulled up and come to a halt, and the girls were already starting to climb in. Scarlett saw them out of the corner of her eye and she put her hands on Archer's cheeks, pulling him down to her. She kissed him, very sweetly, a couple of times.

"You're wonderful and sweet," she whispered, "but let's give each other a little space. This is all happening way too fast and I don't want either of us to make a decision we'll regret. Okay?"

His eyes were closed, savoring the sensation of her hands on his face. It was more than he could bear. "Okay," he murmured. "Then what?"

"You get things straightened out with your mother. That's not a request."

"Things *are* straightened out."

"Then we'll talk in a couple of days, I promise."

"I'm sorry if she offended you; I really am."

"She didn't offend me. She was right."

He just started shaking his head, grasping her hands when she pulled away and kissing the palms reverently. Scarlett had to literally yank her hands from his grasp because he wasn't willing to let go. He just stood there, looking away, as she climbed into the taxi and the vehicle took off back down the drive. Only when it was well on its way did he dare look, watching it go with a heavy heart. He felt sick about everything, blaming himself completely.

But he knew she was right.

FOUR

SCARLETT AWOKE the next morning in the hotel, rising and showering even though the girls were still asleep in the next room, wondering why she was even bothering with getting dressed when she really had nowhere to go and no one to see. As she dried her hair and put on makeup, she had a distinct sense of depression although she couldn't put her finger on it until she forced herself to admit that it was because she wouldn't be seeing Archer. Her sense of depression grew.

But along with the depression came a sense of guilt; guilt that she wasn't focused on the house or her daughters or their new life. She was thinking about a man she just met. So she forced herself to shift focus and get her priorities in order, the top one being that she needed to head out to the rectory and see how things were coming along. If they had running water, then she was going to move the girls in that day. Electricity wasn't necessary, but running water was.

Dressing in jeans, white tennis shoes and an oversized gray cardigan that was lightweight and rather sexy, she wrote a note for the girls, collected her purse, and headed down to the hotel's lobby. As she got off the elevator, she noticed that there was a continental breakfast spread out so she collected an apple and a muffin. She picked at the muffin, noticing it was a sunny day outside. As she chewed a bite of muffin and rummaged through her purse for her car keys, one of the hotel's employees approached her.

"Mrs. Ward?" the girl greeted her.

Scarlett turned to the young, pale woman. "Yes."

The girl smiled and pointed over to the front desk. "Those were left for you this morning. We were instructed not to wake you to deliver them."

Scarlett looked at the front desk with some curiosity. She could see the usual things; the desk, an employee behind it, a couple of computers, and a gigantic flower arrangement. It took her a moment to realize that the girl meant the flowers and her eyes widened as she made her way over to the desk.

"*Those* are for me?" she asked, incredulous.

The young woman was grinning as she pointed to the enormous bouquet of roses, lilies and other flowers carefully arranged in a cut crystal vase. "They were delivered all the way from York."

Scarlett's jaw dropped as she inspected the arrangement which, if placed on the floor, would have almost been as tall as she was. She could see a card shoved down into the bunch and she reached in to pluck it out. Opening it, she read the neat writing:

Miss you already
A

Scarlett couldn't help but smile as she read the message, at least three times, and put the card and the envelope in her purse. Looking at the explosion of flowers once more, she turned to the concierge.

"I'm sorry if these are in the way," she said, "but I'm not sure there's enough room in my hotel room for them right now. Can I leave them here for everyone to enjoy until I get back?"

The young woman nodded. "Of course."

With a smile of thanks, Scarlett slipped outside into the cool sunshine and headed to her rental car in the car park. Starting the car up, she very carefully pulled out and headed for the rectory.

It wasn't so bad driving on the wrong side of the car once she got the hang of it, but the narrow streets with hedgerows right up against the shoulder were a little unnerving as she made her way into Newton Kyme.

It hadn't rained in a couple of days so the ground was drying up nicely as Scarlett pulled up the drive to the old rectory. There were a few contractor vehicles and a very nice motor-cycle parked out front, and she pulled up next to them and parked her car. Climbing out of the vehicle, she went inside.

She could hear banging and pounding, and men's voices talking to each other. Sticking her head into the main living room, or reception room as the British called it, she noticed right away that the windows were new. As she went from room to room, she noticed that all of the windows on the lower level were new, including the broken window in the kitchen.

More than that, she could see new piping in the kitchen under the sink and in the small toilet off the entry vestibule. Additionally, portions of the walls were pulled away and it was clear they were doing work on the wiring. Scarlett finished her inspection of the lower floor and took the stairs, hearing the voices grow louder and suddenly realizing that one of the voices sounded very familiar. Curious, she paused at the top landing and listened.

It was Archer. Curiosity growing, she followed the sounds of the voices to her left where the only bathroom in the house was located. There was a tiny separate toilet room, then the room with the actual bath and shower. But there was no one there and she realized the voices were coming from the other side of the wall, which would make it the master bedroom's dressing room. She wound her way out and went into the master bedroom.

"... and it looks to me that whatever happened here must have happened years ago," Archer's voice was muffled, faint. "Look at the condition; it's slumped up against the wall where it was either left or where it died. It's hard to say if it was alive when this was all bricked up."

Scarlett was standing in the doorway between the master bedroom and the dressing room. The space for the dressing room was an annexed section of the big northwest chamber that had been divided up into the bathroom and shower room. At the far end of the dressing room was a small door, which was open to reveal a very small room, like a big closet, with a window at one end. But it was then that she noticed that back near the window, part of the wall had been torn away to reveal a very old staircase. The voices, including Archer's, were coming from of the top of that very tiny stairwell.

Timidly, she took the stairs, watching her feet hit each old wooden step and hoping it wouldn't collapse under her small weight. By the time she reached the top, she was in a very small room with a window that had been partially boarded over. Cobwebs hung from the ceiling and it appeared like junk was everywhere. Archer was standing directly in front of her, his back to her, talking to a couple of men who were crammed into the room, also. They were obviously studying something on the floor very intently.

"What room is this?" Scarlett asked.

Archer whirled around, as did the other two men, spying her at the top of the steps. Immediately, Archer went to her in an attempt to not only block her view of the room, but to also herd her back down the stairs.

"The contractor was replacing the windows when he found a seam in the wall and these stairs behind it," he said, sounding rather startled. "There's just a small room up here. It must have been where the servants slept long ago."

Scarlett wasn't oblivious to the fact that he was trying to move her back down the stairs. "Oh," she said to his explanation as she began to back down the flight. "But what are you doing here? What were you talking about? I heard you when I came upstairs."

"I was in the neighborhood so I thought I'd drop by."

"I didn't see your car."

"I didn't drive my car."

They were halfway down the stairs when Scarlett suddenly came to a halt and dug her heels in. Archer plowed right into her.

"Archer, *stop*," she commanded. "What's going on? What are you doing here and why can't I see the room?"

He was pressed up against her, unmoving, so she couldn't go back up the stairs. He was prepared to give her an evasive answer and try to get her back down to the first floor but if he knew one thing about Scarlett Ward, it was that she was an intelligent and stubborn woman. They could argue about it for the next hour and all the wheedling in the world wasn't going to convince her to do what he was trying so hard to get her to do. He'd give in to her eventually and tell her the truth. So he surrendered and gave a heavy sigh.

"I got a call from the contractor about an hour ago," he told her in a low voice. "He'd just found this hidden staircase and the room above, and he needed me to come out and take a look."

"Why did he call you? It's *my* house."

Archer put a big, gentle hand on her shoulder. "Because it

would seem that there's a very old corpse up there," he said quietly. "As near as I can figure out, the staircase was bricked up and whoever is in that room was either left there to die or was dead already. I'm going to have to open a case file on it."

Scarlett's eyes bugged. "Oh, my God," she breathed. "A body?"

He nodded, seeing the anxiety and horror in her face. "Love, I don't want you to get worked up about this, please? I'll take care of everything. I'll have the body out by tonight and have my inspectors comb over this place and the history of it to try and figure it out. You're not living here, anyway, so...."

Scarlett didn't want to hear anything more. She whirled away from him, nearly tripping down the stairs in her haste to put distance between her and the room upstairs. She was running by the time she hit the dressing room of the master suite, hearing Archer calling her name but unwilling to stop. She ran all the way downstairs and out of the rectory, running to her car and throwing open the door. She was breathless and frantic, but she knew what she had to do. The camel's back had just broken.

By the time Archer reached her, Scarlett was on the phone to someone, furiously but concisely outlining the issue. Archer guessed within the first few sentences that she was talking to the real estate agent.

"... and you deliberately, willfully and with complete foresight and knowledge sold me a home that was completely uninhabitable," Scarlett was speaking through clenched teeth. "Everything you sent me via email or told me about the property was a complete and utter lie simply so you could get a commission. Don't talk while I'm speaking to you. Shut up and listen or I promise you will be very, very sorry. Are you listening? Good. Now, this is what's going to happen. I don't care how you do it, but you are going to buy back this rectory or sell it to someone else within the next month, or I will charge you and your entire brokerage with fraud. Is that clear? Because I promise you that the bad publicity you'll get from my suit will collapse your business and you will lose your real estate license, pure and simple. Once I present the facts to a court, you'll be lucky if you don't end up in jail. Secondly, you are going to find me a deal of a perfectly habitable house in the areas of Tadcaster, Wetherby or York, and you're going to do it today. You're going to kiss my ass like I'm your one and only client or I'll rattle your cage so hard that your fake blond hair is going to fall out by its dark roots. Do you understand me?"

Archer was trying very hard not to grin as Scarlett beat down the real estate agent within an inch of her life. It was impressive and completely justifiable. He was very glad she was finally standing up for herself and not simply trying to live with the situation. Once Scarlett was off the phone, she turned to Archer and struggled to calm down.

"There," she took a deep breath. "Now things are in motion. I'm going to buy a real house and not this broken down crypt. Honestly, I was okay about everything until the body was found, but I can't take anymore. I'm over it."

He let his grin break through. "You're really something," he exclaimed appreciatively. "So beautiful and so full of fire."

Scarlett grinned in spite of herself. "Speaking of beautiful, thank you for the flowers," she said, forcing herself to smile and veer away from the harrowing subject of the rectory. "They're gorgeous."

His smile grew. "You're welcome." He looked at his watch. "You should be getting a gift basket right about now."

Her brow furrowed. "Gift basket?"

He nodded. "About every couple of hours, you'll be getting a delivery from me. I couldn't help myself. I didn't think I was going to see you today and I wanted you to know I was thinking about you every second of the day."

Scarlett laughed loudly; she couldn't help it. "We just saw each other last night, Archer."

His smile faded. "I know, but we didn't part under the best of circumstances." He sobered completely. "I really am terribly sorry if my mother offended you. I wouldn't have knowingly hurt your feelings for anything. I hope you know that."

Scarlett's smile eased as she gazed up into his handsome face. "I do," she assured him. "But I still think she was right. Things are moving awfully fast."

He nodded. Then he shrugged. "I don't care," he declared. "I really don't. I can't go a minute of the day without thinking about you. Every moment I've spent with you has made me feel like I've never felt in my life, and it's a feeling that only gets better with time. Please have dinner with me tonight. I can't stand the thought of not seeing you."

She sighed heavily, eyeing him indecisively but being swayed by his pathetic, yet hopeful, expression. "I thought we were going to cool it for a couple of days?" she said weakly.

He nodded patiently. "I know, but I can't stand it. Please don't make me stay away."

Scarlett tried to hold out but it was no use. She wanted to see him, too. Finally, she grinned and shook her head with regret.

"All right," she gave in. "What time do you want me to be ready?"

Archer couldn't help it; he threw his arms around her and planted a fairly amorous kiss on her mouth. It was warm, lingering and delicious.

"Six," he told her breathlessly. "Thank you, Scarlett. You've made me a very happy man."

She giggled, all wrapped up in his big arms and not entirely troubled by it. She rather liked being held by him because he was big and strong and warm. It made her feel very safe and very secure.

"You're a big crybaby, you know that?" she tried to sound serious.

He nodded like a man who was used to being hen-pecked but didn't mind one bit. "I know."

"Do you always cry and beg until you get what you want?"

"Mostly."

She just shook her head reproachfully, but there was humor to it. "Am I bringing the girls tonight?"

He hesitated. "Would you be upset if I said I just wanted to take you out?"

She shook her head. "No."

"Then we'll take the girls out another time, I promise."

She simply nodded, without much to say to that, and he kept her wrapped up in his arms, gazing down at her with a warm expression. It seemed like he wanted to say something more to her but before Scarlett could ask, he interrupted her thoughts.

"So you're really going to buy another house?" he asked.

She nodded. "I'm not going to live in this place," she said resolutely. "It's been nothing but bad karma since we arrived and I just get the feeling that we're not supposed to be here."

"You're not going to move far away, are you?"

"I hope not, but I would like to find a nice house where the girls and I would be happy. If that means moving far away, I suppose I'd be open to it."

He loosed his grip on her, the big arms unwinding themselves but he still managed to find one of her hands and hold it.

"I think I know of something you might like to see," he said.

She was interested. "Really? What is it?"

He grinned evasively. "Do you have an hour or two?" he asked. "I'd like to show you something."

Scarlett nodded. "I've got the time," she said, then gestured to the house. "But don't you have to stay and handle... this?"

He shook his head. "I'm off today," he told her. "I just came over because the contractor called me, not knowing who else to call. I'll have my inspectors come over now and take care of it."

She cocked her head, studying him a moment because he seemed very willing and eager to leave the scene of a dead body, old as it may be, and take off with her. "Are you sure you didn't plant that mess up there just so I'd have to come over here?"

He grinned. "If I was going to lure you into a trap, it wouldn't be with old corpses. It would be with wine and roses."

She laughed softly. "So where are we off to?"

He didn't answer her directly. "Let's take your car. I don't have an extra helmet for you for my motorbike."

Scarlett looked over at the very nice motorcycle next to the rectory entry. "That's yours?"

He nodded. "I have lots of toys, I admit it. It's my one and only vice."

"It could be worse."

"How's that?"

"You could have lots of women," she said, watching him laugh. "If you've got to have a vice, let it be motor vehicles and not slutty tarts."

He laughed louder as he opened her car door. "Who says I don't?"

She giggled. "Somehow, I don't think your mother would let you."

He winked at her as she climbed into the passenger seat of the car. "You would be correct, madam."

As they left the old rectory under increasingly cloudy skies, Archer got on the phone to the contractor and told the man to stop all work on the house for the day while he sent his inspectors over. Then he made a call to his office and made arrangements for a police paleontologist and two inspectors to head over to the rectory to see if they could piece the puzzle together. Old finds like the one in the rectory weren't unheard of in England and they had procedures to follow. By the time Archer hung up the phone, they were back on the road heading south into Tadcaster.

He talked up a storm as they drove to through Tadcaster and headed east. Scarlett mainly kept quiet and listened while he talked about Henry and the boy's determination to pick out a suitable horse for Alexandra, about the fact that he was on-duty for the next couple of days, and about the two racehorses on his property that he was shipping up to Catterick Racecourse in North Yorkshire. Scarlett listened to everything with interest, sensing that the man was in a very good mood with all of his chatting and suspecting it was because the day had unexpectedly brought the two of them together. She was in a pretty good mood herself, happy to be sitting with him, wherever he happened to be taking her.

Scarlett watched the scenery go by as conversation flowed easily. She had no idea where they were going, or what direction they were heading in, but to tell the truth the rolling green hills started looking all the same so she simply sat and enjoyed it.

"You mentioned the horses you were shipping to Catterick Racecourse," she said, watching a few horses in a field whiz by. "You have racehorses, too?"

He nodded. "My grandfather was heavily into racing back in the day when movie stars made it glamorous," he told her. "Right now, we're breeding sixth generation racehorses from Phipps stock. They're pretty well known on flat courses throughout the empire."

She turned to look at him. "Flat courses?"

He glanced at her. "That's what the Americans race; flat courses. We race flat courses and National Hunt, or steeplechase. Phipps horses are usually flat course, built for speed."

She was impressed. "Wow," she exclaimed. "You really are into a lot of different things, aren't you?"

He shrugged. "It's all inherited," he said. "I didn't start anything. I'm just continuing it."

She smiled. "So what contribution will Archer Phipps bring to his family tree?"

He grinned. "I'm not sure yet, but I'm working on it."

She winked at him as she turned to watch the countryside blow past, endless greenery, little villages and farms. It was bucolic and peaceful. Archer kept glancing at her as they sped along the road.

"You know," he said casually, "you never did tell me what you did for a living. You know all about me but I don't know half as much about you."

She grinned, running her fingers through her dark hair and leaning against the back of the seat. "That's kind of a complicated answer," she said. "I told you that I had a few hit songs back when I was in high school and made money on appearances, which my parents took from me and invested wisely, so I basically live off the income from my investments. Also, when the car company bought the rights to 'Shoes, Shoes, Shoes' and turned it into their jingle, they paid me a bundle. I'm very lucky that I don't have to work for a living, but I still write songs and sing. I guess it's just in my blood. It's something I will always do."

Archer was listening seriously. "Did you go to college?"

She nodded. "I did, and I have a degree in Musical Theater. But it really doesn't pay the bills. I did it because I loved it."

"Do you have any big goals for the rest of your life, then?"

Again, she nodded, turning to watch the scenery go by. "I'm

writing a musical right now and I want to have it produced on Broadway. Musical theater is such a love of mine. I think... I hope... I can do it."

"So you came to England to finish your musical and get it produced?"

"Something like that. Like I told you before, I came to England for the adventure of it. I came for a lot of different reasons."

He slowed the car down and took a left on a small road. "I must admit something."

"What?"

"I looked you up on the Internet last night after you left," he confessed. "I saw every one of your videos on YouTube. You're absolutely amazing and talented. You have a beautiful voice."

She grinned. "Thank you."

"If I asked you to sing something for me, would you?"

She laughed. "Sure," she said. "What do you want to hear?"

"Can I pick anything?"

"Anything."

"Do you know any Beatles songs?"

"Every one of them. My dad is a huge fan."

He was watching the road ahead, silent for a moment, and Scarlett wondered what was going on in his head. When he finally spoke, it was three soft words.

"If I fell."

She grinned, watching his face as she lifted her lovely and trained contralto voice in soft strains of a very sweet song.

"'If I fell in love with you/would you promise to be true/and help me understand/cuz I've been in love before/And I found that love was more/Than just holding hands'."

She trailed off and he sighed heavily, closing his eyes a

moment even though he was driving. It was like he was savoring every note from the warm timbre of her voice. When he opened his eyes again, his deep baritone floated soft and smooth.

"'So I hope you see/that I would love to love you/And that she will cry/When she learns we are two/If I fell in love with you'."

By the time he was finished, Scarlett's smile had vanished. She was staring at him in astonishment.

"You have an amazing voice," she declared. "Where'd you learn to sing like that?"

He gave her a half-grin. "You're not the only one who has done musical theater," he said. "I did several plays when I was a young lad but that ended when I went to Sandhurst."

"What's Sandhurst?"

"A royal military academy near London."

She regarded him a moment, remembering what the bartender had told her about Archer being such a bully that his father sent him away. "Did you do any singing there?"

"I was in the choir."

"But nothing else? No professional training or anything?"

He shook his head. "No," he replied. "Like you, I just seem to have a knack for it."

She wriggled her eyebrows. "Archer, I don't know if you realize it, but what you have goes beyond a knack. You have a gift. It's really beautiful."

He grinned modestly. "I will tell you a secret."

"What?"

"I've always wanted to sing lead in *The Phantom of the Opera.*"

She waved a hand at him, as if it were a non-issue. "Oh, my goodness," she exclaimed. "You'd be amazing. Your voice is perfect."

"Then maybe you'll let me sing the lead in your musical."

"The job is yours."

He grinned at her, taking her hand and giving it a squeeze as they entered a small village. There were a couple of main streets, one bisecting the other, and Scarlett noted the typical English buildings with interest. She could see several cute little restaurants, a market, a bank, a petrol station, and a massive Gothic church right in the center of town. There were people on the streets walking in pairs or walking their dogs, enjoying the bustle of small town life.

There were streets and streets of houses, and they passed a school. Scarlett's curiosity finally got the better of her.

"Where are we?" she asked.

He took a left turn which led them down a small street and across some railroad tracks. "This is a town called Ludbourne," he told her. "If you want to get technical about it, it's part of my earldom and my family has owned a lot of the property around here for hundreds of years."

"Oh," she said as they crossed the railroad tracks and headed up a hill into a wooded area. "I'm kind of ignorant about how the nobility works around here, but do you have people who farm your land or rent homes from you? Or was that just something I've seen in movies?"

He nodded. "That's exactly how it works, at times," he replied. "Most of this land belongs to me and I have tenant farmers."

They went up the hill and into the trees for about a half mile before he took another left turn into a residence. Scarlett looked at the house with interest; it was a two-storied stone structure with a neat and tidy stone wall around it, encircling both the residence and the front yard. As they pulled more deeply onto the property, she could see that a small courtyard and two outbuildings were attached to the back of the home, all very neat and updated and clean. When Archer pulled the car next to the big four-car stone garage and put it in park, she climbed right out.

Archer turned the car off and got out, looking at Scarlett, who was standing at the back of the car studying the house and grounds. He went to her and put his big arm around her shoulders.

"This home was part of a larger property that we own," he told her. "Three hundred years ago, I had an ancestor whose sister was granted this land and this village, and she built a massive Georgian mansion just over this hill, and this house was where her caretaker lived. They called it the Deerkeeper's Lodge. The home was added to over the years, and eventually the estate was broken up and pieces of it sold, but this house has remained here all of that time. We had tenants in it until a couple of years ago, and when they moved out I had the home completely renovated to sell it off. Do you want to take a look?"

Scarlett nodded eagerly and he began to walk her towards the house. The structure was picture-perfect on the outside and very typically Georgian in design with its stone walls, peaked slate roof, and bold architecture, and Scarlett was instantly in love with it. When Archer opened the door, however, she audibly gasped.

The beautiful rough walls were white in the entry and reception room, but all of the trim, including the massive mantel, was a gorgeous distressed blue-gray in color. The floor was polished hardwood, dark and spectacular, and the ceiling had been worked on to expose the big oak beams. It was also minimally furnished with white couches to match the walls and beautifully restored tables and other wooden furniture, and as Scarlett walked through it, she had to make an effort to keep her mouth from hanging open. Every room she saw brought a new gasp of delight.

There was a drawing room, a sitting room, a study and a dining room that were all beautifully restored. The kitchen had been completely rebuilt to include a stone floor that was made from spectacular random sizes of slate, and attached breakfast area and utility room. A big island sat in the middle of the kitchen with a brass vegetable sink and two sets of beautiful wooden stairs lined the entry hall and one wall of the dining room, leading to the second floor.

The second floor was more amazing than the first. The original house had three bedrooms, which were gorgeously restored with exposed beam ceilings, and renovations had added three full, beautiful bathrooms with stone tiles and glass. There was an addition to the house which, downstairs, contained the kitchen, breakfast area, another big sitting room and a utility room, but upstairs, the addition contained two more bedrooms, two more bathrooms, and a big open bonus room area. By the time they got to the big bonus room area with a spectacular view of the meadowlands in the distance, Scarlett could no longer contain her awe. She turned to Archer with a look of utter astonishment.

"This is the most beautiful home I've ever seen," she said sincerely. "This is the kind of home I wanted to buy in the first place."

He was standing in the entry to the bonus room, hands in his pockets. "I'm glad you like it," he said. "It's not too far away from the girls' schools, about twelve miles, and it's not too far from me, either. Come on downstairs; I want to show you something else."

Scarlett followed him down the dining room stairs and out into the courtyard beyond. There was an outbuilding on the opposite side of the landscaped courtyard, long and thin, that had been converted into an entertaining room. It was all glass on one side, the walls of rough stone, and it contained a bar, a toilet, a miniature kitchen, and recessed lighting. At one end was an open space with an exposed beam ceiling and a big white leather sectional couch, expensive and pristine. Scarlett stood in the open sliding glass door, inspecting the structure with approval.

"Wow," she exclaimed. "This is a fantastic room to entertain in."

Archer was standing near the bar as he turned to look at her. "Or finish writing a musical in."

She grinned. "Maybe," she replied as his gaze moved over the perfect room again. "I'm afraid to ask how much you're asking for it."

He lifted his eyebrows, making his way back over to her in a thoughtful manner. "May I ask what you paid for the rectory?"

She sighed faintly, looking rather longingly at the room. "*Too* much," she muttered. "A little over a million U.S. dollars. What are you asking for this place?"

He kept a very good poker face. "How much would you be willing to pay?"

She gave him an exasperated look. "That's not a fair question," she said. "If I had just walked off the street to look at this home, how much would you tell me you were asking for it?"

He grinned. "If you just walked off the street to look at it, I'd tell you whatever I thought would keep you here long enough so I could ask you out to dinner."

She giggled but quickly sobered. "You're asking a lot, aren't you?"

"About one and a half million U.S. dollars."

Scarlett's humor left her quickly and she sighed, looking around the place longingly. "Well," she said after a moment. "I'm not sure I can do that."

"I'm willing to listen to any reasonable offer."

She looked at him, mulling over his statement. "I can offer

about one point two million U.S., but that's as high as I can go, and this house is so seriously beautiful that I feel like I'm insulting you with that offer." She suddenly grinned. "You wouldn't be willing to take the difference out in trade, would you?"

He didn't miss a beat. "Absolutely," he said seriously. "What did you have in mind?"

She giggled and waved him off, but he wouldn't let her back down. He moved towards her, his demeanor very intense.

"For every kiss, I'll knock off fifty thousand dollars," he told her. "For a hug, I'll knock off twenty-five thousand dollars, and for anything more than that, I'll just give you the damn house."

He was saying it rather dramatically, which only increased her giggles. "If I sleep with you, you'll give it to me?"

"I'll give you everything I own."

She snorted. "How are you going to explain that to your mother?"

"We'll be married by then so it won't matter."

Still giggling, she continued to wave him off and put a few feet of distance between them because he was moving in too close and, knowing her attraction to him as she did, she wasn't entirely sure she could fight him off if he made a grab for her. So she wandered over to the big glass entryway, pretending to inspect the big entertainment room again. Then she looked at him.

"One point two, Archer," she ran her hand along the custom doorjamb. "That's my final offer."

"Sold."

She looked at him in shock, all of the humor gone from her expression. "Seriously?"

"Seriously."

Her jaw dropped in astonishment. "You'll take well under what you were asking?"

He smiled and started to come towards her again. "Tell you what," he said, shoving his hands into his jean pockets. "I'll take nine hundred thousand U.S. dollars for it and leave you enough money to furnish it the way you want to. All I really wanted to do was recoup the money I put into renovating it, plus a little extra, and the nine hundred thousand more than covers that. You get what you want, I get what I want, and we're all happy. Okay?"

Scarlett was stunned. "I don't even know what to say," she said. "That's the most generous thing I've ever heard of. To say thank you doesn't seem enough."

He was standing right in front of her by this time, very close, his pale blue eyes glimmering warmly at her. "You're having dinner with me tonight. That's thanks enough."

Scarlett still wasn't sure what to say to all of it. She looked around at the home of her dreams, a spectacular residence that she had just bought, and she was thrilled to death. She knew the girls would be thrilled, too.

"Morgan and Alexandra are going to go crazy over this place," she said. "It'll make the stay in the hotel until escrow closes bearable. I don't..."

He cut her off. "Why would you wait until escrow closes?" he wanted to know. "You can move in today. The house is vacant and there's no reason to wait."

Her jaw was hanging open again. "Archer, I can't do that," she insisted. "I have to sell the rectory first before I can purchase this place, and I have no idea how much time that will take. I wouldn't dream of moving into this place before I've legally paid for it."

He cocked his head. "Would you rent it from me, then, until you purchase it?"

The light went on in her eyes. "Yes," she said with some excitement in her tone. "I would do that."

He was back to grinning. "Good," he said decisively. "It's settled, then. You can move in today and rent the place until you sell the rectory and are able to purchase it."

Scarlett was back to being speechless. She looked around the room again, across the beautifully landscaped courtyard to the house beyond, and her relief and excitement exploded. She jumped up and threw her arms around Archer's neck, hugging him tightly.

"Thank you," she whispered into his ear. "Thank you so much for this. I'll never forget what you've done for us."

He gladly wrapped his arms round her, hugging her against him, feeling her curves and softness. It had been quite some time since he last had a woman against him and it reminded him of how badly he missed it. However, Scarlett was no ordinary woman. She set him on fire in so many ways he couldn't even remember how it started. All he knew was that Scarlett Ward had filled his mind since the moment he met her, like nothing else had existed before her and if he had anything to say about it, nothing would exist after her, either. She was the one.

As Scarlett attempted to release him from her hug, he wouldn't let her. He held her in his big, strong arms and as she tried to pull back, he planted a soft, warm kiss on her mouth, feeling her succumb to him almost instantly. There was no hesitation or reservation, as if she were finally letting herself go and responding to the warmth that so easily ignited between them. In fact, she began to grow aggressive, snaking her tongue into his mouth and licking his teeth. Archer groaned, incredibly and instantly aroused. He was overwhelmed with her.

More than twice Scarlett's size, he used that strength to pick her up, holding her fast against him. He had her exactly where he wanted her and she was responding to him, feeding his desire. He tasted her lips, her flesh, his mouth moving across her cheek to her tender earlobe. Her skin, so pale and soft, was sweet and delicious. He suckled on a tender earlobe, listening to her gasp and feeling her tremble. He needed more from her and until she stopped him, he was going to do what felt right and came most naturally.

She was wearing a long sleeved t-shirt that was form-fitting, with a deep V-neck. His mouth moved all over her cleavage, suckling and gently licking, before returning to her mouth and kissing her furiously. As he did so, his right hand moved to her left breast, very gently cupping it. When she didn't stop him, he squeezed harder. Scarlett, overwhelmed with desire she had tried so hard to suppress, ripped her shirt off and tossed it aside. As her mouth fused to his again, she went to work on his shirt.

Archer was on fire. He helped her unbutton his shirt, so impatient at one point that he ended up popping off two buttons when he pulled it open and yanked it off his body. His mouth was on hers, his hands on her naked flesh as he found himself making the most logical move he could think of; he had her up in his arms and was moving for the big leather couch. Scarlett didn't even try to stop him, as she was all wrapped up around him, making out with the man as she had never made out in her life. His masculinity, his charisma, his power had her drowning in him.

Archer laid her down on the big sectional couch, lying down right on top of her. He unhooked her bra and pulled it free, his big hands coming into contact with her full, sweet breasts, his mouth eventually capturing a nipple. Scarlett groaned as he suckled her furiously, incoherent, and began going for his pants. Archer felt her fumbling and his hands moved to her jeans, unbuttoning them and yanking them down her body. Somehow he managed to pull them off with his mouth still attached to her breasts. But once the jeans were off, he planted his face in between her legs and pleasured her.

Scarlett cried out softly as he licked her mercilessly. His

mouth, his hands, were doing wicked things to her, things she hadn't experienced in years, and although somewhere in the back of her sex-hazed mind she knew they shouldn't go any further, the truth was that she didn't want him to stop. She wanted to feel the man in her, experience him on an intimate level, and Archer didn't make her wait very long. His tongue had manipulated her to the verge of a climax but stopped short of bringing on her release. Breathlessly, he pulled his jeans down to his knees and mounted her.

Scarlett groaned as he thrust into her wet and waiting body. Archer was a big man and his manhood was proportionate, full and large, and Scarlett felt every inch as he drove it into her sweet body. She responded to him eagerly, her pelvis moving against his, meeting his thrusts, feeling sparks fly every time he plunged deep. Wrapping her arms around his neck, she pulled him down to her and slanted her lips over his as he continued to thrust.

She was still kissing him deeply as she climaxed, and Archer's mouth absorbed the swift pants of pleasure. As wildly aroused as he was, he kept his pace and his focus, bringing her to another climax a few minutes later. After that, he couldn't control himself and when he felt himself peaking, he withdrew from her body and spent himself on her belly. It was such a glorious orgasm that he nearly blacked out from it, feeling her hands on his testicles as she magnified his pleasure. He'd never experienced anything like it.

But Scarlett apparently wasn't finished. She was still kissing him, grinding her wet heat against him, seeking his spent manhood that was still fairly hard. Knowing what she wanted without her saying a word, Archer plunged back into her very hot and very wet body, feeling her climax again, playing with her nipples as she continued to wriggle her pelvis against his. He didn't think it was possible for him to recover and grow hard again so soon, but it was literally minutes before he was rock-hard again, beneath her as she plunged her body down on him again and again. He just lay there, his eyes half-lidded, watching her exquisite body as she made love to him.

It was like a dream, like a piece of heaven he had never known to exist, and she was magnificent beyond compare. She was doing erotic things to him with her pelvis, with her hands, and in little time he climaxed again, so hard that he bit his tongue. He could feel it coming on and he tried to withdraw from her, but he didn't make it in time and she didn't seem to care, so he took the greatest of pleasure spilling himself into her, loving the hot, slick feel of what he had put into her. It was the most amazing sexual experience he'd ever had.

Eventually, Scarlett climaxed again and collapsed against him, his body still embedded in hers as she lay on his chest. Her dark hair was splayed over them both and Archer lay there with his arms around her, holding her fast and close, thinking on how his life was going to change from this point on. He'd been wildly attracted to Scarlett since the moment he met her but now, there was emotion involved. The intimate act sealed the deal. He knew he loved her; he couldn't remember when he hadn't. So he simply lay there and held her, savoring each and every moment as if it were the best one he had ever lived.

It took Archer a few minutes to realize that Scarlett had fallen asleep on top of him. He would have thought her to simply be dozing until her soft, sweet snores filled the air. With a grin, he tightened his grip around her, holding her close.

He'd never spent a better two hours in his entire life.

FIVE

SCARLETT WOKE up in a strange room, on a strange couch, with a big white duvet covering her up from head to toe.

It was daylight, bright sun streaming in through the windows. Momentarily disoriented, she looked around without moving a muscle, seeing white walls and exposed beam ceilings, trying to clear out the cobwebs as to where she was. Then she shifted slightly and lifted her head, seeing a wall of windows facing out into a beautifully landscaped courtyard and a stone house beyond, and it all started coming back to her.

Very quickly, she realized she was naked underneath the duvet and she rolled over onto her belly to see if Archer was anywhere in the vicinity. A perusal of the room showed that she was quite alone, her clothes folded neatly on the edge of the couch. She lay there a moment, thinking back to the last thing she remembered, and her cheeks instinctively flushed, as did her body. Thinking of Archer made her feel warm and tingly all over. When she should have been appalled at her behavior, or embarrassed at the very least, she found that she couldn't muster the strength. She wasn't embarrassed and she didn't regret it.

A smile crept over her lips as she thought on her encounter

with Archer. She'd been married once, and had a long-term relationship that ended last year, and a smattering of boyfriends throughout her adult life, but she had never in her life experienced such raw, blazing passion as she had with Archer. The man touched her and she turned into a wild animal, unable to control herself. He had an almost hypnotic effect on her. It was an amazing, consuming sensation.

Getting up from the couch, she dropped the duvet as she quickly put her clothes back on – her underwear, bra, jeans and shirt. Once her shirt went on, she used the toilet and cleaned up a little, running her fingers through her long hair and trying to smooth it down so she didn't look like she'd been having sex all morning. She had the Cheshire Cat grin look about her, or so she thought with some paranoia. As she gazed at her reflection in the mirror, she truly had to smile; it was more than sex. It had been an awakening.

She felt good, relaxed, and light of heart. But as she came out of the bathroom and went for her shoes, she began to seriously wonder where Archer was. Maybe he didn't feel the same way she did about their intimacy and was off trying to figure out how to deal with his mistake. He'd just sold her the house; maybe he was re-thinking everything. Maybe he didn't feel the same way she did. Maybe he realized he'd made one giant error.

Bracing herself for the possibility, she was in the process of pulling on her shoes when she heard a door slam. Glancing up, she saw Archer coming from the house with a bag in one arm, crossing the courtyard towards her. Feeling somewhat anxious, Scarlett stood up, her attention fully on him as he entered the big entertainment room. When Archer caught sight of her, standing over by the couch and looking at him, he came to a halt.

For a moment, they just stared at each other and volumes of uncertainty filled the room. Neither one of them knew what to say, afraid to acknowledge the obvious, or perhaps not acknowl-edge it. Either way, it could be a minefield of emotion or confu-sion. Finally, Archer smiled weakly.

"Hi," he said.

Scarlett returned his smile, although there was uneasiness to it. "Hi."

His gaze lingered on her before he indicated the big paper bag in his arms. "I went out to get us something to eat," he said. "It's noon. I thought you might be hungry."

Her smile turned real. "Thank you," she said, "but I really need to get back to the girls. I've been away longer than I'd intended."

"I know," he said quickly, perhaps too quickly. "I just thought you might like something to eat, but I'll take you back to the hotel immediately."

Scarlett could see how uneasy he was. They were both walking on eggshells and she decided to put a stop to it, for both their sakes. She walked towards him, looking him right in the eye as if she had something to say.

"Look," she said softly. "I don't want you to think that you have to...."

"I love you," he suddenly blurted, then cringed when he saw the shocked look on her face. With a heavy sigh, feeling like a fool, he set the paper bag down on the nearest chair. "Scarlett, I'm sorry. I shouldn't have... I guess I'm just blunt. I don't beat around the bush and I come straight to the point, and if that means I lack tact, then so be it. But I was attracted to you the moment I saw you and it's a feeling that's grown stronger by the hour. When I brought you to see this house, I had no ulterior motive other than to show it to you. I truly didn't. I still don't know how we ended up the way we did, but I have to tell you that I'm not sorry in the least. I realize now that I love you madly and I want you to belong to me, because I already belong to you. If that's being blunt, then I'm sorry, but it's the way I feel. So there."

Scarlett was looking at him with astonishment. "You... you *love* me?"

He nodded without hesitation. "I do," he said. "I love your wit, your intelligence, your humor, and the way you seem hell-bent on always doing the right thing. I admire that. I admire your patience and your sweet manner with your girls. You're a wonderful mother. You're also the most beautiful and alluring woman I've ever met. I realize I've only known you a few days, but I can't help it. I've never felt so strongly about anyone in my entire life."

She was gradually overcoming her astonishment, now facing him with some warmth in her expression. "You certainly don't waste any time, do you?"

He looked rather disgusted with himself. "No," he admitted. "It's gotten me into trouble at times."

She fought off a grin. "With women?"

He shrugged. "With a lot of people," he said. "I guess you can say I'm sort of a bully when I feel strongly about something and I feel strongly about you. Now, the question is – how do *you* feel?"

Scarlett lifted her eyebrows and turned away from him, going to the bag on the chair and opening it up to see what was inside.

"I feel hungry," she said. "What did you bring us?"

"That's not what I meant."

He wasn't finding humor in her answer and she paused, turning to look at him. He seemed rather pathetic and anxious. She softened.

"I'm not entirely sure how I feel," she admitted, "but I suspect I'm becoming quite attached to you. You're a wonderful, generous man, and you and I together... earlier... honestly,

Archer, I've never had sex like that in my life. It was an amazing experience for me."

He smiled timidly. "Marry me, Scarlett. Please."

She grinned nervously, off-balance with his proposal. "Based on good sex?" she asked. "Is that really what you would base a marriage on?"

He shook his head. "I didn't mean it the way it came out. I simply meant... I don't ever want to be without you. I knew it when I met you but I'm convinced of it now."

She could see that he was sincere. After a moment, she shrugged. "I would feel much more comfortable if we got to know each other better first before we make any kind of a commitment like that. I think it's only wise, especially with children involved."

"Then you're at least open to the idea of marriage?"

"Of course I am."

His smile bloomed. "I know it was impetuous of me to tell you that I loved you, but it's the truth," he said. "And I furthermore know that you don't love me, but I hope that, in time, you will. I hope you will at least give me the opportunity to earn it."

He was being honest and truthful and earnest, and Scarlett believed him implicitly. She ran to him, throwing her arms around his neck as he picked her up and held her tightly. His hungry mouth slanted over her lips, tasting her, feeling something deeper and richer, more than he had ever felt before. Scarlett was breathless in his arms.

"I will give you the opportunity," she whispered.

"Thank you," he whispered between heated kisses. "You won't regret it, I swear."

Knowing she had to get back to the girls kept them from stripping their clothing off again, so Archer picked up the bag of corned beef sandwiches as they made their way back to the car. Scarlett was distracted by the house, however, and he stood near the garage, watching her as she walked around the courtyard and the front of the house, excitedly inspecting her acquisition. Archer assured her that they would go pick up the girls and bring them back over, so she jumped in the car and they took off for Wetherby.

Since it was a rental car, the normally neat-freak Scarlett didn't have any qualms about eating in it, and they wolfed down the sandwiches as they headed back to the hotel. This time, Scarlett was very chatty, praising the tasteful and true manner in which the Deerkeeper's Lodge had been restored and vowing not to touch what had already been done. All she wanted to do was add some furniture, even though the place was already partially furnished. She did mention that the girls would more than likely want to decorate their own bedrooms, including the paint colors, and Archer listened to her describe how Morgan had painted her last bedroom a deep, dark shade of eggplant.

They passed through York and headed up to Newton Kyme to pick up Archer's motorbike. When they finally pulled into the rectory's long driveway, there were several police vehicles parked along the drive and Archer pulled the rental car up behind one of them. He turned the car off, peering up the driveway to the open vestibule entry.

"I'm going to go in and speak with the inspectors for a moment," he said. "Do you want to come with me?"

She shook her head. "No," she said, her gaze moving moodily over the rectory. "I really don't want to set foot in that place ever again."

He glanced at her unhappy face before leaning over and kissing her cheek. "You don't have to," he said as he opened the car door. "But don't you have some furniture in there?"

She nodded as she climbed out of the passenger side. "Three beds," she said. "We brought everything else with us to the hotel, but the stuff I had shipped from the States will be arriving in a couple of days and this is the address they're being delivered to."

They met at the front of the car, both of them gazing up at the gray-stoned rectory. "Can't you contact the shipping company and change the destination?"

"No," she shook her head. "Not while it's in transit. I'll have to have it delivered here and then arrange to have it trucked over to the new place."

Archer nodded his head. "I'll take care of it when the shipment arrives," he said, just like that, and bent down to kiss her again. "Go back to the hotel and I'll see you in a little while. I assume you're going to want to stay at the new place tonight?"

She shrugged. "If the electricity and water are turned on, then I'd like to," she said. "You already have beds in the bedrooms."

He snorted. "Beds but no sheets. Everything is very superficial for showing to prospective buyers. But I'll send some of my people over to clean it up a little bit and fix up the bedrooms so you can move in tonight."

She just looked at him a moment, somewhat in awe, before shaking her head. "Do you always just take charge of everything like that?" she wanted to know. "You're like a magician with an army of people at your disposal who wash clothes, deliver suitcases, and make up beds."

He grinned. "I get things done, I suppose," he said, handing her the car keys but exacting one last kiss before he released them into her hand. "I'll see you later."

She took the keys with a smile, her gaze lingering on Archer, as she climbed back into the car. Archer stood there and watched her until she backed out and drove away, his mind lingering on her even as he turned for the rectory to speak with the inspectors who were on-scene.

———

At seven-thirty that evening, there was a knock on the hotel room door. Scarlett had been waiting for Archer for an hour and half so she rushed to the door and threw it open. She was about to ask him if everything was all right because he was so late, but Archer wasn't at the door. Mr. and Mrs. Bayse were.

"Oh... hi," Scarlett looked between the pair, concerned. "Is everything okay with Archer?"

Mr. Bayse nodded. "Yes, mum," he replied. "He got called into work and can't make it to dinner, so he sent us over to pack you and the girls up and move you over to the new house."

Scarlett was relieved that Archer was well but disappointed she wouldn't see him. She nodded quickly. "Wonderful," she said, turning to the door that linked her room with the girls' room. "Are you two ready to go? We're going to head over to the new house."

The sounds of squealing girls filled the air along with sounds of a scramble. Mr. and Mrs. Bayse stood in the doorway as Morgan and Alexandra began wheeling out their big suitcases, running back into their room to grab bags and other items from the bathroom. Scarlett already had her two big suitcases ready to go and Mr. Bayse took them down to the car. Mrs. Bayse helped the girls with their smaller bags as they maneuvered the big suitcases. Scarlett did a final sweep of both rooms to make sure they didn't leave anything behind before heading down to the car with her daughters.

The sun was nearly down by the time they reached the new house. As they pulled into the parking area by the big four-car garage, Morgan and Alexandra perked up in the back seat, "ooohing" and "aaahing" at the beautiful new home. There were lights on inside the structure and the entire complex was lit up. The courtyard had big torches burning and a glowing fire pit that was accented by a stone waterfall. It was utterly spectacular and once the car stopped and the girls jumped out, they ran into the courtyard first because the fountain was running and it was all lit up with flaming torches. They inspected the courtyard with glee as the adults lugged the suitcases and bags into the house.

Scarlett dropped her suitcase off in the amazing master bedroom, noting that all of the fireplaces were burning. It made the home so sweet and cozy. She checked the bed, seeing that Archer's people had, indeed, put very nice sheets on it. Making her way back downstairs, she could hear the girls chatting and laughing so, grinning, she went through the kitchen and to the back door that opened out into the courtyard. She could see that the girls were in the big, long entertainment room, the same room she and Archer had found such passion in. She called to her girls.

"Hey!" she waved them over. "Do you want to come in here and pick out your bedrooms?"

With a shriek, the girls raced across the courtyard and into the house, gasping with delight at the beautiful interior just as their mother had when she had first seen it. Scarlett took them through the family room, the big kitchen, the dining room, living room, sitting room and study, before finally taking them upstairs to see the bedrooms.

All of the bedrooms had big bathrooms and Morgan immediately claimed the bedroom across the hall from her mother's room. It was a large room with a roaring fire in the hearth and the bathroom had granite counters, a big white bathtub and a separate shower. The third bedroom in the main section of the house wasn't quite as large but it had a nice window seat, big closet, and big bathroom. Alexandra was in love with it, even before Scarlett showed the girls the other two bedrooms and bonus room. Though the other bedrooms were very nice, the girls stuck to their original choices. They were home.

As Morgan and Alexandra settled into their new bedrooms, Scarlett went downstairs to Mr. and Mrs. Bayse, who were in the kitchen milling around. It took Scarlett a moment to realize that they were cooking dinner.

"Oh, my," she exclaimed when she saw the pair hard at work. "You don't have to do this."

Mrs. Bayse smiled at her as she put fresh rolls in the oven. "Of course we do," she said cheerily. "We work for you now. Lord Phipps says you can't take care of this big estate all by yourself, so he has told us we're working for you. We'll take care of the place for you and do the chores. You don't have to worry about anything."

Scarlett stood in the doorway, a little shell-shocked by the information. "Uh...," she stammered. "I really appreciate that, but... well; I didn't plan on an au pair. I think I can handle this house myself."

Mrs. Bayse winked at her. "You'll have to take that up with Lord Phipps," she said. "For tonight, we work for you and we'll stay until morning."

Scarlett didn't want to argue with her about it, but she wasn't sure she needed or wanted domestics. She was trying to think of a way to discourage the woman without insulting her.

"Well...," she looked around. "Where will you sleep? There are extra bedrooms upstairs, but...."

"Here," Mr. Bayse pulled himself away from salad duty and motioned to Scarlett to follow. "Let me show you."

Hesitantly, Scarlett followed him through the family room, which connected to the utility room, which opened up onto the driveway. Across the driveway was the garage and Mr. Bayse opened the door into the garage, or so Scarlett thought. It turned out that it was a door into a nice sized bedroom and full bath attached to the garage that she didn't even know existed. Her tour of the house had ended at the entertainment room where she and Archer had gotten busy. She never even made it to the garage.

"I'll be damned," she muttered, looking around the cozy bedroom. "So this is where you're staying?"

Mr. Bayse nodded. "I think you'll appreciate our help, mum. This is a big house for one person. You'd have to hire someone to come do the maintenance and garden, anyway, so we may as well stay here and help you take care of it. Have you no need for domestics in America?"

Scarlett gave him a half-grin. "Not really," she said, still looking around the room before her gaze fell on the older man. "But I take it that domestics are normal in England?"

He nodded. "With the bigger homes and estates, they are. Mr. Phipps has a lot of people working for him, so many, in fact, that he was thinking of letting the missus and I go. But he said you needed us, so we're happy to help."

Scarlett lifted an eyebrow. Of course, she couldn't tell them that she didn't need them if they were about to lose their jobs. They were old people and unemployment in England was high. So she simply nodded her head.

"I appreciate it," she said, leaving the bedroom and crossing back towards the house. "I really appreciate everything you and your wife have done so far. The house looks amazing."

Mr. Bayse shut the door to his quarters and followed her. "There's a lot of garden on this property," he pointed into the courtyard with its blazing torches. "The home sits on almost an acre so there will be plenty to do."

Scarlett looked around as they entered the main house. "I like to garden, so I hope you don't mind if I buy plants and flowers."

"I'll plant them for you, mum, if you just tell me where you want them."

Scarlett thought that was a pretty sweet deal, actually. "And I like to cook," she said as they came into the kitchen. "I hope Mrs. Bayse doesn't mind if I want to cook meals on occasion."

Mrs. Bayse heard her. "Of course not, mum," she said. "While you do that, I'll find other things to do. There's always plenty to do."

Scarlett gave her a side-long glance. "If I cook, will you wash the dishes?"

"Of course, mum."

"That's a pretty sweet deal. I'm not sure I can refuse."

"We're here to help you, mum."

Scarlett paused by the big island in the kitchen, looking at all of the food that was spread out. It was obvious the pair had gone shopping along with everything else they had done to get the house ready. She felt a little overwhelmed by it all but very grateful. She'd always done for herself, so this was something of a new experience for her. She wasn't hard pressed to admit she already liked the idea.

"Well," she crossed her arms and leaned against the island. "How much do people like you usually get paid?"

"Mr. Phipps is taking care of our salary, mum," Mr. Bayse said as he returned to his salad duties.

Scarlett was about to contest that but she realized the pair had no say in it. Archer had taken charge and she would have to take it up with him. Truthfully, Mr. and Mrs. Bayse seemed like a truly sweet couple, so Scarlett put her reservations aside for the time being and went back upstairs to her bedroom to begin unpacking. But she made a mental note to talk to Archer about all of it the next time she saw him.

SIX

A YOUNG INSPECTOR in a nice suit found Archer standing in the residence of the crime scene, just staring at the room after the bodies had been removed. Crime Scene Investigation was still on the case, so other than removal of the bodies, nothing else had been touched. There was still blood everywhere and the room was in shambles.

"So...," the inspector ventured, "what are you thinking?"

Archer glanced up at the man, a colleague he had worked with for over ten years. His expression was rather frozen and distant.

"You know what I'm thinking, Calvin," he rumbled. "You're thinking the same thing."

Inspector Calvin Rorsch found himself studying the room just as Archer was. "Same pattern," he muttered. "A mother and her children, alone because Dad's at work. The perpetrator enters through an unlocked window, ties the children up, rapes the mother, then gathers them all in the reception room where he proceeds to slit their throats. Then he rapes the mother again after she's dead and violates the young daughter. We saw this before, ten years ago, but it suddenly stopped. We never caught whoever did it and...."

"And now he's back," Archer cut him off, his jaw ticking as he perused the crime scene one last time. He looked up at Calvin. "I thought we were done with the Yorkshire Cutter. I swear to God, if this is going to go on again, then...."

"There wasn't any note this time," Calvin reminded him calmly. "That was something that never made it into the papers, Archer, so no one knows about that detail. At least there was no note."

Archer just shook his head and turned away from the awful scene. "Yes, I can rejoice because there was no note written to me at the scene," he hissed. Then he ran his fingers through his cropped hair, wearily. "God, this can't be happening again."

Calvin watched him struggle. "You don't need to be involved in this investigation," he said quietly. "You're the Deputy Chief Constable and this is not part of your regular duties. I know you came because you had to, as part of your report to the Chief, but you need to leave this one to the inspectors. When you were working on the Cutter ten years ago, it nearly destroyed you. I know, because I worked on the cases with you and I saw what it did to you."

Archer scratched his forehead and noted the time. It was just past six o'clock in the morning. He knew Calvin was right but he also knew he was going to have trouble separating himself. Ten years ago, he had been a young inspector investigating a series of horrific murders against women and children. The killer, whoever it was, had known Archer was the lead investigator and taunted him at every turn. Every time Archer would get close, another murder would occur and they went back to square one.

That was just the way the murderer worked; calculated, intelligent, always one step ahead. Archer thought he had his suspect years ago but could never make anything stick. The man had been a bus driver, picking his victims out from the people who rode his bus, or so Archer thought. It had been one of the worst times of Archer's life and then it all stopped for some reason. The bus driver still drove his route, still a free man, and Archer kept an eye on the guy for about five years after the murders stopped, at least until the man retired and moved far away. Last Archer had heard, he'd had a massive heart attack and died shortly thereafter. So maybe it wasn't the bus driver. Maybe it was someone else.

Now, Archer didn't want to believe that the nightmare was going to start again. He was trying not to feel sick about it but he felt like he was looking at a crime scene from ten years ago. Rubbing his eyes, he headed for the door.

"Call me if you come up with anything," he told Calvin. "I'm going home to get some sleep. I'll be back in a while."

"Stay away from this, Archer," Calvin called after him. "Let the inspectors handle it."

Archer didn't respond. He continued on to his car as the soft hues of dawn colored the eastern sky, his thoughts shifting from the blood-spattered reception room to Scarlett. He'd missed their dinner date last night because of the crisis, so very disappointed, and even as he climbed into his car he was thinking about heading over to the lodge to see how she was. After the mess he had just witnessed at the crime scene, he had an almost stdesperate need to see her, to remind him of the beauty and happiness in the world. As he got on the cell phone to the Chief Constable to report on the murder, he turned his car in the direction of Ludbourne.

The Chief Constable of the North Yorkshire Police wasn't happy to hear about the violent murder in his jurisdiction and told Archer to keep a close eye on the case. He didn't mention the similarity of the crime to the string of murders they'd had ten years before, and Archer didn't bring it up. He didn't even want to entertain the thought. Hanging up the phone, Archer picked up the pace as he headed south to Ludbourne, entering the sleepy berg just as the sun began to break the horizon.

His phone rang.

"Phipps," he said without even looking at the incoming number.

"You're up early."

Archer recognized the voice. A weary grin spread across his lips. "Why in the hell are you calling me so early?" he demanded. Then, he yawned. "I haven't even been to bed yet."

"I'm going to tell your mother."

Archer burst out laughing. "You always were a horse's arse, Fox," he said, but he didn't mean it. "If you tell her I've been out all night, I'm going to tell her about the time you took two women back to..."

"Easy," Fox Henredon said loudly, interrupting him. "You tell her that and she'll never let us have a play date again."

Archer was still laughing. "Probably," he said. "How have you been? I feel like I haven't spoken to you in a while."

"You haven't," Fox said. "I've been... busy."

"With two women?"

Fox snorted. "With one," he said. "Would you believe me if I told you that I think I'm in love?"

Archer's laughter turned into something that sounded like gasp. "Seriously?"

"Dead serious."

"Do I know her?"

"No," Fox said. "I didn't even know her until a few days ago. She's American, but she just had a great-grandfather die and she's come to clean out his estate. As it turned out, her great-grandparents did a lot of collecting in Egypt back in the 1920s, so she had some things she wants to sell to the museum. Enter me."

"Astonishing," Archer said. "And that's how you met her?"

"That's how I met her," Fox said as if it was the most marvelous of happenstances. "Morgan is her name. You've never seen such a beautiful woman."

Up ahead, Archer could see the road that led to the driveway, at the end of which sat the house where Scarlett and her girls were sleeping in their beds.

"Actually, I have," he said quietly. "I've found an American of my own, in fact. Met her several days ago, and like you, I think I'm very much in love with her."

"Really?" Fox was interested. "What are the chances, Archer? So many years and so little luck for the both of us. I'm ecstatic for you."

Archer grinned. "I'm eager to meet your Morgan sometime."

"What are you doing next week?"

Archer's smile faded. "I don't know," he said. "But something has come up at work... something bad. I have no idea what's coming, Fox, but if you knew... say a prayer for me, mate."

Fox and Archer had been friends for many years and knew the good, the bad, and the ugly about one another. Fox could tell by the tone of Archer's voice that the man was serious.

"Shit," he muttered. "I hope it's not as bad as you think it is."

"Me, too."

"Call me when you've got some open time?"

"You know I will."

"And you'd better call me if you need me."

"If I do, I will. I promise."

"Good," Fox said. "Speaking of schedules, however, I may be going to Egypt soon, so if I don't hear from you in the next couple of weeks, we'll get together when I get back."

"Fair enough."

"Then I'll see you when I see you," Fox said. "Oh, and don't think you're the only one who's been up all night."

Archer's eyebrows lifted. "You?"

All he could hear was laughing before Fox hung up the phone.

With a grin on his face, Archer pulled into the driveway, quietly rolling his car up to the four-car garage next to Scarlett's rental car. He sat in his car a moment, looking over the darkened house, realizing that at this early hour they were all still asleep and not wanting to wake them. He thought about driving home to get some sleep but he didn't want to leave. Wherever Scarlett was, he wanted to be there also, if only to be near her. He was preparing to lay his seat back and sleep in the car for a few minutes when he saw Mr. Bayse emerge from the rear of the house.

Archer climbed out of his car, heading towards the gray-haired man who caught sight of him in the early morning light. Mr. Bayse raised a hand to his employer.

"Mr. Phipps," he greeted. "It's a fine morning."

Archer nodded as he closed in on the man, glancing at the open door that led into the utility room and kitchen beyond.

"Yes, it is," he replied. "Is Miss Scarlett awake?"

Mr. Bayse nodded, pointing towards the house. "She was up when the wife and I got up. She's sitting inside."

Archer thanked him and went in through the back door, being hit immediately by the smell of coffee and something baking in the oven. It was a wonderful, comforting smell, some-thing Archer realized he could get very accustomed to coming home to. He wandered into the family room but it was empty, crossing over into the kitchen where it was warm and smelling delicious. Mrs. Bayse was doing something on the counter and he greeted the woman, asking again for Scarlett. Mrs. Bayse pointed to the front of the house so he proceeded towards the dining room and ended up in the living room. Still no Scarlett. Casually, he strolled into the sitting room opposite the living room and found her curled up on the couch in front of a warm fire, sipping coffee and reading something on her tablet.

Scarlett glanced up when she caught movement out of the corner of her eyes, surprised when she saw that it was Archer. He was dressed in a dark suit, which looked very dapper on his big frame, but she mostly noticed how tired he looked. Their eyes met and he smiled.

"Good morning, my angel," he said.

Scarlett set the coffee down and tossed off the throw she had around her legs. "Good morning," she said as she got off the couch and went to him, putting her arms around his neck for a sweet hug. "What in the world are you doing here?"

He hugged her tightly, savoring the moment, and gave her a gentle kiss on the mouth. "I just got off of work," he said quietly. "I missed not seeing you last night so I just drove over here in the hopes we could have breakfast together."

The more he spoke, the more exhausted and stressed he appeared. The man was strung out, a state Scarlett had never seen him in before. She cocked her head with concern.

"Sure," she said, "but are you okay?"

"Fine."

"You look exhausted."

"You would be, too, if you were up all night."

She raised her eyebrows. "True enough," she agreed, taking him by the arm and pulling him towards the couch. "Let's get your coat off so you can sit down."

Archer let her pull his suit coat off. In fact, he was quite content to let her take charge of everything at the moment. Too often, it was him taking charge, but this morning, he just wanted to be bossed around and told what to do so he didn't have to think about anything. He also realized that he wanted to come home to her from now on. He wasn't sure how he was going to accomplish that, but it was his top priority to figure it out. This life, and her, is exactly what he'd always wanted.

Scarlett gently pushed him down on the couch and took off his tie, not saying a word as she slipped it off his neck, gently ran a hand through his hair, and kissed him sweetly on the forehead. She cast the coat and tie aside and unbuttoned the top two buttons on his dress shirt.

"How do you take your coffee?" she asked.

He grunted, feeling weary but wonderful as Scarlett tended to him. "Black."

Scarlett touched his cheek affectionately before she left the room. He could hear her out in the kitchen speaking with Mrs. Bayse and when she returned less than a minute later, it was with a steaming cup of coffee and a roll. She sat down next to him and put the plate on the coffee table. Archer grasped the cup and took a grateful sip.

"So," Scarlett curled up next to him and pulled the throw on. "I take it you had a busy night?"

Archer couldn't help but think about the grisly mess he had witnessed. He tried to push it out of his mind.

"Yes," he sat back on the couch with the coffee and put a big hand on her leg. "I'm so sorry about dinner. I hope you'll let me make it up to you."

She smiled. "No worries," she assured him. "There will be other dinners."

"I hope so," he said seriously, his gaze moving over her beautiful face. "I've missed you."

Her smile grew as she snuggled up next to him. "I've missed you, too."

He laid his cheek on the top of her head a moment before

kissing her hair and returning to his coffee. He looked around the room, feeling the warmth and charm of it.

"I have a confession to make," he said.

"What?"

"I like your house better than mine."

She giggled. "Your house is gorgeous."

He half-shrugged, half-nodded, sipping at his coffee. "It is," he agreed, "but, honestly, it's more my mother than me. Even though I'm technically the owner, it was her house before it was mine and it's still her house. She oversees everything. I just happen to live there."

Scarlett watched the flames flicker, her cheek on his shoulder. "You and your mother must have a good relationship if you can live together peacefully," she said. "As much as I love my mother, I could never live with her. A home can't have two queens."

Archer began to think about the inevitable – his strong desire to marry Scarlett which, presumably, would bring her and her girls to live at Phipps Hall. Her comment had him concerned about her and his mother living under the same roof. But looking at the Deerkeeper's Lodge, he felt more at home in the place in the first five minutes than he had at Phipps Hall his entire life. He shifted, put his arm around Scarlett, and snuggled up with her.

"My mother feels very bad about chasing you off the other night," he told her. "She's truly not a negative or bitter woman. She's actually very kind and practical. Although she doesn't regret what she said, she regrets that your feelings were hurt."

Scarlett shook her head, sitting up and looking at him. "I told you before that your mother was completely right," she said. "Does she know you sold me the lodge?"

"She knows."

"Have you decided how much you're going to ask for rent?"

"Not yet."

"Whatever it is, I'll pay it. I love this place. Last night, I slept better than I have in years. That bed in the master suite is heavenly."

He grinned. "Perhaps you'll let me try it sometime."

She laughed softly, knowing what he meant, and shook her head coyly at him. "Maybe," was all she would say.

He laughed at her reaction and hugged her tightly, snuggling down as the fire crackled and morning deepened. It was one of the best moments he'd ever savored. Mrs. Bayse came in a short time later and announced that breakfast was ready, so they went into the breakfast room where the woman served them an enormous breakfast of eggs, sausage, bacon, potatoes, mushrooms, scones, and copious amounts of coffee. Scarlett wasn't usually a big eater but she wolfed down an enormous amount of food and then blamed Archer for her misery, since he was the one who hired Mrs. Bayse. He just grinned and burped.

Finished with breakfast, they went back into the sitting room but Archer realized he was deadly tired now that he'd eaten. The food was weighing on him and all he wanted to do was sleep. He yawned repeatedly as Scarlett went on about doing some shopping for artwork and by the time she sat down on the couch, she looked up to see him rubbing at his eyes.

"I'm sorry," she said. "I'm keeping you up and you're exhausted."

He yawned again. "I am, but I don't want to leave you. I'm rather enjoying all of this."

She smiled. "There are five bedrooms upstairs, three of which are empty. If you don't want to drive all the way home, you can pick a bedroom."

He sighed heavily. "That," he said sincerely, "would be much appreciated. I'm not sure I could drive home right now in my current state. That big breakfast is about to send me into a food coma."

Scarlett got up from the couch and took his hand, leading him up the main staircase to the second floor. This was the section where the family bedrooms were, and Morgan and Alexandra were still sleeping as they made their way to Scarlett's bedroom. It was an exquisite room with white walls, exposed beams, and a massive wrought iron bed with a fluffy white duvet. Scarlett went to the bed and yanked the covers back.

"Okay, young man," she teased with a wink. "Get in."

Archer's eyes were twinkling at her as he closed the bedroom door and proceeded to take off every stitch of clothing. Scarlett stood next to the bed, watching the man strip down; in the heat of passion the day before, she hadn't really taken the time to look at him, but now in the weak morning sunlight, she wasn't shy about inspecting the man she felt an overwhelming attraction towards. He was broad chested, with a muscular neck and enormous arms, narrow waist and big, strong legs. He was also semi-aroused by the time he pulled his briefs off. Scarlett took her eyes off him when she realized it, her cheeks growing warm as he came over to the bed. Instead of climbing in, however, he put his big arms around her and began to suckle her neck.

"Lay down with me," he purred.

Scarlett struggled to pull away from him. "If I lay down with you, you're not going to sleep and you know it," she wasn't trying very hard to pull away because the man's attentions had her turning to putty. "Besides, I don't want to do... that... with the girls in the next room. I just don't think it's right, at least not right now. If you and I are going to... well, you know, see each other, then at least let the kids get used to it before they figure out we've been in the same bed."

He pulled back to look at her after a moment. "You're right," he whispered. "I'm sorry. I'm just so consumed with you. I didn't mean to suggest anything inappropriate in front of your girls."

She smiled up at him as he towered over her. "I know you didn't." She wrapped her arms around his neck and pulled him down to her mouth, kissing him softly. "Get some sleep. I'll be downstairs if you need me."

"I need you."

She laughed and pulled free from his embrace, directing him into the bed. He climbed in and she pulled the covers up around him, tucking him in and kissing him on the forehead. When their eyes met, she smiled warmly. There was something more to her expression than there had been before, something that made him feel weak and giddy all over. It was as if her walls of defense had finally broken down and now he was seeing the true warm and wonderful woman emerge. He'd been waiting for just this moment.

"Sleep tight, sweetheart," she whispered.

He sighed, loving the sound of the pet name from her lips. It was the best thing he could imagine. "See you in my dreams, beautiful girl," he murmured.

Scarlett left the room, shutting the door behind her. It was a satisfying and comforting feeling knowing he was sleeping in the house and would be waking up to her face. It had been a long time since she had known that feeling and, with a smile, headed down the hallway towards Alexandra's room because she could hear the girl stirring around. There was a lot to do today and she intended to make the most of it.

———

"This church is really old." Alexandra was standing next to the car, looking at the spire of the church across the street. "It's like something out of a story book."

Dressed in a black pencil skirt that came to her knees, a pretty white blouse, sexy black pumps and a stylish hat she had purchased the day before, Scarlett locked the car and put the keys in her purse. Archer had invited her and the girls to attend church with him and his mother and, although they really weren't churchgoers, Scarlett had accepted the invitation simply to start becoming integrated into her new community. Now, as she looked up at the big Gothic church with the well-kept but creepy old cemetery, she wasn't so sure it was a good idea.

They had parked the car in the car park across the street from the structure, trickling in for the late morning service along with a few dozen other people. Everyone seemed very friendly but Scarlett noticed quickly enough that she was overdressed. Feeling somewhat uncomfortable about the fact that she was very nicely dressed, she was in the process of debating whether or not to remove the hat when Archer's big BMW pulled into the car park.

He pulled the silver vehicle next to Scarlett's rental car and brought it to a halt. He hadn't even turned the car off before Henry was bailing out of the backseat, running straight for Alexandra. The young man was dressed nicely in slacks and a sport coat and when Archer climbed out of the car dressed in nearly the same thing, Scarlett didn't feel so terribly over-dressed. He looked very handsome. Archer's eyes locked with hers as he came around the car and the smile on his lips, the warmth in his eyes, was unmistakable. He went to open the car door for his mother as he spoke to Scarlett.

"Good morning," he said to the three women. "You all look lovely this morning."

Alexandra was already off with Henry and Morgan gave

him her usual bored expression, but Scarlett smiled her thanks. He winked at her as he helped his mother out of the car, who was dressed primly in a yellow suit and matching hat. Arabella looked straight at Scarlett as she got out of the car.

"Good morning," she said.

Scarlett gave the woman a short wave. "Good morning."

Archer still had his mother in hand as he shut the car door and made his way over to Scarlett and Morgan. Arabella clutched her son's elbow, smiling at both Morgan and Scarlett.

"You both look so lovely," she said nicely, focusing in on Scarlett's hat. "Your hat is beautiful. Wherever did you get it?"

Scarlett's fingers fluttered to the black hat perched stylishly on her head. "I found a milliner in Ludbourne," she said. "The owner helped me pick this out. I will admit it's the first hat I've owned. We don't wear hats like this in America unless we're going to the Kentucky Derby."

Arabella laughed. "You were born to wear a hat."

Scarlett was flattered by the compliment, hoping that this meant the woman had forgiven her for trying to move into her house. She still felt very strongly that she wanted peace with the woman, if not her respect. Thanking the woman kindly, she followed Archer and his mother as they walked towards the church.

"Is this your regular church?' she asked as they paused at the road to watch for traffic before crossing.

Archer nodded. "It's part of the estate," he said. "Generations of Phipps have gone to church here, but we divide up our time between this church and York Cathedral. My parents were married at York Cathedral, in fact."

Alexandra and Henry raced up, and Scarlett put out a hand to the children, stopping them before they could rush across the road and get plastered by a car. When it was finally clear of traffic, Archer led his group across the street. Several people were milling outside of the entrance and, seeing Archer and his mother, the men removed their hats in greeting and the women bobbed a brief curtsy. As they neared the door, Arabella let go of Archer's arm and latched on to Scarlett's. Startled, Scarlett was nonetheless pleased.

"Archer tells me that you have purchased the Deerkeeper's Lodge," Arabella said.

Scarlett nodded. "It's the most beautiful home I've seen other than Phipps Hall," she said. "Archer did a wonderful job of restoring it. My girls absolutely love it."

Arabella was pleased. "I'm so happy you like it." She suddenly came to a halt before they entered the church, casting her son a stern expression when he came to a halt as well. "Go on inside, Archer, and take the children. Scarlett and I will come inside in a moment."

With a lingering glance at Scarlett, Archer fought off a grin as he herded the kids inside the church. Scarlett was a little nervous to be left alone with Arabella but she didn't show it. She faced the woman and smiled expectantly. Arabella, in turn, studied Scarlett's face for a moment before speaking.

"I hope you don't mind that I wanted a moment of your time away from my nosy son," she said quietly.

Scarlett shook her head. "Of course not. What can I do for you?"

Arabella paused a moment, thoughtfully, before continuing. "I wanted to apologize for hurting your feelings the night you came to dinner at Phipps Hall," she said. "I was quite rude when my son announced he had invited you and your girls to stay with us, and that was unkind of me. I suppose I was simply caught off-guard."

Scarlett gently cut the woman off. "You were right," she assured her. "I wasn't entirely sure about Archer's offer, either, but your son can be rather persuasive. I was so afraid we had offended you and I'm very sorry if that was the case."

Arabella digested her words, smiling after a moment. "Archer said he pushed you into accepting, and I believe him," she said. "You did not offend me, my dear. I hope we can put the incident behind us and move forward. My son speaks very highly of you and I would like to see what he finds so fascinating. Already, I think I have caught a glimpse of it."

Scarlett smiled modestly. "He speaks highly of you, also."

"Then we can become friends?"

"We already are."

"Good," Arabella said. "I will admit that I am glad Archer has found a good woman. He's a rather lonely man although he won't admit it."

"Lonely? What do you mean?"

"He spends most of his time at work and when he's home, his life revolves around Henry and various projects he has going on. I can't remember when last he enjoyed himself with a woman, on a friendly level."

"I'll make sure he enjoys himself with me."

Arabella smiled and took Scarlett's elbow. Scarlett escorted the woman inside the church, which was rather small but well laid out. It was in the shape of a cross, with a long section and two side sections that branched off on either side of the elaborate pulpit. Archer and the children were seated in one of the smaller branches and when Archer saw Scarlett and his mother approach, he stood up. Seating his mother on one side of him and Scarlett on the other, he had never felt happier or more complete.

Church was something of a long process, the Anglican service different from what Scarlett had experienced in her youth as a Nazarene. The reverend spoke a good deal about tithing and donating to the church before launching into a sermon about the joy of prayer. Scarlett sat next to Archer, listening intently to the sermon, as her daughters grew bored and fidgety. By the time the service concluded, Morgan and Alexandra were ready to explode, so Scarlett allowed them to rush out of the church simply to get outside and into the fresh air. Henry went with them, as their proper escort, as Archer took hold of his mother and Scarlett and approached the reverend.

There were several people milling around the reverend but they backed off when they saw the Earl of Wintringham and Mulgrave and the dowager countess. Scarlett thought it was all very odd the way people just seemed to fall back out of the way so Archer could speak to the reverend. Next thing she realized, Archer was introducing her.

"Miss Ward," he indicated the man in the green and white robes, "this is the Very Reverend Bond Bryan. Reverend, this is Ludbourne's latest resident, Miss Scarlett Ward."

Reverend Bryan was a middle-aged man with thin glasses and a receding hairline. He smiled brightly and extended a hand to Scarlett. "It's a pleasure to meet you, Miss Ward."

Scarlett smiled in return; trying not to stare at the man's yellowed teeth. "Thank you," she replied. "I'm very happy to be here."

The reverend cocked his head. "You're American," he picked up on the accent immediately. "Where are you from?"

"Los Angeles."

That seemed to excite the reverend. "Hollywood!" he gasped. "I'm an old movie buff myself. Do you know much about them?"

Scarlett couldn't help but laugh. "A little," she replied. "My dad was a big fan, so I know my way around Cary Grant, Katharine Hepburn and James Cagney."

The reverend was thrilled. "I would love to sit and talk to

you sometime. I've never been to Los Angeles but I would like to go someday."

"It would be a trip of a lifetime, I'm sure."

"The reverend and his father both served in this church," Archer stepped into the conversation, realizing he was jealous the way the reverend was literally drooling all over Scarlett. "If memory serves, I believe his grandfather serviced this church as well."

The reverend tore his gaze away from Scarlett to focus on Archer. "He did, sir."

Arabella was already pulling Scarlett away. "It was nice to see you, Reverend," Arabella said as they began to walk away. "Your sermon was most interesting. Long, but interesting."

The reverend's face fell somewhat as Archer and his group moved away. "Thank you, mum."

Scarlett found herself a captive of Arabella as they moved out of the church. People treated the dowager with all due respect and Scarlett found herself smiling and murmuring "hello" to the crowd as they passed. The entire pomp and circumstance of the etiquette was odd to her. As they neared the exit, she caught sight of a little girl with a bunch of flowers in her hand. She raced towards Scarlett with her flowers but ended up tripping, going down hard on her knee. Scarlett was the first one by the little girl's side.

"Uh oh," she said lightly, helping the little girl to her feet and handing her back the dumped flowers. "Look; your flowers are fine. They're still very pretty."

The little girl was trying not to cry as she extended the now-damaged bunch. "They're for you."

Scarlett was genuinely surprised. "Me?" she accepted the flowers, hesitantly. "My gosh... thank you. They're so beautiful. Did you pick them yourself?"

The little girl nodded, wiping her nose. "Mummy told me to."

She was pointing behind her to the small blond woman standing just behind her. When Scarlett looked up, the mother bobbed a brief curtsy. Scarlett looked around to see who the woman was curtsying to as she stood up with the flowers in her hand.

"Uh... thank you," she said to the tot's mother.

The woman beamed. "Welcome to Ludbourne."

Scarlett smiled. "Thank you," she said sincerely. "It's a beautiful village."

At this point, Archer had her by the elbow and was gently escorting her through the crowd of people. Scarlett let him pull her along as they continued on to the edge of the road. Archer emitted a piercing whistle to the children, who were hanging out in the old cemetery adjacent to the church, and the kids came running; even Morgan. Together, they headed across the road to the car park and headed for their respective vehicles.

Back at the church, Reverend Bryan was standing in the church entry, watching the earl's group in the distance. As he stood there and watched, the mother of the girl and a few other ladies came up to him, turning to see what he was looking at. In fact, they all watched Archer and his group climb into their cars and head off towards the east.

"Do you know who she is, Reverend?" the girl's mother asked.

"Phipps introduced her as Scarlett Ward," he said. "She's American."

Another older lady with a bad haircut and a purple suit spoke up. "Who is she?" she asked, rather stuffily. "Do we know anything about her?"

The reverend shook his head. "She's American but that's

about all I can tell you," he replied. "Phipps introduced her as the newest Ludbourne resident, so she must have moved in somewhere around here."

"Phipps owns some property on the edge of town," the child's mother put in. "I know because my husband did some concrete work when Phipps was restoring it. Maybe she moved in there."

"Maybe," the reverend shrugged and turned back towards the church. "If you'll excuse me, ladies, I need to go about seeing about that roof. It looks like it's going to rain again and I don't want a mess on my hands."

The women let the reverend go but they continued to stand on the steps of the old Gothic church, watching the crowds around them disburse and go on about their Sunday afternoon.

"Scarlett Ward," the child's mother repeated quietly. "I'm going to see what I can find out about her. She's a looker, I reckon."

The woman with the bad haircut snorted. "She's beautiful, all right," she agreed. "Phipps wouldn't look at a sloucher."

"Still," the mother said suspiciously. "I'm going to 'Google' her name and see if I can find out anything. Don't all Americans have something on 'Google'?"

The other woman began to turn and walk away. "Maggie, you're simply jealous because Phipps had no interest in meeting your single sister," she scolded. "Your sister is single for a reason; she's a nasty old shrew and smells like garlic all the time."

Maggie frowned. "That's not true," she insisted, yelling as the woman got further away from her. "She doesn't smell like garlic all of the time!"

Maggie could hear the other women laughing. Frustrated, she grabbed hold of her daughter's hand and quickly walked in the direction of her car. She was going to head home, put the baby down for a nap, and look up what she could on Scarlett Ward. When she found out who the woman really was, *she'd* be the one laughing in the end.

SEVEN

LUNCH AFTER CHURCH was at Phipps Hall. Scarlett and the girls had swung by the lodge to quickly change clothes before they headed out to Archer's home. Archer had his mother in the car with him and Scarlett didn't want to make the woman wait in the car while she changed clothes, so Archer gave her very specific instructions on how to get to Phipps Hall.

Having learned her driving skills in Los Angeles, Scarlett was more than up to the task and after changing into a white French-cuff button down shirt that hugged her torso, coral-colored Capri-cut slacks and adorable coral peep-toed pumps, she looked sleek, stylish and sexy, and when she arrived at Phipps Hall, Archer couldn't take his eyes off her. In fact, when Henry collected his harem of Alexandra and Morgan with the intent of taking them to the barn to show them his pony, Archer swooped in on Scarlett and wrapped an arm around her slender waist to pull her close.

"You," he whispered in her ear, "look fantastic. Any chance I can get you alone sometime today?"

Scarlett grinned. "Oh, I don't know," she said coyly.

"Maybe. I'm sure there's any number of nooks and crannies in this place that could swallow us up for a couple of minutes."

He laughed, his arm still around her as they followed the children around the side of the manse, where a broad stone path led off into the trees to the east. Scarlett could see buildings on the other side of the greenbelt. The children were several yards ahead of them with Henry pulling Alexandra along.

"Where is Henry taking the girls?" she asked.

Archer was happy and content strolling along with Scarlett under his arm. "He wants to show them Nero."

Scarlett put her right hand up to grasp Archer's hand resting on her right shoulder. "Alex is going to want to ride now," she said. "You should have waited until after we ate. I'll never get her away from the barn."

He smiled, watching his son tug on Alexandra on up ahead. "No worries," he said, fondling her fingers. "We'll bring luncheon down to the stables, then."

Scarlett smiled up at him and he gave her a little squeeze. "You're very easygoing with children."

He shrugged. "I've had to learn, raising Henry alone as I have. My mother has helped enormously, however. She's a good role model."

"Yes, she is," Scarlett agreed. "She raised a fine son."

"Thank you very much."

"You're welcome."

They just grinned at each other until Archer bent down and kissed her on the forehead. The man was so thrilled to be with her that he was walking on air, so happy that his life was taking the path that it was. He'd never known such joy.

They reached the barn and as the children went on ahead to Nero's stall, Scarlett quickly realized she couldn't walk on the rain-soaked ground of the stables. She stopped at the edge of the stone path and pointed to the muck beyond.

"I can't walk on that," she said apologetically.

Archer didn't miss a beat; he swooped down and picked her up in his big arms, carrying her off across the mud in pursuit of the kids.

"We don't want to get your beautiful shoes dirty," he murmured, nuzzling the side of her head. "Besides, this is good practice for me."

Arms wrapped around his neck, Scarlett looked at him curiously. "For what?"

"For when I carry you across the threshold after we're married."

She just grinned and looked away. "I will admit," she said, "that I wasn't particularly comfortable with all of those people at church and the way they treated me like I was some sort of royalty."

"If you're with me, then they're assuming you are," he said. "You're going to have to get used to it."

"Are you related to the royal family?"

He nodded. "Distantly," he replied. "My ancestor had an affair with one of Edward the First's daughters, a young lady who was destined to become a nun in fact, and their son was christened the first Earl Wintringham by Edward the Second. My heritage is very old on both sides of the family."

"You mentioned your mother was from an old family."

"Very old. Her ancestor, many centuries back, was a bloodthirsty warlord with a reputation like Vlad Dracul. Do you know who he is?"

She grinned up at him. "Yes, I've heard of Dracula," she said. "Unfortunately, I don't have such a colorful family tree. My family has been in America since the Revolutionary War, mostly in Virginia, Texas and California."

"Any brothers or sisters?"

"Two brothers," she replied. "And you?"

"Just my brother and me," he said as they neared the children, now fawning over a black pony who was sticking his head out of his stall. "My father was an only child, as was his father. Oddly enough, my family doesn't seem to produce a lot of children. As far back as we can trace the family lineage, there have never been more than two children and there has always been a male."

Archer came to a halt when they reached the stall, still holding Scarlett in his arms. All of the children were petting the black pony, who kept trying to nip at Alexandra. She giggled with delight as she avoided nosy pony lips.

"Do you want to ride him?" Henry asked excitedly, looking at his father. "Dad, can we ride him now?"

Before Archer could decline for the moment, Alexandra chimed in and, between the two of them begging, Archer was a pushover and caved in.

"All right," he sighed heavily. "Henry, go find Edward and tell him to saddle your pony and also saddle Miss Daisy for Alexandra. Morgan, do you want to ride, also?"

Morgan wasn't beyond showing some excitement. "Well," she said reluctantly, looking between Archer and her mother. "If the horse is really super gentle, then I will."

Archer returned his attention to his son. "Tell Edward to saddle Sunny for Morgan."

Henry was wildly excited. He grabbed Alexandra by the hand. "Come on!" he shouted. "We can help him saddle the horses!"

They were off, running for the end of the barn where the head groom had a small office. Scarlett and Archer watched them all go, even normally-morose Morgan. Scarlett finally shook her head.

"I told you we should have waited until after lunch," she said.

He grinned. "They'll be fine for now with Edward," he said. "Let's go up to the house and tell my mother that the location for lunch has been moved."

"I hope she doesn't get upset."

"She won't."

They headed back up to the house. Everything on the grounds was gorgeous and landscaped, and he took her up a set of very old stone stairs before arriving on a terrace. He could have set her down at any point but he continued to hold her as he passed through the terrace furnished with stone benches and topiaries, across a big driveway, and on towards the house.

There was a set of very big gates that looked as if they were embedded right in the side of the house and as Archer walked through them, Scarlett could see that there was a courtyard beyond. The house, so old and well designed, had a courtyard built right in the middle of it. Scarlett looked skyward, seeing at least three stories of the house towering around her.

"Wow," she exclaimed. "I had no idea there was this big open space in the middle of your house."

He was walking towards one of the many doors surrounding the courtyard. "Back in the old days, this was the equivalent to a garage," he told her. "Carriages would pull in through the gates, or supply wagons, or whatever, and would be protected from bandits or the elements, or whatever. Back when I was a child, all of the rooms on this level were kind of dark and foreboding and forbidden to me because they hadn't been touched in hundreds of years. They'd been left to deteriorate. When my mother restored the home, I had some input and we put in a gym, a bar and a couple of party rooms, a wine cellar, a billiard room, and other store rooms. All of the rooms at this level are fortified, and enormous, because when the house was originally built, this was the level that could be breached if there was an attack. The walls in some places are a couple of feet thick."

He set her down as they reached a door and he opened it for her, ushering her into the cool depths. It was a maze of rooms until he took her up the stairs to the main living level. They found Arabella working on something in the big, dark-paneled study, and she wasn't distressed at all that lunch had been moved to the terrace so they could watch the children ride. In fact, she seemed rather excited about it.

Fortunately, the weather cooperated and it was a fairly balmy day. A beautiful lunch of broiled chicken, salads and sandwiches was set out on the exquisite terrace overlooking the stables and small park-like arena below, and down-wind, where the adults sat and watched the children ride around the arena on their horses. A tall, thin man stood at the edge of the arena, watching the children like a hawk, and Archer told Scarlett that it was the stable master, Edward Feller. As the birds sang and a soft breeze blew, Scarlett sat next to Archer, picking at her salad and watching Alexandra and Morgan ride circles on two small mares. She could hear Alexandra laughing, knowing the girl was having the time of her life. Finally, some happiness over their move to England. She was coming to feel so much better over the whole thing.

It would be a short-lived feeling.

———

Archer had been dreaming when his cell phone woke him up. Scarlett had been in his dream, something warm and erotic no doubt, but he was awake quickly and answered the phone. He didn't like what he heard on the other end.

This one was off of Elvington Lane near Grimston, to the south and east of York in a mostly unincorporated and rural area of Yorkshire. A single mother and her young son had been found dead by the boy's grandmother, and the old lady was still hysterical and being tended to by emergency personnel when Archer arrived. Inspectors were already on the scene and the officers had secured the modest row home. It was a cold night, mist off the moist fields hanging heavy in the air and lending credence to the dark and foreboding atmosphere. As Archer entered the dimly lit house, he could already smell the coagulated blood.

Calvin met him in the small, neat reception room. His handsome features were taut with fatigue. "Hi, Archer," he greeted him quietly. "I told them to call you in on this."

Dressed in slacks, a pullover knit shirt and overcoat with his badge clipped to the breast pocket of the coat, Archer struggled against the sick feeling in the pit of his stomach.

"Why?" he asked. "What's the situation?"

Calvin sighed heavily, pointing back to the kitchen. "Mrs. Reisler, the grandmother outside, had been calling her daughter all day but the woman never answered her phone," he explained. "She made her last call at eleven pm and still no answer, so she decided to come over and see what was going on. She let herself in and found the mother dead in the kitchen and the boy dead on the landing at the top of the stairs. Both of them have been shot in the head."

"Why did you call me in?"

"Because the boy's throat has also been slit," Calvin lowered his voice. "The police surgeon also thinks the mother was raped postmortem. You know the chief is going to want a report as to whether or not this is another Cutter murder."

Archer gave Calvin a tense, if not apprehensive, expression. "Have you gotten a good look at both victims?"

Calvin nodded. "It's hard to say. You're the expert."

Archer sighed heavily, his gaze moving to the staircase. He could see a pair of legs hanging over the top of the stairs as the police technicians worked around the body.

"God, I wish I wasn't," he muttered.

Archer took the stairs to the top, seeing that the murder victim was probably no older than Henry. Sense of nausea increasing, Archer pulled out a pair of latex gloves from his coat pocket and put them on, kneeling next to the body of the child and paying close attention to the corpse without touching anything. The child had a head wound on the left side of his head, with blood and brain matter pooling, in addition to a gaping neck wound. Archer stared at it a moment, digesting everything he was seeing, before realizing that Calvin was standing behind him. He pointed to the child's neck.

"Did you see the wound on his neck?" he asked.

Calvin nodded. "I did."

Archer stood up. "Did you notice how ragged it is?" he asked, pushing past Calvin and making his way back down the stairs. "The Cutter's incisions are almost surgical in their precision. That wound looks hasty and ripped. Not the usual work."

Calvin followed him down the stairs, not saying anything to that end because it sounded to him as if Archer was attempting to talk himself out of the fact that this could be the second serial death in as many days. He knew how much that possibility was eating at Archer. By the time they reached the kitchen, the police surgeon, or medical examiner, was investigating the mother, who was on the floor spread-eagle. There was so much blood that it was difficult to tell where it was all coming from. The woman, the floor, the cabinets were covered with it.

Dr. Ross Davis had been a colleague of Archer's at Sandhurst. They knew each other well. When he glanced up and saw Archer standing in the doorway, he immediately stood up from his stooped position.

"Hello, Archer," he greeted with warmth. "Sorry to drag you out of bed in the middle of the night."

Archer forced a smile. "Don't feel sorry for me," he said.

"I'm feeling sorry for you, in fact. What a mess you've got to sort through."

Davis grinned, nodding as he looked at his feet. His smile faded. "Mess, indeed."

"Can you tell me anything?"

Davis shrugged and knelt down again, pointing to the woman with a gloved finger. "She's been dead awhile," he said. "I would estimate since this morning, at least. The boy upstairs has only been dead eight hours or so."

Archer's brow furrowed. "So she was killed first?" he glanced over his shoulder at the base of the stairs. "What are the chances that that boy came home from school and the killer was waiting for him?"

"Every chance in the world," Davis looked up at him. "Look at this floor; blood everywhere. There was no blood on the sole of the boy's shoes, yet there are bloodied footprints in the living room. Someone was waiting for that boy, he must have come in through the front door, saw whoever it was, and then ran upstairs to try and get away. Only he didn't make it."

"How do you know he came in through the front door?"

"Because there are only two doors; the kitchen door and the reception room door. Had he come through the kitchen, he would have tracked blood all over the place."

Archer was silent for a moment, gazing down at the young mother who had been so brutally murdered. He sighed heavily.

"You were part of the Cutter murders, weren't you?" he asked Davis.

The doctor nodded. "I was a very young and impressionable surgeon at the time," he was looking over the body. "You don't think he's resurfacing, do you? I was at the murder scene last night on Pipter Road, but I left before you got there. It sure looked like a similar scene."

"But no note," Archer said.

Davis shook his head. "No note."

They all knew about the notes. Since it was something that had nearly driven Archer over the edge, no one acknowledged them more than briefly in passing. As Archer knelt down to get a better look at the mother, someone shouted from upstairs.

"Hey!" it was one of the police technicians. "Inspectors! Help!"

Archer bolted, as did Calvin, both of them racing up the stairs, following the sounds of the shouting. They leapt over the body of the boy to get to the back bedroom where the tech was. The man was pointing to a closed closet.

"There's something in there," the tech was breathless as he ran to the door, cowering behind the officers with their guns drawn. "I've been hearing noises since we got here and something just thumped on that door again."

Archer was the first one to the door, his gun drawn, with Calvin right behind him. He put his hand on the door knob, nodded at Calvin to silently let the man know he was going to open the door, and then jerked open the panel. But what came forth was not what they expected.

A small child fell out of the closet, a little girl covered with blood. She was barely conscious, horribly weak, and apparently unable to open the closet door. All she had been able to do was thump at it and hope someone heard her. Archer carefully turned the child onto her back, seeing that her throat was slit even though she was still alive. Horror surged through him.

"Get the medics up here!" he roared. "Get them *now*!"

———

Both girls started school the next day, Monday. The day dawned clear, bright and chilly, typical English weather, as the girls from Southern California agonized over what to wear. Because of the move and commute, Scarlett had decided against sending the girls to the schools they had originally chosen and Archer was instrumental in getting them enrolled on short notice at the same school Henry was attending, Fulford Academy in York. He'd done it yesterday after their lovely Sunday luncheon, and the school's Head Master was more than happy to do business with the earl on a Sunday.

The school was actually much closer to Scarlett's new home and many children from Ludbourne went there as well. Scarlett arrived with the girls early Monday morning and went to meet with the Head Master, filling out all of the enrollment paper-work and figuring out their curriculum since American school courses were slightly different from the British. But the school dean was very helpful in getting the girls set up and Scarlett left them to find their classes and get acclimated, telling them that she would pick them up promptly at three in the afternoon. As she watched her daughters walk down the hall of the old, formal building, she felt some trepidation. She prayed it went well.

Unfortunately, it didn't, at least for Alexandra. Morgan seemed to find a few friends right away, but Alexandra climbed into the car in tears. Concerned, Scarlett tried to find out why she was so upset but Alexandra wouldn't say a thing. She just sniffled and wiped her nose. By the time they got back to the lodge, both girls ran up to their rooms and slammed the doors. Scarlett was left following them in, hearing doors slam and concerned as to why Alexandra was so upset. As she passed through the kitchen, Mrs. Bayse was busy at the stove.

"I'll have tea ready in a few minutes," she said cheerily.

Scarlett smiled weakly and thanked her, heading to the staircase in the dining room that spilled out almost in front of Alexandra's door. Standing in front of her daughter's closed door, she knocked softly. She heard Alexandra reply, although she wasn't sure what she said, but she took it as a cue to open the door anyway.

Alexandra was standing in her bathroom, brushing her long hair into a ponytail. She looked over when she saw her mother.

"Mom," she said, "can I please go riding with Henry?"

Scarlett nodded, leaning against the doorjamb and watching her daughter primp. "I'm sure you can," she said. "But not before you tell me what happened at school."

Alexandra's face fell. But rather than burst into tears, she just looked angry as she stormed out of the bathroom and plopped down on her bed.

"I'm not going back there," she declared. "Those kids are dumb and mean."

"Why? What happened?"

"They just are."

"If you can't tell me what they've done, then you're going to have to go back. You're not giving me anything to base your decision on."

Alexandra's angry face turned to her mother. "There's some girl in my class who goes to the church we went to," she said. "I saw her yesterday. She wasn't very nice."

"What did she say?"

Alexandra lowered her head. "She said...," she shrugged. "Stuff."

"*What* stuff, Alex?"

Alexandra sighed heavily. "Stuff about you."

"Me?" Scarlett was genuinely surprised. "How in the world would she know anything about me?"

Alexandra fell back on her bed. "She said her mom said you were a slut," she said. "She said her mom said all Americans were sluts and idiots, and when she saw your videos on the internet, she said you were one, too. She said that her mom said that you must have used your pussy to get Archer and he doesn't know any better."

Shocked to the bone, Scarlett slapped a hand over her mouth to keep from laughing or, better yet, screaming with outrage. She struggled to keep her composure. "Do you know what that means, Alex?"

Alexandra shrugged. "I think so," she said. "When we lived in California, I think I heard some boys in my class say pussy and laugh. It's not very nice, is it?"

Scarlett took her hand away from her mouth and shook her head. "No, it's not," she said softly. "It's not a very nice name for a woman's vagina."

Alexandra sat up. "Really?" she looked perplexed as well as angry. "Then I'm going to slap that girl next time she says that."

Scarlett shook her head and sat down on the bed next to her, putting her arm around her daughter. "Don't," she hugged her youngest, feeling sad and shocked. "So she mentioned my videos, did she?"

Alexandra nodded. "Her mom must have looked you up on the internet and saw you singing. You weren't a slut back then, were you?"

Scarlett laughed. "No way," she said. "Grandma and Grandpa would have killed me."

Alexandra was gradually becoming less angry and more distressed. "I really don't want to go back to school. Those kids were all laughing at me and no one wanted to eat lunch with me except Henry."

"Did he hear what the kids said?"

"I think so."

Scarlett stroked her daughter's dark head sadly. "Well," she said after a moment, "I don't think we should run. I think we should stand up for ourselves. Those people don't know us and they're saying a lot of bad things about us. I'm not afraid of them and you shouldn't be, either. Jealous people will say a whole lot of bad things just to upset us and if we run away, then they win. Do you want that girl to win?"

Alexandra thought about that. "No," she said firmly. "I don't."

Scarlett hugged her. "That's my girl," she said. "Maybe I should have a talk with that girl's mother to straighten her out. What's the girl's name?"

"Adriana Rorick."

Scarlett thought on the name. "I don't remember meeting anyone with that name," she said. "I'll ask Archer. He should know."

"Are you going to tell him what she said?"

"Probably not."

"Mom?"

"What?"

"You didn't get Archer, did you?"

"What do you mean?"

"I mean... are you two, you know, like you and Jerry were? Do you love each other?"

Scarlett thought carefully on her reply. "Would that upset you?"

Alexandra shook her head firmly. "No," she said. "Because we could move into that great big house and I could have all the horses I want, and Henry and I could ride all of the time."

Scarlett laughed and got up off the bed. "That sounds like a great plan," she said. "But for now, we're going to stay in this house. Okay?"

"Okay. I like this house."

"So do I."

Scarlett left her daughter with a reminder to come down for tea in a few minutes, which intrigued the girl because she really had no idea what "tea" was, as she went back down to the kitchen where Mrs. Bayse had a lovely tray of goodies, little sandwiches, and tea set out on the breakfast table. Morgan was already wandering around the front of the house chatting on her new cell phone, and Scarlett was happy that at least one of her girls had a good experience at school. But the whole "pussy" thing really had her upset. She made up her mind quickly to seek out the child's mother and straighten her out, but good. Better yet, she might even ask Archer to do it. He knew the people, after all, and they respected him.

Morgan and Alexandra loved tea. They scarfed down the scones and jam, and ate all of the little chicken salad sandwiches. Scarlett was sitting at the table with a cup of tea, watching her girls eat with a grin, when Mr. Bayse opened the door leading out into the courtyard and announced he'd found some baby quail. Thrilled, the girls bolted up from the table and charged out of the door just about the time Archer was coming in. Morgan missed him but Alexandra didn't; she plowed right into him and he grunted as she smacked into his belly. Then he laughed as he righted her on her feet, watching her race off after her sister and Mr. Bayse. He shook his head as he watched them all go.

"Where in the world are they going?" he wanted to know.

Grinning, Scarlett set her teacup down and went to greet him. "Apparently, the lure of baby animals is very strong," she said. "Mr. Bayse is going to show them a nest or den or something."

Archer was still smiling as he looked down at her. He took a moment just to study her, drinking in that gorgeous face. Then he bent down to kiss her softly on the lips.

"Hello, my angel," he said, kissing her again because she tasted so good. "How was your day?"

Scarlett felt a thrill run through her as he kissed her and, had Mrs. Bayse not been standing in the kitchen behind her, might have quite possibly put her arms around his neck and kissed him deeply. But she refrained, at least for the moment.

"It was good," she said, gazing up into his handsome face. "More importantly, how are you? Did you work today?"

He nodded as they headed into the house. "Actually, I was called in on a case last night," he said as she directed him to the breakfast table and Mrs. Bayse brought forth a new pot of tea. "I've been up all night and most of the day."

Scarlett sat down next to him at the round table. "Oh, my," she frowned. "You must be exhausted."

He nodded, running a hand through his cropped auburn hair as Mrs. Bayse poured him a cup of tea. He thought on the horrific night, struggling not to let the dark memories drag him down.

"I am," he agreed. "But I wanted to see you. How did the first day of school go?"

Scarlett eyed Mrs. Bayse, who was busy over at the sink. She flicked her eyes in the direction of the woman and shook her head briefly at Archer, who took the hint somewhat.

"Morgan seems to have made friends already," she said for Mrs. Bayse's benefit. "Alex is a little more of a challenge."

Archer didn't even touch the tea. He stood up, pulling her with him, not wanting the housekeeper to hear a private conversation. They walked into the dining room and on out into the sitting room with its exposed beams and off-white, rustic furniture. Archer had Scarlett by the hand as he fell back on the couch and pulled her down with him. She ended up lying on top of him.

"Now," he sighed, half-asleep already as he snuggled with her. "Tell me what happened with Alex."

Scarlett got comfortable from her position splayed on top of him, gently stroking his forehead as he grunted with pleasure.

She couldn't help be touched that, as weary as he was, he was still concerned for her daughters.

"It seems that there's a girl in her class who was at church yesterday and somehow knew my name and knew who my girls were."

"Why is that a problem?"

"Because she said some pretty nasty things about me."

Archer's eyes opened up and he looked at her. "What's the girl's name?"

"Adriana Rorick."

Archer stared at her a moment and she could see his expression tense up. "What happened?"

Scarlett was matter of fact about it. "Apparently, her mother either met me or knew enough about me to look me up on the internet," she said. "According to Alex, this girl said that her mother said I was a slut and that all Americans were sluts and idiots."

Archer's eyes widened with outrage. "Are you kidding?"

Scarlett shook her head. "It gets worse," she lowered her voice. "Adriana told Alex that her mother said I must have 'got' you with pussy because you didn't know any better."

Archer was up off the couch. Before Scarlett realized it, she was on her feet, looking at Archer as he built up a significant rage.

"What that woman won't do," he hissed. "I can't believe she... I'm so sorry, my angel. I promise I'll take care of this. Where's Alex? I need to apologize to her as well."

Scarlett could see he was completely agitated and she went to him, putting her hands on his big arms in an attempt to calm him down.

"Honey," she was firm but soft. "You don't need to apologize to Alex, but I would like to know who this girl's mother is so I can talk to her. I can't have Alex dealing with this kind of crap her first day in a new school."

Archer shook his head, putting his arms around her. "I'll talk to her," he insisted. "Maggie Rorick is one of the worst gossips around. She tried to set me up with her sister last year and will never get over the fact that I had absolutely no interest in her ugly spinster sister. So she's going to bad-mouth anyone that is seen with me, including you. You'd better let me deal with her."

Scarlett was very patient with him. "I appreciate that," she said evenly. "And I will take you up on your offer. However, I would like it if we could both speak with her. If I'm going to live in this community, I can't hide behind you. I need to establish relationships or at least rapport with people. But nothing is going to happen right this minute so I want you to lie down for a while. You look like you're ready to fall down."

Hearing her words, he stopped raging and looked at her. It was as if all of the fight suddenly drained out of him, so much pressing on his mind, tearing at his thoughts.

"Will you lie down with me?" he asked hoarsely.

Scarlett looked at his expression, his body language, thinking that he suddenly looked so vulnerable and weary. Weary more than in the sense that he needed rest; it was his expression and his voice that conveyed something more than that. The man seemed spiritually beat to hell.

"What's wrong?" she whispered, cocking her head with concern. "This is the second time you've come to the house, having been up all night and all worn out. What's got you so strung out?"

Archer just looked at her for a moment. Then, he held out his hand to her and she took it. Kissing her fingers, he silently led her upstairs and into the master bedroom. He went to sit on the fluffy, oversized king bed, letting go of her hand long enough to pull off his shoes. Then, he lay back on the bed and pulled her down with him, collecting her in his big arms and holding her sweetly and snuggly against him.

For that brief moment, he forgot about his troubles, something that Scarlett seemed to suck right out of him. She eased his mind more than he could comprehend. All he could think of was her, lost in her soft warmth against him.

"I wish I could tell you," he whispered, his lips against her forehead. "I don't even want to voice it. I don't want to bring that hell into these walls."

Scarlett was all snuggled up against him, smothered by his big body. "You're scaring me."

He kissed her head. "I'm scaring myself, trust me," he confessed. "This house, this room with you in it, is my sanctuary and I don't want to let anything bad in here. So for now... just know that something very dicey is going on and I'm a part of it. Leave it at that until I have the courage to tell you more."

Scarlett lay there a moment, digesting his statement. Then, she lifted her head to look at him. "Of course I'll respect that," she whispered. "I didn't ask to be nosy. I asked because I'm concerned. If you feel that you want to talk about it, or vent, or just get it off your chest, I'll be happy to hear whatever it is. That's what people do who respect and adore each other, and I am coming very much to adore you."

His weary face smiled up at her. "I love you, my angel," he purred. "You make me so happy... I haven't known much of that in my life, and I've never known anything like what I feel for you. It's the most wonderful thing I've ever experienced."

She returned his smile, kissing his chin, his eyes, his forehead, and running a gentle hand over his face. Archer closed his eyes, truly relaxing for the first time in a very long while, and was asleep almost instantly. When he began to snore, she carefully climbed off the bed, pulled the curtains, and quietly shut the door behind her.

EIGHT

ARCHER DIDN'T WAKE up until Scarlett got up the next morning and went into the bathroom, shutting the door. Momentarily disoriented, he lifted his head in the dark room, seeing the light from underneath the bathroom door and then looking at his watch. *6:10 am*. He blinked at his watch as if trying to figure out just how long he'd been asleep, realizing it had just been over fourteen hours. Shocked, he was just starting to sit up, wearily, when Scarlett came out of the bathroom.

"Well, well," she saw him sitting up and flipped on the light. "Sleeping Beauty awakens."

Archer grinned and scratched his head. "Good morning, my angel," he yawned. "Sorry I passed out on your bed last night."

Scarlett came near the bed, giggling when he whipped out a big arm and pulled her onto his lap. In her silky pajamas, she curled up on his lap, hugging him.

"No problem," she said. "I didn't mind. Morgan and Alex kept coming in to check on you to make sure you were still breathing. At one point, you stopped snoring and slept like a corpse. Alex even took your pulse."

He wriggled his eyebrows. "Sorry that the girls saw me

here," he said. "Well... you know, in your bed. That wasn't very tactful of me."

Scarlett laughed. "You were fully clothed on the top of the covers," she said. "They didn't think anything of it."

"Did you?"

She kissed his nose and stood up. "I was *under* the covers," she said, her sleepy eyes twinkling at him. "I was sound asleep, too. But I will say one thing."

"What?"

"I liked sleeping next to you."

He grinned and reached out an arm to grab her again but she dodged him. "Not now," she batted at his hand as it came close. "I need to get dressed so I can take the girls to school."

Archer yawned again as she turned for the bathroom. "Hold on," he told her, standing up from the bed when she paused to look at him. "I need to drop Henry off at school, so let me take the girls. That way, I can seek out Mrs. Rorick and have a little chat with her."

"I thought we were going to do that together."

"I want you to let me do it alone. Please. This woman's vendetta is against me and I need to deal with it."

Scarlett's gaze lingered on him a moment, seeing how serious he was, before lifting her shoulders. "All right," she said, turning for the bathroom. "If that's the way you want it."

Archer followed her into the bathroom. He was dressed in a pullover shirt, white t-shirt underneath, and jeans. His shoes were over next to a chair near the fireplace that had his overcoat on it. As Scarlett went to brush her teeth, he stood in the doorway and looked around the big, modern bathroom he had helped design.

"I don't have a toothbrush," he said somewhat pathetically.

Scarlett grinned and dug around in a drawer, pulling forth a new toothbrush. Happy, Archer took it from her and brushed his teeth at the basin next to her even though there were two basins, thinking that he wanted to wake up every morning like this for the rest of his life. He had a beautiful bedroom at home with a bathroom that was the size of Scarlett's bedroom and bathroom combined, but it didn't mean anything to him without her in it.

"Scarlett?" he asked.

She was scrubbing her teeth. "Yes?"

"Please marry me."

She stopped scrubbing, surprised, and looked at him. "Now?"

He was scrubbing his own teeth. "You're more beautiful now than I've ever seen you. I'd marry you this very minute if I could."

She eyed him, grinning, and finished up with her teeth. Then she went over to the big stone shower and turned the water on to warm up.

"I won't get married in my pajamas," she told him flatly.

He finished brushing his teeth, too. Then he began pulling his clothes off. "I don't care what you get married in," he told her. "I'm marrying you, not your wardrobe."

Scarlett turned her back on him and began unbuttoning her pajama top. She wasn't entirely sure just how serious he was about the subject so she just kept talking.

"If you and I get married, will...?"

"What do you mean 'if'?" he interrupted her, pulling off his white t-shirt and moving to remove his socks. "Please don't say 'if'. Say 'when'."

Scarlett peeled off her pajama top and stepped out of her pajama bottoms, kicking them aside and entering the big glass and stone shower.

"Okay, *when* we get married," she said, taking the hand-held shower fixture and hosing herself down with steaming water, "do my girls inherit any titles? I'm assuming I will be the countess. Oh, but wait; your mother is already the countess, isn't she?"

Archer was naked as he stepped into the shower behind her and flipped the lever that sent water through the giant showerhead located at the top of the shower enclosure. Water poured down over them both like a waterfall and Scarlett turned around, surprised to see him standing behind her. But her split second of surprise vanished as she put the hand-held shower fixture back in its bracket, pulled out her poof and body wash, and began to soap up. So what if he was in the shower with her; it was easily big enough for two and she quickly realized she liked nothing better.

"You will be the Countess of Wintringham and Mulgrave, as my wife," Archer told her, shaking the water out of his eyes. "My mother is the Lady Arabella, Dowager Countess of Wintringham and Mulgrave, and Henry is Viscount Sheffield. Unless I legally adopt Morgan and Alex, they'll just have courtesy titles of Lady Morgan and Lady Alexandra."

Scarlett had finished soaping herself up and was now going to work on Archer as he stood there and let her run soap all over him that smelled like oranges.

"And if you were to adopt them?" she asked.

Archer thought on that. "There are some obsolete titles that my family still holds," he said. "My aunt, as the sister of my father, had the title of Katharine of Thixendale, and his younger sister was Bridget, Lady Stamford. They've both passed away and left no heirs, but it's within my power to grant those titles to Morgan and Alexandra if I were to adopt them. Morgan of Thixendale and Alexandra, Lady Stamford have a nice ring to them."

There was a stone bench in the shower and Scarlett made him sit on it so she could wash his hair. He was far too tall for her to try to reach up and do it. She stood between his legs as the water rained down, scrubbing his auburn scalp.

"Interesting," she said. "It's really amazing how England, after all of these centuries, still stands on the formalities of hereditary titles. What if you and I were to have children?"

"Then they would be a lady or a lord, with whatever title my hereditary rights allowed me to bestow upon them." He closed his eyes with bliss as she gently washed his hair. "They would be my descendants and entitled to inherit a very big part of the estate."

Scarlett digested the information as she finished washing his hair and rinsed it. Then she took a bar of white soap from the soap dish, lathered up his stubble, and very carefully began to shave his face with her expensive ladies' razor. Archer sat stock-still, watching her concentrate on shaving him. His hands were on the backs of her wet thighs, drifting up to gently cup her buttocks.

"What's the deal with the girls' father?" he asked.

Scarlett, tongue between her teeth as she concentrated, shrugged. "Tom and I got married right out of high school," she told him. "We met when we were both freshmen. He was with me through all of the singing and fame and all that, and everyone expected us to get married, so we did. We had the girls and just grew apart, really. We divorced when Alexandra was two and he met a woman who had a couple of little boys, and he just assumed them as his family. He always wanted boys and was disappointed when we had girls. It's sad, really. Other than pay child support, it's like he can't be bothered with his daughters. When I told him we were moving to England, he couldn't have cared less. The girls have just learned to deal with it, which is really tragic. I think that's why they've quickly warmed up to you; you're a male figure that takes interest in them. They haven't had much of that."

Archer sighed, listening to her story. "They're beautiful and intelligent girls," he said. "I can't believe their father doesn't want more to do with them."

Scarlett shrugged. "Much like Henry's mother, I don't think Tom was really cut out to be a father. He has a hard time relating to children."

Archer was still and silent a moment as Scarlett carefully shaved his neck. "What about this man you had a long relationship with? How was he towards your girls?"

"Jerry?" she thought a moment, shrugging. "He was good to them, but he was also a lot older than I was and had kids and grandkids of his own. His attention was spread pretty thin as a result, but he took care of Morgan and Alex. They never wanted for anything."

"How long were you with him?"

"Five years."

"Did you love him?"

"I did."

"Do you miss him?"

She shook her head. "Not anymore," she said. "I've done my grieving. Jerry and I had a good relationship but I'll be honest when I tell you that it wasn't an all-consuming, passionate romance. He was a good man, good to the girls, and fun to be with, and we had a routine. It was a good life but I wasn't crazy about him. When he was killed on his motorcycle, I grieved, of course, but all of the fighting with his kids afterwards just wore me out. I don't even want to think about that part of my life anymore. It's done and buried."

Archer digested the information, pondered it. "I'm sorry to hear about all that," he snorted ironically. "And now you have more drama to deal with in the person of Mrs. Rorick"

She grinned at him. "I think my boyfriend is going to take care of her."

He looked at her with big eyes. "Am I your boyfriend?"

Her eyes twinkled. "*Are* you?"

"I'd certainly like to be."

"Me, too."

He smiled broadly and she had to take the razor away or risk cutting him from the animation on his face. "I'm very glad to hear that," he said sincerely. "It'll make getting married a little easier if you're already my girlfriend."

She giggled and finished shaving a strip on his neck. "Probably," she agreed.

Archer was still fixated on the fact that she wanted to be his girlfriend, feeling joy in his heart like he'd never know. He reflected back on their conversation, thinking of all of the things they'd talked about, before fixating on one subject in particular.

"Your ex-husband," he said thoughtfully. "Do you think he would object to me adopting the girls?"

Scarlett rinsed off the razor in the shower stream. "Probably not," she said. "Why? I wasn't fishing when I asked you those questions. I was just... talking."

"I know," he said, eyeing her nude and delicious body as she began to wash her own hair under the big showerhead. He stood up and made his way over to her. "But your ex-husband is an idiot. It's incomprehensible to me that any man could grow apart from you, and as for your girls, they deserve much better than what they've been dealt. When we're married, I will remedy that."

Scarlett's eyes were closed as she rinsed off the shampoo but she could feel him up against her. As she lifted her arms to run her hands through her hair, he came up behind her and cupped her breasts from behind, his mouth moving to her wet shoulder. She shuddered and tried to lower her arms.

"Not now, Archer," she whispered. "I need to get the girls up and ready for school."

He was all pressed up against the back of her, a full erection rubbing against the small of her back. As Scarlett protested very weakly, he picked her up and took her back over to the shower bench where he proceeded to position her on all fours on top of the shower bench and mount her from behind. Wildly aroused, Scarlett groaned softly as he thrust into her, feeling more heat and lust than she had ever experienced.

When his hands weren't on her breasts, they were between her legs, fingering her, bringing her to a climax more quickly than she had ever come in her life. Her multiple orgasms were followed by his own as he quickly withdrew and spilled himself on her buttocks. But his hands, his fingers, were still between her legs as his mouth suckled her shoulder, fingers probing intimate and sensitive places. Scarlett climaxed again simply from the stroking of his fingers and as her pants of pleasure died away, he grasped her around the waist, flipped her over so she was facing him, and proceeded to kiss her deeply.

"We will never be without one another," he whispered against her mouth. "I will love you and your girls as if you have all belonged to me since the beginning. You went to England looking for a new life and I am thrilled to offer that to you. I wasn't even looking for a new life but I found one, better than anything I could have dreamt of."

Scarlett opened her eyes, watching him as he kissed her face. "This is all happening so fast," she murmured. "I still can't believe it. I'm afraid I'm going to wake up tomorrow and this all will have been a dream."

He pulled back to look at her, a big hand stroking her wet head. "It's no dream," he assured her, "but it feels like one to me, too."

She studied him closely as the water pounded down around them and the steam rose. "Are you *sure* about all of this?"

He nodded before she even finished her sentence. "I was sure the moment I saw you." When she lifted her eyebrows in doubt, he grinned. "Well, I was sure after I'd spent about ten minutes with you. I knew I wasn't going to let you get away."

She grinned, snuggling against him as he kissed her forehead and gave her a big hug. It was a sweet, heavenly moment, all bundled up against each other as the steam and heat cleansed them. Eventually, Scarlett pulled away from him and turned off the shower, exiting to collect a towel and begin drying off. Archer followed her, pulling another fluffy white towel off the shelf.

"I need to go into the office this morning but I was hoping we could lunch together," he said as he dried off his big frame. "Do you have plans for the day?"

Scarlett shook her head. "Mrs. Bayse was telling me about a furniture store in York," she wrapped her head up in a towel. "It's called Wall to Wall. I was thinking of heading over there to start picking out some stuff for the house. You've got it so beautifully decorated that I don't want to mess with it too much, but I do want to put a few of my own touches on it."

He nodded, heading over to the sink and inspecting her shaving job in the mirror. "Of course you do," he agreed. "Wall to Wall is a good store. There's also another one called MacDonalds for furniture, and still another called Homebase. If you want to wait for me to show you around, we can go together after lunch."

Scarlett found her bathrobe and wrapped up in it. "Sure, I can wait," she said. "But I need to pick the girls up by three."

She had walked up to the sink and he leaned over and kissed her on the cheek. "What a coincidence," he said as if surprised. "I will need to pick Henry up at the same time."

They looked at each other with mouths open, feigning

shock, until Scarlett broke down in giggles. As she turned for the mirror to inspect her face before putting on some makeup, she changed subjects.

"I was thinking about the rectory yesterday," she said as she examined nonexistent wrinkles around her eyes. "I need to pay the contractor for the work he's done up to this point, but he hasn't contacted me. I should probably give him a call."

"Don't bother," Archer pulled the towel off his waist and began rubbing it over his head. "I took care of it."

Scarlett looked at him, brow furrowed. "Why did you do that?"

He shrugged. "So you wouldn't have to worry about it," he said. "You tied a lot of money up in that heap so until everything gets settled with this house and that house, don't worry about the contractor. When your accounts are settled, we can talk about what you owe me."

Scarlett just looked at him as he briskly dried off his auburn head and tossed the towel aside. "Seriously, Archer?" she demanded. "You just paid for the contractor just like that? Why in the world are you so good to me like that?"

He grinned at her, opening up a couple of drawers until he came across her hairbrush. He pulled it out and combed through his hair. "Because you belong to me," he said as if it weren't a big deal, tossing the brush back into the drawer and going in search of his clothes. "I think I smell coffee. Hurry up and get dressed, love. I'll go wake up the girls."

Scarlett just stood there, mouth hanging open in awe and some shock, as the man pulled his pants on, his shirt, and opened the bedroom door. Just like that, he was knocking softly on Morgan's door, asking if she was awake, before moving down the hall to Alexandra's door and tapping gently on that one as well. Scarlett could hear him. He was acting as if he'd been doing it all his life, assimilating into their little family as if he'd always been there.

Scarlett moved out into the bedroom to hear better when she heard voices down the hall, listening to Archer's gentle bass voice and Alexandra's sleepy tone. It warmed her heart to hear it. He was already so good with her girls and she could tell they were responding. Scurrying back into the bathroom, she hurried to put on her makeup and dry her long dark hair, pulling on skinny jeans, knee-high leather boots and a body-skimming cream-colored lightweight sweater. She came downstairs as the girls and Archer were halfway through the big breakfast Mrs. Bayse had cooked.

"Mom," Alexandra got out of her chair with a jam-filled scone in her hand and went to hug her mother. "Archer says I can ride this afternoon with Henry after school. Is it okay?"

Scarlett stroked her daughter's long hair. "Of course it is," she said, "but make sure you get your homework done after dinner. I'll be checking."

Alexandra nodded eagerly and shoved the rest of the scone in her mouth as Archer stood up and took a last gulp of coffee.

"We have to go pick up Henry before heading over to school," he told Scarlett, setting the coffee cup down. "I'll see you at lunch."

Scarlett nodded her head as the girls bolted up and grabbed their backpacks and lunches that Mrs. Bayse had made them. Morgan kissed her mother as she blew by and Alexandra hugged her once more as both girls headed towards the door that led out to the courtyard. Archer went over to Scarlett and put his arms around her, kissing her sweetly.

"I'll be back by noon," he whispered, kissing her again. "Have a good morning."

Scarlett hugged him tightly. "You, too."

He winked at her and followed the girls outside. Scarlett wandered after them, standing in the doorway as they all climbed into Archer's BMW and he pulled out of the driveway. When all was said and done, and the house was suddenly very quiet, Scarlett closed the door quietly and went back into the kitchen. Mrs. Bayse was there, washing the dishes.

"Now you have some time to yourself," Mrs. Bayse said cheerily.

Scarlett looked around the big kitchen. "I guess," she replied. "I feel kind of useless, actually. Archer takes my girls to school, you do all of the cooking and cleaning, your husband does all of my gardening and maintenance, so what do I have to do?"

Mrs. Bayse laughed. "You can read a book or go for a walk."

"That's not a bad idea. Maybe I will go for a walk and start getting myself acclimated to this village."

"There's a coffee house in town," Mrs. Bayse said helpfully. "Perhaps you could walk there for a cup of coffee."

Scarlett liked that. "Good idea," she said, heading upstairs to get a jacket. "I'm going to walk into town."

She did, on a perfectly lovely but cool morning that was quintessentially English. The fields were brilliant green and damp, the road cold beneath the canopy of trees and hedgerows. Scarlett found a big branch as she walked along, picking it up and using it like a walking stick. She passed by a field where sheep were against the stone wall, grazing, and she reached over to pet their wooly coats. Then she was startled by a fox and two kits running across the road, laughing at her jumpiness. But as she walked, it underscored one thing; her growing love for the new country she had come to and the new life that had enveloped her. She was coming to deeply love it all, in spite of the gossipy neighbors or derelict old rectories. Archer and her new lodge house were the best things she could have hoped for.

The village was about a mile from the lodge and she entered the outskirts, walking along the main road, peering into the rows of little houses and shops that lined the avenue. There was a bakery and she was lured inside by the smell of fresh bread and cinnamon. The baker greeted her kindly and she introduced herself, and he was more than happy to sell her a giant cinnamon roll that she happily tucked into.

Continuing on, she passed by a real estate office, a curio shop, a shoe store and a chemist. She wandered into the chemist's store and ended up buying lotion, perfume and a few other things she didn't need. Moving on, she finally came across the coffee house with its charming stone patio and a few tables and chairs set up. She bought a tall coffee to go with her almost finished cinnamon roll, and sat on the patio to finish the rest of the pastry and sip her coffee. As the sun rose, she watched the traffic and people go by, thinking she was pretty happy to be there. Life, for the first time in a very long while, was pretty darn good.

The coffee shop had complimentary newspapers and she ended up sitting and reading for about an hour. On the back page of the paper was a big advertisement for a garden shop with a beautiful array of new flowers and plants. She read the advertisement carefully, inspected the flowers, and thought it would be a very good idea to go back home and discuss it with Mr. Bayse. She wanted to plant flowers in the courtyard and around the fountain, so maybe this morning was a perfect time to start on that project. Collecting her paper and the rest of her coffee, she headed home.

Scarlett passed by the church as she headed home, slowing down to admire the beautiful old structure. As she peered over the wall at the old graveyard, the reverend suddenly appeared from a side door. Scarlett waved at the man when he caught her eye.

The reverend waved back and made his way over to her through the old headstones of the green, lush graveyard. He stuck out a hand as he drew close and she shook it.

"Good morning," she said.

"Good morning," he replied happily. "You're out early."

She smiled. "With the girls in school, I have a bit of free time on my hands so I was just walking."

Reverend Bryan looked at the sky above. "It's a lovely morning for it," he said before looking back at her. "How do you like your new home? I knew the place when it wasn't nearly so nice but I've heard that the earl had it beautifully renovated."

Scarlett nodded. "I love it," she said sincerely. "Archer did a beautiful job on it. Would you like to come and see it? I'm just heading back right now."

The reverend was thrilled at the invitation. "I would love to but I have a few things I have to attend to this morning," he said. "Perhaps this afternoon?"

Scarlett shook her head. "Archer and I will be out and about," she said. "But maybe tomorrow morning you'd like to come for coffee and I'll show you around?"

Reverend Bryan eagerly agreed. "Thank you very much," he said. "When I was a child, the Deerkeeper's Lodge was sort of old and run down. An old man lived there – he must have been a hundred years old – and he would scare the kids who came around. He'd shake his stick at us and yell."

Scarlett giggled. "I won't shake a stick at you, I promise," she said, her gaze drifting around the church yard. "This is such a beautiful church. There's nothing like this where I come from."

Reverend Bryan looked over his shoulder at the big Gothic beast behind him. "Beautiful, yes, but also expensive," he sighed. "There's so much wrong with the church right now and donations aren't what they should be. I spend much of my time trying to figure out how to pay for things."

Scarlett looked seriously at the church. "What's wrong with it?"

The reverend looked at her. "Quite a bit," he answered with dismay. "First and foremost, the roof leaks terribly and I'm afraid it's going to start damaging the interior if we can't get it repaired. We also have a plumbing problem and there's a host of other things that need to be fixed or repaired."

"Have you told Archer any of this?"

The reverend shook his head. "Not lately, no," he admitted. "Last year, we were in need of a new front door because the old one was literally falling off its hinges, and he and his mother donated the door. It was a huge expense."

Scarlett's gaze moved over the church again, so beautiful in the early morning light with its brown stone and soaring bell tower. "Have you had any fundraisers?"

Bryan cocked his head curiously. "Fundraiser?"

She nodded. "To raise money for the repairs," she said. "You could have a festival or carnival or something. Have you tried anything?"

The reverend shook his head. "I have thought about it, but to be truthful, everyone around here already gives what they can and any event we held would be directed at the community. I don't know if we would make any money begging from the same people who tithe to the church every week."

Scarlett shrugged. "Then you have to reach out to the entire countryside," she said. "Have you applied for grants or things like that?"

Reverend Bryan looked rather contrite. "I haven't, I admit it," he said. "I'm not very good at that sort of thing."

Scarlett's gaze lingered on the man for a moment while all the time, her mind was working furiously. What better way to become integrated with the community than to help out the church with a big fundraiser? She'd done plenty at home for her kids' school, but she realized this was a little different. Still, her mind was mulling over the idea. She needed to flesh it out a bit.

"How much money do you think you need for everything?" she asked.

The reverend shrugged. "Somewhere in the neighborhood of two hundred thousand pounds," he said. "The roof is very expensive to fix."

Scarlett sipped at her coffee; eyes now back to the church. "Let me think about it and talk to Archer," she said. "He might have an idea as to how to raise money."

Reverend Bryan appeared somewhat hesitant. "I don't want him to think I put you up to it."

"He won't." She waved at him and turned away. "I'll see you tomorrow for coffee, Reverend. We can talk more about raising funds. Come over about nine or so."

Bryan lifted a hand and gave her a half-hearted wave. "I will," he said. "Thank you again."

Scarlett continued on along the avenue, feeling energized with a project on the horizon. As she walked, she began to hum a song, and within the first few bars an idea occurred to her; she'd done a lot of singing at malls and race tracks and other venues. She once did a concert for fifty thousand people at the Coliseum in Los Angeles. Maybe she could do a concert to help raise funds, or even a music video to ask for donations. She wanted to utilize something she was good at and she was good at music. Plus, she still had some connections in the music industry. An idea began to form and she was growing increasingly excited about it.

By the time she got home, she went straight into the study and got on her laptop computer. Ideas were flowing fast and hard, and she needed to write everything down.

Ludbourne was going to rock.

———

"You don't even want to know," Calvin was shaking his head. "It's one of the worst things I've ever heard of."

Archer was standing in the pediatric unit of the National Health Service York Hospital, the same hospital they had brought the injured little girl the night before from the crime scene. The six-year-old girl was in intensive care after having been operated on the previous night to close two stab wounds. After taking care of some business after dropping the children off at school, Archer had come by the hospital for a report but what he was hearing from Calvin wasn't something he was ready to hear.

"Spill it," he commanded, his jaw ticking.

"Forensics has it now," Calvin replied. "God, Archer, I hate to even tell you this, but we found a note on the girl. A note to you."

Archer had to make a conscious effort to keep from reacting, but the tick in his jaw grew worse. "Where did you find it? I didn't see anything on the girl and I'm the one who held on to her until the medics arrived."

Calvin sighed heavily, glancing over at the two uniformed bobbies who were guarding the little girl's door. He pulled Archer with him so they could speak more privately and they ended up over by a window overlooking the parking lot. Calvin lowered his voice.

"This sick bastard, whoever he is, took one of the mother's tampons, pulled out the tampon part, and reinserted it with a note," he muttered. "He inserted the whole thing into the little girl's anus. When the doctors pulled it out, they found the note addressed to you inside."

Archer couldn't help it; he closed his eyes tightly, briefly, as if to ward off such disgusting horror. "What did the note say?"

Calvin pulled a rumpled piece of paper out of his pocket and began to read.

"'She walks in beauty like the night;
I pray this time you get it right.
Scarlet lips are yours to kiss;
Revolutionary lady is in our midst.
Phipps, Phipps, you will cower;
Now it is the killing hour.'"

Archer stared at him in horror. He was having trouble breathing, terror such as he had never known sweeping him.

"*That's* what it said?" he hissed.

Calvin nodded. "The Chief Constable already knows," he said quietly. "He'll be here in a little while to talk to you. You know he's going to take you off the case, Archer. You can't go through this again."

Archer's hands were on his face, his heart pounding painfully against his ribs. "Oh... my God...."

Calvin didn't sense the depth of Archer's horror. "He's back," he whispered. "At least now we know what...."

Archer grabbed his wrist, so hard he nearly snapped bones. "I already *knew* he was back," he hissed. "But that note... scarlet lips...."

Calvin tried to pull his arm away without getting it broken. "Do you know what he means? It sounds like a reference, doesn't it?"

Archer was trying very hard not to panic. Still holding on to Calvin, he began to walk back towards the elevator banks, dodging doctors and nurses as they went.

"Walk with me," he commanded quietly.

Calvin had no choice. Archer remained silent until they got

on the elevator, just the two of them, and the door closed. Then he turned to Calvin.

"About a week ago, I met a woman named Scarlett," he explained quietly. "I'm in love with her, Calvin. We're going to be married as soon as I can talk her into it. It's too much of a coincidence for the word 'scarlet' to be in the note and not be a referenced to my Scarlett, which means he's been watching me. Whoever this person is, he's been watching me and if he knows my movements, he knows hers."

Calvin's brow furrowed. "Watching you for ten years?" he countered. "The man stops killing for ten years and suddenly he's back again and after your girlfriend? How is that possible?"

Archer was grinding his teeth, a hand on his head as he tried to calm down. He snatched the transcription of the note out of Calvin's hand and read it again, a few times. Eyes still on the note, he spoke.

"It has to be her," he muttered with disgust. "This is not a coincidence. He also mentions revolutionary lady, and she's American. You know – the American Revolution? He knows her, damn it, or he's at least seen her. And... oh, Christ...."

He faded off and suddenly looked very pale just as the elevator doors opened to the lobby. Calvin's brow furrowed.

"What's wrong?"

Archer swallowed hard and forced himself to start walking out of the elevator en route to the car park.

"She's a single mother with two young daughters," he said hoarsely. "She's exactly the type of victim the Cutter preys on."

Calvin stared at him, finally beginning to sense the man's horror. He had some horror of his own, for Archer's sake. The nightmare had just grown worse.

"Go," he slapped Archer on the shoulder as they reached the doors that led out to the car park. "Go to her and stay with her. I'll tell the chief what's happened and call you later."

Archer didn't need to be told twice.

————

Scarlett was sitting in the study at the old rustic desk when she heard a car barreling up her driveway. Curious, she stood up to look out the window and saw Archer bring his car to a screeching halt near the garage. In fact, he hit the brakes so hard that the car actually skidded a few feet. Then he was out of the car, slamming the door and making haste towards the house. Concerned, Scarlett went to the front door and opened it.

"Archer?" she called.

He had been heading for the kitchen entry but quickly shifted direction when he heard her voice. He ran the last few feet towards her, sweeping her up into a crushing embrace as he entered the house and slammed the door. Then, he just stood there and held her in the entryway, her feet dangling about a foot off the ground. In his embrace, Scarlet swore she could feel him trembling.

"Hey," she whispered, kissing his earlobe. "What's the matter?"

Archer didn't say anything for a moment. He just stood there and held her. When he finally set her on her feet, he pulled back and cupped her lovely face in both big hands, gazing intensely into her hazel eyes. He studied her closely as if reassuring himself that she was well and safe. It was necessary, considering the entire drive over had been filled with terrifying scenarios in his mind.

"Are you okay?" he asked.

She was confused as well as concerned. "Fine. Why?"

"Have you been here all morning?"

She shook her head. "No," she replied. "I went for a walk into the village. I got back an hour ago. Oh, and I had a really interesting talk with Reverend Bryan. I want to talk to you about some ideas I have for...."

He had her by the hand, cutting her off and pulling her up the stairs. "I need to talk to you."

She had no choice but to let him tow her up the steps. "Uh... okay."

Archer didn't say a word until he took her into the master bedroom and closed the door. By that time, he had released her hand and Scarlett wandered over to the big overstuffed chairs that flanked the fireplace. She perched on the edge of one of them expectantly as Archer turned in her direction. He just stood there and stared at her.

"Oh, my God," he finally breathed. "My angel, I am so very sorry for all of this."

Scarlett cocked her head. "Sorry for what?" she asked. "Did you talk to Adriana Rorick's mother?"

He shook his head. "I must have missed her. I didn't see her at all when I dropped the children off at school."

"Then what are you sorry for?"

He sighed heavily and made his way, rather laboriously, over to the other chair. Sitting heavily, he seemed like a man with a great deal on his mind and Scarlett was quickly losing her calm. He was obviously very upset.

"Archer, what's the matter?" she asked, concerned. "Has something happened?"

He was struggling, debating how much to tell her without terrifying her. Still, she had to understand the seriousness of what was going on. It was very serious, indeed.

"Yes," he said after a moment. He made sure to look her in the eye as he spoke. "I'm not even sure where to start with this so I'm going to start from the beginning. It's very important, so please listen carefully. All right?"

She nodded seriously. "Of course."

He sighed and began pulling his coat off. "About ten years ago when I was an inspector with the North Yorkshire Police, we had a rash of murders," he laid the coat across the arm of the chair, still looking at her. "They all had the same patterns and were concentrated in and around the New Earswick borough of York. I was put on the case and followed it to the end, so much so that I became rather obsessed with it. That was made worse by the fact that the killer knew I was on the case and began to leave notes for me at the crime scenes. It was like some sick game and we played it back and forth; the closer I'd get to him, the more he taunted me."

By this time, Scarlett was listening with some horror. "That's awful," she whispered. "What happened?"

He sighed heavily and sat back in the chair. "The killer was nicknamed the Yorkshire Cutter because he would slash the throats of his victims," he said, omitting much of the other grisly details. "He was brutal, to put it mildly. He was also very clever. I spent six months of my life entrenched in every aspect of this twisted fool's mind, trying to anticipate him, and I thought I had our man at one point but we couldn't get enough evidence for an indictment. And then, the murders stopped... just like that."

Scarlett was hanging on every word. "You were never able to arrest anyone?"

He shook his head. "No," he said. "When the murders stopped, I didn't give up, but after another six months working the case, my chief finally pulled me off because I just wasn't getting anywhere. I was still trying to put the same suspect behind bars and either he really wasn't the killer or he was just too clever for me, I don't know. But I will tell you this; the case very nearly ruined my life. At least, I almost let it ruin my life. I had a girlfriend at the time and she left me over it. She said it changed me. I was young and enthusiastic, and determined to make a big name for myself catching the killer. It was a bitter pill to swallow to realize I couldn't do that."

Scarlett thought on that a moment but realized there had to be more to it if he was here telling her the story. "Is that what's had you so upset over the past couple of days?" she asked. "Has something about the case resurfaced?"

He nodded slowly. "We've had two murders in two nights that fit the same pattern as the Yorkshire Cutter," he said. "The first one didn't have a note to me, but the second one did."

Scarlett's eyes widened. "Oh, God," she breathed. "Is he back?"

Archer sighed heavily, feeling sick and apprehensive. He rubbed his eyes wearily. "Scarlett, my sweet angel, he has apparently been watching me, or at least keeping track of me," he explained. "The note he wrote to me with the latest murders mentions you by name. Somehow, someway, he's resurfacing again and he's watching me and watching you."

Scarlett just looked at him. She didn't react for a moment or two, but that was the extent of her remaining calm. As Archer watched, tears filled her eyes and spilled in rivers down her cheeks.

"What does that mean?" she whispered tightly.

He clucked softly, with sorrow and regret, and got out of his chair. He went to her, taking a knee beside the chair and putting his enormous hands on her cheeks. He kissed her face gently.

"Please don't cry," he whispered. "I know you're frightened but I had to tell you for your own safety. No more walks into town, no more banging about alone. I have no idea what's in this man's mind but I do know he's clever. I will be honest when I say that I am fearful of what he might do. Therefore, I'm going to be with you every minute of every day until this man is finally caught. You'll never be without protection."

She nodded, struggling not to cry, but the tears kept coming. "What about the girls?"

"I'll have an inspector assigned to each of them," he assured her. "They'll travel with protection always."

She was trying not to sob. "What do I tell them?" she wanted to know. "They'll be terrified."

He shook his head at her patiently, trying to calm her fears, dragging his thumbs across her cheeks to wipe away the tears.

"I'll explain everything to them," he said. "I'm not sure how much I'm going to tell them, but I'll tell them enough so they realize that they need to be careful about going anywhere alone or straying from the house without an escort. Meanwhile, all of us are going to be joined at the hip, all right? I want you and the girls to come live with me at Phipps Hall. I think it would be the safest place for us."

Scarlett broke down into soft sobs and he held her, rocking her gently as she spent her fear. He felt so badly about everything, knowing he was completely to blame. He kissed her ear, her hair, stroking her head until she finally pulled away and struggled to compose herself.

"I don't want to move to Phipps Hall," she said, sniffling. "I love this house, Archer. I'm so happy here. I feel like it belongs to me and I belong here. I promise I won't wander around and I'll be very careful. I really don't want to move to Phipps Hall."

He had a feeling that would be her answer and was prepared. "Then Henry and I will move in here with you," he said. "If you won't go to Phipps Hall, then Phipps Hall will come to you."

She sighed heavily, wiping at her nose. "Are you sure?" she asked. "What about your mother?"

He shrugged and stood up, going into the bathroom. "I'll give her some story that makes sense," he said, emerging from the bathroom with tissues in his hand. "I'm not sure I'll tell her the truth, but I'll tell her something sensible. Besides, Henry will love it here. This is such a warm, cozy home, something I think he's been missing in his young life."

"But there are no ponies here."

"We'll bring them with us."

"How are you going to do that?"

He threw a thumb in the general direction of the courtyard and wooded fields beyond. "All of that land is mine," he said. "I'll have a section of it fenced in and we'll put up a few stalls. Alex and Henry can ride to their hearts' content. I'm also going to alarm the house and hire a patrol. We'll be very safe and very cozy here."

He was trying to make her feel better and it worked, at least marginally. Archer anxiously watched her expression, trying to gauge how she was handling everything and, for the most part, she seemed rational. He was pleased to see this side of her, the side that, although frightened, didn't fall into hysterics. He liked that very much; she was a strong woman. He already knew she wasn't afraid to defend what was hers, as he'd seen the night they'd met and she had lashed out at the intruder at the rectory, but this accepting grace she seemed to possess endeared her to him all the more. He glanced at his watch, noting the time.

"Let's go have lunch, okay?" he gently encouraged. "Then we can take a look at a couple of furniture stores before we pick up the children."

She looked up at him. "Are you seriously going to stick to me like glue until this is over?"

The smile faded from his face. "Like glue."

"What about your work?"

He averted his gaze. "Because of the note found today, I fully expect to be taken off this case," he replied. "I really wasn't involved with it, anyway, but now with this latest happening... I'm sure the chief will want me far away from what's going on, so I'll just take a leave and spend it with you until everything is over."

She regarded him. "Do you think this killer is targeting you somehow?"

He shook his head. "No, not me," he said. "But he and I had a rapport ten years ago. Maybe if I'm out of the picture, he'll get careless and lazy. I seemed to have challenged him and he liked that."

Scarlett thought on that a moment, still not entirely comfortable with everything, but she needed to digest it all. She didn't feel like shopping for furniture much but it was better than sitting around the house, so she changed into a figure-hugging black and white striped top, white Capri-cut jeans, and strappy black sandals with a four inch heel.

As Scarlett dressed and fixed her makeup, Archer went down to the study and got on his cell phone. He was still down there, chatting, when Scarlett came downstairs looking sexy and lovely. Archer grinned at her from his position behind her desk and quickly wound down the conversation. He hung up the phone and went over to her.

"You look beautiful, as always," he took her hand and kissed her cheek. "How is it that you look better each time I see you?"

She smiled weakly, fussing with her purse. "Being happy has something to do with it, I guess."

He lifted an eyebrow at her. "You're happy? Even after everything we just discussed?"

"It's just a little glitch in the road." Scarlett stopped fussing with her purse and faced him. "Archer, none of that has any bearing on how I feel about you. You have gone out of your way since nearly the moment I met you to make me happy. You've gone above and beyond the call, in every way, and I'm constantly amazed at your thoughtfulness, kindness, and generosity. You're an amazing human being. Of course I'm happy. People in love usually are."

His somewhat grinning expression faded as her words sank in. "Say that again."

"Say what again?"

"What you just said. Tell me again."

She realized what he was driving at but wasn't going to come right out and say it. "I'm happy?"

"After that."

"You're generous and thoughtful."

He could see her hazel eyes twinkling and knew she was toying with him. "Scarlett," he rumbled. "Don't make me beg."

She deliberately turned her nose up at him and turned for the door. "I have no idea what you're talking about."

He grabbed her before she could take a step, whipping her into his powerful embrace, listening to her giggle as he nibbled her neck.

"People in love are usually happy," she whispered against his ear. "Is that what you wanted to hear?"

"Can you tell me that you love me?"

"I love you."

He picked her up and spun her around, listening to her squeal. When he set her to her feet, he kissed her all over her face until she pulled away because he was smothering her.

"I love you, too," he whispered. "I'm so happy right now I could just shout it to the world."

She touched his cheek, smiling when he captured her hand and reverently kissed her palm. "Let's go get some lunch and celebrate, okay?" she said.

They headed back out to his car and Archer took her into Ludbourne and to a pub called the Pig and Fiddle. Scarlett discovered that it was a wonderful gastropub and she enjoyed a delicious salad while Archer tucked into a big Angus burger. It was fairly crowded at lunchtime and a few people came by the table to greet Archer and be introduced to Scarlett. It seemed that everyone knew who Archer was in this small little village.

A pair of very old men sauntered up to the table with beer in hand, already sloshed at noon, and tried to talk Scarlett into running away with them. Archer just shook his head as Scarlett laughed, finally shooing the pushy pair away so they could finish their lunch in peace. The old men fled in good-natured fear of the big earl.

It had been a lovely lunch, something that restored their good moods and spirits, and as Archer escorted Scarlett out to the car, her cell phone rang. She dug around in her purse for the phone as Archer opened the car door for her. She climbed into the car with the phone on her ear.

Archer closed the door as she began to speak, going around to the driver's side and getting in. Turning the car on, he pulled away from the curb and headed for the first store on their list, Wall to Wall. He wasn't paying much attention to what Scarlett was saying, his mind drifting back to the hospital, the note, the savage way in which it was delivered. He was thinking about what he was going to say to the chief and how he really had no intention of being kept out of the loop with the investigation. He'd make sure Calvin updated him regularly.

At some point, he realized that Scarlett had hung up the phone. He glanced over at her to see that she was looking at him. The expression on her face was somewhat appraising.

"Archer?" she asked.

His eyes were on the road as he made a right hand turn. "Yes, my angel?"

"What did you do this morning?"

He thought quickly on that question, suspecting what she was driving at as a result of the phone call. He hadn't known who she was talking to but he could guess simply by the question. Still, he played the game.

"I went to work."

"What did you do at work?"

He shrugged. "Work," he said casually. "Why?"

Scarlett was still looking at him, now with some suspicion. "That was the real estate agent calling about the rectory."

"Really? Good news, I hope."

"It is. She says someone bought the property for my asking price. No haggling, no negotiating, no nothing. They just called up, said they wanted the property, and made arrangements for their legal team to handle the transaction."

"That's great."

"Yes, it is. She couldn't tell me who the buyer was, however."

"Why not?"

"She said because they wanted to remain anonymous. She thinks it's a Saudi prince. But do you know who I think it is?"

"Who?"

"A particular constable I happen to know."

"Why would you think that?"

"Because this is too coincidental. The house isn't even listed back on the market yet."

"Maybe the Saudi prince happened to drive by and fall in love with it. Perhaps he had his people call the real estate agent and make an offer."

"How would he know what agent to call if there was no For Sale sign?"

"Good question. You'll have to ask him."

"I don't have to. I know who bought it."

"Who?"

"I told you; a particular deputy chief constable. In fact, I happen to know he would do something like this just to make my life easier. He's afraid I'm going to spend months or years worrying about how to unload that old wreck of a house and he would do it to help me out. He's just that way."

"Sounds like a very nice gentleman."

"He is. But I think it's a very sneaky thing to do."

He looked at her, surprised. "Why?"

"Because now he's on the hook for almost a million pounds for that heap of rocks that's not worth the property it sits on. Doesn't he know how guilty I'm going to feel about that? I wonder why he didn't talk to me about it first."

"Maybe he wanted it to be a surprise."

"Do you think so?"

"I do."

"Do you think he bought it?"

"Given your reasoning, it's very possible."

"Ah-*HA*!" she pointed a finger at him accusingly. "You *did* buy it, didn't you?"

He burst out laughing, a great booming laugh that had Scarlett laughing too even though she was trying not to. She couldn't help it; he was infectious.

"I plead the Fifth," he said.

She poked him in the arm. "You *can't* plead the Fifth," she said. "Only an American can plead the Fifth Amendment of the U.S. Constitution against self-incrimination."

He looked at her. "I'm going to marry an American," he said. "Doesn't that entitle me to plead it by proxy?"

"No."

He shrugged, grin still on his lips, as he noticed their destination up ahead and began to look for a parking space.

"Then I refuse to answer," he said. "It doesn't matter who bought it so long as it's sold. Now you can buy the lodge and everything is wonderful."

She sat there staring at him even as he parked the car and

turned it off. When he turned to look at her, he could see the warmth sparkling in her eyes even though there was no smile on her lips. He grinned at her.

"Let's go look at some furniture," he said.

"Will you tell me the truth?" she countered.

His grin faded. "I will always tell you the truth."

"Did you buy the rectory?"

He hesitated. "It wasn't as bad a deal as you think," he said. "I can restore it and sell it just like I did the lodge. It was a business investment."

She shook her head at him reproachfully but at the same time, she reached across the seat and put her hands on his cheeks, holding his face between her two warm palms. Her lovely hazel eyes were intense.

"I don't even know what to say," she whispered. "You've done so much for me and I have no idea how I can ever repay you or show you how much I appreciate what you've done."

He put his big arms around her, pulling her against him as much as he could in the restricted space of the car. He kissed her cheek, her lips.

"I don't do these things to keep a scorecard," he insisted. "I do them because I want to, because I want to take care of you and see you happy. I want to come home to you every night and see that bright smile light up when I come in through the door. I want to laugh with you and love you. I want to give you my all. I can't love half-assed, Scarlett. I love with everything I have. Is that so hard to understand?"

She shook her head. "No," she whispered. "But... this is all happening so fast. I know I've said that before, but it's true."

"Does it feel wrong?"

"No."

"I feel like this is where I'm meant to be, with you."

"I'm starting to feel the same way."

"Then you're not angry with me for buying the rectory?"

"I can't be mad at a noble intention, even if it was impetuous."

His grin returned. "Speaking of impetuous, I'm eager to buy some new furniture."

"*I'm* buying the furniture, big boy."

"That remains to be seen."

She had to laugh at him as he very nearly pulled her out of the car.

NINE

THE CALL from the school hadn't been a social one.

Archer had received a call from Fulford when they were twenty minutes into their furniture shopping spree. Apparently, Henry had been in a scuffle and was in the Head Master's office, so Archer and Scarlett cut their trip short and headed over to the brown-stoned school about four miles away. The kids were still in session so it was fairly quiet as they made their way inside. When they both walked into the secretary's office, they were greeted by Henry sitting against the wall with a hell of a black eye. Scarlett had to slap a hand over her mouth so she wouldn't audibly gasp, but Archer remained calm as he went to his son.

He put his big hand under the boy's chin and tipped his head up so he could get a good look at the purple and red bruise that covered most of the left eye and part of the temple. Henry gazed up at his father fearfully.

"What happened?" Archer asked evenly.

Henry was contrite, trying to lower his head but his father wouldn't let him. He kept looking at Scarlett out of the corner of his eye. "I... I...."

"Speak up," Archer said in a tone that suggested he wouldn't tolerate any disobedience. "What happened? How did you get this?"

Henry was becoming red-faced. "I don't want to tell you in front of," he flicked his eyes in Scarlett's direction, "her. Please, Dada."

Archer's brow furrowed, confused, but Scarlett heard him. She promptly turned for the office door.

"I'll wait outside," she said cheerily.

Archer called after her but she ignored him. When he returned his attention to Henry, it was with a distinct expression of disapproval.

"That was very rude," he scolded quietly. "What did I tell you about bad manners?"

Henry seemed to be much more at ease now that it was just him and his father. "But it was *about* her," he insisted. "Some kids were saying bad things and made Alexandra cry, so I hit them."

Archer stared at him, shocked. Before he could reply, the Head Master's door opened up and Mr. Preston stood in the archway.

"Hello, sir," he held out his hand to Archer, who shook it. "Sorry to have to call you over like this, but young Henry has had a bit of a scuffle. He wouldn't tell me why, so I called you. Perhaps you can get it out of him."

Archer put his hand on his son's shoulder and turned him around. "Let's go into your office," he said to Mr. Preston. "I think we need some privacy to sort this all out."

Mr. Preston invited them in and shut the door. Archer set his son down in one of the guest chairs and took the other for himself. Mr. Preston resumed his seat behind his big, cluttered desk with the big candy jar on the corner.

"Now," Archer looked at his son. "I want you to tell me

what happened. No one is going to get angry with you, but I need to hear what happened. Please."

Henry was very hesitant but he complied, mostly because he knew he didn't have a choice. He hadn't wanted to say anything in front of Mr. Preston when the whole situation started, but now he was stuck. He began to get defensive.

"We were in the yard and I saw Alexandra crying," he said, his brow furrowed as he looked at his father. "She was off by herself standing near the fence so I asked her what was wrong."

"What did she tell you?" Archer asked.

Henry glanced at Mr. Preston before continuing. "She said that Adriana Rorick was saying very bad things about her mother. I asked her what and she said that Adriana said her mom was a scrubber. So I went to find Adriana and she was with Billy Teedle and his friends over by the oak tree near the play sets. I asked Adriana what she said and she told me. She said that Americans didn't belong here because they're all scrubbers and whores, and Alexandra must be one too if her mother is a whore, so I pushed her and told her it was a lie and that she was evil. Then Billy Teedle hit me and knocked me down, but I got back up and hit him."

"He loosened three of Billy's teeth, I'm afraid," Mr. Preston interjected. "Billy wouldn't say why Henry hit him, only that he had started it. I'm sure you know that we can't have that type of behavior at our school, Lord Phipps. Henry is usually such a good boy and I am shocked by his behavior."

Archer turned on the old Head Master who, in fact, had been his Head Master when he was in school thirty years before. He knew the man and knew that he was generally fair, but this episode had his blood boiling.

"He was defending a young girl from a gang of schoolyard bullies," he pointed out. "You would punish Henry, but what are you going to do about those children who bullied a young girl and called her and her mother names? There's your problem, Mr. Preston. It's not Henry; it's those self-absorbed little bullies like Adriana Rorick and Billy Teedle that give schools a bad name and if you don't do something about it immediately, I'm pulling Henry out of this school and with him go my donations. Am I making myself clear?"

Mr. Preston was sitting straight in his chair by the time Archer was finished, looking sickened and shocked. He could see that this meeting was taking a direction he hadn't intended. An angry Archer Phipps was an intimidating thing, indeed.

"As rain, Lord Phipps," Mr. Preston sighed with resignation. "Clear as rain."

———

Scarlett was standing out in front of the school at the edge of the walkway, watching a little rabbit dig a big hole in the flower bed. It was a nice day outside, temperate, and she could hear the kids inside the classrooms, their voices wafting from the windows. She looked around, wondering which classroom her girls were in, when she noticed some mothers gathered over near the street, apparently waiting for their children to get out of school. Glancing at her watch, she saw that it was a few minutes before three.

Wandering over to the edge of the grass where the walkway met the street, she was passing the time by kicking at the dandelions when a voice caused her to turn around. A woman and a young girl were standing there, smiling timidly at her, and Scarlett realized that the little girl was the same child who had given her flowers at church. She smiled at the pair.

"Hello," she said.

The woman bobbed one of those stiff, brief curtsies. "Good afternoon," she said. "We met you at church last Sunday and...."

"Of course I remember you both," she looked down at the little girl. "Hello, there. I never did know your name."

"Alyce," the child said.

"Hello, Alyce," she responded. "I loved your flowers."

Alyce beamed and the mother took over. "I had heard your daughters were in school here," she said. "We weren't properly introduced, but my name is Maggie Rorick."

Scarlett's smile vanished. She stared steadily at the woman, struggling not to lash out at her but it was extremely difficult. Being forthright and at times blunt, Scarlett wasn't going to back down from what she had been told by Alexandra. Now was the perfect time, before they were swarmed with children begging to go home after a long day at school. Archer hadn't been able to confront the woman, but she was certainly going to take the opportunity to defend herself.

"Your daughter is Adriana?" she asked.

Maggie nodded. "Yes," she replied. "I believe she's in the same grade as your daughter."

Scarlett lifted an eyebrow. "So I've been told," she said coldly. "Your daughter has been very outgoing towards mine."

Maggie didn't catch on to the icy tone. "That's nice to hear. I told her to be friendly."

"Did you also tell her that all Americans were sluts and idiots?"

Maggie's cordial expression vanished and her eyes widened. "I... uh," she stammered. "Of course I would never...."

Scarlett cut her off. "You'd better be glad that your toddler is here because if she wasn't, I'd really have some choice words for your stupid ass," she snarled. "You listen to me and you listen well; if I hear that your daughter has spouted off anymore crap about me or my children, from your mouth no less, I'm going to take it straight to the Head Master or school board, or anyone else I need to go to in order to get your child expelled from school. What kind of parent tells their child that someone used pussy to get a man, for God's sake? Are you truly so vulgar?"

By this time, Maggie was pale with shock and fear. Her big eyes were so large that they threatened to pop from her skull and she took a step back, away from Scarlett, because she was truly stunned by what was flying out at her. She looked around to see if anyone else had heard and she could see a few of her friends looking at her curiously. She was cornered.

"I...," she stuttered, "I don't... don't know what you mean."

Scarlett's eyebrows flew up. "So you're telling me that your daughter is a liar? That she made up that stuff all on her own?"

Maggie was backing up as Scarlett advanced. "I... I...," she sputtered.

"Are you willing to swear on the Bible that you never said that stuff about me?" she demanded. "I'm going to run straight to Reverend Bryan with all of this and you can swear in front of him that you never said a bad word about me and that your daughter is making it all up. Are you willing to do that?"

"No!" Maggie exclaimed, pulling Alyce with her as she backed up. "I wouldn't... I never...!"

"You're a liar," Scarlett stopped advancing, watching the woman back away. "And tell your evil little daughter to keep her mouth shut about me and my girls. Make sure she knows what a gossiping low-life her mother is who spreads lies about people she doesn't even know. For a woman who goes to church, you sure don't act like much of a Christian."

Maggie just tucked her head down and scurried off with Alyce in hand. Scarlett watched her go, so furious that she was shaking. After watching Maggie lose herself in a group of other mothers, who would undoubtedly hear only Maggie's side of the story, Scarlett turned away and went back to her side of the grass where she could watch the rabbit dig. She was trying to think of a way to tell Archer that she was pulling her girls from the school because she knew if they stayed here, it would be an uphill battle all the way. That wasn't fair to the girls.

So she stood by herself and waited until school let out and students in their neat little uniforms began filtering out. Eventually, she caught sight of Morgan, who was surrounded by three teenaged boys and looked as if she was having a marvelous time. Scarlett waved at her daughter, who caught sight of her, and the entire group came sauntering over to her. Scarlett could hear her daughter laughing as she approached, something that Morgan didn't normally do.

"Hi, Mom," Morgan was unusually cheery. "I want you to meet some friends. This is Matt, Patrick and Christopher. Guys, this is my mom, Scarlett Ward."

The three boys were nice-looking and very polite. They shook Scarlett's hand, which helped her calm down tremendously from the encounter she had just had with Maggie Rorick. Matt was a big, strapping lad with dark hair and blue eyes, and he zeroed in on Scarlett.

"I can see where Morgan gets her beauty," he said. "It's nice to meet you, Mrs. Ward."

Scarlett grinned at the smooth-talking young man. "It's nice to meet you, also."

"We've invited Morgan to go with us to get something to eat," he said. "Do you mind? I'm driving. I'll bring her right home afterwards."

Scarlett wasn't so sure but she looked at Morgan, who was alive with hope. "Please, Mom?" she begged.

It had been a long time since Scarlett had seen her daughter so happy and she was deeply torn. Not knowing these boys, she didn't trust them, so it was difficult for her to turn her daughter over to them. As she opened her mouth to speak, she could see Archer and Henry coming out of the school. Thankful for the distraction, she waved at them.

"There's Archer," she said, avoiding her daughter's pleading expression.

Archer saw her standing there surrounded by teenagers and made his way over to her. Morgan was still looking at her mother for an answer but the boys turned in Archer's direction. Archer focused in on Matthew.

"Summerlin," he shook the young man's hand. "How's your father doing? I heard he had surgery a little while ago."

Matthew nodded. "Yes, sir, he did," he replied politely. "He's doing much better."

"Good," Archer said. "I'll stop by and see him one of these days. Tell him I said hello."

"I will."

Archer glanced at the other two boys, extending a hand in greeting. "Degare," he shook the first boy's hand and then the second, "and Aubrey. Staying out of trouble?"

The young men nodded firmly. "Yes, sir," Christopher Aubrey replied.

Archer cocked an eyebrow, fighting off a grin. "You'd better," he threatened, but the boys seemed to know he was teasing them. Then he looked at Scarlett. "Has Alex come out yet?"

Scarlett shook her head. "Not yet," she said, glancing at Henry and his black eye but refraining from asking what happened inside, at least for the moment. "I'm sure she'll be out any minute."

"Mom," Morgan wouldn't be ignored. "Can I go get something to eat with them? Please?"

Scarlett was back on the subject she was trying to avoid, but this time, Archer was in the mix. He looked between Morgan and the three young men.

"Where are you going?" he asked.

As Morgan shrugged, Matt spoke up. "Just down the street,"

he told him. "There's a place that does American burgers. We asked Morgan if she wanted to come."

Archer was in fatherly mode, like Morgan was his daughter and he'd been protecting her all of his life. He lifted a stern eyebrow at the trio.

"Behave as gentlemen or you'll have to answer to me," he demanded, glancing at Scarlett and giving her a knowing wink. "What did Mother say?"

Scarlett felt much better that Archer knew the young men and didn't see any reason to withhold permission. If he thought it was all right, then she would trust him. Besides, Morgan was happier than she'd seen her in a very long time, no longer a lonely American transplant in a foreign country. It was hard to resist.

"I haven't said anything yet," she replied. "But I suppose it's all right. But be home before dinner, okay?"

Morgan nodded eagerly just as another girl, a young blond, joined the group. She was giggly and bright-eyed, and Archer seemed to know her as well, so Scarlett watched as her daughter went off with four happy strangers. She must have had an apprehensive look on her face because Archer put his arm around her shoulders and gave her a squeeze.

"She'll be fine," he assured her quietly. "At least she's making friends."

Scarlett looked up at him. "Do you know all of the kids who go to this school?"

He shrugged. "It's a small community," he said. "I've done some anti-drug programs the past couple of years and have gotten to know some of the students. I also volunteer from time to time. I grew up with Summerlin's father, so I know the family. He's a good lad."

Scarlett didn't reply other than to shrug and Archer gave her another quick squeeze for reassurance before dropping his arm. He was very conscientious of public displays of affection and didn't want to put on a show for the gossips. In fact, he happened to glance over at the group of mothers on the other side of the walkway and spied Maggie Rorick. Before Scarlett could stop him, he was crossing the walkway in Maggie's direction. Henry, seeing his father walking off, started to go with him but Scarlett stopped him.

"No," she grasped the boy by the shoulder. "Stay here. Let's wait for Alex."

Henry did as he was told, watching his father as he walked up to Adriana Rorick's mother and began to engage her in conversation. Scarlett watched as well, her hand on Henry's shoulder, as Archer seemed to do all of the talking and Maggie seemed to do all of the listening. Kids continued to filter out of the academy and she eventually turned her attention towards the front door as the stream of students thinned out. Still no Alexandra, and she began to grow concerned.

"Henry," she turned to the young boy. "Will you please go inside and see what's keeping Alex?"

He nodded eagerly and ran on inside. Scarlett stood by herself, not looking over at Archer anymore because she didn't want it to seem as if she had sent him over there on her behalf. She wished Archer had said something to her before charging over there, but it couldn't be helped now. She would just have to see how it panned out.

She waited a few minutes before Henry emerged from the school with Alexandra in tow. Her youngest daughter had her head down, quickly walking after Henry. When she saw her mother, she ran to her and threw her arms around her. About the same time, a young girl with long blond hair emerged from the school also and headed straight for Archer and Maggie. Archer saw the young girl coming and left Maggie before the child came close. He headed towards Scarlett, Alexandra and Henry.

Scarlett, meanwhile, hugged her child, having no idea why she seemed so upset, although she could guess. She stroked her daughter's dark head.

"Alex?" she asked. "What's wrong? How was school?"

Alexandra just shook her head. Then, Scarlett noticed Henry standing next to her, his frowning gaze on Alexandra.

"Tell your mom what happened," he urged her. "Hurry up and tell her."

Scarlett's brow furrowed as she gently peeled her daughter off of her. "What happened? What is Henry talking about?"

Alexandra wiped her red eyes; she had been crying. "Well," she was clearly reluctant. "Because... well, because Henry pushed Billy Teedle, Adriana pushed me. I fell back into the bathroom and hit my elbow."

Scarlett's jaw dropped and, furious, her gaze found Maggie Rorick just as she and Adriana began to walk away. She let go of her daughter and began storming in Maggie's direction, only to be circumvented by Archer. He grasped her before she could get too far.

"Hey," he demanded. "What's the matter? Where are you going?"

Scarlett was all fury and fight in defense of her child. "That woman's daughter pushed Alex in the bathroom and she hurt herself," she was pointing at Maggie and Adriana. "I'm going file assault charges against that girl, Archer. This is going to end here and now."

Archer's head snapped in Maggie's direction. "Did Alex tell you that?"

"Of course she did!"

He still had a hold of her, now trying to soothe her. "All right, my angel," he said calmly, trying to pull her back over to the children. "I'll take care of this. Let's take the children back...."

"No," Scarlett dug her feet in. "I'm taking care of it *now*. If you don't call the police to take a report, I will. I'm serious, Archer. She's not going to get away with this. That little girl assaulted my child and I'm filing charges."

Archer faced her, seeing how upset she was. He didn't blame her. But the situation was more complicated than she realized.

"Did you see Henry's eye?" he asked.

"Of course I did."

"He got it defending Alex," he told her quietly. "We've got a little mess on our hands, not the least of which is Adriana pushing Alex. We need to go home and talk this out and decide what we're going to do. Filing charges against a nine-year-old isn't going to solve the problem."

Scarlett cooled down, sadness now gripping her. "Oh, God," she breathed. "Now Henry is involved?"

Archer shrugged. "He was defending Alex," he repeated. "It's very noble of him, but now he's in trouble, too. Come along, love; we need to go home and figure out how we're going to handle this."

Scarlett was struggling not to tear up. "I'm pulling Alex out of this school," she whispered hoarsely. "I know it's a wonderful school and Morgan seems to have made some friends here, but I can't let Alex go through this."

"I understand," he said patiently, putting his arm around her shoulders and turning her back for the children.

"I'm finding another school for her tomorrow."

"Of course you are. I'll help you."

Scarlett was wiping at her nose, upset, before reaching out to pull Alexandra into an embrace as the four of them headed back to Archer's car.

—————

Scarlett was sitting on the rail of the arena at Phipps Hall, watching Alexandra and Henry ride in circles. Henry was astride his black and white pony, Nero, but Alexandra wanted to jump so Archer put her on a gentle white mare named Chalkdust who was very nimble over the one-foot barriers.

Scarlett watched her daughter ride the horse around the arena, taking the small barriers and delighted in doing so. The girl was actually smiling, challenging Henry to a jumping contest on his small pony, and laughing when he told her Nero would out-jump the old mare. It was good to see Alexandra in good spirits after such a rough day and Scarlett stuck close to her, feeling as if she had somehow let her daughter down by enrolling her in a school apparently filled with bullies and gossips. Her guilt was great.

Arabella sat several feet behind Scarlett on a small stone patio set, sipping lemonade as she watched the children frolic. Every so often, Scarlett would go back and sit with her, chatting about the weather or gardening or some past adventure involving the children, but she would always return to the rail of the arena to watch her daughter play while Edward, the lanky stable master, stood in the center of the arena in case anyone got into trouble.

Archer had been up in the house since nearly the moment they arrived. He had spent the drive back to Phipps Hall calming both Scarlett and Alexandra and when they arrived, he took the children down to the stables and had Edward saddle up a couple of horses. That distracted the children enough from their bad day so all he had to deal with was Scarlett. She was a bit trickier, but a few gentle kisses and sweet words managed to do it, and then he turned her over to his mother while he took care of a few things.

He had been in the house over an hour and Scarlett kept glancing up to the big manse, wondering what he was doing. She was sure it had everything to do with what happened at school and she appreciated his take-charge personality. It made her feel as if he really cared about her and her girls, as he was so willing to do what he could to make sure they were all happy and healthy. She trusted him. As she hung over the railing and watched Henry and Alexandra jump over small barriers, she heard another voice in their midst.

Scarlett turned around in time to see a man with dark red hair kiss Arabella on the cheek. He was good-looking, fairly tall and well built, and when he turned to look at Scarlett, she could see that he bore a faint resemblance to Archer.

"Scarlett," Arabella was holding on to the man's hands. "You haven't met my middle child. This is August, Archer's younger brother. Auggie, this is... well, how can I phrase this? Scarlett, how would you phrase your relationship with Archer?"

August Milford de Velt Phipps, Baron Heslington, grinned broadly and pulled his hands from his mother's grip. He extended one of them to Scarlett.

"I already know about her," he told his mother, focusing on the truly lovely and delicious Scarlett. "Hi there. It's nice to finally meet you."

Scarlett was grinning. "It's nice to meet you as well."

"So when's the wedding?"

Scarlett's eyes widened and she threw up her hands, laughing. "You'll have to ask your brother, since he apparently has this all mapped out. I think I'm just along for the ride."

August snorted. "I have news for you – you *are* the ride," he teased, eyeing her more closely. "But I will give Archer credit; he didn't lie about you."

"What do you mean?"

"He said you were gorgeous. He was right."

Scarlett laughed. "Thank you very much," she bowed her head humbly, not sure what more to say to that so she shifted the subject. "I seem to remember hearing that you were a barrister."

August nodded. "That would be me," he said. "My brother arrests them and I put them in jail. It's a neat little arrangement. But enough about me; I hear you're a celebrity."

Scarlett laughed again, rolling her eyes. "Maybe that was true twenty years ago," she said. "Now, I just bum around and stir up trouble."

August chuckled; he could already see what his brother saw in the woman, beautiful and charming as she was. He was, truthfully, quite envious. As he was warming up to the conversation, a deep voice suddenly entered the mix.

"Well, well," Archer was coming down the big stone steps leading down from the house. "I've come just in time. Trouble has arrived."

August looked at his older, bigger brother. "You know me well," he grinned, managing to get a look at his brother's face and seeing how weary the man appeared. "What in the hell is wrong with you?"

"What do you mean?"

"You look as if you haven't slept in weeks."

Archer made his way over to Scarlett as he spoke. "Work has been very busy, I suppose."

August tilted his head in Scarlett's direction. "Just work?"

Archer put his arm possessively around Scarlett's shoulders. "Don't get any funny ideas. Keep your distance from her."

August snickered. "She's too good for you."

"I know."

August had a bit of a rascally streak in him, the goofy little brother to serious Archer. Scarlett could see the mischief in his eyes as he grinned.

"I asked her when the wedding was but she said you were in charge of that," he turned back to his mother and sat down beside her on the big stone bench. "Please don't tell me you're bullying this woman into marrying you."

Archer fought off a grin as he looked at Scarlett. "Am I bullying you into marrying me?"

"Not so far."

Archer looked at his brother and made a face at him. "So there."

He pulled Scarlett over to where his mother and brother were sitting and pulled a white metal chair out for her to sit in. Scarlett gratefully accepted the glass of lemonade that Arabella handed to her while Archer took a seat next to Scarlett. He took his own glass of lemonade.

"How do you like England?" August asked, popping a cookie in his mouth. "It must be a big change from America."

Scarlett nodded. "It is," she agreed. "I wasn't so sure I'd like it the first few days I was here, but it's growing on me."

"Where are you from in America?"

"California."

"Scarlett's a singing star," Archer pointed out. "She's come to England to get away from nosy people like you, so don't ask too many questions."

August popped another cookie in his mouth, grinning. "I looked you up online," he told her. "I know those songs you sing. That's quite an accomplishment."

Scarlett smiled humbly. "I was very lucky the way it all happened," she turned to Archer. "Which reminds me; I had an interesting chat with Reverend Bryan earlier today. He was telling me how badly the church is falling apart and how much he needs to raise money to fix it. Did you know about that?"

Archer nodded, taking a cookie for himself. "It's an old

church, love," he said. "There's always something that's going to need to be fixed."

"Yes, I know, but he said the roof is in serious disrepair and there are other things that need to be fixed. I asked him if he had done any fundraising or applied for grants, but he said he really hadn't. It seems like he just depends on donations from parishioners, but that's not going to get him the kind of money he needs."

Archer had one arm around the back of her chair as he looked at her, chomping on the cooking. "My family donated brand new doors last year," he said. "I haven't really looked at the roof and Reverend Bryan hasn't said anything to me about it."

"And he didn't want me to speak to you about it because he was afraid you'd think he'd put me up to it," she said. "Rather than beg donations from you, I have another idea."

"What's that?"

"I was thinking that we should put on a festival of some kind," she said. "I'd be willing to give a concert and donate all proceeds to the church, which might bring in more money than just depending on tithing and donations from the locals. We could advertise it all over Yorkshire, you know, like the Glastonbury Music Festival, and see if we can get a decent crowd. We can sell tickets for ten bucks a piece. Even if we only get a couple hundred people, that's still two thousand dollars. It would help."

Archer was smiling at her. "You'd be willing to do that?"

She shrugged, setting her lemonade down on the big glass and iron patio table. "Of course," she said. "If this is my new community, then I want to do something to help it. I didn't grow up here so I feel like I need to do something to contribute and to get to know people around here. What do you think?"

"I think that's very generous," August spoke before Archer

could. "But something like that will take a lot of people to put it on, won't it?"

Scarlett shrugged. "If the people who attend the church help, then I should have enough help," she turned back to Archer. "I put together a proposal this morning after I talked to Reverend Bryan, outlining the volunteer and monetary needs, but the site is the next step. I'm assuming you own a lot of the vacant land around here and I'm further hoping you would consider letting the festival use the land. I've got clean-up built into the budget so we would try to leave the site the way we found it as much as possible. What do you think?"

Archer was leaning back against the chair, seriously listening to her. When she finished, he simply grinned and shrugged his shoulders. "How can I refuse?" he said. "Let me see your proposal, but I think it's a wonderful idea."

Scarlett beamed. "Really?" she was flattered. "I was hoping you would."

"I can hardly wait to see you perform."

"Will you sing with me? We could do a duet."

He snorted. "I'm not sure about that. I'll have to think about it."

"We could do Phantom of the Opera. I'll be Christine and you can be the Phantom."

He shrugged his big shoulders, somewhat reluctantly, and affectionately stroked her shoulder, glancing over at his brother to see that August's focus was intently on Scarlett. He knew what the man was thinking; August had an eye for pretty women and although he'd never been married, he'd had his share of lovely ladies. Odd how he felt jealous with even August's attention on Scarlett. He felt incredibly possessive and struggled to shake it off. However, when August caught his brother looking at him and devilishly wriggled his eyebrows, Archer's eyes narrowed dangerously.

Oblivious to the Phipps men posturing around her, Scarlett had turned her attention to Alexandra and Henry as they left the arena with Edward and headed back to the barn. Arabella and Archer were back on the subject of the old church, discussing something about new pews, and Scarlett watched Alexandra and Henry fade back towards the stables until she lost sight of them. Then she happened to glance at her watch, noticing it closing in on dinnertime.

Archer noticed that Scarlett had glanced at her watch and the arm that was resting on the back of her chair moved to her shoulders.

"What's the matter, love?" he asked.

Scarlett looked up at him. "I was just wondering if Morgan is home yet," she said quietly, turning her head so she was whispering in his ear. "I really don't mean to be unsociable, but I'd like to get home. The girls have homework and all that."

Archer was nodding even before she finished her sentence. "I know," he said. "Alex and Henry are done riding so we can head back to the lodge as soon as they've packed the horses away."

"What are you two whispering about over there?" August asked.

Archer looked at his brother. "We're going to collect Alex and Henry and head back to Scarlett's house," he replied. "Are you going to be all right here with Mother?"

August waved him off. "I'm going to take over your bedroom and have wild parties," he said, patting his mother firmly on the knee. "Isn't that right, old girl? We're going to have a crazy time, you and me."

Arabella gave her son a deadpan look. "God help me," she muttered, looking over at Scarlett and Archer. "Scarlett, dear, I really wish you would reconsider staying here with us. We have plenty of room and we could all be together."

Scarlett had no idea that Archer had apparently arranged for his brother to stay with Arabella while he and Henry moved over to the lodge. Now, August's appearance was starting to make some sense. She smiled weakly at Arabella, turning to Archer because she had no idea how to respond. She really didn't know what Archer had told his mother about his reasons for moving over to the lodge. Archer took the hint.

"Scarlett's been displaced enough, Mother," he said. "She and the girls need to settle into the lodge. She doesn't want to be moving her children around like a band of gypsies."

Arabella sighed, her attention still on Scarlett. "I'm still not sure why... well, there's so much room at Phipps Hall. We could all live here quite happily."

Archer didn't want to get into it with his mother at the moment. She knew very little about why he was moving over to the lodge and he'd meant it that way. He'd made it seem like it was because he and Scarlett were madly in love and wanted to be together, which upset and confused his mother somewhat. Still, she was respectful of his adult decision and accepted the fact that Archer had asked August to come stay at Phipps Hall with her so she wouldn't be alone. August, however, knew the whole truth. Archer trusted his brother and felt it was important to be honest about the situation with him.

"I appreciate your point, Mother, but you'll forgive me if I make my own decision about this for now," he said, a gentle rebuke. "Besides, if Auggie is moving in here, I'm keeping Scarlett far away from him. I'd have to worry about my brother waiting in the wings to snatch her away from me."

Scarlett giggled as August tried not to appear too much in agreement. Before Archer and August could go at it, Alexandra and Henry suddenly came into view from the stable block, scurrying around the edge of the big arena as they headed for the adults. Scarlett watched her daughter approach, realizing the girl had something in her arms. Henry was running alongside of Alexandra as if he was trying to get a glimpse of what she was holding. As the pair drew close, Scarlett could see that her daughter was carrying a puppy.

"Alexandra Vivienne Ward," she scolded. "What in the world do you have?"

Alexandra was in heaven. She cuddled the little black puppy as Henry tried to pet it. "Edward's dog had puppies," she said. "Isn't he cute?"

Scarlett had a soft spot for dogs and she reached out, petting the little puppy's dark head. "Adorable."

"Can I keep him?"

Scarlett gave her daughter a disapproving expression even as she continued to pet the dog. "Honey, we're not really set up for a puppy," she was trying to be firm but could feel herself fading. "We're just moving in ourselves. Why don't we wait a little while before deciding whether or not we want a dog?"

Alexandra hugged the puppy, who licked her face furiously. "Please, Mom. Morgan has a bunch of new friends but I don't have any. Can't I please have the puppy so at least I have someone to spend time with?"

Her little statement shot holes in Scarlett's willpower. She knew she was about to give in to her pathetic daughter, angry at herself, and all she could do was shake her head.

"This dog will be your responsibility, Alex," she said sternly. "You feed him, you take him outside to go to the bathroom, and you are responsible for where he sleeps at night. Do you hear me?"

Alexandra was already smiling, hugging the dog happily. "I promise I'll take care of him," she assured her dubious mother. "Can we go get him some dog food on the way home?"

Archer could already see his evening was cut out for him. They had some things to do and he was truthfully thrilled.

There were kids and women and dogs to worry about, make comfortable, and settle in for the evening. It was the life he'd always wanted but never truly thought he'd have. Regardless of the circumstances as to why they were all thrown together, they were together and that was all that mattered. He stood up, snapping his fingers softly at Henry.

"Upstairs, young man," he instructed. "Go get your bag and bring it down to the car."

Henry took off, thrilled to death that he was going wherever his father and Alexandra were going. August and Arabella walked Archer, Scarlett and Alexandra up to the car parked in front of the hall. Arabella was still trying to convince Scarlett it would be best for her to come and stay at Phipps Hall, but Scarlett was politely stubborn. She was very sweet as she thanked Arabella, but no amount of persuasion could convince her to remain at Phipps Hall. She wanted to go home. More than that, the girls still hadn't been told and neither had Henry. Henry just thought it was all some kind of adventure and Alexandra had been too wrapped up in her own world to pay much attention to the suitcases Archer and Henry were bringing.

Leaving Arabella and August behind at the massive mansion the Phipps family had called home for over five hundred years, Archer and Scarlett headed back to the lodge.

TEN
MID-OCTOBER

"AUGGIE, I swear I'm going to kill you if you don't stop messing with the shopping list," Scarlett threw a balled sock at him as she came from the utility room with a basket full of laundry. "Put the pen down and go somewhere else; anywhere but the kitchen. Get out of here."

August was grinning as he hovered over Mrs. Bayse's shopping list with a pen in hand. Archer was off picking up the children from school so, as had been the routine for the past couple of months, August was in the house with Scarlett whenever Archer wasn't. Usually she went with Archer to pick the children up, but she had been suffering from migraine headaches off and on over the past couple of weeks and this morning had been a particularly bad one. She was only now feeling well enough to get up and move about. Now, she could feel the headache coming back as her frustration with August bloomed.

"You're going to be sorry you're so mean to me," he told her, although he set the pen down and moved away from the counter. "I'm on a case starting next week so you won't see me around so often."

"Good," Scarlett said firmly, setting the laundry down on

the couch in the family room. "Maybe then I won't have to worry about Mrs. Bayse buying personal lubricant or five gallon tubs of ice cream. Do you have any idea how horrified that woman was that 'warming sex lubricant' was written on the shopping list?"

August snickered like a bad kid. Then he went to the couch where Scarlett was folding clothes and sat down so hard that a pile of towels toppled over. Frustrated, Scarlett picked up a hand towel and began beating him with it until he rolled off the couch to get away from her. He was just escaping her angry smacking when the back door of the utility room opened up and people began to come in.

Alexandra and her new best friend, Maisie, were the first ones into the kitchen with Henry tagging along behind, walking the growing puppy on a leash. Alexandra and Henry had been enrolled in a local school called St. Lawrence since the mess at Fulford, and both of them were doing extremely well. Alexandra had more little friends than she could handle, as did Henry, but Henry always wanted to hang around with Alexandra, which made for a frustrated young lady at times. Already, they were getting along like brother and sister and it was sweet to watch.

Following Alexandra was Morgan and her bubbly blond friend with the silly giggle, Laura. Morgan was still at Fulford and had been the steady girlfriend of Matt Summerlin for the past month. Scarlett truly liked Matt and he spent a good deal of time at the lodge. Behind the group of kids came Archer, closing the back door and entering the kitchen. He glanced over at his brother and Scarlett as he put his keys and wallet on the kitchen counter, noting his brother was getting off the floor. His brow furrowed.

"What in the hell are you doing, Auggie?" he asked.

August brushed off his knees and perched on the edge of the

couch. "Your girlfriend was beating the snot out of me for toppling her laundry."

Archer fought off a grin as he made his way over to Scarlett, who was folding his t-shirt. He bent over and kissed her.

"I told you to leave her alone," he told his brother, then looked at Scarlett. "How's your head, love?"

She shrugged. "At least I can move around," she said, putting the neatly folded t-shirt on the pile and collecting another. "Auggie was over at the counter writing on the grocery list. You'd better see what he wrote and get rid of it so Mrs. Bayse doesn't have a stroke because she has to buy extra-large condoms or a one hundred pound bag of dog food."

Archer rolled his eyes and went over to the pad of paper, making sure there wasn't anything questionable on it. Noting that it looked normal enough, he made his way back over to the couch and sat down next to the laundry without toppling anything. He just sat there a moment, watching Scarlett fold and thinking over the past two months.

It had easily been the best time in his life. He and Scarlett had settled into a beautifully normal routine, getting along as if they'd been doing it all their lives. She and Archer would take the children to school together and then return to the lodge, usually to go on a long morning walk with Freddie the puppy, strolling through woodlands and fields that had belonged to the Phipps empire for hundreds of years. They would chat about anything and everything, becoming acquainted with each other on a level that Archer had never known before. Within the first two weeks of knowing Scarlett, he realized he was so deeply in love with the woman that he couldn't even verbalize it. Every day saw that love grow.

Nearly every morning they would also go into town once they were finished walking the fields, getting coffee and sitting with Freddie watching the world pass by. The people at the coffee shop had their coffee waiting for them by about nine in the morning, knowing they were coming, and the baker had warmed cinnamon rolls set aside for Scarlett. Reverend Bryan would sometimes walk with them and the town constable's wife, Victoria Leggett, had become a friend to them both. They had actually met Victoria one morning when her dog got loose and Archer had managed to corral the beast. A ten minute chat-fest between Scarlett and Victoria had turned into a three hour conversation back at the lodge. Archer was thrilled that Scarlett had found some quality female companionship after her rocky beginning with Maggie Rorick.

Scarlett had also thrown herself into volunteering at Alexandra and Henry's school, mostly just helping out in the classroom, and had made several friends there also. There was always someone calling for her on the phone or women over at the lodge. The Head Master of the school, having found out what Scarlett had done in her youth, had asked her if she'd be interested in doing music workshops after school, and Scarlett had quickly agreed. Now, she taught students how to sing and read music twice a week, something that thrilled her. They were starting to work on a musical that they hoped to perform during the holidays.

But no matter where she went or what she did, Archer was by her side. He never left her alone for a minute and, fortunately, they'd gotten along so well that it hadn't been an issue. He'd taken eight weeks off of work, time now drawing to a close, and he loathed to even think about going back to work. In fact, he'd taken a phone call from his chief on the way home from school regarding his return and it was something he needed to discuss with Scarlett. The pressure was on him to return to work and he knew they'd reached that point where a decision had to be made.

"Well," he finally grunted, stretching out on the couch.

"You're not going to have to worry about Auggie much longer. He's heading back to work and will get out of your hair. I should get back to work, too."

Scarlett looked up from folding a towel. "I was wondering when they were going to make you go back," she said. "You've been off a couple of months. If you don't go back soon, they're going to fire you."

Archer gave her half-grin. "Not quite," he said. "But I did talk to the chief constable today. He wanted to let me know that there hasn't been any activity on the Cutter case since the two most recent murders, so he's encouraging me to come back to work."

"How soon?"

"Next week."

Scarlett nodded as she folded the last of the towels. "You should," she agreed. "Auggie's going back to work and you need to go as well. I feel really awful that you both have upended your lives because of me. You need to go back to work so we can all move on."

Archer glanced at August, who was watching Scarlett with a surprisingly serious expression. "The threat's not over, love," Archer said quietly. "I've already arranged for a private security company to patrol the premises twenty-four seven, so even if I'm at work, there will be two armed security guards on the grounds."

Scarlett stopped folding and looked at him. "I appreciate that," she said. "And please don't get me wrong; I appreciate everything you and Auggie have done, except for Auggie screwing with my shopping lists, but the fact of the matter is that we're letting that guy, whoever he is, rule our lives. He has the control – not us. You and Auggie need to go back to work and give us that control back over our lives. I don't like the fact that somebody, somewhere, has had control over how we live."

Archer could only nod, almost in resignation. "Auggie didn't have anything better to do, anyway," he prodded his brother, "and I got to spend time with the woman I'm going to marry, so it all worked out. But the time has come for us to go back to our normal routine. I can't say I'm totally comfortable with leaving you, but the time has come."

August opened his mouth to say something but Morgan and her giggly girlfriend were down in the kitchen looking for something to eat. So the adults stopped talking for the moment because the kids still didn't know very much about the real reason behind Archer staying at the lodge. Scarlett eventually gathered the folded laundry and carried it upstairs. When Morgan and her friend snatched a bag of cookies and raced back upstairs, August turned to his brother.

"What did the chief really say?" he asked quietly.

Archer glanced over towards the kitchen area and the stairs to make sure Scarlett wasn't in earshot.

"He really does want me to come back to work," he said quietly. "As for activity on the case, I wasn't entirely truthful. There haven't been any more murders, but it seems as if new forensic evidence has seen some breakthrough. I'm going into the office tomorrow to meet with him and the inspectors about it."

"Do you really feel comfortable enough to leave Scarlett alone?"

Archer shrugged. "The armed patrol starts tomorrow at six in the morning," he said. "I feel much better that they'll be here, but the trick will be keeping her inside the house. She likes to wander."

Scarlett started coming down the stairs into the kitchen. August caught sight of her before wriggling his eyebrows at his brother.

"Good luck with that," he muttered. Then he stood up and

stretched out his lanky body. "Scarlett, darling, I'm heading out. Will you miss me?"

Scarlett was at the kitchen counter, giving him a look of impatience. "No," she said flatly. "But thank you for babysitting me today."

August flashed a grin. "You're welcome," he looked at Archer. "Talk to you later."

Archer waved him on, listening to the door slam in the utility room as August headed out to his car. Scarlett was still banging around in the kitchen as Archer picked up the remote for the television and turned it on to a football game. Manchester United was beating the crap out of some other team and he was instantly hooked, but not so hooked that he didn't realize that Scarlett was beginning to pull out pots and pans. He glanced over.

"Are you making dinner?" he asked.

Scarlett nodded. "I'm going to try to," she said. "Mr. and Mrs. Bayse had something to do tonight so I told them to take the night off."

Archer tore himself away from the television and got up of the couch. "Can I help?" he asked, making his way into the kitchen.

Scarlett was already pulling ingredients out of the refrigerator. "No, honey, but thank you," she said. "You go watch your game. I'll take care of dinner."

Archer didn't reply but it took her a minute to realize he was still standing next to the island, watching her work. She glanced up as she began to chop some garlic.

"What's wrong?" she asked.

Archer had a faint smile on his lips, his pale blue eyes twinkling at her. "I need to ask you something."

"What?"

"Will you marry me?"

Scarlett grinned and stopped chopping. "Uh... about that...," she sighed, setting the knife down. "I was thinking about that the other day. I need to talk to you."

"Of course. What about?"

"Us getting married."

His smile faded, thinking he didn't like the tone of her voice. "What about it?"

"Do you think we can do it soon?"

His smile was back, bigger than before. "I was hoping you'd say that," he said. "Reverend Bryan will marry us whenever we want. How soon did you have in mind?"

"Before I start looking like I'm pregnant. That would be embarrassing."

Archer was all set to give her a happy, glib answer, but her unexpected statement had him faltering. Her first sentence sank in and his eyes widened, but when the second sentence registered, his mouth went agape.

"*What?*" was all he could think to say.

She fought off a grin at his shocked expression. "You're not going to back out now, are you?"

Archer's expression only grew more astonished. "What are you...?" he had to grip the granite countertop for support. "Scarlett, are you *pregnant?*"

Scarlett laughed. "I think so," she said. "The last time I had headaches like this was when I was pregnant with Alex. Some women have morning sickness, but I have headaches. Plus, I haven't had my period since we moved to England, so that's a pretty strong indication. I was thinking maybe we could go to the chemist tonight and buy a pregnancy test. I didn't want to put that on Mrs. Bayse's shopping list for obvious reasons."

Archer was pale with shock. But in the next breath, he was rushing at her, his arms going around her, wanting to touch her and hug her but not wanting to hurt or upset her. He ended up running his hands all over her arms like an idiot because he didn't know what to do.

"Oh, my God," he breathed. "Are you serious?"

"Yes."

"But... but you're so *calm* about it!"

She laughed. "Why shouldn't I be?" She sobered, her hazel eyes glimmering up at him for several long moments. "What's going through your mind, Archer? You don't look very happy."

His roving hands moved over her arms and shoulders until he got to her face. Then he cupped it, gazing down into her beautiful features.

"I... I'm speechless," he murmured. "I never thought... Scarlett, are you *serious*?"

"Of course."

"Really?"

"Really."

He suddenly kissed her, so forcefully that he nearly bent her over backwards. When he was done sucking the life out of her, he hugged her so hard that he cracked her back.

"A baby," he breathed. "Oh, my God... a *baby*. Even as I say it, I want to laugh hysterically and jump around like a fool. You can't even imagine how happy I am right now. Words cannot express it. I'm just... gobsmacked."

Scarlett had her arms around his neck. "Is that good?"

"That's very, very good. It's better than good. It's the happiest thing in the world."

Scarlett took a moment to study his handsome face, a faint smile on her lips as a lot of different thoughts rolled through her head.

"You know," she said casually, "I never imagined I'd come to England, shack up with a guy I'd only known a week, and then get pregnant after knowing him just a couple of months. I told the girls that moving here would be an adventure and it surely has been that. But this also underscores something else."

"What?"

"The church fundraiser I've been working on? We'll need to move the performance date up because I'm not going to be on stage at nine months pregnant singing my lungs out."

He was very serious. "I'm not sure I want you performing at all, love. You need to take care of yourself and the baby."

"I'm perfectly fine," she insisted. "What concerns me, however, is getting enough volunteer help. I've had two meetings about this fundraiser and the only people who showed up from the church were Reverend Bryan and your mother. I can't do this all by myself."

Archer sighed faintly, not wanting to say what he was thinking. The incident with Maggie Rorick a couple of months back had pretty much turned the local parishioners against Scarlett, as the outsider. Maggie hadn't been shy about crying her side of the story all over the place and people were more apt to side with her than the flashy woman from America, even if she was Archer Phipps' fiancée. So the jaded churchgoers grew even more jaded and suspicious, and when it came to helping Scarlett with her fundraiser, everyone was suddenly very busy or out of town.

Archer had offered to set everyone straight, once, but Scarlett had shot him down. She was convinced that she could win people over on her own merit and she had tried very hard, but so far, she'd made little headway. Still, she wouldn't admit defeat. She kept plugging forward and Archer was forced to stand in the wings, heartbroken, and watch. She didn't want his help and he didn't offer, no matter how hard it was for him. She still thought she could do it on her own.

"Maybe you should think about putting the fundraiser aside

for the time being," he said gently. "With a baby on the way, you'll have enough to deal with. I don't see that...."

She waved him off, interrupting him. "I can deal with a baby and other activities just fine," she said firmly, pulling away from him to return to her garlic. "I'm healthy and there's no reason I can't finish with this fundraiser. After dinner, we can go get a pregnancy test and then we'll know for certain, okay?"

He snatched his keys off the counter. "I'm getting it *now*," he declared. "I'll be right back."

He was off before Scarlett could stop him. With a giggle, she returned to making dinner, which turned out to be pasta with gorgonzola sauce, salad and garlic bread. In fact, dinner was on the table and the kids and their friends were eating by the time Archer got back from the chemist. He pulled Scarlett away from the kitchen and in the privacy of their bathroom upstairs made her take the pregnancy test. When she was finished peeing on the stick, she came out of the bathroom and handed it to him so he would be the first one to know.

Scarlett had never seen the man so happy.

———

Archer was up early the next morning, getting ready for work. Scarlett woke up with him but her head was pounding so badly that she stayed in bed. Archer made her promise that she'd see a doctor as soon as possible and she miserably agreed. He planned on calling his practitioner as soon as the office opened up to get a referral to an obstetrician. Just like everything else in their lives, he was taking charge of even the baby business and loving every minute of it.

So Scarlett lay in bed, listening to the house becoming awake as the sun rose. Archer got the kids up and on to breakfast, and she could hear them running up and down the stairs.

Pots and plates were banging around in the kitchen and the smell of coffee wafted up to the second floor. Forcing herself to get out of bed, she popped a couple of Tylenol and headed downstairs to see everyone before they were off for the day.

Alexandra and the dog were over on the couch, eating bacon together while Morgan and Henry sat at the table with Archer. Archer saw Scarlett come into the kitchen and he got out of his chair.

"Why are you up?" he asked, going to her. "Go back to bed, my angel. I've got the kids covered."

Scarlett smiled wanly, patting him sweetly on the cheek. "I know you do," she said. "But I'd really love some coffee. I can smell it all the way upstairs."

"Go back to bed and I'll bring it to you."

"I'll go back to bed after you leave, I promise."

He smiled, conceding defeat that he hadn't been able to send her back to bed right away, as Mrs. Bayse poured a cup of coffee and handed it to her. After doctoring it up with cream and sugar, Scarlett pulled a fork out of the drawer and stood at the stove, eating scrambled eggs straight out of the frying pan, as Alexandra and Freddie the dog bolted off the couch and ran at her, begging to go to Maisie's house after school.

Scarlett held up a hand to silence her pleading daughter. "Archer, are you going to be able to pick the kids up from school?"

He was leaning back against the island in the center of the kitchen, sipping at his coffee and speaking with his son about something. But he heard her over the commotion.

"I'm fairly certain I can," he told her. "If I get hung up, I'll give you a call. Will you feel well enough to get them?"

"Sure." Scarlett looked back at her daughter. "Call Maisie right now before you leave to make sure it's okay with her mother."

Alexandra did as she was told and in minutes had the situation cleared up. Archer moved over to the stove where Scarlett was still standing, his arm around her shoulders as she picked at the eggs and he finished his coffee. Morgan was on the cell phone, chatting even at this early hour, as Alexandra, Henry and the dog were running up and down the stairs collecting book bags for school. With the television blaring the morning news, the chaos from the kids, and all of the other smells and sounds of morning, Archer knew he had never been happier in his life. This was how he'd always wanted his life to be, happy with a family and children. He loved Scarlett more every day and now with the pregnancy, he was figuratively walking on clouds. Life was good.

Glancing at his watch, he set his coffee cup down. "Is everyone ready?" he announced to the group. "We need to pop off."

Alexandra and Henry collected their books and lunch sacks as Morgan, still on the phone, did the same. Scarlett kissed her children, gave Henry a hug, and finally kissed Archer as everyone headed out of the door. Archer pointed a finger at her before he got completely out the door.

"If you go anywhere, you take one of the security people with you, okay?" he said.

Scarlett nodded. "I will."

"Promise?"

"Yes."

"They're supposed to follow you if you go out, so don't leave without them."

"I won't."

"Thank you. I love you."

"Love you, too. Have a good day at work."

Satisfied, at least as much as he could be, Archer winked at her and continued on to the car. Scarlett stood in the doorway leading out towards the garage, watching the four of them climb into Archer's BMW. She also noticed a small, white car with a security company's logo parked off near the fence. She knew the security people were around even though she didn't see them. It was the one reminder that things weren't all as rosy and normal as she would have liked.

Victoria rang her about an hour later to see if she wanted to meet her in town for coffee in about fifteen minutes. Remembering her promise to Archer, she told Victoria she'd meet her at the coffee shop and upon hanging up the phone, went to quickly change her clothes. The weather was growing cooler now that they were in October so she put on jeans, a white camisole and a body-skimming tunic top with long sleeves that laced up the front. It covered but her cleavage, now filling out in early pregnancy, strained against the lacings.

Scarlett looked at the way her bustline was growing, giggling because she looked really sexy without the baby bump that would very shortly follow. It was a little too much flesh for the sleepy English town of Ludbourne but she shrugged it off because she liked the top and liked the soft material of it. Pulling on her flat-soled leather boots, she plucked a jacket and her purse out of the closet and headed back downstairs.

Once downstairs, she told Mrs. Bayse where she was going and headed outside to the new Audi that she had purchased last month. As she reached the car, she saw one of the security patrol over near the gate and she waved the man over, letting him know that she was heading into town. The man ran back to the little white security car and followed Scarlett as she drove on into town.

Scarlett didn't pay much attention to her bodyguard as she got out of the car and headed over to the coffee shop. Victoria was already on the street, a tall blond with big blue eyes and a bright smile. She waved Scarlett over and the two came together with a hug.

"It's cold out here," Scarlett took the woman's hand as she turned for the coffee shop. "Let's get inside."

"Wait a minute," Victoria held her in check. She pointed over to the church across the street. "I wanted... well, I need to show you something. Do you see anything over there you recognize?"

Confused, Scarlett looked across the street to the church. It looked the same as it always did, with its well-kept old cemetery and dark-stoned walls. She had no idea what Victoria meant until she realized that there were several cars in the parking lot, one of them being Arabella Phipps' Aston Martin. Curiosity swept her.

"What's going on over there?" she asked.

Victoria sighed faintly, took her hand, and began to lead her across the street. "I was wondering that myself a couple of weeks ago when I saw all of these cars parked here," she said. "You know I don't attend church here; I go with my parents to the church over in Heslington. I also don't go here because this church has a bad reputation for being pretty closed in on itself. They don't welcome outsiders."

Scarlett gave her a quirky smile. "No joke."

Victoria grinned in return as they hit the sidewalk on the other side of the street and began to walk up the steps towards the church. "I know about Maggie Rorick," she said. "You told me and I've also heard rumors to that effect. Maggie's a bitch, everyone knows she's a bitch, yet they all seem to stand up for her because she was born here. It's just the way it is."

Scarlett's smile faded. "I know," she agreed. "I wouldn't go to church here at all if it wasn't for Archer. It's his church and I do it to support him."

They made their way through the old cemetery to the side

door of the church, which was slightly cracked open to allow for airflow. Voices were wafting from inside. Victoria came to a halt next to the door and lowered her voice to a whisper.

"I saw this group here a couple of weeks ago when I came over to drop off some canned food for their annual food drive," she whispered. "They didn't see me at the back of the church but I saw them. And I heard them, too. I think you need to hear what's going on."

Curious, Scarlett leaned against the door crack and listened. She could hear several female voices overlapping one another, and that's all that went on for the first few minutes. But she listened harder when she suddenly heard Arabella's voice chime in. The woman was very distinctive in her speaking.

"... but I think it's imperative that we have this festival to coincide with the anniversary of the founding of the church," she was saying. "That would put the date at August 1. Everyone has their assignments and knows what needs to be done, so it's simply a matter of pulling it all together from this point. We need to have pre-sale tickets at ten pounds each, and I will personally purchase the first one hundred."

Everyone congratulated and thanked her. As Scarlett listened, increasingly baffled, she could hear Reverend Bryan speak up.

"I would be remiss if I didn't remind the committee, again, that Miss Ward has already spearheaded a fundraising effort for the church," he sounded strained. "She came up with the idea and has been asking for support. I think the fact that you all took her idea and turned it into your own, while excluding her, is somewhat underhanded. She's going to find out eventually. What will you tell her?"

The women started to respond at the same time but Arabella's voice was heard above everything.

"Scarlett means well," she insisted. "But she doesn't know

our country or our people. What works in America will not work here. She doesn't understand that people don't want to see a half-naked woman on stage singing about sex. They want something more conservative and I think it's up to us, as a committee and long-time members of the church, to provide that. Scarlett had a very brilliant idea and I will not let any of you condemn her for her efforts, but I would not trust this to her. I think it would fail simply because she's not one of us. She doesn't understand."

There was a buzz about as people agreed or debated. Reverend Bryan spoke up again. "She is trying to be one of us but those of you with very un-Christian attitudes have spurned her attempts." He sounded like he was scolding. "The woman is kind and dedicated to her children, and I think the way you're treating her in this instance is deplorable. The Christian thing to do would be to include her."

"I agree that the way people have shunned Scarlett is disgraceful," Arabella confirmed. "I have spoken of this before and you all know my feelings on the matter. I would expect that at least some of you will amend your ways and be more welcoming in the future."

An unfamiliar voice spoke. "But what she did to Maggie...."

"Maggie Rorick is a gossip and a troublemaker," Arabella said sternly. "You know this, yet you side with her. Scarlett is twice the woman Maggie could ever hope to be and if some of you brought your noses out of the clouds for a moment, you would realize that."

"Then why do you support stealing the woman's idea for a fundraiser?" Reverend Bryan asked.

There was that mumbling buzz again as the subject was debated. Finally, Arabella spoke. "The truth is that I like Scarlett very much and think she has been very good for my son," she said. "But she is also American and thinks like an American.

Give her a few years in England and she'll assimilate into our culture. For something as critical as this, I simply do not trust her to see it through for reasons I have already explained."

"She's going to marry your son, Lady Arabella," Reverend Bryan reminded her quietly.

"And Archer will mold and control her," Arabella replied. "If he can't, I will. You needn't worry. I think she'll make a fine wife for Archer and then, I am sure, more widely accepted."

There was more discussion going on but that was all Scarlett needed to hear. Her eyes were already filling with tears as she turned away from the door and headed back across the cemetery.

"I'm sorry," Victoria was following her. "I thought you should hear. They've been meeting twice a week here for almost a month talking about the fundraising festival they're going to put on. I just thought you should know."

Scarlett could only nod. She could feel the sobs coming and she didn't want to make a fool of herself. She took the steps down to the street too fast and ended up slipping. As Victoria grabbed her jacket to keep her from falling, the jacket slipped from her grip and Scarlett ended up rolling down four big, stone steps before landing on her bum at the bottom.

"Oh, my God," Victoria rushed to her side. "Are you okay?"

Bruised, Scarlett picked herself up with Victoria's help. "I'm fine," she whispered tightly. Then she looked to her friend. "Thank you for... well, letting me in on this since no one else would. I appreciate it."

Victoria had her gently by the arm. "Let's go get some coffee, okay?"

Scarlett shook her head. "I don't feel much like it now," she said, patting Victoria's hand. "I think I'm just going to go home."

"Want some company?"

Scarlett forced a smile and hugged her. "No," she said. "But thank you. Thank you for being a friend."

Victoria walked with her back to her car and made sure she got in. She didn't notice the private security car that pulled away when Scarlett did and even if she had noticed, it wouldn't have meant anything to her. Archer and Scarlett had never discussed the situation involving the Cutter or the notes. All Victoria could think of was how badly she felt for her new friend. She was trying so hard to be accepted and finding it a huge uphill battle, now with Arabella Phipps involved.

As Victoria wandered back to her car, she called Archer. The man needed to know.

ELEVEN

ARCHER WAS home within a half hour of receiving Victoria Leggett's phone call.

She had filled him in on everything that had happened and even as he drove home, he could feel an inordinate amount of anger and the fact that his mother was in on the deceit nearly sent him through the roof. But first and foremost, he needed to get home to Scarlett. He could only imagine how hurt she was and he was desperate to comfort her.

What he hadn't expected to find was the master bedroom torn apart. He walked into the usually clean and tidy room only to find clothes and other items in piles all over the floor. It was a mess. Stepping further into the room, he didn't see Scarlett anywhere. However, he happened to glance at the open bathroom door and spied her sitting in the giant stone bathtub. Her head was down, her dark hair covering her features, as if she were staring down at the water. She was still and unmoving. Concerned, he moved quickly into the bathroom.

"Scarlett?" he asked hesitantly. "Are you...?"

It was then he saw that she was sitting in what looked like a bathtub half-filled with blood. The water was a rich red color. Seized with panic, Archer fell to his knees and reached into the tub to pull her out. She was limp and barely responsive as he lay her down on the stone floor to check her for injury.

"Scarlett," his voice was quivering as he checked her wrists for cut marks, her body for any signs of trauma. "Love, can you hear me? Talk to me, angel, please. What happened?"

Scarlett seemed to come around somewhat and tried to sit up. "I couldn't... couldn't get to the phone," she whispered, falling back against the stone when she was too weak to rise. "I fell."

Archer had tears in his eyes as he raced into the bedroom for the house phone and called emergency services. He was on his knees beside Scarlett, struggling to stay calm as he gave his address and Scarlett's condition. He really didn't know what the matter was other than she seemed to be bleeding heavily from somewhere. As he hung up the phone, he could see a trickle of blood pooling up under her thighs and, taking a closer look, realized it was coming from her vagina. Horror such as he had never known seized him.

"You said that you fell?" he was grabbing for towels. "Angel, what happened? When did you fall?"

Scarlett was nearly unconscious from blood loss, a pure miracle alone that she hadn't passed out and drowned in the bathtub. She tried to sit up again.

"Outside the church," she murmured. "I fell down the steps. I heard your mother...."

She faded off, unable to continue. He began to wrap her up in towels, moving her away from the bathtub and bloody floor so he could make an attempt to stop the bleeding.

"I know," he whispered, kissing her forehead, her cheeks, as he cleaned her up. "I know what happened."

Scarlett began to cry as Archer took a big white towel and

put it between her legs, clamping her thighs down over it to hold it in place.

"She went behind my back," she sobbed. "They all went behind my back. I hate this damn country. I want to go home."

Archer bent over her and hugged her as tightly as he could, trying to soothe her. Truth was, he was terrified and verging on tears, but he couldn't think about that now. He had to help Scarlett. He didn't even care about the obvious miscarriage; he was simply afraid that she was bleeding to death in front of him and he had no way to stop it.

"I'm so sorry," he whispered, kissing her forehead again. "I know what happened. I'm going to get to the bottom of it, I swear."

"Don't bother," she wept. "I'm going back to America where I belong. I was trying to pack but I felt so cold that I took a bath. What are you doing home?"

She wasn't thinking clearly; he was coming to understand that simply by the way she was talking. Bolting to his feet again, he raced to the master bedroom door and shouted down to Mrs. Bayse, who had been in the utility room when he came in the house and apparently oblivious to what was going on upstairs. He ran back to the bathroom, pausing by a pile of clothes and picking out a bra, panties, a pair of yoga pants and some kind of tank top. He wanted to get her dressed before emergency services arrived and at least somewhat preserve her modesty.

He had just put her bra on when Mrs. Bayse appeared in the bedroom, gasping when she saw all of the blood in the bathroom. Archer caught sight of the woman.

"Emergency services should be here any moment," he told her in a shaking voice. "Please let them in. Also, I will need for you and Mr. Bayse to pick the children up from school."

"Of course," Mrs. Bayse was horrified, near tears. "What on earth happened? Can I help?"

Archer shook his head. "I've got her," he murmured. "But when you pick the children up... please don't tell them about this. I will tell them what happened when I know more."

"I won't," Mrs. Bayse said fearfully. "Are you sure I can't help?"

Archer was focused on pulling the tank top over Scarlett's head. "Not at the moment, "he said. "Please go downstairs and watch for the rescue."

Mrs. Bayse nodded and fled. Scarlett was becoming more lucid, realizing he was trying to dress her and further realizing there was a big white towel in between her legs. As Archer tried to sit her up, she pulled the towel out and saw all of the blood.

"Oh... no," she moaned faintly. "There's a lot of blood."

"I know, love," he was trying to stay composed. "Let's get you dressed. We're going to the hospital."

She helped him pull on her underwear although she was very weak and uncoordinated about doing it.

"Why is there all of this blood?" she wanted to know. "What about the baby?"

Archer lost it. He kissed her forehead, her cheek, tears running down his face as fast as he could wipe them away.

"Not this time," he comforted. "I'm more concerned about you. We need to get you fixed up."

There was nothing like childbirth and the realities of it to bond two people together or, in this case, the loss of a baby. With Scarlett still in one big arm, he reached over into the cabinet and began hunting around for sanitary pads. He didn't find anything but tampons and he really wasn't sure that was a good idea considering the copious amounts of blood she had lost, so he ended up opening up the first aid kit that was under the sink and pulling out big gauze pads.

Scarlett had pulled on the yoga pants and sank back down

to the bathroom floor. Archer sat next to her, holding the gauze pads in one hand.

"You're going to bleed all over yourself unless you...," he gestured towards her pelvis, "... use these."

Scarlett gazed up at him with a blank expression. She was so very pale. But after a few moments she realized what he was saying so she took the gauze from him.

"I'm really cold," she whispered. "Can I have my jacket, please?"

As Archer got up to get her big fleecy jacket, Scarlett used the gauze like a sanitary pad. By the time he came back, she was just lying on the bathroom floor, eyes closed in her pasty face. He sat down beside her and put the jacket over her, all the while gazing down into her delicate face. So many thoughts were rolling through his head, so much turmoil he could hardly contain it. When Scarlett opened her eyes, she looked up to see his eyes swimming with tears. Startled, she tried to sit up again.

"What's the matter?" she asked as he forced her to lie back down. "Why are you crying?"

Archer couldn't even answer. He just shook his head, falling forward until his face was on her breasts, weeping softly. Weak and disoriented, Scarlett put her arms around him. She still wasn't completely cognizant of the trouble she was in. Blood loss had seen to that. She didn't really have a clue why he was crying.

It seemed like a matter of moments later that they heard the rescue siren. By that time, Scarlett had closed her eyes again and had drifted into unconsciousness. When the rescuers came upstairs, they nearly had to pry Archer away so they could get a look at her. He had been in moderate control until they arrived but now he felt panicked. They separated him from Scarlett while they hooked her up to IVs and examined her, and he didn't like that one bit. When she was heavily sedated, the rescue ambulance took her to the York Hospital with Archer following behind in his police-issued BMW with the rotators lit up.

He wept the entire way there.

———

Victoria sat next to Archer in the waiting room of the emergency department at York Hospital. She had called Archer while he was following the ambulance and the man sounded as if he were coming apart, so she met him there a few minutes after the ambulance pulled in. Medical personnel were there to greet Scarlett and assess her, and they whisked her away into an examination room, leaving Archer and Victoria in the waiting room.

Archer was shook up but he managed to give the admitting nurse the information she needed. He'd spent more than his share at the hospital during the course of his job so some of the employees knew him on sight. It also happened to be where his ex-wife worked, a vascular surgeon he had met years ago during a case. But his ex-wife didn't cross his mind more than fleetingly as he filled out the financial responsibility portion of Scarlett's admission paperwork and put himself down as the man with the checkbook. He didn't even know if she had insurance but he suspected she didn't.

When the paperwork was done, he sat down next to Victoria to play the sickening waiting game. About a half hour into it, he called August to ask the man if he could go over and spend the evening with the children and tried to explain the circumstances without breaking down. Until he knew how Scarlett was, he wanted someone with the kids other than domestics in case things got dicey. He was especially concerned for Alexandra and Morgan, and knew they had come to like Uncle

Auggie a great deal. He would comfort them. August, horrified by the tale his brother told, agreed to stay with the children, but after he hung up the phone with Archer, he immediately called his mother. That call brought Arabella to York Hospital nearly two hours after Scarlett had been brought to the Emergency Department.

A doctor had come out to tell Archer that Scarlett had been stabilized and that they were waiting for Gynecology to examine her. They let him see Scarlett, briefly, but she was doped up and passed out, so she didn't even know he was there. So he kissed her hand and tried not to cry as a nurse ushered him back out of the room.

As he was sitting in the hallway outside of her room, alone, as Victoria had left him to go and pick up her children from school, he heard soft footfalls approach. Glancing up, he recognized his mother and just as quickly looked away.

"I can't even look at you right now," he said. "If I'd wanted you to come, I would have called you."

Arabella was genuinely perplexed. "Why on earth would you say such a thing?" she demanded. "Auggie called me. How's Scarlett?"

Archer was still looking away. "She's doing better, no thanks to you," he said. "Go home, Mother. I don't want you here."

Arabella was becoming annoyed as well as perplexed. "Archer, what in the world is wrong with you?"

He stood up, quickly, to put some distance between them. When he faced his mother, it was with restraint. God, he wanted very much to unload on her.

"I hear you're doing some fundraising for the church," he said after a moment. "Scarlett heard about it, too. Do you have any idea how betrayed she feels?"

Arabella lost some of her confusion, being replaced by a distinct sense of foreboding. She was shocked, cornered, struggling to come up with a reply that wouldn't anger Archer even more. She could see by his expression that he was positively furious and she labored to get the upper hand.

"Sit down, Archer," she commanded. "This is not a subject we are going to discuss in a hospital corridor. Will you tell me how Scarlett is?"

Archer wasn't going to sit down. He put his big hands on his hips, a gesture of pure frustration. "She's stable."

"What happened?"

His frustration was ready to explode. "Your betrayal is what happened," he fired back. "Scarlett was in town today at the same time you were having your fundraising meeting at church. She heard all about it, first hand, because she listened in on the committee meeting and she heard you in particular talk about how she wasn't capable of running a fundraiser so you were going to hold your own and leave her out of it. She was very upset and apparently slipped and fell outside of the church, and by the time she got home she was hemorrhaging. When I got home, there was blood all over the damn place and it's a bloody miracle that she didn't bleed to death."

Arabella was shocked and sickened, losing some of her defiance. "I don't understand," her voice was considerably weaker. "Did she cut herself?"

Archer lost some of his rage, looking at his mother and suddenly feeling very much like weeping again. He swallowed away the lump in his throat.

"No," he whispered. "She lost the baby she was carrying. We were going to surprise you with the news before all of this happened."

Arabella's hand flew to her mouth, stunned and horrified. "She was pregnant?"

"*Was.*"

Arabella struggled to control her reaction. "Oh, Archer," she finally breathed. "I'm so terribly sorry. I don't even know what to say."

Archer looked at his mother, feeling his anger abate but not his resentment. He didn't know what he was feeling at the moment except for great and painful confusion.

"Just... go home," he turned away from her, unable to look at her. "I really don't want you here right now."

Arabella's pale blue eyes welled, trying to frantically come up with a way to salvage the situation. She wasn't going to leave unless he bodily threw her out and she knew her son well enough to know he wouldn't do that. As she backed away, the door to Scarlett's room opened and a young Asian doctor appeared. She was tiny and sharp, moving quickly towards Archer.

"Are you Mr. Phipps?" she asked.

Archer nodded quickly. "Yes," he replied. "How's Scarlett?"

The doctor indicated for them to take a seat in the plastic chairs that lined the corridor. Archer planted himself as did Arabella, eager to hear how Scarlett was. Archer couldn't even summon the energy to tell his mother to go away again; all he cared about was Scarlett's health.

"We did an ultrasound scan of her uterus," the doctor said. "Unfortunately, she did miscarry, but most of the blood seems to be coming from a ruptured ovarian cyst. We need to clean her out to make sure there's no infection or residual bleeding as a result of the miscarriage."

"Clean her out?" Archer asked anxiously. "How do you do that?"

The doctor used her tiny fingers to demonstrate. "We dilate the cervix and suction her out," she replied. "It will help her heal faster. She lost a significant amount of blood, unfortunately, but she's stable now and we're going to keep her here a day or two. She should be fine."

Archer let out a huge, pent-up sigh of relief. In fact, he almost started crying again. "Thank you," Archer shook the woman's hand gratefully, almost crushing it with his big grip. "I'm so glad to hear that. Thank you so much."

The doctor grinned as she pulled her hand away from his and rubbed it. "We'll probably do the surgery later tonight and, providing all goes well tomorrow, you should be able to take her home in a day or two. It just depends on how she responds. I know that a big question on your mind after a miscarriage is when you can start trying for another baby, but give her at least six weeks or so before you start trying. Give her time to heal."

Archer nodded, but in truth, he wasn't even thinking about another baby. That hadn't really been a concern. He was only thinking of Scarlett's health.

"Can I see her?" he asked.

The doctor shrugged. "She's still asleep and probably will be until tomorrow morning, but you can sit with her if you want to. Just don't wake her up. Let her sleep."

"I won't, I promise."

Without a hind glance to his mother, he followed the doctor into the examination room and the door shut softly. Archer sat with Scarlett for two and a half hours, until the orderlies came to wheel her off to surgery. When he emerged from the room, he noticed that his mother was still sitting in the dark hallway all alone, patiently waiting. He was still angry and really didn't want to talk to her, but the part of him that was relieved by Scarlett's recovery was a little more magnanimous.

Slowly, he made his way over to the woman, gazing down at her in the dimly lit hallway. After a moment, he extended a hand to her, one she gratefully accepted. Together, they made their way to the floor below where the surgical waiting room was located.

Scarlett was going to be all right.

TWELVE
DECEMBER

ARCHER DROVE up to the big garage, noticing that nearly every light in the house and in the courtyard was on. The entire compound was brilliantly lit, a beacon of light in the dark winter's night. It was Friday evening in the middle of December and they'd had heavy snow the week before, now melted into the over-saturated ground and making for ice and mush. As he climbed out of the car with bags in his hands, he headed for the utility room door.

As he crossed the courtyard, he could see a bunch of kids in the entertainment room. It was noisy and fun, and there was a big fire blazing in the fireplace. As Archer watched, Mr. Bayse came hustling out of the room, shutting the glass door behind him and heading towards the house. When he noticed Archer and all of the bags in the man's arms, he hurried and opened the back door for him.

"Thank you," Archer said as he entered the house, setting the packages down on the counter in the utility room. "Hide those things, will you? If Scarlett finds them, she's going to open them all up before Christmas."

Mr. Bayse chuckled. "She's a tricky one, sir."

Archer grinned. "That's a nice way of putting it. She's nosy as hell and worse than the children. So hide those presents well if you know what's good for you."

As Mr. Bayse did what he was told, Archer entered the kitchen that was warm and cozy and smelling like bread. Alexandra and Henry were watching television in the family room, Henry leaping to his feet when he saw his father.

"Dad!" he rushed his father. "Edward called and said that Ginger is going to give birth tonight. Can Alex and I go watch? Please?"

Archer glanced at Alexandra, who was sitting on the couch with the dog on her lap, looking rather hopeful. Archer had avoided going to Phipps Hall for the past couple of months, ever since Scarlett's accident, mostly because he still wasn't ready to speak to his mother yet. The woman called daily, leaving messages, and speaking to Henry when she was lucky enough to get him on the phone. Archer suspected this was another of his mother's ruses to get him over to the house.

"Maybe," he told his son. "Let me change clothes and eat dinner, and then we'll talk about it."

Henry wasn't satisfied with the answer. "But, Dad...!"

Archer cut him off. "Later," he said firmly.

Henry went into pouting mode but kept his mouth shut. Archer took the stairs in the dining room and ended up in the master bedroom, pulling his overcoat off as he entered. The first thing he saw was Scarlett sitting on the bed with a laptop computer on her thighs. As he came over to the bed, she looked up from the computer monitor and smiled at him.

"Hi, honey," she said sweetly.

He leaned over the bed and kissed her on the lips. "Hello, my love," he kissed her again before standing straight and pulling off a shirt. "It looks like we've got a party downstairs in the entertainment room."

Scarlett nodded as she refocused on her computer screen. "Some of Morgan's friends are here," she confirmed, although multiple teenagers in the house was pretty much a weekly occurrence. "Plus, we were rehearsing for the Christmas program at Alex and Henry's school. There's a whole gang of kids in there having takeout Chinese food for dinner. How was your day?"

"Long. How was yours?"

"Good."

"What are you doing on the computer?"

"None of your business."

He grinned at her as he pulled off his undershirt. "Why not?"

"Because I'm doing some Christmas shopping. That's all you need to know."

She was being snippy in a funny sort of way, so he chucked as he went into his closet to change clothes. Then he came out of the closet in jeans and a sweater, holding something behind his back. Scarlett was focused on the computer and didn't see him trying to be very obvious that he was hiding something from her. When Archer realized she was basically ignoring him, he rolled onto the bed and snatched the computer away from her.

"Hey!" she tried to grab it back. "Give me that. I'm not finished."

He set the computer on the floor on his side of the bed, grabbing her around the torso when she tried to crawl over and get it. He flipped her onto her back and covered her up with his big body, nuzzling her neck.

"Not now," Scarlett tried to push him off. "The kids are around and the door is wide open. What's the matter with you?"

He wouldn't let her up. "You'd better be nice to me."

"I'm always nice to you."

He chuckled. "Yes, you are, but you'd better be nicer."

"Why?"

He suddenly held up a small ring box. "Because I'll sell this to the gypsies if you don't properly worship me."

Scarlett froze in her struggling, a smile spreading across her lips as her gaze fell on the small black box. Playing the game, she wound her arms around his neck and kissed him tenderly, so much so that Archer forgot his teasing and went in for a big, passionate kiss, but she stopped him.

"Later," she whispered, hand over his mouth. "Give me what's in the box and you can have whatever you want afterwards."

He lifted his eyebrows. "That's an offer I can't refuse."

He put the black satin box in the palm of her left hand and she popped the top open, gasping when she saw the contents. Scarlett found herself looking at an 8 millimeter platinum band with a three carat diamond perched on it. It was big, sleek and gorgeous, and as she sat up and looked at it, her eyes began swimming with tears. Archer's expression as he watched her face was gentle and warm.

"What's wrong?' he asked. "Don't you like it?"

She swallowed her tears, her eyes still on the ring. "It's not that," she whispered. "It's just... Archer, do you realize you've been asking me to marry you since nearly the moment we met? Up until this point, all of it has been talk."

His smile faded somewhat. "Didn't you believe me?"

She tore her eyes off the ring and looked at him. "I always believed you," she murmured. "I didn't mean it the way it sounded. I always knew we would, eventually, but this ring somehow makes it real. We're really getting married."

He laughed. "Of course we're really getting married, silly girl," he said, stroking her cheek. "These past few months have been the happiest of my life. I want to thank you for that. I never believed I could be so happy or so in love with someone. I wake up every morning and thank God for you."

She kissed him and threw her arms around his neck, squeezing him tightly. "So do I," she concurred. "I never knew I was missing anything until I found you. Now I can't imagine my life without you."

He smiled broadly, stroking her cheek again before gently kissing her. He was about to do it again when Henry suddenly appeared in the doorway.

"Dad," the boy wandered into the bedroom. "Grandmother is downstairs. She wants to see you."

Archer looked at his son, surprised. Then he looked at Scarlett, who still had her arms around his neck. Silent words and expressions passed between them until she quietly unwound her arms and he stood up from the bed.

"Where is she?" he asked.

Henry threw a thumb over his shoulder. "With Alex and Freddie," he said. "She brought Christmas gifts with her."

Archer's gaze lingered on his son a moment before looking over his shoulder at Scarlett. She was fishing the computer off the floor as if nothing was amiss, returning to whatever she had been doing before Archer interrupted her. She had set the black box with the ring in it on the night stand, which disturbed him a little. His romantic proposal had been interrupted by the touchy subject of his mother's arrival, but it couldn't be helped. He'd make it up to her. He put his hand on Henry's shoulder and turned the boy around.

"Let's go down and see what she wants," he said.

When Archer made it into the family room, he found his mother sitting next to Alexandra on the couch, both of them watching some kind of Christmas cartoon show. Freddie had his head on his mother's lap, which almost made Archer laugh because his mother didn't like dogs. But he kept a straight face as he approached the couch and Arabella caught sight of him. She immediately pushed the dog off of her and stood up.

"Hello, Archer," she said, sounding somewhat timid. "Merry Christmas."

"Merry Christmas," Archer replied, but he didn't say anything more. He wouldn't in front of Henry because for all the kid knew, nothing was amiss between his father and grandmother. They'd kept that part of it very quiet. "Uh... come on into the living room. We can talk in there."

Arabella followed her son through the warm and cozy home, beautifully decorated. There was a gorgeous Christmas tree in the living room with stacks of presents underneath it. Arabella paused in the doorway between the dining room and the living room, taking in everything around her.

"The house looks beautiful," she said. "I've only been here once, you know, back when you were renovating it. It's really a lovely place now with all of the homey touches."

Archer paused by one of the two big couches in the room. "I think so."

"Scarlett has a good eye for color and decorating."

"Yes, she does."

"Are you happy here?"

So much for pleasantries. Arabella was going to get right down to business. Archer silently indicated for his mother to sit before he took a seat himself. It was good manners, something he was so stringent about, and habit. He had mixed feelings as he faced her.

"Extremely happy," he said quietly. "I've never been happier in my life. Is that what you came to ask?"

Arabella shook her head. "I came to ask how we can solve this separation between us," she said. A prideful woman, it was difficult for her to swallow her ego. "I have spent the past two months missing my son and grandson very much, and very hurt that you would choose to side with a woman you're not even married to over your own mother. Can you explain why I should not feel this way?"

Archer sat back on the couch. Thinking on how to reply without becoming angry, he sighed heavily.

"Mother, I want you to understand something very clearly," he said quietly. "It doesn't matter if Scarlett and I aren't married yet. She is the center of my world and I love her more than anything. It's not like she did anything wrong to cause this separation; she's a good woman with a good heart, and you did something very underhanded that hurt her deeply. If she's hurt, *I'm* hurt. I'm hurt that you would do this to the woman I love. I'm hurt that you were capable of such betrayal. So in answer to your question, Scarlett and I have done nothing wrong. Your actions brought this about and the sooner you accept responsibility, the better chance we have of moving past it."

Arabella looked at her hands, all bundled up in wool gloves against the cold December night. She fell quiet, contemplative. Archer watched her, convinced she was going to fight him on it.

"I honestly didn't think it would be such a huge issue," she finally said. "Scarlett had a wonderful idea to raise funds for the church, but she's so new to our community. I thought I could do a better job since I know everyone and have their respect. I thought Scarlett would just forget about the idea and move on to something else when she realized she didn't have any support. I didn't think it would hurt her so badly."

Archer's brow furrowed and he struggled not to become enraged. "Why on earth would you think that?" he wanted to know. "You knew she was having a difficult enough time blending in and being accepted, and by deliberately going behind her back like you did, you validated Maggie Rorick and everyone else who has shunned her. If they see you alienating Scarlett, then you have only supported their cause. Do you have any idea how badly that hurt her? What you did was horrible and I'm ashamed of you."

Arabella looked up from her hands, studying her son's hard expression, before averting her gaze again.

"What do you want me to do, Archer?" she asked. "How can I make this up to you both?"

"You can start by apologizing to Scarlett. I can't promise she'll accept your apology, though, and I wouldn't blame her if she didn't. You've done a lot of damage."

Arabella's expression turned remorseful. "I truly didn't mean to hurt her."

"I find that hard to believe."

"May I at least speak with her?"

Archer sighed faintly, watching his mother's hopeful features, before raising his eyebrows in resignation.

"I'll see if she wants to talk to you," he replied. "If she doesn't, don't push it."

"I would appreciate it if you would ask her."

Archer got up and went into the dining room, to the second set of stairs that led to the upper floor. But before he took the steps, he begrudgingly went into the kitchen and asked Henry to find Mrs. Bayse and ask her to make Arabella a cup of tea. It was a hospitality thing and the right thing to do on such a cold night. Even if he was mad at his mother, he wasn't beyond being concerned for her comfort.

He found Scarlett where he had left her, sitting on their bed working on her computer. He stood next to the bed, hands in his jeans pockets, hoping his mother's request didn't upset Scarlett too much. He'd come to know a woman of supreme patience over the past four months, but he also knew that when she was pushed beyond her limit, she could get very fired up. He remembered that aspect of her personality from the night in the rectory when she almost beat Declan Knobbs within an inch of his life.

"My mother wants to speak with you," he said quietly.

Scarlett looked up from the computer screen. "What about?"

He shrugged. "I think she wants to apologize for the whole fundraising thing," he said. "She's reached that point where she realizes what she did. Will you come downstairs and hear her?"

Scarlett's gaze lingered on him a moment before looking back to the computer screen. But she didn't try to type or move the mouse around. She just stared at it.

"I don't know," she murmured. "I'm just so over it, you know? She did what she did and it happened, but I don't want to go back and hash it all out. That all happened during a very bad time, with the baby and all, and I really don't want to relive it. I'm not sure I want to talk about it, not even to hear an apology."

"I know, love."

"But I can't go through the rest of my life playing the victim of your mother's behavior. At some point, I'm going to have to be the bigger person."

"I'm not going to advise you either way. If you don't want to talk to her, you don't have to."

She looked up at him. "Be honest with me," she said. "What would *you* do?"

He drew in a long, pensive breath and sat down on the edge of the bed. "Well," he said after a moment. "My mother isn't going to go away. When you and I get married, she's going to be a part of your life for the rest of your life and, God willing, grandmother to any children you and I have. You can't ignore her. My mother isn't a bad person at heart, Scarlett. I think she just made a very bad choice. I'm as angry with her as anyone, probably more, but even I've come to the point where I'm willing to forgive and move on. Anger is such a destructive emotion and I don't want it in our lives."

Scarlett listened to him seriously. "I don't feel anger," she said. "I just feel hurt. And disappointed, wondering what I did to deserve her betrayal. Other than being American, I really don't know what I did. I can't figure it out."

"The only way you'll find out for sure is if you ask her."

He had a point. Scarlett set the computer aside and got off the bed. Dressed in cream leggings and a big cream-colored sweater that hung to her knees, she pulled on a pair of slipper booties and headed downstairs with Archer behind her. By the time she entered the living room, Mrs. Bayse was just bringing in a tray with a tea service on it. As she set it down, Arabella caught sight of Scarlett and Archer, and she rose to her feet.

Scarlett was struck by the woman's expression. There was such apprehension and sorrow in it. Before she could say anything, Arabella spoke.

"Scarlett, I'm sorry," she said. "I didn't mean to hurt you by excluding you from the church fundraiser. I suppose I couldn't understand why someone so new to our community would want to raise money for our church and I suppose if you get down to it, I really didn't think you were serious. No, wait; that's not entirely true. I think the truth of the matter is that I didn't want anyone but me in control of such an effort so I stole it from you. Yes, I did. I did and I'm truly and deeply sorry."

Scarlett hadn't been expecting such a speech. A little surprised, she suddenly didn't feel so defensive or hurt. Arabella had let her guard down and that told Scarlett that the woman was sorry, indeed. Even if she was only really sorry that her actions had caused a rift between her and her son, still, she was making the effort to apologize. And it was Christmas, after all. Scarlett just didn't have the energy or desire to keep up the fight or continue the hurt.

"You know," she said thoughtfully, crossing her arms. "You and I haven't had such a good beginning. Things seem to have gone wrong since the moment we met."

Arabella nodded timidly. "I suppose it's my fault," she said. "I do speak my mind at times and I've been known to make hasty decisions."

Scarlett shrugged. "Maybe," she said. "I do know that you were right about my girls and I not moving into Phipps Hall after having only known Archer a matter of days. I agreed with you on that point. And as for the fundraiser, I will admit that I've been wracking my brain trying to figure out what I did to cause you to undermine me. I'm sure there must have been something."

Arabella shook her head. "No, dear. You did nothing."

"Not even take Archer away from you?"

Arabella looked stunned by the question. "What do you mean?"

Scarlett uncrossed her arms and planted herself in a winged-back chair near the hearth. "You had your son and your grandson all to yourself for many years," she said. "Suddenly, he meets a woman he's crazy for and you feel neglected and ignored. Maybe you stole my fundraising idea to get back at me for taking Archer away."

Arabella sank to the couch, her expression wracked with thought. After several moments, she sighed. "Oh... my," she muttered. "Perhaps it's possible. Perhaps there is some jealousy there. I hadn't consciously thought on it but now that you say that... it's very possible."

Scarlett was in a particularly forgiving mood. "It was never my intention to take your son away from you, Arabella," she said. "He's *your* son. I would never do that. But I fell in love with the man and we have a very happy life together. We want you to be a part of it, but I want there to be total honesty and trust between us or that relationship is going to be very difficult for all of us, Archer most of all. He loves you, and he loves me, and he wants us all to get along."

Arabella was nodding in agreement, her gaze moving between Scarlett and her enormous son. "You're right," she agreed. "But... but in my defense, if I did feel jealousy, perhaps it was because I am very protective of Archer. His first wife put him through hell and I didn't want to see that happen again."

Scarlett looked over at Archer, who was slowly shaking his head at his mother. "It's not about me," he told her quietly.

Arabella didn't back down. "This *is* about you, Archer," she insisted. "I'm sorry if this isn't an appropriate forum for this, but if we're going to put everything on the table, then let's put all of it out. I don't want to see you go through with Scarlett what you went through with Christiana. Perhaps some part of me doesn't trust her, or any woman, when it comes to you. Christiana was emotionally and verbally abusive to you and to Henry, and I'll be damned if I'm going to stand by and watch that happen again."

Archer was starting to turn red in the face but a soft gesture from Scarlett stopped his building anger.

"Do you really think I would ever treat Archer or Henry poorly, ever?" she asked. "Look around you, Arabella; look at this home. It's a happy home with happy children and happy parents. It's warm and wonderful. We love each other and you are simply going to have to trust me and be happy for your son. I understand you're protective of him; I understand that you are jealous of me because of him. But please don't penalize me for something another woman did to him. That's not fair. I love your son very much, and I love Henry very much, and I'd like to love you, too, but you really haven't given me a reason to."

Arabella was looking at Scarlett with sorrow. After a moment, she pulled the glove off of one of her hands and reached over to the tea service, taking a cup of tea. Her hand was shaking as she held it up to her lips and took a timid sip.

"I'm sorry," she finally said. "I shouldn't have done what I did. The festival is still several months off and I would be honored if you would co-chair it with me. I would sincerely love your help and guidance."

Scarlett smiled faintly. "That's very nice of you to ask," she said. "But I've got my hands full doing music workshops after school and I'm afraid it's all I can handle. But thank you for asking; I appreciate it."

Arabella was disappointed but she forced a smile. "Maybe... maybe we can do something together in the future."

"I'd like that."

Arabella sipped at her tea, unsure what more to say or where the conversation should go from there. Archer finally stood up and poured Scarlett a cup of tea, which she gratefully accepted. As they sat there in odd silence, the door that led in from the courtyard opened and several teenagers spilled into the utility room and eventually the kitchen.

Noise filled the house and Archer left the quiet living room, heading into the kitchen where Morgan, her boyfriend, and several other young people were beginning to raid the refrigerator. Archer stood in the doorway and put his hands on his hips.

"What's going on in here?" he demanded. "Who let in the herd of cattle?"

The kids giggled, chuckling at Morgan's gigantic stepfather. "We're hungry," Morgan declared.

Archer watched her dig into the refrigerator and hand stuff out to waiting boys. "Hold on there," he pushed the door shut. "I thought you lot just ate takeout?"

Morgan made a face. "We didn't get any," she said. "Some of the other kids hogged it all up."

Archer shook his head, reached into his pocket, and pulled

out his wallet. He fingered three ten pound notes and handed them over to Matt Summerlin, standing next to Morgan.

"Go into town and get something to eat," he said. "Get what you can for thirty pounds. And drive carefully, Summerlin; the roads are slick."

Matt nodded eagerly as he, Morgan, Laura and a couple of other kids fled to the door. Alexandra suddenly jumped up from the couch.

"Can I go, too?" she begged.

Morgan sneered at her sister. "No!"

Alexandra turned her pleading eyes to Archer. "Why can't I go?"

Morgan chimed in and the two began arguing as Archer stepped out of the way. Fighting females intimidated him. He poked his head into the dining room, catching sight of Scarlett and his mother still sitting in the living room.

"Scarlett," he called. "A little help, please."

Teacup in hand, Scarlett stood up and went into the kitchen. When the girls saw her, they immediately quieted because their mother didn't like it when they argued. Between the two of them, they explained the situation from opposing sides and Scarlett made the decision that Alexandra would remain while Morgan and her friends went out. Unhappy, Alexandra went back to the couch to sit with Freddie and Henry, who was still pouting himself.

Archer watched the younger children on the couch, being more of a softy than Scarlett was. He felt rather sorry for them. As he turned to say something to Scarlett, he noticed his mother standing in the doorway to the dining room, watching all of the happenings.

"Mother," he said. "Edward called and said that one of the mares is in foal tonight. Henry wants to watch."

Arabella nodded. "That is what Edward told me as well,"

her gaze found her grandson, sitting over on the couch. Her expression grew wistful. "He's grown so much since I last saw him."

Hearing his grandmother's voice, Henry jumped up from the couch and ran over to her, taking her hand.

"Can I go home with grandmother?" he asked his father eagerly.

Archer looked at his son, seeing in that moment two distinct things; Henry had missed his grandmother very much. He also referred to Phipps Hall as home. Archer was coming to think that the move to the lodge might have affected Henry more than the boy let on. Henry was a quiet, polite boy, and more than likely just rolled with the punches as his father moved him into a house with basically three strange women. Feeling somewhat uncertain and guilty in his treatment of his son, Archer nodded his head.

"If you want to," he said.

Alexandra heard the conversation and she, too, jumped off the couch with Freddie trotting beside her.

"Can I go, too?" she begged.

Archer looked at Scarlett, who gave a smile and nodded. "Get your coat," he told the girl.

The kids ran excitedly upstairs, followed by the dog. They could hear running overhead, doors slamming, and a dog bark. It was joyful chaos. Arabella set her teacup down and pulled tight on her gloves.

"Shall they return with me, Archer?" she asked. "Or do you want to bring them over?"

Again, Archer looked to Scarlett, who didn't seem to have any opinion on the subject. He turned to his mother.

"You can take them," he said. "I'll be over in a while to bring them back."

Arabella nodded, fussing with her gloves as she looked between her son and Scarlett. Her fidgeting slowed.

"I...," she stopped, then started again. "I want to thank you for seeing me tonight. I hope the situation between us is better from now on. I will try to do my part."

Archer didn't say anything. After a moment, he simply hugged his mother. "Thank you for coming over. It means a great deal to us both."

Arabella was softened by the hug, by the fact that she was again on speaking terms with her beloved Archer. Flushed, she fought to keep the smile off her face because she just wasn't the type to show a lot of emotion. Uncomfortable, yet relieved and happy, she shifted the subject because she didn't deal well when it came to speaking of her feelings.

"When are you two planning on getting married?" she asked. "I fear I've been on the outskirts a bit and haven't heard when the happy event will take place."

Archer looked at Scarlett with a grin. "Ironic you should ask that question," he said to his mother. "I was in the process of proposing tonight when you showed up."

Arabella's eyes widened. "Truly?" she looked between her son and Scarlett. "What's the happy word?"

Scarlett laughed and went to Archer, wrapping her arms around his waist. He put a big arm around her shoulders, hugging her.

"The happy word is yes, of course," she said. "But we haven't talked about a date. Maybe after the holidays."

Arabella threw up her hands. "Why not *during* the holidays?" she wanted to know. "What better way to celebrate the new year? Why not have a Christmas day wedding? We'll all be together, anyway. It would be the perfect time."

Scarlett and Archer looked at each other. "I don't know," Scarlett finally said. "I hadn't really thought about it. I wanted my parents to attend but I suppose we could do it at Christmas without them."

Archer hugged her gently. "We can wait until your parents can make plans," he said quietly. "We don't have to rush it."

Scarlett thought on that a moment. "Actually," she said, "I think Christmas day would be perfect. Can we do it at Phipps Hall?"

Arabella beamed; she couldn't help herself. "Of course, my dear," she said. "Would... would you like for me to help you make arrangements or do you want to do it all yourself?"

Scarlett smiled at the woman, thinking it might be a good time to show some faith. She needed to establish a relationship with Arabella and maybe this was a good start. Besides, she didn't care about the details too much other than her dress and her vows. She could leave the rest up to an old woman who was very eager to help.

"Would you mind planning it?" she asked. "I'm so busy these days. It would help me so much if I knew you were taking care of everything. Archer and I will just show up; you can handle the details."

Arabella was thrilled to death. "Thank you," she said gratefully. "I would love to plan it. Archer, are you all right with that?"

Archer had Scarlett all wrapped up in a big bear hug. He sighed dreamily. "Ecstatic," he said. "Do your worst, Mother."

Arabella's eyes twinkled. "I most certainly will."

THIRTEEN
EARLY FEBRUARY

"I DIDN'T GET a chance to congratulate you on your wedding," Calvin was standing on the curb as Archer climbed out of his car.

Archer gave him an impatient look. "You're joking, right?"

"What do you mean?"

"We're at a crime scene and you're congratulating me on my wedding?"

Calvin flinched. "Bad taste, eh?"

"Rotten taste," Archer said with some disgust, his gaze drifting over the neat, brick row house in York about three miles north of Ludbourne. "I thought I wasn't to be called in on any more of these."

Calvin nodded sorrowfully, his gaze moving over the house and yard. "I know," he said, "but the chief wanted you to know about this one. There was another note."

Archer already knew that. He'd suspected as much. But it didn't prevent him from sighing heavily in something that came out sounding like a growl.

"Bugger," he hissed. "We've gone months without anything. Why now? Why again?"

Calvin shook his head as they began to walk towards the house. "This one is bad, Archer," he said quietly. "A mother and her two daughters. Word has already gotten out and the press has been all over this site this morning."

Archer looked down the street, noting the people grouped up on the other side of the police caution tape. "Neighbors?"

Calvin saw where he was looking. "They're terrified," he said. "But no one saw or heard anything unusual last night, just like with the other murders. Everything was quiet. More than that, forensics has determined that this murder, as well as the previous two, had no signs of forced entry."

"That means the killer had easy access."

"They knew him."

"Possibly."

They continued on towards the house, each to their own thoughts, although their thoughts at this point differed somewhat. Archer was thinking about the message that was once again left for him while Calvin was thinking something entirely different yet something Archer needed to be aware of.

"Before we go inside, I need to mention something," Calvin said, stopping Archer at the door. "If you map out the past three murders, each one draws closer and closer to Ludbourne. Didn't you say that's where you're living now?"

Archer nodded slowly. "Scarlett bought a home there and that's where we've been living as of late."

Calvin sighed heavily. "Archer, the chief already knows this and he's asked me to tell you," he lowered his voice and pulled a piece of paper out of his pocket. "This is what the Cutter's note says verbatim:

'Darkling, I listen; and, for many a time
I have been half in love with easeful Death
To take into the air my quiet breath;

Now more than ever seems it rich to die.
Die, my Scarlet bird, as thy wings are clipped
Never to fly again'."

Calvin looked up from the paper in his hand to see that Archer had turned ashen. He just stared at Calvin for a long, painful moment before turning away from the front door, wandering back out into the yard. Calvin followed.

"That first part of the note," Archer was shaken and struggling not to show it. "That's not original... I think it's Keats. He did that before, years ago, using passages from Shelley."

"I know," Calvin said quietly.

"He mixes classic prose with his own sometimes," Archer was trying to work through the clue and not let his fear get the better of him. "But again, he mentioned Scarlett. He's baiting me again. He knows I'm showing up at these crime scenes and he's baiting me."

Calvin sighed heavily. "Get her out of York," he said quietly. "You have other property, Archer. Move her somewhere else and keep her safe."

"And then what?" Archer turned to look at him, struggling with his composure. "Calvin, you need to understand that this sick bastard made my life hell ten years ago. Now he's resurfaced and he's determined to make my life hell again, only this time, he's threatening my family. What do I do? Do I keep moving around the rest of our lives, hoping we stay one step ahead of a killer, or do I take a stand and stop this bloke once and for all?"

He was agitated and Calvin didn't blame him. "If it were me, I'd...."

Archer cut him off as he began marching back towards his car. "Where's the chief?"

Calvin was trailing after him. "He was here a little while ago," he said. "I would imagine he's gone back to headquarters."

Archer opened his car door so hard that the entire car bobbed sideways. "That's where I'm going," he snapped. "Like hell I'm off this case. I'm on it now and I'm lead. This isn't going to happen again, do you hear me?"

Before Calvin could answer, Archer slammed the door and put the car into gear, pulling a screeching U-turn and heading off in the opposite direction.

—

"Mom!" Alexandra was shouting as she rode a big, chocolate brown horse around the ring. "Look!"

The first of February had dawned a bright day amidst weeks of snow and overcast skies. It was also the first day that Alexandra had been able to truly ride her Christmas gift from Archer, a big beautiful jumper named Snapdragon. The weather had been so bad following Christmas day that all Alexandra had been able to do was walk the horse in the shed row around the barn. But with the weather clearing up this morning, Edward saddled the silky brown horse and Alexandra had been riding for two solid hours.

Scarlett waved at her daughter. "I see you."

Alexandra was beside herself with joy. "I'm going to jump her!"

Scarlett just waved her daughter on with a grin, watching as Alexandra took the horse over a series of one foot barriers. The horse had a smooth gait and smooth lines as it lunged over the barriers and Alexandra was thrilled. She took the horse in a big circle and took the barriers again.

"Aren't you cold?" Arabella approached from the big stone stairs that led up to the house. "It's chilly out here."

Scarlett grinned at the woman. "Look at me," she opened up her arms, showing her the heavy coat, boots, scarf, hat and gloves. "I look like a tick ready to pop."

Arabella laughed as she came to the rail, watching Alexandra jump barriers. Together, she and Scarlett watched the girl ride 'round and 'round.

"She certainly loves that horse," Arabella said.

Scarlett nodded, eyes glued to her daughter. "I have a feeling we're not going to get her off of it today," she said. "She's waited thirty-seven days since she got the horse for the weather to clear up. She's going to keep riding until we drag her off."

"I'm surprised she didn't try to sneak the horse into her bedroom."

"I think she did. I found hay in the kitchen the other day."

They shared a chuckle until Arabella sobered. "I come with a message, Lady Phipps."

Scarlett gave her a quirky grin at the use of her new title. "From whom?"

"Your husband," Arabella replied. "He called the house looking for you a few minutes ago and I was forced to tell him that you were still outside watching your daughter. He says to tell you to get inside because it's too cold."

Scarlett snickered. "Call him back and tell him that I said 'make me'."

Arabella lifted an eyebrow, although it was in good humor. "Do you really want me to?"

"Yes. It will make him come home faster if he thinks he's going to get a chance to spank me."

Arabella snickered and turned for the house. "He's already on his way home. You're going to need a horse yourself to escape him once he arrives."

Scarlett let the woman go, turning to watch her daughter so joyfully ride. Freddie the dog was beside Scarlett, unhappy because he was on a leash and not allowed to go in the ring with Alexandra. Scarlett finally sat down on one of the stone benches that lined the arena, petting the frustrated dog as they both watched Alexandra jump her new horse.

Eventually, Henry came outside, all bundled up against the weather. Scarlett caught sight of the boy on the other side of the arena, heading for the barn, and she knew he had sneaked out without his grandmother's knowledge because he was sick with a cold and had been told to stay in the house. When he came out astride his black and white pony and joined Alexandra in the ring, Scarlett didn't have the heart to scold him. They'd all been cooped up for weeks because of the foul weather. She didn't blame the boy for wanting to get out.

"Henry," she called as he trotted by the rail. "Your father is on his way home. What do you think he's going to say when he sees you out here?"

Henry was trotting his pony in big circles. "He'll think I'm feeling better!"

Scarlett just wriggled her eyebrows and let the boy ride. She sat there, watching the kids and petting the dog, as the wind picked up and the afternoon advanced. Clouds were starting to form overhead and Scarlett glanced up more than once to see how the weather was progressing. Just as she was thinking about calling a halt to the kids riding circles in the arena, she heard footsteps over her left shoulder. As she turned around, Archer put his hands on her shoulders and kissed her forehead.

"Your skin is cold, love," he said as he took a seat beside her and put a big arm around her. "How long have you been out here?"

She snuggled against him. Even the lonely dog put his head on Archer's thigh. "A while," she said. "I can't get Alexandra off the horse."

Archer grinned as he watched the young girl jump the horse

tirelessly. "I'm glad she's finally able to enjoy the animal," he said. "She had to wait a long time to ride her Christmas present."

"Which you should have cleared with me first, by the way."

He sighed contritely, biting his lip to keep from grinning. "Are you going to berate me again?"

"Probably."

"When will the beatings stop?"

"When I have satisfaction."

He laughed low in his throat. "My angel, I have already apologized profusely for gifting my stepdaughter with a new horse and not letting you in on the surprise. I guess I wanted it to be a surprise for everyone. What more can I do?"

She grinned and shrugged, and he hugged her fiercely, kissing her cheek. The horse surprise had been a running gag between them since December twenty-fifth, when Archer had surprised Alexandra with the animal. Scarlett couldn't get too angry about it, considering how happy it had made her daughter, but she wanted to make sure Archer understood she wasn't happy about the fact that she wasn't consulted on such a major gift in her daughter's life. He understood, all too well, but was usually able to get out of it with some humor and groveling, like today. He continued to hug her until he noticed his son ride by.

"I thought Henry was sick?" he said, concerned.

Scarlett remained casual. "He says he's feeling better."

He watched his son trot around on the pony. "Henry!" he called to the boy. "Come over here!"

He stood up and Scarlett stood up next to him. "Don't be harsh with him," she put her hand on his arm. "It's the first day in weeks that the weather has been good enough for the kids to come out in. It's not fair that he's cooped up in the house while Alex is out here riding."

Archer patted her hand. "I'm not going to be harsh with him," he assured her. "I just want to see how he's feeling."

They both came to the rail, standing there as Henry dutifully plodded over with his pony. The boy looked contritely at his father.

"Hi," he said.

Archer cocked an eyebrow. "Hi," he replied. "Come over here. Let me feel your forehead."

Unhappy, Henry climbed off the pony and went to the rail, where his father put his big hand on the boy's forehead to feel for fever. He had Scarlett feel the boy, who was reluctant to agree he still seemed to have a slight fever. That was all Archer needed to bundle everyone, including Alexandra, up into the house.

The weather was clouding up by the time both horses were cooled, watered and stabled, and Archer had two unhappy kids on his hands as they went into the house. Giant Phipps Hall opened up before them as they entered through the courtyard, into the bottom level of the house where the billiard room and other store rooms were located. By the time he got them up into the kitchen, Alexandra was complaining of extreme fatigue and Henry was starting to cough. Archer put on the kettle while Scarlett took temperatures and gave both kids a dose of cold medicine. When the tea was ready, the kids took theirs in big mugs upstairs as Scarlett put Alexandra into the bathtub and down the hall, Archer did the same with Henry.

Once the younger kids were bathed and in pajamas, Archer and Scarlett met up in the hall outside of the master suite. Archer took one look at his wife, saw how exhausted she appeared, and swept her into his arms, carrying her off into the enormous bedroom. Scarlett giggled at his impetuousness, her arms around his neck as he used his foot to slam the door behind them. He didn't put her down until they reached the enormous bed and even then, he fell down on the bed beside her.

"How was work?" Scarlett asked, a usual question to him at the end of a work day.

He kicked his shoes off and snuggled up with her. "Not too good," he admitted. "You and I have things to discuss."

She looked at him seriously. "What?"

He sighed, pushing a piece of stray hair off her forehead as he studied her face. "It would seem that the Cutter has committed another murder."

Scarlett's warm expression transformed into one of fear. "Oh, God," she breathed. "I didn't see anything on Skynews."

"You will eventually," he said. "We can't keep it under wraps forever. The media is already sniffing around, guessing that we've got a serial murderer on the loose. They just don't know that we believe it's the Yorkshire Cutter."

"So what are you going to do?" she asked seriously.

He shifted on the pillows, lying on his back as she propped herself up on his chest, looking down at him. "I know you love the lodge but I believe it will be better if we all stay here," he told her. "This place is like a fortress, alarmed, and we've got four full-time security people that patrol the grounds. I'd feel much better having you here rather than at the lodge where there simply aren't as many security measures."

She watched him a moment. "He said something about me again, didn't he?"

Archer couldn't lie to her. "Yes."

"What?"

He shrugged. "The usual rhetoric. It doesn't matter. But I have requested to be lead inspector on this case and the chief has allowed it. I'm going to catch the bastard this time, I swear it. The fact that he mentions you... when I find him, he'll be lucky if I don't kill him myself and call it self-defense."

Scarlett stared at him for a moment before rolling off his chest. Lying flat on her back, she gazed up at the ornate plaster ceiling above the bed.

"Who *is* this guy, Archer?" she demanded. "He ran you ragged ten years ago and now he's back... but the question is why? What made him come back?"

Archer was looking at her as she stared up at the ceiling. "I've been thinking the same thing, which is why I asked to be put on the case," he said. "This isn't about killing. It's about me, for whatever reason. The last time he showed up was ten years ago when I was new as an inspector and, not coincidentally, Christiana and I first got together."

Scarlett looked at him. "Did he ever mention her in his notes?"

Archer nodded reluctantly. "He did."

She sat bolt upright and looked at him. "So it's someone who's been watching you for God knows how many years and starts killing when you get serious with a woman?" she raised her voice. "Is that it?"

He put his hand on her arm, trying to keep her calm. "It looks that way, but there's more to it than that, I'm sure."

"What more can there be?" she was off the bed, growing agitated. "Did you ever stop to think that the killer isn't a man but a woman? Someone who's jealous every time you get into a relationship? From what you've told me about these cases, it really seems that it's all about getting your attention, don't you think?"

He watched her as she paced. "We've been all through these theories, love," he said quietly. "It's hard to say if the killer is male or female because we've never been able to get DNA from the crime scenes to match up to a database. The killer, whoever he is, is either very careful or has no criminal record and isn't in our data base. They know who I am, watch my life on a daily basis it seems like, and writes notes for me at crime scenes that seem more like a rage killing than anything else."

By this time, Scarlett had cooled somewhat. "Rage killing? What does that mean?"

"It means the victims aren't targeted as individuals, but more as an object to release violent emotion. They're just objects."

"Do you think the killer is thinking of you when she kills these people, taking her frustrations out on innocent people?"

He lifted his big shoulders. "It's possible," he said softly. "Anything is possible."

"Do you think she's going to try to kill me or the girls?"

He shook his head firmly. "That's not going to happen."

"How do you know?"

He stood up from the bed. "Because it's not," he was starting to get agitated. "Angel, I go through that exact same fear on a daily basis and I'm telling you that nothing is going to happen to you. I won't let it. Don't you trust me anymore than that?"

"It isn't about trusting you. Of course I trust you. But there are times when you're going to be at work and I'm going to be here with the kids, alone. What's going to stop this killer from getting into the house?"

He could see this was heading into an argument. She was upset and he was becoming upset, so he slowed down and took a deep breath.

"I told you that this house has a full time security force and a state of the art alarm system," he said calmly. "What more do you want me to do, Scarlett? Please tell me so I can make sure you feel comfortable and safe."

She just shook her head and turned away, feeling increasingly frightened and upset. "I think the killer is a woman and I think this is her way of controlling you," she said. "Maybe it's an old girlfriend or some woman who has admired you from afar.

This isn't about murder; it's all about control, and she's controlling you completely."

"That's not true."

"Yes, it is. We have to change our entire life because of this person, so it's not just you she's controlling, but me and my girls, also. My girls have had a hard enough time on this move to England without having to deal with this bullshit on top of everything."

"I'll repeat my question; what do you want me to do?"

Scarlett didn't know. She was unnerved and ruled by fear at the moment. Without another word, she crossed the room and went into the enormous master bathroom. Archer didn't follow her but he listened very carefully to what she was doing; he could hear her banging around a little bit, opening cabinets, and then he heard the bathtub faucet turn on.

Water was pouring like a fire hose into the massive bathtub and he continued to stand next to the bed, listening, debating on whether or not he should go into the bathroom. He was fearful that their argument would only continue should he follow her so he backed off and went into his closet, changing into his casual pajama bottoms as he turned on the television. There was an all-sports channel that had a hockey game on so he lay back on the big couch in the master suite to watch it.

———

Archer woke up on the couch. The last thing he remembered was closing his eyes as he listened to the hockey game. Now the television was off, as were the lights. Glancing at his watch, he saw that it was almost three in the morning. With a hissed curse, he sat up on the couch and wiped his eyes.

Glancing over his shoulder at his enormous king-sized bed, even in the dark he could see that it was empty. He tried not to be concerned as he stood up and looked around for Scarlett, wandering into the giant sitting room adjoined to the master suite to see that it was empty, too. At that point, he began his methodical search of the house for his wife.

He didn't have far to go. He found her in Alexandra's room with her and Alexandra in one double bed and Henry sound asleep in the other. As Archer quietly made his way towards the beds, he could see books strewn about and one lying on the pillow next to Scarlett's head. He stood there a moment, gazing down at her, wondering if he should wake her. After a moment, he bent down and gently kissed her cheek. He couldn't help himself.

Scarlett stirred and her eyes rolled up. She turned slightly to see Archer standing over her, his big arms braced on the bed. When their eyes met, he smiled.

"I was missing you," he whispered, leaning down to kiss her again on the chin. "Do you want to come to bed?"

Scarlett didn't say a word as she rolled away from Alexandra and sleepily sat up. Archer bent over and scooped her up, carrying her silently out of the room as she wrapped her arms around his neck and held him tightly. Once they reached the master bedroom, Archer closed the door with his foot and continued to carry her into the bed chamber.

"I'm sorry I got mad at you," Scarlett murmured. "I shouldn't have done that."

He squeezed her. "No need to apologize," he whispered. "I'm sorry to have upset you so much."

"I'm just scared," she yawned as he laid her down on the bed. "When I get scared, I get mad."

He climbed into bed after her, snuggling down with her. "I've seen you when you get scared and mad," he snorted. "Remember the night I met you? I thought you were going to take Declan Knobbs' head off."

She smiled, sleepy, her eyes closing. "That was mostly because I was mad, not scared. If you hadn't stopped me, I probably would have beaten the crap out of him."

He laughed low. "You're a tough woman, Lady Phipps."

She rolled over so she was facing him in the bed, putting her arms around him as he pulled her close.

"Are you sure we can't go back to the lodge?"

He sighed, his face in the top of her head. "I'd prefer we didn't."

"Can we at least go over and pick up our stuff?"

"Of course," he replied. "We'll go over tomorrow when I get off work."

"What's your schedule going to be now that you're on this case?"

"Hard to say. Probably a three – twelve; three days a week, twelve hours a day, but given the notoriety of this case, it's hard to say. I'll probably be putting in several days a week."

It was her turn to sigh as she began to drift off again. "Can I still teach the music workshop after school?" she asked, muffled by his chest. "We're working on something right now and I really don't want to disappoint the kids. I really love doing this."

He was quiet a moment. "I know it makes you happy," he said. "I don't see any reason why you can't keep doing the workshop, but I will be adamant about you not going anywhere alone or doing anything alone. If I have to hire a bodyguard for you, I will."

"That's your call, honey. You're the security expert."

The conversation died and she drifted off to sleep, little baby snores filling the still night air. Morning was just a few hours away and Archer forced himself to stop thinking about security measures and Scarlett's safety, and shut his mind down for the night.

FOURTEEN

HE WAS KIND OF CREEPY.

Well, not exactly creepy, but more like a shadow, as strong and silent as the grave. It was odd having someone so close to her that she didn't even know, but Archer knew the man and had gladly hired him to protect Scarlett. Two weeks after the latest note from the crime scene, Archer had come home after work one night with one of the biggest men Scarlett had ever seen.

His name was Ryan Sheffield and he was a private detective who also did some bodyguard work for big-name politicians, which is how Archer knew the man. They'd worked together a few times in the past. Ryan stood a little over six feet tall but he was built like a bull. Bald, with a very heavy Lancaster accent, he was difficult to understand and didn't say much, which was a good thing considering he spoke as if he had marbles in his mouth. His job was to mirror Scarlett's movements and to be aware of her whereabouts every hour of the day that Archer wasn't with her. He was also the chauffer, something Scarlett had to get used to. She was an independent American woman so the introduction of Sheffield took some getting used to. She tried not to hate it, knowing it was necessary.

On a rather bright and cold day in late February, Scarlett had spent the morning at the big piano in the giant main parlor of Phipps Hall, scripting out some music for her after school music workshop. When she first started the workshop, she'd had a brilliant idea; much like the church fundraiser idea that never happened, she had the same idea for a fundraiser for St. Lawrence and using the kids as advertisement was a great tool for that purpose.

Even though they were a private school, they were still in need of newer computer equipment and other items. She thought it might be fun to do a music video, post it on YouTube, and get people to donate to support the school. She also hoped her name might carry some weight to those who would remember her from her mall days. That was the "something special" project she had told Archer about, an endeavor the kids had been working very hard on. Moreover, focusing on the fundraiser gave her something to do and took her mind off the psychopathic killer who seemed intent on harassing her husband. It kept her mind off being scared.

The vast parlor was still and silent this clear morning as she worked. Ryan stayed out of the way. He was off in the kitchen reading the newspaper and eating whatever Mrs. Bayse would feed him. It was rather comical because Mrs. Bayse was leery of the newest addition to the Phipps household and she fed him regularly as if making offerings to an angry god. So while Ryan ate, read the paper, and paid vigilant attention to whatever Lady Phipps was doing in the parlor with her music, Scarlett's cell phone went off close to lunchtime. Seated in front of the piano with a pencil in hand as she wrote on sheet music, Scarlett set the pencil down and answered the phone.

It was Fulford School calling, the nurse's infirmary to be

exact. Morgan was apparently in the infirmary with bad menstrual cramps so Scarlett let the nurse know she'd be over to pick up her daughter shortly. As she stood up from the piano, her shadow was already in the doorway, having heard the phone ring, and she informed Ryan that they would be heading out to Fulford to pick up Morgan. He went to get the car as Scarlett went upstairs to get her shoes on.

Scarlett still wasn't entirely comfortable being driven around by a bodyguard but she settled in and forced herself to get used to it. It just seemed weird riding in a car with another man. Ryan drove her along the main road leading into York, heading south of the city where Fulford was located. He parked the car on the curb in front of the tree-shrouded institution, climbing out when Scarlett did and following her up the stone walkway to the main entry where she would check in.

As they neared the front entry, a body emerged. Scarlett glanced up, moving aside reflexively so she wouldn't run into the person, realizing too late that it was Maggie Rorick.

Truthfully, Scarlett was a little shocked to see the woman. She'd gone months without seeing her, even at church, mostly because Maggie had decided to attend another church in the next town given the fact that Archer Phipps had made his displeasure with her known.

Since the initial flare-up of gossip had occurred, there really hadn't been anything else, at least from what Scarlett knew, mostly because she kept herself away from the parents of Fulford. Her friends were all at St. Lawrence so she didn't give a second thought to those rough early days at Fulford.

Until now. Face to face with Maggie, who looked equally surprised to see her, she knew the smart and tactful thing would be to simply keep going without a word to the woman. That would have been to take the high road. Moreover, she was now Lady Phipps and had a station in the community to uphold. She didn't want to embarrass Archer. But the feisty American in her just couldn't let it go, not when the woman standing in front of her had made those early days in England so awful. She seriously resisted the urge to punch her right in the face.

Maggie was tight-lipped and pale as she bobbed in a stiff curtsy. "Ma'am," she greeted purely because protocol dictated.

Scarlett watched the woman as she dropped her head and scooted away as fast as she could without actually running. Maggie reached the bottom of the steps when Scarlett called out to her.

"Maggie?" she said, rather firmly.

Maggie came to an unsteady halt, turning hesitantly in Scarlett's direction. When their eyes met, Scarlett could see that the woman was rattled, and that knowledge gave her confidence. Something deep inside her was calling for some kind of satisfaction at having been hurt by this woman. Although she hadn't reflected on those days since they had happened, now they were weighing heavily upon her.

"Ma'am?" Maggie responded reluctantly.

Scarlett stared into that plain, round face, cocking her head thoughtfully after a moment. She wanted to say so much but only one thing truly came to mind. "Can I ask you a question?"

Maggie was nervous. She was also very aware of the mammoth man standing a few feet behind Scarlett like a guard dog.

"Of... of course," she replied.

"How is Alyce?"

Maggie looked shocked at the question; it sincerely hadn't been what she had been expecting. "She... she is very well, thank you for asking."

"Is she in school today?"

"No, ma'am. She still has another year yet before she'll be in school."

"She's a very sweet little girl. You'll tell her I said 'hi', okay?"

"Of course."

"One more thing."

"What's that, ma'am?"

"Why in the world were you so awful to me when my girls and I first moved here? You didn't even know us. I'm just curious what your motivation was."

Maggie was back to being nervous and pale. Her gaze shifted anxiously between Scarlett and the bodyguard.

"I...," she stammered. "I don't know what you mean, Ma'am."

Scarlett rolled her eyes. "Cut the crap, Maggie," she said. "For God's sake, at least take responsibility for what you said and did. Give me a reason to at least have an inkling of respect for you. Even if I don't like what you did, and even if you did hurt people you didn't even know, at least take ownership of your actions and explain them to me. Maybe you had a reason I didn't even know about. Maybe I offended you somehow and you were angry with me. Was it something like that?"

Maggie was backing away, shaking her head. "You... you never offended me, Ma'am."

"So it was just because I was new and because Archer showed me attention. Is that it?"

Maggie nearly tripped over her feet trying to back away. She shook her head, struggling with her denial. "I... I'm not sure what you would have me say, Ma'am."

"The truth. I just want the truth."

Maggie stopped backing away but she wouldn't look Scarlett in the eye. She just stood there. Scarlett finally came down off the steps, gazing at the woman intently.

"Look," she said, lowering her voice. "I'm not trying to start anything, but I want you to know how badly you upset my daughter. I'm a big girl; I can take criticism and bad gossip. I can even take your petty bullshit. But when it involves my child, that's where I draw the line. Thank God that your attempts to hurt my family didn't work. We're happy and well-adjusted, and I wanted you to know that. Nothing you can say or do can hurt us, but for your own sake, I suggest you get over this gossipy trait you seem to have and grow up. You have two very beautiful daughters and I'm sure you don't want them growing up to be petty and vindictive, do you? Do you even realize that's the example you're setting for them?"

Maggie was looking at her by this time, her blue eyes big and guarded. She really didn't have anything to say so she simply shrugged her shoulders and averted her gaze. Scarlett sighed faintly.

"We don't ever have to be friends," she said quietly, "but I at least want a truce between us, okay? I won't bother you if you won't bother me. Deal?"

Again, Maggie simply shrugged and Scarlett continued.

"I'll take that as an affirmative," she said. "If we run into each other in the future, considering our children attend the same school, I'll be cordial and I expect the same from you. But I'll tell you one thing – if you bad-mouth me ever again, to anyone at this school or in this whole damn country, Archer's not the one you'll have to worry about. It's me, and I promise you'll regret it for the rest of your life. I can make you miserable like you've never known misery, I swear it. Do you understand me?"

Maggie was looking at the ground but managed a gesture that looked something like a nod of the head.

"I'm glad we had this little chat," Scarlett said softly and turned away. "I hope to see Alyce next time. Have a good day."

Content with the rules that had been established and what she had said, she was at the top of the stairs when a thin female voice rang out behind her. Scarlett came to a pause, having to peer around Ryan's bulk to catch a glimpse of Maggie still standing where she had left her.

Maggie was wrapping her sweater tightly around her body, protectively, looking rather small and forlorn. It was almost enough to make Scarlett feel sorry for her. Almost.

"Your older daughter...," she said, struggling over her words. "She tutors my Adriana in math here at the school. My daughter likes her a lot."

Scarlett's eyebrows furrowed. "I didn't know that," she said. "Morgan never told me. I knew that she tutored at lunch time, but I didn't know Adriana was one of her students."

Maggie's nervous twitching was growing worse. "She says your daughter is very helpful," she said. "Adriana is getting good marks in math now. I... I am appreciative."

"I'm glad. Have you told Morgan that?"

Maggie shook her head, overcome by her nerves and giving up altogether. She was a guilty, weak-willed, and repentant woman.

"Goodbye, Ma'am."

With that, she rushed off into the bright spring day. Scarlett watched the woman go, surprised by the revelation that Morgan was apparently tutoring Adriana. Scarlett wasn't sure why her daughter hadn't told her, but upon reflection, perhaps that was a good thing. Perhaps it meant that Morgan hadn't known or hadn't been affected by the rough beginning at Fulford the way Scarlett and Alexandra had been. In fact, Scarlett couldn't remember if she'd even told her daughter what went on. Those days had passed in such a rush. She was rather pleased to see that Morgan had, unwittingly, improved Maggie Rorick's opinion of the American invaders.

With a smile playing on her lips, Scarlett retreated into the school to collect her miserable peacemaker.

––––––––

Archer pulled up in front of St. Lawrence. It was getting dark outside, the March weather fairly moderate, so as he got out of the car, he left his overcoat in the car. He walked towards the front of the old school, noting the lights were on in the multi-purpose room off on the north side of the campus. He knew that was where he could find his wife, staying late with her music workshop.

He'd been working late when he received her call, asking him to swing by the school. He knew the kids had been working hard on their spring musical, their second musical event since the Christmas program that had been an overwhelming success. St. Lawrence had even put Scarlett on the payroll as the Music Director, but she only worked after school three days a week, and she was always home in time for dinner. She loved it.

As Archer walked towards the open door to the multi-purpose room, he could hear the kids and his wife's voice beyond. The sound of her made him smile. He found himself reflecting on the past seven months of his life, since the moment he walked into The Calcaria and saw Scarlett for the first time. So much had happened, a lifetime of things, like he couldn't remember what his life was like before he knew her. He felt so happy and settled and at peace, so in love with the woman that he didn't have words strong enough to describe how he felt. All he knew was that he felt very, very blessed.

As he entered the room, he saw Ryan seated vigilantly near the door. He also saw an entire gaggle of teenagers and pre-teens. They were gathered somewhere down near the end of the room. Then he saw his wife, dressed in jeans and a pretty top, her long dark hair gathered back in a chic ponytail. She happened to catch a glimpse of him and quickly issued instructions to the children, who looked as if they were taking positions around the end of the room.

As Archer approached the group, he noticed Morgan and her usual crew of friends as well as Alexandra. Then he saw Henry, who was jumping up and down with a big smile on his face. Archer came to a halt and pointed at his son.

"What are you doing here?" he demanded. "You're not a part of this group, are you?"

Henry looked like a jumping bean, ready to explode at any minute. "It's a surprise!"

Archer lifted an eyebrow. "Surprise?"

"Yes," Scarlett said as she approached him, a smile on her face. "We have a surprise and we were hoping you'd want to be a part of it."

He smiled at her, giving her a kiss in greeting as she came close. "What kind of a surprise?"

"Well," she said thoughtfully, glancing over her shoulder at all of the grinning faces. "I had an idea."

"What idea?"

Scarlett wound her hands around his big forearm. "This sort of goes back to your mother and the church fundraiser," she lowered her voice when discussing the touchy subject. "Your mother asked me to co-chair the event with her but I told her I was too busy with my music activities, which was true. However, when the Christmas program was over, I was left trying to decide what our new project would be. And I figured it out."

He fondled the fingers that were gripping his arm. "Is this what you were talking about not giving up?"

"Yes."

"What is it?"

Her smile grew. "I'm going to have my own fundraiser that doesn't require any help from anyone at that snooty church," she said. "Forget about those people. I'm having a fundraiser for St. Lawrence. We're going to do a music video and I'm going to post it online and get sponsors for it. I know enough people in the music industry, still, that I think we can get some sizable donations. This school has a big need for newer computers for the classrooms and other things, so we're going to see how much money we can raise. And I need your help."

His smile widened because hers was. "What can I do?"

"You once asked me to give you a job in my musical. So I'm going to give you a job."

"You are?"

"You're going to sing the lead with me in the video."

He was still grinning but shook his head, quickly, as if the idea had just zinged past his head and caught him off-guard.

"Me?" he was a little hesitant, glancing around at all of the grinning kids. "Scarlett, I don't know if I...."

Scarlett cut him off. "Of course you can," she insisted. "The kids are ready to do this and I've got a video crew coming over from Liverpool tomorrow to shoot the video after school. We're going to do it in the field behind the school."

The information was coming too fast and he was having trouble keeping up. "We are?" he looked around. "I'm not sure... I haven't rehearsed this or anything. I don't want to mess up all of your hard work."

"You won't." She was no-nonsense. "Just read your lyrics, we'll practice tonight, and you'll be good to go tomorrow."

His grin was gone and he just looked at her with his mouth hanging open. "Why didn't you let me in on this earlier?"

She smiled brightly. "Because we wanted to surprise you. And also because I didn't want to give you the opportunity to turn me down." She suddenly turned to the rear of the room and lifted a hand. "Hey!" she shouted to people back in the shadows. "Hit it!"

Lights switches were thrown and big spotlights, hung from the ceiling, fired up the room. The kids scattered and took position, giggling and dancing around, obviously thrilled. As Archer looked around, a little stunned, Scarlett took him by both hands and pulled him with her towards a young man who was approaching them with microphones. Suddenly, music began to fill the room.

It was as if a great unseen hand threw a switch and, abruptly, the kids of St. Lawrence began to dance in a very practiced routine, Henry and Alexandra included. In fact, they were dancing together, swinging each other around, as Scarlett handed Archer a microphone and took one for herself.

Archer was a little disoriented by it all, but within the first few bars of the song, he recognized the tune. He'd heard it before, about thirty years before. It had been the anthem of a movie about a girl spending the summer with her family at a camp in the Adirondacks where she met a bad-ass dancing teacher she ended up falling in love with. It had been an iconic American movie and the strains of *I've Had the Time of My Life* filled the cavernous multi-purpose room.

"Here," Scarlett had sheet music. "Sing the lyrics with me."

Archer was nearly beside himself. "Love, I can't dance and...."

Scarlett cut him off. "Do you know this song?"

"I've heard it. But I can't...."

"Sing," Scarlett commanded. "Here's your cue... 1, 2, 3... now."

Fearful what would happen if he didn't obey, he read the lyrics in front of his face and began to sing the ballad-like introduction.

"'Now I've had the time of my life
No I never felt like this before

Yes I swear it's the truth
And I owe it all to you...'."

Smiling at his gorgeous baritone, Scarlett kicked in with her part.

"'Cause I've had the time of my life
And I owe it all to you...."

The dancing commenced in double time behind them as the ballad introduction transitioned into a disco beat. Chuckling at each other, Archer and Scarlett turned to watch the kids kick off with their dance routine. Morgan was up in the air, being held aloft by Matt Summerlin, as other girls were lifted into the air by big, strong boys. The kids were having a blast as they went through their well-rehearsed routine, with a lot of swing dance moves and slick action. Even Henry and Alexandra were twirling around. They were having a ball.

Initially surprised and off-guard, Archer couldn't help but grin at the kids having such a good time. It gave him a very warm, very happy feeling. Plus, he was singing with his wife and her beautiful mezzo soprano, and he figured he had nothing to lose. He really liked the song and as he read through the lyrics, it began to occur to him that they completely summed up his feelings for Scarlett. He was having the time of his life and he owed it all to her. When his cue came for the next chorus, he was ready.

"'I've been waiting for so long
Now I've finally found someone to stand by me'."

Scarlett smiled, gazing into his eyes as she sang her part.

"'We saw the writing on the wall
And we felt this magical Fantasy'."

Now it was the duet part and Archer took the melody while Scarlett took the harmony. She already knew the words, so it was matter of watching her husband's face as he read the lyrics and sang in his strong, deep voice.

"'Now with passion in our eyes
There's no way we could disguise it secretly
So we take each other's hand
'Cause we seem to understand the urgency
Just remember
You're the one thing
I can't get enough of
So I'll tell you something
This could be love
Because I've had the time of my life
No I never felt this way before
Yes I swear it's the truth
And I owe it all to you....'"

The next day, true to Scarlett's word, a video crew shot the entire video in two hours in a spring-filled field behind St. Lawrence. It had been quite a production with twenty-six kids who'd had the time of their life doing it. When it was all said and done, Archer felt like he had accomplished something wonderful, fun and thrilling with Scarlett and the kids. Whether or not the video did what it was intended to do, he still had a great time doing it. No fear, no Cutter horror, no reasons behind the burly bodyguard hanging out in the shadows... only joy and love like he'd never known it.

When the video was finally uploaded and had over a hundred thousand views within the first three weeks, he felt even more accomplished and proud. By the end of the month, donations, as a result of the video, totaled nearly five thousand American dollars and new computer equipment was on order. Lady Phipps' fundraiser for St. Lawrence was an unmitigated success.

When Reverend Bryan heard, he sincerely wished he hadn't listened to Arabella Phipps. He could have done quite a bit for the church with five thousand dollars.

FIFTEEN
LATE APRIL

IT WAS POURING RAIN OUTSIDE, a thunderstorm that had the countryside in its grip since last night. It was the weekend and a bad time for such bad weather. Alexandra had tried to talk her mother and Archer into letting her ride her horse in the horrible weather but they both had turned her down, leaving her and Henry to figure out how to entertain themselves as the weather outside worsened.

It wasn't like the house wasn't big enough. It had forty-six rooms, not including the bathrooms, and the lower ground floor alone had twenty-five rooms in which to lose oneself. It was a great place to play hide and seek, down in the dank and dark bowels of the old home, and once the pair grew bored of cartoons in the morning, a serious game was afoot.

Henry had the advantage, having been raised at Phipps Hall, but Alexandra had become very familiar with the house since the family had moved over from the lodge three months before. Down on the lower level, she and Henry were able to find some good hiding places. Then they'd jump out and scare each other. That went on for a couple of hours while Scarlett went up and down the stairs with laundry and Archer headed into work for a few hours. Morgan and her boyfriend were in the cinema room, basically a giant family room with a giant television in it, and Morgan yelled at the younger kids when they'd try to hide in there. They scampered out and left the love birds alone.

Arabella had a couple of lady friends over up in one of the massive parlors so the kids stayed clear of the ground level. Mr. and Mrs. Bayse had moved back over to Phipps Hall when everyone moved out of the lodge, and Mrs. Bayse made everyone some lunch as she worked around Arabella's snooty cook. Scarlett had come to depend on Mrs. Bayse a great deal and had the woman's back when the cook tried to pull rank, because no rank she could pull was greater than Scarlett's rank as Lady of the House. Not even Arabella. Scarlett and Mrs. Bayse would grin while the cook fumed at the usurpers.

So as the rain poured on the gloomy Saturday and Phipps Hall stayed busy, Alexandra and Henry played down in the lower ground level, inspecting every nook and cranny of the place, imagining ghosts and other scary creatures popping from the walls. At one point, they were messing around in a small interior study that was sandwiched in between the store room and the wine cellar.

It was kind of dark and dingy, with a very old desk that was well used, and a massive shelf unit against the wall that had all kinds of books and papers on it. The light didn't work very well and, at one point, they accidentally shut it off, screaming with giggles and fright until Henry found the switch again.

With the light on, they messed around for a couple more minutes until they got bored and decided to move on. Henry moved first, however, which Alexandra took offense to, so she pushed him out of the way while she went through the door first. Henry banged back into the wall shelf unit, knocking over some books in the process, and abruptly the entire shelf unit swung out and an opening in the wall appeared.

The kids gasped, staring open-mouthed at the ajar shelf unit. Henry started to run but Alexandra grabbed him.

"We broke it!" he declared.

Alexandra held on to his wrist so he couldn't get away. "I don't think so," she said, looking at the shelves both fearfully and curiously. "Look... it just came away from the wall."

Henry wasn't trying to get away anymore. Timidly, they approached the wall unit, seeing that there was, indeed, a doorway beyond. They became less shocked and more intrigued as they peered inside.

"It's a room," Henry said, his big blue eyes beholding the dark chamber beyond. "It's got furniture in it."

Alexandra was also studying the room without actually stepping inside. She was curious but caution had the better of her.

"Look at the desk," she said. "There's paper on it."

Henry was over any initial fear he might have had and, lured by his interest, stepped inside the room that was perhaps eight by ten feet. It was windowless, dank from the stone walls, and had books and paper strewn about in some kind of orderly chaos. It didn't look like old materials, either; the paper was new and fresh, as were the pens that littered the desk.

Alexandra wandered up to the desk as Henry moved around the small chamber, inspecting walls and crevices. Alexandra picked up a couple of the pieces of paper, seeing that it was half-written poetry. She began to shuffle through the pieces of paper, noticing there were some pieces on the floor and in a paper sack that looked like it had been used for a trashcan. She pulled out more pieces of paper, reading the poetry and thinking she had scored a big find.

"Look at this," she held a piece of paper up to Henry. "It's poetry."

Henry came over to the paper bag and, seeing that she was digging in it, dug around in it, too. "Maybe this stuff is valuable, you know?" he said. "Maybe one of my ancestors wrote it and it's worth something."

Alexandra was about to scoff at him when she caught sight of something on one of the pieces of paper. Her brow furrowed.

"Look here," she said, somewhat excitedly. "This one has your dad's name on it."

Henry snatched it out of her hand, seeing his father's name on the paper. He was confused. "Who wrote that?"

Alexandra shook her head and began digging around some more through the discarded scraps of paper. "This one has his name, too," she pointed out. "Someone's been writing poetry about him."

"Look!" Henry shoved another piece of paper in front of her face. "This has your mom's name on it."

Alexandra pulled the paper out of his hand and read it. After a moment, she shook her head. "That's not her name," she said. "She doesn't spell it like that."

"But it says 'Scarlet'."

"It's a color, dummy. Maybe the poem is talking about a color."

"We should show my dad. Maybe this stuff belongs in a museum and he'll be happy we found it!"

Alexandra agreed. The kids gathered up several pieces of the half-written or crumpled up poetry and left the little room, more interested in whether or not the poetry they found was important than the little room they found. They wandered out of the lower level and headed upstairs, past the parlor where Arabella was having tea with her friends. Henry wanted to tell his grandmother what they found but he knew better than to interrupt her, so he continued up to his room but before he could take it into the chamber, Alexandra snatched it all from him and took it into her room, instead.

The pieces of paper were forgotten as the afternoon dragged on and they ended up back in front of the television again.

———

"But it's Saturday night," Henry was whining. "I don't want to go to bed!"

Archer historically had issues with getting Henry to bed. That was nothing new. But tonight, he was being double-teamed as Alexandra put up a fight as well. Sitting on the couch in the family room with a glass of wine in her hand, Scarlett fought off a grin as Archer took on the two younger children in a losing battle. When he pointed a finger up the stairs, both children giggled and scattered. Archer boomed at them but only Henry came to a reluctant halt. They could hear Alexandra giggling upstairs as she ran away.

"Now what?" Archer looked at his wife. "I have one but not the other."

Scarlett sipped her wine and set it aside, rising off the couch. "You chased her off," she said, moving to Henry and taking the boy's hand. "You can go catch her. I'll take this one."

Archer frowned, although it was without force. "That's not fair."

"Yes, it is. Go find Alex."

He made a face at her, letting her know of his displeasure, but she simply winked at him and walked off with Henry. With a grunt, he went off in search of the giggly girl.

She wasn't hard to find. Alexandra had a habit of panting loudly when excited or giddy, so all he had to do was follow the sounds of heavy breathing. Alexandra was hiding in an upstairs closet near her bedroom door and Archer yanked it open to her screams. Then he growled like a bear, bent over, and slung her over his big shoulder. Alexandra alternately screamed and giggled as he carried her, still growling, into her bedroom. Taking her over to one of the big queen-sized beds, he gently laid her on top of it.

Alexandra was wound up and tried to escape, but he caught her and tossed her back on the bed, much to her delight. That went on twice until Archer finally called a truce.

"You may as well give up because you're not going anywhere," he told her. "Be a good girl and get ready for bed. If the weather clears up a little tomorrow, you can go riding."

That seemed to settle her down. "Even if it's sprinkling?"

"Even if it's sprinkling."

Excited at the prospect, she calmed sufficiently and ran to her wardrobe to grab her pajamas. Seeing that his work was finished, Archer turned to leave the room, brushing past her dresser as he did so. He knocked a book, which in turn knocked a bunch of paper off the dresser and scattered them. He paused to pick up the mess as Alexandra, pajamas in hand, went over to help him.

"I forgot," she said as she picked up a few pieces. "Henry and I found these today. We also found a secret room. Did you know there was a secret room downstairs?"

Archer wasn't particularly intrigued one way or the other; the house had dozens of rooms and he wouldn't have been at all surprised if there was a blocked-off one or a hidden one they didn't know about. Houses like this had a way of keeping secrets.

"I don't think I did," he said casually, putting the paper back on the dresser. "Where did you find it?"

Alexandra was looking at the pieces of paper. "Next to the wine cellar, I think," she said. "I'm not sure what the rooms are down there. We were in a room with an old desk and the bookshelf came away from the wall and there was a secret room behind it. We found all of these papers there. They were poems. Some of them had your name on them."

That caught Archer's attention for some reason. "Really?" he started looking at the papers he was picking up. "What did they say?"

Alexandra leafed through the jumble of papers now on her desk. "Here," she announced, pulling out one and handing it to him. "Your name's on it."

Archer looked at the paper. It was a thick bond, just a scrap, as if it had been torn from a bigger sheet. It looked like it was older paper, perhaps stained with age and improper storage, and the faded blue ink writing was done in carefully crafted yet almost childish writing. Some words were crossed out, some were misspelled.

Archer was halfway through the group of sentences when the room suddenly began to rock unsteadily. His heart was pounding in his chest, so hard that he could hear blood surging through his ears. The more he read, the more horrified he became.

She walks in beaut ~~ie~~ y like the night;
I pray this time you get it right.
Scarlet lips are yours to kiss;
~~Walking~~ Revolutionary lady is in our midst.
Phipps, ~~my boy~~ Phipps, of noble thrill;
Now again my time to kill.

He couldn't breathe. The world was moving under his feet and it was difficult to stay upright. Shaking, he reached out and pulled more sheets of paper off the dresser, each one revealing something more horrifying than the first. There were scraps of poems that had been crossed out and discarded, words scratched out, entire lines rewritten, but each one of them contained wording he'd heard before in the darkest hours of his life. Each scrap of paper like a horrific memory, a nightmare he couldn't awaken from. He'd heard two of them in the past six months, but others he remembered ten years ago.

Oh, God... this can't be happening....

Archer's mind was reeling as he read but retained sense enough to realize he shouldn't be touching any of the scraps of paper. They were evidence. He dropped what he had in his hand. Then he read a scrap of paper that had been blown away from the rest, lingering on the edge of the dresser.

Wayfaring warrior soul – still wild
The archer stands
Arrow measured to the goal – sing of
Strong and living man
In his mind there is a vision wand'ring
a woman of flesh, lust and longing
Blood of scarlet flows through her veins
Now she's dead; e'er feel your pain

Archer struggled to keep a level head, prioritizing what he needed to do. He was drawing on every ounce of training he ever had, crisis control, and everything else that the Royal Marines and Police training had taught him about remaining calm in a crisis. He wanted so badly to panic. But he couldn't. He labored to think straight.

"Will you show me the room, Alex?" he asked, his voice shaking.

Alexandra didn't notice the quiver in his tone. She was still looking at the poem. "Henry might know better than me. I kind of get lost down there."

"Henry saw these, too?"

"Yes."

Taking her by the hand, he had her leave her pajamas behind as he led her up to the second floor where Scarlett and Henry were. By the time he entered Henry's bedroom, he was pale and his upper lip was sweating. Scarlett and Henry were sitting on Henry's bed examining a new comic book that Henry had just received, both looking up when they saw Archer and Alexandra enter the room. Scarlett smiled at her daughter.

"So he caught you," she said.

Alexandra grinned at her mother but her attention turned to Henry. "I showed your dad those poems we found," she said. "He wants to see the room but I'm not sure I remember where it is."

Henry was happy to show them; anything to get out of going to bed. He leapt out and went hunting for his slippers.

"It's downstairs next to the wine cellar," he told his father. "Alex and I were playing and she must have done something to make the shelf break so it came away from the wall. We'll show you!"

Alexandra was outraged. "I did not break it!"

Henry found his slippers and the children were already running to the door. Archer held out a hand to his wife, who took it as she climbed off the bed. Scarlett noticed his hand was damp but didn't think much of it until she looked up and saw his face. He looked like he'd seen a ghost with an oddly pale expression.

"What's wrong?" Scarlett squeezed his hand. "You don't look very good."

He looked down at her as the followed the kids down the stairs. "I want you to do me a favor," he said quietly. "Please don't ask me any questions right now and do exactly what I say. Okay?"

The smile faded from her face. "Sure, honey. What's wr-? Oh, sorry. No questions."

He didn't respond other than to give her hand a squeeze. They followed the children down to the lower ground level where a maze of rooms spread out before them. Alexandra and Henry were giggling as they raced down a corridor, took a couple of turns, and then ended up in the small, windowless room with the desk. The bookshelf was still ajar, revealing the small secret room beyond, dark and foreboding and cobwebby. It looked like a crypt.

"Stop," Archer barked at the children before they could touch anything more than they had already done. When two pairs of apprehensive eyes turned to him, he motioned sharply out of the room. "Alex, go out in the hall and stand there. Don't move until I tell you to. Henry, go upstairs and get the cordless phone from the kitchen and bring it down to me. Don't talk to anyone, don't stop for anything. Get the phone and bring it to me now."

Henry scooted off as Alexandra, with big eyes, moved out into the corridor and stood against the wall. She was looking at her mother fearfully, as if she had done something wrong. Scarlett could only smile reassuringly at her daughter as she turned to Archer.

"I know you told me not to ask any questions," she said softly. "But if Alex is to be punished for this, then I think you need to at least consult me. What did she do?"

Archer was looking at the small study, dank and smelling like dirt, and the nearly-black secret room beyond. It was creepy beyond belief, phantoms of memories and evil reaching out to grasp at him. It was every horror he'd ever felt as the possibilities swarmed; *notes. Death. Scarlet blood.* It was as if he were transfixed, as if something else had taken him over and when he turned to look at Scarlett, for a brief moment, she didn't recognize the man looking back at her. There was no warmth or recognition in his face. It frightened her.

"Archer," she hissed. "What's wrong?"

Archer looked at her for a long moment before seeming to break from whatever trance enveloped him. Then he put his arms around her, holding her tightly.

"I'm sorry," he whispered. "Please don't be upset. I'm not angry with Alex. But..."

He trailed off and she pulled away from his embrace, studying his features. The man was deeply upset.

"You're really scaring me right now," she murmured. "You told me not to ask questions, but you're acting really strange and it's scaring me. Please tell me what's going on. What's wrong with this room?"

He just looked at her, seeing Alexandra's scared face in the hallway beyond. As anxious and bewildered as he was, he nonetheless struggled to calm down and put his thoughts into a format that wouldn't terrify Scarlett. He didn't want to have to worry about her freaking out, too.

"It's not the room, my angel," he said. "I'm not really sure what's going on right now so I'm not sure I can explain it to you. I'm not angry with you, or the children, but I need for you to trust me and just do what I tell you for now. That would help me tremendously."

Sufficiently satisfied, at least for the moment, Scarlett simply nodded her head and went to stand with Alexandra out in the hall. As she did so, Henry returned with the cordless phone and Archer took it from him. He had Henry stand out in the corridor with Scarlett and Alexandra, all three of them looking somewhat confused and apprehensive.

Things were only going to get worse.

SIXTEEN

THE NORTH YORKSHIRE police descended on Phipps Hall less than an hour later. Police officers were everywhere and Scarlett was introduced to the Chief Constable and Archer's boss, a man about ten years older than Archer named Tom Midwick. He was slim and lanky, with a sharp wit, and after a few moments of cordial conversation with Scarlett, he gave quiet orders to a few inspectors, including Calvin, who swung into action.

Scarlett and the children were taken upstairs to Morgan's room and kept there by a female constable. When Morgan got home after her date with Matt, she was also taken up to her room and sequestered. All of the household employees were rounded up and taken to a room down on the lower ground level, while a female inspector woke Arabella up and kept her isolated in her bedroom.

Scarlett truly had no idea what was going on and she was, quite frankly, terrified. She didn't know where Archer was and after an hour of sitting and wondering with three frightened children, she finally convinced them to go to bed. Alexandra and Morgan slept in the king-sized bed with Freddie the dog while Henry fell asleep on the couch. That left Scarlett alone in the dim room, gazing out of the window over the Yorkshire countryside and wondering what in the hell was going on.

The night dragged on and Scarlett, weary and upset, lay back on a big purple chair and covered up. She lay there staring at the ceiling before finally drifting off to sleep. She had no idea she'd even fallen asleep until Archer gently woke her, nuzzling her neck and putting his big arms around her. She awoke with a start and he put his hand over her mouth.

"Shhh," he whispered. "The children are sleeping. I need you to come with me."

Groggy, she struggled up from the chair with a good deal of Archer's assistance. He took her out of the bedroom, which was now guarded at the door by both a male and female constable, and took her into the master bedroom. Scarlett glanced at the clock, yawning, and saw that it was nearly five in the morning. She was exhausted and edgy.

"What's going on?" she demanded. "Can you please tell me something?"

He pulled her over to the arrangements of couches in the sitting room. He set her down and disappeared into the bedchamber, returning with a blanket, which he tucked around her on the couch. He didn't sit next to her, however; he sat across from her so he could look her in the eye.

"I'm sorry this has been so frightening and confusing," he said.

Scarlett was exhausted and upset. "Just tell me what's going on."

Archer sighed, sitting back in the chair as he collected his thoughts. He decided to get straight to the point; he didn't think she'd appreciate anything else.

"You saw those scraps of paper in Alex's room."

"Yes."

Archer's expression was intense. "Do you remember the discussions we've had about the Yorkshire Cutter?"

Scarlett was listening seriously, now somewhat confused. "Of course I do, but what specifically? What does that have to do with anything?"

His expression tightened. "Those notes that the children found... those were the same notes, or variations of them, that had been found at the crime scenes ten years ago and then recently."

Scarlett stared at him as the information sank in. She wasn't sure what she had expected him to say, but that hadn't been in the realm of possibility. When she realized what he was saying, her eyes widened dramatically and she nearly came off the couch.

"*What?*" she hissed. "Those are the notes... oh, my God! Are you serious?"

"Unfortunately, yes."

"But... but that's not possible, is it? I mean, why are they here? How did they get here?"

Archer remained calm. "That's why I called my department," he said. "I have no idea what's going on and I have to remove myself from the case, considering the circumstances. That's why I kept you and the children away from the room once Henry showed us where it was, and why I kept you all corralled together until the police arrived. Right now, everyone in this house is being sequestered from each other and the inspectors are methodically interviewing everyone while the crime lab goes over the secret room, the notes, and pretty much the entire house. Nobody knows what's going on, least of all me. I'm a little... confused right now."

Scarlett's hand was at her throat, her breathing coming swiftly, as she listened to Archer. As frightened as she was, it took her a moment to realize he was taking all of this very hard. He looked pale and drawn, and she went over to him, going to her knees in front of his chair. She put her hands on his legs, her expression open and anxious as she gazed up at him.

"Honey, I'm sorry," she said softly. "I know this can't be easy for you, but... what do *you* think happened? Is it possible that someone in this house is actually the Yorkshire Cutter?"

He put his big hands over hers. "I don't know what to think," he said honestly. "But it would make sense that it's someone here. The Cutter was watching me; we always knew that, and when you came along, he or she knew about you as well. We always wondered how or why the Cutter knew so much about me, but if they were in the same house as me... that would explain everything. The possibility never even occurred to me."

"I still can't believe it. How is all of this even possible?"

Although Archer was looking at her, his mind was still going a million miles a minute. It had been since he first saw the notes. He was entertaining all possibilities, running scenarios through his head, but over the past hour, he was coming to nail down one possibility in particular. It was the one that, unfortunately, made the most sense to him although he couldn't truly believe it.

"I'm not sure," he said, collecting her hand and gently squeezing her fingers. "But I need to talk to my mother."

"Haven't you spoken with her yet?"

He shook his head. "No. The inspectors have been busy with her. From what I've been told, she hasn't spoken much."

"You need to go to her. She's probably really frightened."

He nodded reluctantly, not wanting to leave Scarlett but knowing she was right. "I should," he muttered, standing up and pulling her to her feet. "I'll take you back to Morgan's room so you can stay with the children. I want you all together."

He seemed edgy, uncertain, so Scarlett merely nodded. "Whatever you say."

He led her back out of the bedroom and headed for Morgan's room. "You stay there until I come for you, okay? Don't leave for any reason. Any reason at all."

"I won't."

They descended the stairs to the mezzanine and he opened the door to the darkened bedroom. "Get some sleep," he murmured, bending down to kiss her. "I'll be back as soon as I can."

"Okay."

Archer could see a hint of fear come to her eyes. "Please don't worry."

"I won't."

He waited until Scarlett went into the room and closed the door. He could hear the lock gently thrown. Looking to the female constable who was guarding the door, the silent implications of his expression were obvious. *Guard that door with your life.*

His mother's room was on the floor above and to the left, a large suite with two entrances. There was a female constable at each entrance and he went to the first entrance he came upon. Admitted by the rather large female constable, he entered the vast chamber to find his mother awake and alone. The room was dark at dawn and she sat in a lovely winged-back chair with a single light on overhead, reading a book. She looked up when Archer entered.

"Finally," she said, closing the book. "You have decided to make an appearance. What on earth is going on, Archer?"

Archer made his way over to the chair, which sat in front of a large fireplace. He knelt down and began to stoke up wood from the woodbin next to it. The eerie stillness of the air surrounding them was making him uneasy for some reason. There was something very cold about the room.

"No one told you anything?" he asked.

Arabella snorted. "Not a bloody word," she said, using an unusual curse word. It was indicative of her emotions at the moment. "All they want to do is ask me a bunch of foolish questions but not tell me why. They have asked me many questions about you, Archer. What have you done?"

Archer was focused on starting a fire in the fireplace, sparking a long match and lighting the kindling. "Nothing," he said, blowing out the match. "But something peculiar is going on in this house and we must get to the bottom of it."

"Peculiar?" Arabella repeated. "Peculiar how?"

Archer wasn't sure where to start. He sighed heavily and stood up, seeking out another chair in the dark and chilly room. When he sat, it was with all of the confusion and weariness he was feeling. He was having a difficult time keeping his thoughts together.

"Do you remember about ten years ago when I spent an inordinate amount of time chasing after a suspect that the press called the Yorkshire Cutter?" he asked.

Arabella's expression didn't change but she laid the book down in her lap. "I remember."

"You'll recall I spent a good deal of time on the cases."

"I do. It was back when you and Christiana first met, as I recall."

He nodded, sighing heavily as he continued. "Perhaps you will also recall that the Cutter left notes to me at the crime scenes," he said quietly. "That was also made public. The press had a field day with it."

Arabella nodded patiently. "I remember."

Archer's focus was on his mother's calm face. "Last fall, we believe the Cutter began killing again," he said. "There were three murders in a row, two of them with notes meant for me. Remember when I stayed with Scarlett over at the Deerkeeper's Lodge for those months? It was because those notes mentioned her by name. Whoever was doing the killing was watching me and, consequently, her, so I moved there to protect her because she didn't want to stay at Phipps Hall. I never told you the truth about it because I didn't want to frighten you, but now you know the real reason. You *do* recall all of this, don't you?"

"Of course I do. What's happened?"

He sighed again, trying to phrase his next sentence carefully. "When Henry and Alex were playing yesterday, they came across a secret room down on the ground floor level. It was purely by accident. However, the room contained notes, or versions of the notes, that had been left for me at crime scenes. Same paper, same writing, and variations of the same prose. Mother, someone in this house is the Yorkshire Cutter. That's why my department is here. That's why they've been questioning you."

Arabella studied her son very carefully. "That's why they've been asking me questions about you."

He nodded faintly. "It is."

"They think it's you."

He lifted his big shoulders. "They can't rule out anyone, even me."

Arabella sat still for a few moments. Nothing moved on her person and her breathing was even and shallow. Her bright blue gaze was on her son and Archer gazed back at her, waiting for the inevitable fear and shock. But Arabella remained still. When she finally spoke, he barely heard her.

"Rubbish," she muttered. "You would never do anything like that. You're not a murderer."

Archer shook his head, feeling very weary at the moment.

"No," he mumbled. "But finding those notes downstairs… you can't imagine the shock and revulsion I feel right now, but in the same breath, it makes so much sense because the killer seemed to know my every move and everything about me. Those notes mention Scarlett, so whoever it is knows about Scarlett. I'm scared to death for her because one of the notes mentioned something about her death."

Arabella remained still, silent, and unmoving. She simply stared at her son. Then, she looked away, staring off into the darkness of the room. The sun was just starting to crack the horizon and gray light strained to enter the room from beyond the blinds. Archer finally reached over and took his mother's hand.

"What are you thinking about?" he asked. "Do you know anything about that room downstairs? It's right off the wine cellar, linked by a door built into the wall. Who knows about it and, more importantly, who has access to it?"

She didn't say anything for a moment but when she finally turned to look at her son, she suddenly looked quite weary herself. Gone was the inbred arrogance that was her habitual expression. She simply looked old and worn.

"You weren't supposed to find the room," she murmured.

Her words didn't mean anything to him, nor did they make sense. "What? Why not?"

"It's all very explainable," she said. "But you mustn't get worked up about it. You must stay calm."

Her statement didn't register with him at first. He was still holding her hand, still waiting for the explosion of fright. Her softly uttered words didn't sink in for several long seconds and when they finally did, his expression screwed up with confusion.

"What do you mean?" he asked.

Arabella was eerily calm. "When you were first promoted to

inspector those years ago, your father got ragingly drunk one night, like he always did, and began to plot out how we should advance your career and make you a hero. He thought perhaps we should pay someone to go on a crime spree so that you could catch them and make yourself look good. He was joking at first but then he grew serious about it. Your father was very determined to better your career, you know. He didn't want his son to be a common bobby forever."

Archer dropped her hand. "What in the world are you talking about?"

She continued, almost casually. "Obviously, your father wasn't going to do anything himself so he hired a man to commit that first crime in east York, your jurisdiction at the time," she said. "Do you recall? It was a woman and her young son. The man was only supposed to rob her but he accidentally killed her. The boy saw what happened and the man panicked and killed the boy as well. So your father paid the man a goodly sum and sent him out of the country, mostly because he was fearful what would happen if you really did find the killer and he was somehow linked to us. Your father thought perhaps nothing would come of the investigation if the man was sent away, but that wasn't the case at all. The case became yours, as we'd planned, but the newspaper got a hold of your identity and suddenly the Viscount Inspector was all over the news. Do you remember that? It made you famous."

Archer was sitting stiff against the back of the chair, hardly believing what he was hearing. It was like a nightmare, ghastly truths vomiting out of his mother's mouth that were making him physically ill. He couldn't believe it.

"You...," he choked, then started again. "You did *what?* You and Father paid someone to...?"

Arabella waved him off calmly. "When your father saw how his little plan had helped your career, he found someone else to commit the next crime. Actually, this man committed all the rest of them, including the most recent ones. Those notes in the wine cellar... well, he couldn't very well write them on his own so your father and I helped. When your father passed away, I took over and told him what to write. How on earth do you think such a common criminal would know of Keats and Shelley and Baudelaire? They *were* rather clever notes."

Archer stood up unsteadily from the chair, his hands over his mouth. He turned away from his mother, sharply, and moved across the room as if he had somewhere to go but the truth was that he had nowhere to go and nowhere to hide. The agony that had consumed so much of his career, at times, had apparently been homespun. He was dizzy with the possibilities.

"No," he hissed, bumping aimlessly against a wall in the darkness and slumping. "It's not true. It simply cannot be true."

Arabella stood up, her focus riveted to her son. "Tom Midwick is retiring in a few years, Archer," she said, very matter-of-factly. "Don't you understand? We must make you shine once again so, perhaps, you will be promoted to Chief Constable. It's what your father would have wanted and what he would have been so proud of. He was never proud of you as a child, Archer, you know that. You were a big, mean bully and he was convinced you were incorrigible. But you went into the military service and then to the police force and he was very proud of you for that. All he wanted was for the world to know how wonderful you were. He wanted to be proud of you. What's wrong with that?"

Archer's face was pasty white. "What's *wrong* with that?" he nearly shouted. "My God, Mother, do you realize what you're saying?"

"Stop yelling, Archer," she scolded, moving in his direction. "The Yorkshire Cutter has given you a career like no other officer on the force. You will be forever associated with it and, when you finally solve the murders and bring the killer to justice, you'll be a hero."

Archer could hardly breathe. He was horrified that his mother seemed to think everything she spoke of was perfectly justifiable. His mind was reeling with the truth.

"No," he finally hissed. "This is all some big mistake. This cannot be happening, any of it."

Arabella came to within a few feet of him and came to a halt. "You're a very clever boy," she said quietly. "I have always known that. Now everyone will know it."

He slapped his hands over his ears and moved away from her. "Stop," he roared. "I don't want to hear any more of this madness."

Arabella frowned. "Calm yourself," she snapped. "You might attract attention. Those nosy inspectors will want to know why you're yelling."

He whirled on her, grabbing her by the arms. "Are you mad?" he hissed. "Do you realize what you've told me... my God, I can't believe any of it. Tell me you're fabricating all of this. Please, God, tell me that you're joking."

Arabella cocked an eyebrow. "The man you want is Edward," she said calmly. "He has been carrying out the crimes. He wasn't certain about murder at first, of course, but it had to be done because that's what that first man did. We had to make them look all alike."

Archer felt as if he'd been struck. He let go of his mother, stumbled back and ended up down on one knee. He just stared at his mother as if she had completely gone insane.

"You....," he gasped. "*Edward?*"

"Yes."

"He committed the crimes?"

"Yes," Arabella said evenly. "Your father made sure he was quite well compensated, of course, and I have seen to that compensation since your father's death. Edward is a very wealthy man."

Archer's eyes began to fill with tears; he was so over-whelmed that emotion was coming out of every pore in his body. It was coming out of everywhere.

"But…," he breathed. "But… why did you… I followed clues. I did my police work; bloody hell, I worked my ass off trying to find the killer. For years, I did this. *Years!*"

He was shouting again by the time he was finished. Arabella remained cool. "You did your best, I understand," she said, almost softly. "But Edward's not a criminal. He doesn't have a record. There was no way you could find him or know who it was, and we always made sure he was extremely careful – gloves and all that. He would take the bus lines and not a car, nothing that people could recognize or single out. It's not your fault, but it certainly kept you busy and made you look strong and knowl-edgeable."

Archer was having a horrible time comprehending what she was saying. "But I caught the wrong man," he groaned, over-come with the implications of that statement. "The man I was convinced was the killer was the *wrong* man."

"That's true, but you were close. He actually looked a good deal like the first man your father hired. Your eyewitnesses were very close."

Archer just shook his head. "But I don't understand why this is happening again. Are you trying to make me run in circles again?"

"I told you why," Arabella said. "Because Midwick is retiring in a few years and you must be in a prime position to assume his job."

Archer stared at the woman, open-mouthed, before strug-gling to his feet. "My dear God," he muttered, struggling to get a hold of himself now that everything was becoming clear.

"You did all of this just to make me look good?"

"Yes. Go now and arrest Edward; it will make you a hero."

Archer's heart was pounding against his ribs as the news sank deep. He was reeling, struggling to grasp at coherent thought, laboring to put a plan of action together of what must be done. All he could see was jail for his mother and disgrace to the family name. That was the reality of it. No glory, no promotions... none of it. All he could see was the Phipps name in ruin and his career a laughing stock.

"Do you realize what you have done?" he finally rasped. "You are an accessory to murder, Mother. You and father... you both planned and executed murders."

"We did no such thing."

"Do you have any idea what you've done?" Archer raised his voice, watching his mother jump at the volume. "Everything you've ever held dear and every good thing the Phipps name has stood for has now come to an end. You've taken everything that was sane and strong about this family and threw it into a swamp where it can lie with the other families who have thought they were above the law or somehow akin to God himself. You've destroyed us, Mother. God help you, you have."

Arabella's mouth was in a flat, angry line. "I haven't done anything except give my son opportunities to excel," she snapped. "Any mother would do the same."

He gazed at her, steadily, gaining control over his emotions and feeling such sorrow, such disgust, that he couldn't verbalize it. All he knew was that his entire life was destroyed. He was sickened by it. He turned for the door.

"Edward should be in the stables," Arabella called after him. "His fingerprints will be all over those notes. I never touched them. And I will trust that you will keep this conversation a secret. I'm sure you won't dare turn in your own mother, Archer. Not when I did all of it for you."

He came to an unsteady halt near the door, his back to her. He didn't respond to her; he couldn't. He quit the room without another word.

Arabella waited a nominal amount of time before heading to her medicine cabinet.

SEVENTEEN

"YOUR MOM'S ASLEEP," Henry whispered. "It's morning and I'm hungry. I want to go see my pony."

Alexandra was lying next to her sleeping sister as Henry stood next to the bed. She rubbed her eyes, glancing at the window with its gray light streaming in through the cracks in the curtains. It was very early, the dawn of a new morning after an eventful night.

"I don't think we can leave," she yawned. "We're supposed to stay here."

Henry eyed Scarlett, sleeping soundly on a chair across the room. The woman was sleeping like the dead.

"I'm not staying here," he whispered determinedly. "I'm going to get something to eat and see my pony. Then I'll come back and they'll never know I was gone."

Alexandra sat up in bed, carefully, as not to wake Morgan. "You can't do that!"

"Yes, I can!"

Very quietly, Henry skittered across the room in the darkness, grabbing for his clothes that he had neatly folded on the dresser near his bed. He continued on into the bathroom as

Alexandra, still sitting up in bed, waved her hands at him. She was fearful and frustrated. But there was a larger part of her that was bored, and hungry, and didn't want to stay cooped up in her sister's bedroom any more. She missed her horse. Perhaps Henry was right; perhaps they really *could* sneak out and sneak back without anyone having seen them. She was unfortunately willing to take the chance.

She changed her clothes quickly and quietly while Henry was still in the bathroom. When he came out, she was ready to go. Henry motioned her to silently follow him.

From Morgan's room, they went back into the bathroom, which had a pocket door built into the wall that could only be locked from the bathroom side. He unlocked the pocket door, which really blended seamlessly into the architecture of the bathroom, and slid it open. Beyond was a sort of closet, a linen closet, which opened up into a small laundry room tucked in between the rooms on this level. Henry quietly opened the laundry room door that opened up into the corridor outside and peered into the hall.

It was dark outside but to his right he could see the female constable guarding Morgan's door. The woman had a chair and was sitting outside the door, reading something with her torch to illuminate it. To his left was an empty corridor that led off into the darkness. Motioning for Alexandra to follow, the two of them slipped from the laundry room and disappeared down the hall.

They were giggly with their disobedience, racing down the hall towards a servant's staircase that led down to the kitchen. They quietly and carefully took the stairs, descending in darkness to a panel door that opened up into the kitchen. Henry carefully opened it to discover it dimly lit but a kettle heating on the stove. Someone was heating water. Not wanting to be discovered when the person returned, Henry threw open a cabinet, grabbed the first thing he came across, which happened to be a package of crackers, and raced out with Alexandra on his heels. Taking another staircase to the lower level, they ended up on the terrace.

They made a break across the misty yard for the stables.

———

"She told you *that?*"

August was leaning against the hood of his car, his face as pale and gray as the sky above. Archer's car was across from his, the front ends facing one another. They were at the entrance to Phipps Hall, the mouth of the long and manicured drive that led to the great house itself.

His brother had called him at sunrise and told him to get the hell over to the house because something had happened. August had tried to ask questions but Archer had hung up on him. Panicked, he drove at breakneck speed from his home in York to find his brother waiting for him at the entrance to Phipps Hall. He was a fixture in the fog, a silent sentinel, as the misty York moors enveloped him. But what he heard coming out of Archer's mouth was not what he had expected, and even now he found himself reeling as much as his brother was. He felt ill.

"Yes, she did," Archer was bundled up against the cold, his pallor a sickly pasty color. His hands were shoved in his pockets as he gazed up at the slate-colored sky. "I... I don't even know what to say. I can't think clearly about this, Auggie. I'm in total shock."

August gazed at his brother, deeply concerned, deeply sickened. After several long and painful moments, he simply shook his head and slumped against the car.

"Christ," he hissed. "What the... are you sure you understood her correctly?"

"I'm sure."

"I don't believe it!"

"Believe it."

August shook his head, perplexed. "But it doesn't make any bloody sense," he said. "It's pure madness!"

"I know."

August threw up his hands. "I have to speak with her."

"Go ahead, but she'll just tell you the same thing."

"But there has to be another explanation."

"Like what?"

"Like the old girl has lost her marbles!"

Archer cocked an eyebrow. "I told you what she told me, verbatim. I left nothing out. I changed nothing. You know as well as I do that Mother, and Father for that matter, always had a sense of...."

August finished for him because they both knew the answer. "Entitlement."

"Exactly. They believe that law and justice and all that was for those who didn't have eight hundred years of heritage behind them. Do you recall the time when Father got that speeding ticket in York? Do you remember that fuss he put up?"

August was nodding his head before Archer could finish. "Over by the church?"

"Yes."

"He was doing about sixty KPH in a thirty zone and had a bloody heart attack when he was cited for it." August shook his head. "He fought that citation like a madman. He even tried to pay off the judge but we stopped him. He had to pay one hundred and forty three pounds for that citation but you would have thought he had to pay a million. He didn't think he should have to pay anything because he was the bloody earl."

Archer remembered well that moment in time twelve years ago. He had still been a corporal on the police force and August had just gotten out of law school. Both of them had been hugely embarrassed by their father's behavior. But as August began to reflect on that incident, it became clear that he no longer thought his mother was mad. He was coming to very much believe his brother.

"Oh... God," August muttered, wiping his hands over his face. "It's true, isn't it?"

"Yes," Archer whispered.

"I think I'm going to be sick."

Archer looked at him. "Hold off on that for now," he said. "Right now, we have to decide what to do about it. She's an accessory to murder, you know. When this gets out, it'll drag the Phipps name through the mud for eternity. There's no way to redeem the family name or family honor after this. We're finished."

August's jaw ticked as he stared at his shoes. "What do you want to do, Archer?" his head came up, looking at his brother. "What's your gut telling you?"

Archer met his brother's gaze steadily. After a few moments, he simply lifted his shoulders. "I'm a cop," he muttered. "The bottom line is that I'm a cop and I know right from wrong. What she did, what father did, was wrong. I... I just can't let them get away with it, not even for the sake of family honor. They have to pay for their crimes. I couldn't live with myself if I did it any other way."

August nodded slowly. "I agree," he sighed. "Neither could I."

The brothers fell silent for a time, each pondering their own thoughts and the course of the future as they saw it. It was a very painful future.

"So what now?" August finally asked. "What do we do?"

Archer sighed faintly. "I need to speak with the chief," he said. "He'll understand the need for discretion in this. And then we'll pin Edward down and interrogate him. Maybe he'll come up with something more than what Mother told me. In any case, I need to detain him right away. If what Mother said was true, then he's our killer."

"Where is he?"

"Down in his quarters at the stable," Archer replied. "He's being held there by a constable, in his rooms, just like everyone else."

"Do you think he knows why?"

"Doubtful. The only people who know what's really happening are the chief and the inspectors. Not even the constables know why they're here. All they know is that they are to keep the occupants of the house contained and separated, and that includes the domestic help."

August thought on that a moment. "Then you'd better move quickly before he starts to become suspicious. If that man is capable of such horrific killings, then there's no telling what he'll do if he suspects you're on to him."

Archer nodded his head. "I realize that," he replied. "And I intend to move quickly. But first, I think... I think I need to see my wife. I just need to have a moment of peace and calm before all hell breaks loose."

"Does Scarlett know any of this?"

"No, but I'm going to have to tell her at some point. I'm really not sure how she's going to react knowing my mother was behind all of her fear and stress."

August was pensive and drawn. It occurred to Archer that his brother looked older than he'd ever seen him, just like their mother had earlier when the confession had come out. Distress and regret had a way of aging people.

"I want to talk to Mother," August finally said. "It's one thing to tell you everything, but from now on, she needs to keep her mouth shut."

Archer shot him an exasperated look. "Auggie, she confessed everything to me. I can't keep it secret, nor will I. I'm a cop and she confessed a crime."

"Did you advise her of her rights before she started talking?"

"Of course not."

"Then it's inadmissible."

Archer was about to explode when he thought better of it, for a very good reason. He cocked his head. "You're right," he said. "I can't use the confession against her."

August shook his head, an expression suggesting that all may not be lost, at least where their mother was concerned. "From this point on, the police department conducts all communication through me. I just appointed myself her lawyer and she's not saying another bloody word."

"Good enough."

With that understanding, Archer and August got into their cars and proceeded down the two and a half mile drive until they came to the silver-stoned manor house that they had been raised in.

After today, Phipps Hall would never be the same.

EIGHTEEN

BECAUSE OF THE security of the situation, August was forced to remain in the large parlor while Archer went upstairs to see Scarlett. The house was oddly still at the early hour because usually the help was up and in the kitchen, and the smells of breakfast could be sniffed throughout the manor. Archer took the main stairs up to Morgan's room, being ushered in by the female constable who had been guarding the door all night.

The room was dark and he took a moment, his eyes adjusting to the weak light. The first thing he saw was his wife sleeping in a big, fluffy chair, all spread out across the arms of the furniture. He grinned at the sight, feeling his heart lighten as he gazed upon her, but it also brought tears to his eyes. He was so mentally crippled at the moment that he just needed five minutes with her, being the weak one for a change, being comforted as only she could do.

The tears started to come before he could control himself and he went to his knees beside the chair, tenderly wrapping her up in his arms as he buried his face against her shoulder. Scarlett wasn't startled awake. In fact, she was used to the man wrapping her up against him as they slept. She put her arms around him and nestled her face against the top of his head, smelling his distinctive musky scent that had a tendency to make her heart flutter wildly. Warm, half-asleep, and sweetly blissful, it took her a moment to realize that her shoulder and part of her cleavage was wet. When he sniffled, she came to realize he was weeping.

"Archer?" she mumbled, startled awake. "Honey, what's wrong?"

He just shook his head. He didn't even want to talk about it at the moment. He just wanted to hold her. Frightened, she tried to sit up and force him to lift his head.

"Archer?" There was fear in her voice. "What's the matter? Tell me what's wrong?"

He finally lifted his head, shushing her softly as he wiped at his face. "Don't wake the children," he murmured. He cupped her face in his big hands and kissed her cheek. "I'm okay. There's just a lot going on and I need to talk to you. Auggie's here."

Scarlett was sitting up in the chair, concern all over her face as she wiped moisture from Archer's cheeks. "Why is he here?"

"I called him. I asked him to come. It seems that there are some issues concerning my mother and I wanted him here."

Scarlett wasn't particularly clear on anything he was talking about. She lifted her eyebrows at him. "Your mother?" she said with concern, almost in a normal speaking tone, and then put her fingers over her mouth as if to acknowledge she had spoken too loudly. She looked over Archer's shoulder to see if she'd woken the children but realized, as she peered at the bed containing her two daughters, that there was only one dark head on the pillows. Her features twisted with confusion. "Where's Alex?"

Archer's head snapped around, looking at the bed with only Morgan in it. He immediately stood up and went to the second bed, tossing back the bunched-up covers and seeing that Henry was not in that bed, either. Fear surged in his veins, terror such as he'd never known flooding him. He could feel Scarlett standing next to him and he turned to look at her with apprehension all over his face.

"They're both missing," he hissed. "How... oh, my sweet God...."

He bolted for the bathroom with Scarlett right after him. This was his house, after all, and he knew all of the nooks and crannies in it. He knew where the secret doors and hidden stairs were, and he knew of the pocket door in the bathroom. As he rushed to the panel and slid it open, he heard Scarlett gasp behind him.

"What's wrong?" she demanded. "What are you doing? Where did they go?"

Archer knew his son and knew there was only one place the child would go on the grounds – a favorite place where his beloved pony was housed. It wouldn't be the first time he had snuck out to go visit his pony. In fact, it happened quite regularly. More than that, now Alexandra had a stake in all of this because she had a horse she wanted to visit, too. *The stables.* He felt as if all of the air had been sucked out of him but he collected his wits, knowing what had to be done. Those two silly kids had put themselves in a world of danger. He could hardly believe it.

Whirling on Scarlett, he grabbed her by both arms and struggled to stay calm. "I want you to stay here with Morgan and bolt all of the doors from the inside," he told her. "Please don't ask any questions right now because it would take too long to answer them. Just do what I say and stay here until I come back for you. Don't leave for any reason. Okay?"

Scarlett gazed up at him with fear in her eyes. He could see the tears starting to well. "Why?" she begged. "Where's Alex?"

He could see how terrified she was and he hugged her tightly, kissing her cheeks to reassure her. "Nothing has happened to her," he said. "I need to go find her and Henry and bring them back, that's all. But you stay here. Promise?"

She nodded, sniffling. "Yes."

He kissed her again, this time on the lips. "Thank you," he murmured, letting her go and making a break for the bedroom door. "I'll be back."

He slammed the door in his wake, which roused Morgan. She sat up, sleepily rubbing her eyes.

"Who's making all the noise?" she demanded, grumpy.

Scarlett was standing in the middle of the room, gazing at the door Archer had just slammed with tears in her eyes. She couldn't even answer Morgan, who fell back on the bed, grumbling, and tried to go back to sleep.

Eventually, Scarlett lost the battle with her tears. She didn't know why she was so frightened, but she was. Maybe it had something to do with Archer's tears, tears he wouldn't explain, or maybe it had something to do with the total expression of horror when he realized Henry and Alexandra were missing. The situation at Phipps Hall was going from bad to worse and she was genuinely terrified.

She stood there and sobbed.

NINETEEN

"I WANT TO RIDE MY PONY," Henry said, hanging on the stall door and looking in on his pony. "We can ride really fast and get back upstairs before they know we're missing."

Alexandra was standing at the next stall, watching Snapdragon nose around his hay. It was dawn and neither animal had been fed yet. In fact, all of the horses seemed hungry and restless.

"Where's Edward?" Alexandra wanted to know. "Doesn't he usually feed the horses now?"

Henry wasn't paying attention. He just wanted to ride his pony. He opened up the stall door and went inside, cooing to the animal. Then he came out of the stall leading the pony by his halter.

"I want to ride him," he said again. "Let's go get his saddle."

Alexandra took a stand. "No," she said firmly. "Archer told us not to leave the room, but we did because I wanted to see my horse, too. If we go and ride in the arena, they'll see us and we'll get in a lot of trouble, so I'm not going to do it. I'm going back inside."

Henry lost some of his confidence. "No," he said, pleading. "Don't go. I... I won't ride, I promise."

Alexandra was dubious. "Then put him back in his stall," she said. "I want to go back inside."

Henry, ever the gentleman, reluctantly bowed to the lady's wish. He turned back for the stall and led the pony inside. Alexandra followed, watching him as he petted the pony and explained that he would ride him later. The pony went to his feed bucket and began banging around in it.

"He's hungry," Henry said. "We should at least find Edward and see if he's going to feed them."

Alexandra wasn't sure about that. "He'll feed them," she said, growing increasingly anxious about returning. "We should...."

Above their heads, something heavy banged against the floor, so much so that both children jumped with fright. There were two more bangs and the sound of something breaking. Then, there was dead, still silence. Eyes wide, the children were gazing up at the ceiling in fright.

"What was that?" Alexandra asked.

Henry shook his head unsteadily. "I don't know," he said. "Edward lives up there. He has a flat. Do you suppose he's okay?"

"Maybe we should go see."

From Henry's perspective, the girl was suggesting something that would take some bravery, so not wanting to be less brave than a girl, he nodded in agreement and took the lead. Alexandra followed.

Cautiously, the children made their way to the staircase that led up to Edward's flat. The fog had grown heavier now that the morning was deepening and it was difficult to see even twenty feet in front of them. Everything was cold, damp, and eerie. As they reached the exterior wooden staircase painted to match the stables, a tall and lanky body appeared at the bottom of the steps.

Both children yelped with fear until they realized it was Edward. Henry ran to the man. "Edward!" he said. "We heard banging. Are you okay?"

Edward, skinny and pale as if he were bordering on perpetual malnutrition, nodded. "I'm fine, young Henry," he said. "What are you children doing out so early?"

"We came to see our horses," Henry told him. "They're hungry. Can we help you feed them?"

"Henry," Alexandra shook her head at him. "We have to go back inside."

"I can feed the horses, Master Henry," Edward told him. "You go back inside and get your breakfast."

It was then that the children noticed that Edward was carrying a satchel. Henry pointed at it. "Are you going somewhere, Edward?"

Edward simply shook his head and set the bag down on the steps. "No," he said. "But perhaps you should go inside like Miss Alexandra said."

"But I want to feed my pony first," Henry begged. "Please? It will just take a moment and then I'll go inside, I promise."

Alexandra was already backing away. She thought Henry was being rather spoiled and childish, and she really didn't want to get into any trouble. Already, they had disobeyed and she was coming to feel badly about it. So she turned for the house, or at least the direction she thought the house was in, as Henry followed Edward into a utility closet that held all sorts of implements for a smoothly running stable – buckets, feed, pitchforks for the hay, shovels, and other things. They were digging around in there as Alexandra turned the corner of the stables and ran straight into Archer.

She shrieked as they bumped into each other. Archer

grabbed the girl to steady her but Alexandra started babbling before he could say a word.

"Archer, I'm sorry," she pleaded. "We just wanted to see the horses. We were coming right back."

Archer couldn't spare the time to be angry about it. He was in professional mode – calm, cool, and collected, a far cry from what he had been only minutes earlier. His three minutes with Scarlett had worked the desired effect; it had calmed him, centered him, and now he was ready to do what needed to be done.

Half of the police officers at Phipps Hall were behind him, tactically spreading out over the grounds to surround the stables, including the Chief Constable and Calvin. Archer had explained that the stable master was their man, grabbed everyone he could from the downstairs command post, and now all of them were descending on the stable block, shrouded by the heavy mist upon the moors.

How Archer knew that Edward was their killer would have to wait. Right now, they were moving forward purely because they trusted the man. If Archer said he had the killer, then they believed him.

"Where's Henry?" Archer asked the girl.

Alexandra pointed over her shoulder. "Back there with Edward," she said. "He wanted to feed his pony. I told him we needed to go back to the house but he wanted to feed his pony first."

Archer didn't say anything. He simply turned Alexandra over to the nearest constable and continued around the corner, straining for a glimpse of his son. He saw him right away, coming out of the utility closet with Edward. Henry had two buckets and Edward had a shovel.

Archer had to make a split-second decision, one that could quite easily decide the fate of his son. The man was in the presence of a killer and, if cornered, there was no telling what the man would do. So Archer decided the best course of action would be to pretend nothing was wrong. As far as he knew, Edward still had no idea why the police were still there but in the same thought, Archer wondered why Edward was moving about freely when he was supposed to be kept to his rooms like everyone else. That realization brought a creeping sense of fear. *Why wasn't he in his room?* Archer kept his manner cool as he strolled towards Henry and Edward.

"Young man," he said sternly to his son. "I told you to stay to the house. What are you doing out here?"

Henry looked like a rat caught in a trap. His eyes grew big as his father approached. "I wanted to feed my pony," he said, knowing he was in a good deal of trouble. "I...I was helping Edward."

As Archer came within ten feet or so, Edward, who was essentially standing behind Henry, shifted the shovel in his hands and lifted it like an axe. Archer saw the movement and came to a halt, sensing the threatening position. As he gazed into the dark eyes of the man he'd known for years, he began to see something different in the murky depths. He began to sense blackness, like nothing he had ever experienced before.

"Edward," he greeted, struggling to keep an even tone. "I'm sure you can feed the horses yourself. Henry belongs back in the house."

Edward didn't say anything at first. But then he put his hand on Henry's shoulder, possessively. It was the beginning of lines being drawn. Archer could see it and he fought down his natural protective instincts for his only child. *Don't show him your fear!*

"I could use Henry's help, sir," Edward replied. "I shall bring him up to the house in a few minutes if it's not too much trouble."

So he's going to be polite about it, Archer thought. He shook his head. "I'll take him," he waved a hand at Henry to come to him. "He's in a bit of trouble. He must be punished."

Henry couldn't move because Edward had a very strong hold of his shoulder. He was a bit confused but something in his little heart told him things were not well. Something wasn't right, he could feel it. He didn't know why Edward was holding on to him so tightly.

"I should go, Edward," he told the man, trying to pull from his grip. "You can feed the horses without me."

Edward didn't say anything. He kept his focus on Archer, who was focused on him in return. They were simply staring at each other. Archer thought he might be able to get Henry away from him with perhaps a bit of persuasion but the moment he moved, Edward brought the shovel far too close to Henry's head.

"Stay where you are, Lord Phipps," Edward said. "That's far enough."

And so it begins. Archer sighed faintly. "Edward, I just want my son," he said quietly. "Please let me have him."

Edward didn't reply for a moment. When he spoke, it was almost casually. "When the police came last night, I suspected what had happened."

"What are you talking about?" Archer gave the ignorant stance one last try, for Henry's sake. "How would you know anything?"

"What else could it be?" he asked. "Did your mother finally tell you what I've done?"

So the man wouldn't be fooled. He knew what was going on, somehow or someway. Archer decided that his ignorant stance would not bode well for Henry if Edward became enraged. After a moment, he nodded his head. "She has confessed."

Edward regarded him a moment, thinking. Those murky dark eyes grew distant, perhaps pondering things in the past, thing he knew he shouldn't have done. Things that Henry Phipps, Archer's father, had proposed to him one night when the man had imbibed too much drink. That had been a dark and stormy night, stormier than most. He thought on his decision, of the events that had happened since then. He thought of his life and his future.

"'Darkling, I listen,'" he murmured, "'and, for many a time, I have been half in love with easeful Death'. I love Keats. Your father introduced me to his works. His words have such meaning... *easeful death*. Such a calm way to die."

Archer could see madness in his expression, in his words, traits he'd never seen in the usually quiet man. He sought to gain control of the situation; he didn't dare look at his son's expression for fear he would lose his composure. He knew Henry must be confused and that confusion would soon turn to terror. He had to acquire control.

"Edward, I want you to listen very carefully to me," he said after a moment. "I know everything. It has been explained to me. I've come to hear your side of the story."

Edward acted like he hadn't heard him. "I would like to go to Africa."

"Why Africa?"

"Because you could not force me to come back. I would like to go there now, please."

"You're not going anywhere until you give me my son."

"He is the only thing preventing you from claiming me. I will keep him with me."

"Edward, it would be wise for you to turn him over. You cannot go anywhere at the moment and I'll certainly not let you leave with him. Think carefully about your answer."

Edward sighed pensively, apparently thinking it over, but

the shovel remained too close to Henry's head. When Edward spoke again, it was very quiet.

"I was only doing what I was told to do," he said. "The earl asked it of me. I will not be blamed for what I was told to do."

"I realize that," Archer replied calmly. "Let's go inside and have some tea and talk this over. I would like to know what's gone on."

Edward still had a grip on Henry, though it was lessening. "It was all for you," he said after a moment. "Your father... he wanted you to look good to your superiors."

"I know."

"I didn't want to do these things, you understand. I was told to."

"I know that, Edward. Please let Henry go and we'll talk."

"Your father told me it wouldn't matter," he muttered. "The people... they were people I didn't know. It made it easier, you know. Not knowing them. It was like putting an animal down at times. I just couldn't look at their faces."

Archer's stomach was in knots, thinking of the ghastly murders the man had committed. It made sense, however – the murders had been so brutal that it was clear the from the killer's profile arc that he viewed his victims as inanimate objects. They weren't human. Archer simply couldn't believe that Edward, meek and silent Edward, had been capable of such things. But there was a sociopath below the surface, one that was proficient at astonishing gore. Bearing that in mind, he knew he had to get Henry away from the man, even if it cost him his own life. He just couldn't let the man maintain his hold of Henry any longer.

"Edward, I understand all of this," he said, startled when Edward caught sight of more police out of the corner of his eye and yanked Henry back against him. Archer raised his voice firmly. "Edward, look at me. Look at *me*. That's better. Now, you know there are police everywhere. You can't escape, so the best course of action would be to let Henry go and we'll go inside and talk about all of this. I want to hear your story, Edward, I really do. I've been chasing you for the better part of ten years, so I think I deserve some answers. Are you listening?"

Edward was frightened by all of the police around him. He could see several. Holding Henry against him, he dropped the shovel and put his forearm across the boy's neck. Archer could see that one good squeeze would snap his son's neck and he took a step towards Edward, holding out a hand.

"Don't do anything to him," he commanded, though there was pleading in his tone. "Do you hear me? No one is going to hurt you, but you must let Henry go. He's done nothing. Let me have him."

Edward was looking around, skittishly. From the corner of his eye, Archer could see Tom Midwick himself motioning the officers back and out of sight. Archer moved extremely slowly towards Edward and Henry, who by now was starting to weep quietly. Archer kept his gaze off his son and on Edward's face.

"Please," he said softly. "Just give me Henry. You have my word that no one will hurt you."

Edward looked at Archer with tears in his eyes. "My mum," he whispered, his lower lip trembling. "I want to see my mum."

"And you shall," Archer assured him. "But only if you give me Henry. Look at him, Edward; you're frightening him. Let him go and let's end this."

Edward was fighting off sobs. But he suddenly burst out. "Damn your father," he spat, spraying saliva on Henry's head. "He told me that nothing would ever happen to me, that I would be safe. I carried out the man's dirty deeds and see what's happened now? I'm caught. I don't want to go to jail."

Archer wasn't sure what to say to that. He took another step and Edward suddenly tightened his arm on Henry's neck, causing the boy to squirm.

"Not another step, Phipps," he said, sounding strong all of a sudden. "I want out of here. You will take me out of here right now or... or Henry will suffer."

"Don't do anything to him, please."

"I'll kill him!"

"Don't do it," Archer was reduced to pleading. "Edward, we can work this out. We can...."

Edward let out a yell, a primal bellow of pain and anguish, and threw his other arm across Henry's neck. It was evident what he was preparing to do and Archer made a lunge, intending to use brute strength to grapple his son out of Edward's arms. There was nothing else he could do; he didn't have a weapon. He only had his power and the wild desire to save his son's life. There was no more time left, for anything. But as he lunged, a shot rang out. Archer watched in shock as half of Edward's head exploded.

Henry shrieked as blood and tissue rained down on him, but he was able to break away as Edward collapsed on the ground. He propelled himself into his father's arms, who was caught off balance and tumbled on to his left side with Henry safely protected in his embrace. The boy was weeping hysterically as Archer rolled onto his back with Henry clutched to his chest.

"Are you all right?" he demanded, running trembling hands all over Henry's head and neck. "Did he hurt you?"

Henry shook his head, sobbing and sputtering. "I'm sorry," he cried. "I'm sorry, I'll never disobey you again, I promise!"

Archer had to laugh, relieved and nervous laughter, as he wrapped his arms around his son and cradled him. He couldn't even speak at the moment, overwhelmed with what could have happened but didn't. As he sat up and hugged his son, Calvin, with the smoking revolver still in his hand, came up behind Edward. He gazed down at his handiwork before looking at Archer.

"I had to," he said, his gaze moving between Archer and Henry. "He was going to kill him, you know that."

Archer nodded, his head up against Henry's. "I know," he whispered. "Thank you. From the bottom of my heart, thank you."

Calvin simply nodded, his gaze returning to Edward's dead corpse. As the other police began to close in, coming out of their hiding places, he kicked the body.

"Bloody asshole," he grumbled. "He killed the constable who had been assigned to watch him. We found the man's body up in Edward's flat."

Henry's head came up. "We heard banging," he said to his father, to Calvin. He wiped at his running nose. "Alex and I heard banging. We thought Edward had hurt himself."

Archer looked at his son. "Banging?" he repeated. "Like what?"

"Like something fell."

"It looks like there was a fight up there," Calvin put in. "Your stable groom smashed a lamp across the back of the constable's skull. There are pieces of broken lamp everywhere."

Archer thought on that a moment. "He suspected what all of this was about," he muttered, mostly to Calvin. "He knew we would close in on him, eventually."

Calvin was still looking at Edward as he was joined by Chief Constable Midwick, who was listening carefully to the conversation.

"But how?" Calvin wanted to know. "I'm still not clear on any of this. How did you know it was him?"

Archer wasn't prepared to tell him everything in front of Henry. The boy was his priority at the moment and he wanted to get him back up to the house and safe before returning to deal with the aftermath. He stood up and pulled Henry to his feet, keeping the child turned so he couldn't see the mess behind him.

"Let me get Henry back up to the house before we go any further into this," he said, wiping the last of Henry's tears from the boy's face. "I'll be back in a few minutes."

As Calvin and the Chief Constable acknowledge him, Henry gazed up at his father.

"I promise, I'll stay in my room," he said. "I won't go anywhere, ever."

Archer smiled weakly. "I'm sure that's a bit severe, but I would say from now on you should probably listen to me when I tell you not to do something."

Henry nodded eagerly. "I promise, I will." He tried to look behind him but Archer wouldn't let him. "What happened to Edward? Why was he... why did he hold me like that?"

Archer didn't even know where to start. There was only so much a six-year-old could understand, but he felt the child deserved an answer considering he had been involved in it. Taking his son firmly by the shoulder as the constables and inspectors closed in to seal off the scene, he simply shook his head.

"I'll explain it to you later," he said. "Right now, we...."

He was cut off by a distant scream. Everyone seem to freeze, ears peaked, listening to see where the sound came from. In the mist, it was difficult to plot a direction, but Archer was already heading for the house. He rounded the stable block just in time to hear another one, louder than the first.

He took off at a dead run.

TWENTY

ARCHER BURST into the kitchen where Mr. and Mrs. Bayse and Arabella's arrogant cook were hovering in uncertainty and fear. Several constables were behind him, all prepped to do battle. They made a rather charging group, which scared the kitchen help even more.

"Where did the scream come from?" Archer boomed.

Mr. Bayse pointed upstairs, but that's really all he could tell them. The police that had been in the parlor had charged up the stairs with August leading the way as soon as the first scream had been heard. August had been born and raised here, after all, and this was his house. He knew it like Archer knew it, deep and intimate. He knew where the screams were coming from.

By the time Archer and his group hit the main staircase, August and the other constables were already up on the second floor. He could hear voices and running feet and, as he drew closer, he could hear distant crying. The first thing he did was run into Morgan's room to find the girl sitting up in bed, frightened.

"Where's your mother?" he demanded.

Morgan burst into tears. "I don't know," she said. "I woke up and she was gone. Who's screaming?"

Archer took a second to comfort her, stroking her dark hair. He could see how scared she was. "I don't know," he said, turning for the door. "I'll find your mother, but you stay here, please. Everything will be all right, I promise."

He left her sniffling. The truth was that even though he sounded calm for Morgan's benefit, he was nearly hysterical by the time he hit the second floor. The sounds of men on the radio calling for a rescue ambulance became clearer and all of the commotion seemed to be coming from his mother's room.

Archer charged into the flowered bedroom, nearly bowling over a couple of constables standing near the door. The room was full of police and the crying was coming from the pink and yellow bathroom. He ran into the room only to be confronted by a horrific scene.

Scarlett was on the floor with the unconscious Arabella in her arms. She was weeping loudly as August and a couple of other police officers tried to lay the woman on the ground, but Scarlett wasn't easily letting go. Archer rushed in and helped them pry his mother away from his wife.

"What happened?" he demanded.

August was hugely distressed, slapping his mother lightly on the face to try and get her to come around.

"I don't know," he said. "We heard the screams and came in to find Mother and Scarlett on the floor. Mother? Can you hear me?"

Archer watched with anguish as two policemen felt for his mother's pulse and tried to see if she was breathing. He went to his wife, still sitting on the floor, being pushed around by those trying to help Arabella. He pulled her out of the way, swept into his strong embrace.

"Are you all right?" he asked her, more gently. "What happened?"

Scarlett was a mess. "I'm sorry...," she sobbed. "I'm sorry, but I didn't stay in the room with Morgan. I was worried about your mother and I just wanted to check to make sure she was all right. I didn't leave the house or anything, I swear, but I just wanted to check on your mother. She was on the floor when I found her. Archer, I don't think she's breathing."

She faded off into tears and Archer struggled against his grief. He held Scarlett, tightly, his gaze moving from August to his mother to the police trying to help her. One of the officers started CPR on her. But his gaze continued to move upward to the bathroom counter and the medicine cabinet on the wall. The cabinet was partially open. He let go of his wife and went to the medicine cabinet. He didn't know why his attention was drawn there, but it was. Call it a hunch.

He didn't even want to open the cabinet. It was a hugely laborious task, like he didn't want to know. But on the other hand, he had to do everything he could to save his mother's life so he yanked the cabinet open and was confronted by a good deal of bottled items – eye drops, prescription drugs for both his father and mother because Arabella couldn't seem to throw away Henry's cholesterol drugs, lotions, creams, and other items. Archer began fingering through the bottles, eventually coming across an empty bottle. He pulled it out and looked at it.

"Here," he turned for the cops who were trying to save her life. "An empty bottle of Valium. It was just filled a week ago."

Someone was on the phone to the hospital, speaking with the emergency department. The rescue ambulance was apparently on its way but Archer knew it was too late. The bottle contained thirty capsules and everything was gone. He just stood there, staring down at his mother, knowing that this was all very calculated.

He was devastated on the deepest level as he watched two constables, and then a third, work on his mother, but he was also bloody furious – furious about the Cutter revelation, furious over the fact that she chose the coward's solution to the problem rather than facing the consequences for her actions. He could hardly believe it. Truth be told, he was numb and overwhelmed by all of the events and confessions that this day had brought. As he watched all of the action going on, he felt like he was on the outside looking in. He felt detached.

When the rescue ambulance finally came to take Arabella to the hospital almost a half hour away, August went with her but Archer didn't. He had a whole mess on his hands at Phipps Hall and whether or not he went to the hospital with his mother would not ultimately make a difference in whether she lived or died. He could do nothing for her except clean up the mess she left in her wake.

After settling Scarlett back in the bedroom with the girls and Henry, he found it easier not to think about the emotional aspects of the day by focusing on the facts. He was an inspector, after all, and a very good one at that, so focusing on the details of his job made it easier for him. When he finally received the call from August that Arabella had passed, he and his brother had a brief conversation in which they both came to the same conclusion, and Archer went straight to Tom Midwick and told him everything.

It was the Chief Constable who decided to let the dead lie. In his view, there was no point in implicating the dead woman's role in the horrific events of the Yorkshire Cutter. As far as he was concerned, what Lady Arabella had told her son was hearsay. Nothing could be proven, but Edward Feller's fingerprints were eventually proven to be all over the secret room, the notes, and were connected to two of the crime scenes. Edward

Feller had acted alone, at least as far as it could be proven, and that was all anybody ever knew, including Scarlett.

Archer had decided not to tell her the truth as the last act of decency towards his mother. He didn't want Scarlett living with that knowledge, perhaps that anger, for the rest of her life. Besides, it wouldn't have mattered, anyway. It was pointless to upset her about it.

The real secret of the Yorkshire Cutter was buried with Arabella Phipps.

EPILOGUE
THREE YEARS LATER

IT WAS POUNDING rain by the time Scarlett and Archer exited the York Theater Royal, a beautiful Edwardian theater that had opened in the early part of the century. Archer had already called for the car and was opening up his umbrella when he caught his wife staring at one of the massive advertising posters lit up at the entry of the theater. With a smile on his lips, he walked up behind her.

"Can't get enough of it, eh?" he asked.

Scarlett grinned, shaking her head, but her eyes were still on the poster. "It's like a dream," she sighed. "I know I keep saying that, but it's true. I still can't believe it."

Holding the open umbrella in one hand, Archer put his arm around her shoulders and kissed her dark head. "Believe it," he said quietly. "You did it."

Scarlett couldn't stop smiling. "I guess I did."

Archer watched her run her hand over the glass that covered the enormous poster, his gaze moving from his wife to the vibrant announcement of the play she had written. The hope, the dream, she had told him about back when they had met had finally become a reality.

"Starr" the poster screamed. Scarlett had ended up writing a play about her rise to fame back in the nineteen eighties in Los Angeles, and the play was a rip-roaring visit to that period in time of big hair, torn jeans, lace gloves, and white high-top Reebok tennis shoes. Along with several songs she had made famous during that time, she'd written eleven more and on this opening night, the comedy-drama had attracted a sell-out crowd who had laughed, danced, and loved every one of the one hundred and eighteen minutes. It had been an overwhelming success.

Scarlett had taken several bows with the cast afterwards and remained to take pictures. Archer had purposely stayed in the shadows, grinning from ear to ear as he watched his wife receive well-deserved accolades. The fun part had been that some of her workshop students from St. Lawrence, including Morgan, Alexandra, and Henry were in the play, in the ensemble, so it had been a true family affair. It was summertime and the play was scheduled for an eight-week run, but based on the reaction of the crowd, Archer suspected it might be much longer than that. More than that, he wouldn't be surprised if it moved down to London's West End at some point. He could not have been prouder.

As Scarlett stood there and studied the poster that advertised her most personal and heartfelt work, August exited the theater with his latest girlfriend on his arm. He was laughing and happy, thanks to a great show and nearly a bottle of champagne following the close of the curtain. He spied Scarlett and Archer waiting for the car.

"Scarlett, darling!" he cried happily. "I'm so happy for you, my love, truly. Are you going to the after party?"

Scarlett grinned at her drunken brother-in-law. "I wish I could but I can't," she said. "We have to get home to the babies."

August shook his head, nearly throwing himself off-balance.

"The children are in good hands, Mother," he said. "You've got built-in babysitters at that house – the kitchen staff, the housekeeper and her daughter – so what are you worried about?"

Scarlett laughed softly. "Do you really want to know?"

"Of course I do! What is preventing you from partying with me, my fine American woman?"

Archer shook his head reproachfully at his enthusiastic brother. "Leave her alone," he said. "But you go on and have a good time. Try not to embarrass the family too much."

August was gearing up to do verbal battle with his brother when Morgan, Alexandra, and Henry emerged from the theater. The children had finished cleaning off make up and changing out of costume, now bundled up against the inclement May storm. Morgan, seventeen and an exquisitely maturing beauty, ran up and threw her arms around her mother.

"Can we please go to the after party?" she begged. "Please?"

Scarlett was doubtful. "I'm not sure," she said reluctantly. "I have to get home to the babies and I can't let you go off by yourselves."

"But it's *your* party," Alexandra insisted. Over the past year, she had sprouted up and was now taller than her mother. "You should go. Everyone will be expecting you."

Scarlett shook her head. "I really can't," she insisted. "The baby will be waking up soon for his feeding and when he wakes up, the twins will hear him and get up as well. I need to get home."

The girls looked at Archer for support, but he was torn. He put his hands on Scarlett's shoulders.

"Well," he tried to explain tactfully, "the baby is only a couple of months old and your mum is still breastfeeding him. Plus, the twins can be a handful when they're wound up. Mrs. Bayse is fine with them but Mr. Bayse gets a little flustered. I'm not sure...."

"But this is mom's party," Alexandra reiterated. "She hasn't been out since Bryce was born."

Archer shook his head. "It's not Bryce I'm worried about," he said. "It's Ward and Havilland. Ward is at the stage where he can't stand for your mother or me to be out of his sight, and Havilland is even worse. You know how she is."

As the girls nodded with some understanding, Henry simply rolled his eyes. "All she does is hang on to your neck," he muttered. "You carry her around everywhere."

"That's because she screams if I don't."

"Was I ever that spoilt?"

Archer lifted his eyebrows at his eldest son. "When you have children, you'll understand why you do what you have to do in order to keep them happy. I can't explain it to you. You'll just have to experience it for yourself."

Henry wasn't interested in the rearing of the twins that had been born almost two years earlier on a cold and snowy night two days before Christmas. In fact, he remembered very little of that night, as he had been asleep when his father had rushed Scarlett to the hospital in York where she had given birth to a girl and then a boy shortly before sunrise. All Henry remembered was that he had awoken to the news of a new sister, Havilland Harper Arabella Phipps, and a new brother, Ward de Velt Bottreaux Phipps.

Then, six weeks ago, Scarlett had given birth to another boy, Bryce Rossheimer Phipps. Babies were everywhere now at Phipps Hall, not exactly something that interested a nine-year-old boy. These days he was into theater and singing, and he liked it just fine. He was also very interested in attending the party that his stepsisters were so excited about. Like them, he was growing up.

"What about the party?" he wanted to know. "Can we please go?"

Scarlett could see how badly the kids wanted to attend. The after party was being held at a restaurant nearby and she knew there wouldn't be any craziness because the theater crowd just wasn't like that. These were people she knew and trusted for the most part, having worked with them almost daily over the past eleven months in preparation for this night. It was a big night for all of them. She turned to Archer.

"Why don't you go with them over to the restaurant for a little while?" she said. "I'll head on home. Give everyone my regards, okay?"

He shook his head. "Love, it's *your* party," he said. "Alex is right; you should go, if only for a few minutes. Mr. and Mrs. Bayse can handle the babies for a little while longer."

Scarlett was in the process of refusing when a car pulled up with several of the actors, including the girl that played Scarlett's role. The dark-haired beauty jumped out of the car and ran for Morgan, pulling her back towards the car. Alexandra followed simply because she didn't want to be left out and Henry ran after them as well. There was a good deal of laughing and chatter going on as the rain pounded, all of them swept up in the excitement of the opening night. Eventually, Scarlett relented and attended her after party for about a half hour, returning to baby Bryce in plenty of time for his midnight feeding.

Archer returned in time, too, holding the cranky and sleepy twins who always woke up like clockwork when Bryce was fed. They were nosy busy-bodies, curious about everything and incredibly brilliant. Archer sat in an overstuffed chair in the master bedroom, watching Scarlett feed the dark-haired infant, growing heavy-lidded as he observed the tender scene. By the time Scarlett was finished feeding the baby, he was fast asleep in the chair with two sleeping toddlers cradled against his broad chest. Dad was out like a light.

Scarlett had to grin at the Chief Constable of the North Yorkshire Police Department. An accomplished man, no doubt, with ancestral titles and a new position that he richly deserved. But all of it paled in comparison to the two titles he truly held dear over all the others; husband and father. As Scarlett had known from nearly the moment she'd met the man, he was focused, compassionate, and dedicated beyond anything she'd ever known.

When she and the girls had come to England on their adventure three years ago, she could have never imagined how that undertaking had turned into the fulfillment of dreams she didn't even know she had, and all of those dreams centered around the man snoring in the chair. She had everything she had ever wanted and couldn't ask for more. Life, for Scarlett, had come full circle. Bending over, she kissed him gently on the forehead and turned out the light.

Archer and the twins slept there all night.

ABOUT THE AUTHOR

ABOUT KAT LE VEQUE

KATHRYN LE VEQUE is a critically acclaimed, USA TODAY Bestselling author (having hit the list over 30 times), an Indie Reader bestseller, a charter Amazon All-Star author, and a #1 bestselling, award-winning, multi-published author in Medieval Historical Romance with over 150 published novels. Kathryn also writes Romantic Suspense as Kat Le Veque.

Kathryn has received praise for her writing and has won several awards for her work, including two nominations for the Holt Medallion. Her books have topped bestseller lists, and she has gained a loyal fan base that eagerly anticipates each new release.

Kathryn is a talented author who has made a significant impact on the world of historical romance fiction. Through her captivating storytelling and meticulous research, she has enchanted readers with her tales of love, adventure, and the enduring power of the human spirit.

Kathryn loves to hear from her readers. Please find Kathryn on Facebook at Kathryn Le Veque, Author, or join her on Twitter @kathrynleveque, and don't forget to visit her website at www.kathrynleveque.com.

ALSO BY KAT LE VEQUE

The Unholy Angels

Hour of Surrender

Trent Chronicles

Valley of Shadow

The Eden Factor

Canyon of the Sphinx

The Eagle Brotherhood

The Sunset Hour

The Killing Hour

The Secret Hour

The Unholy Hour

The Burning Hour

The Ancient Hour

The Devils Hour